WOLFBLOODED SERIES NOVEL

MADISON CHASE

Other Works by Madison Chase

The Wolfblooded Series

Pack or Prey

The Road to Hell Series

Dance with the Devil

First Published by Melissa A. Graham 2013

(Melissa A. Graham is now writing under the pen-name Madison Chase)

Cover by Madison Chase

Illustrations by Madison Chase

ISBN: 979-8-3256093-8-1(paperback-amazon)

ISBN: 979-8-9927182-1-8(paperback)

ISBN: 979-8-9927182-2-5(e-book)

Published by Madison Chase Books

www.madisonchasebooks.com

Author Notes

This book contains scenes that may depict or discuss: abduction, abusive relationships, blood & gore, emotional abuse, extreme violence, misogyny, murder, physical abuse, racism, sexual harassment, strong language & stalking.

To everyone sick of hearing me whine, cry, and gush about this book, thank you for sticking with me. From the sweetest whispers of encouragement to the threats of bodily harm if I didn't stop bitching, you all have helped me through this. This is for you.

And especially to my Unicorn. For your guidance, your laughs, your middle fingers, and your tea. Especially the tea. #TeamDuckicorn

Chapter 1

April 7th 2008, 4:18 p.m.

THE TROUBLE WITH TROUBLE is it is one sneaky son-of-a-bitch. If it came at us with a flashing neon sign screaming for us to run the other way, most people would be smart enough to heed its warning. Sadly, for others—read: me—trouble seems to come out of nowhere and is often disguised as everything we think we want.

My own brown-eyed, leather-clad flavor of trouble could have rode in on a pale horse, signaled by a procession of trumpets while hellfire rained down around us, and I'd be doomed just the same. There were no horses or trumpets, but there *was* the deafening roar of ten or so motorcycles pulling into the field.

I stared at the line of machines as we entered the fairgrounds and imagined what it would be like to jump on one and burn out of this city with middle fingers blazing. I found myself full of envy as I watched the men and women hanging around the bikes. Something in their ease of simply existing seemed unchained and unobligated.

I had never felt so comfortable in *my* existence. I wondered what it would have felt like to fit in with my family the way they seemed to fit with each other.

The relationship between my parents and I was strained at best. My relationship with my sister was, well, non-existent. I learned long ago that we would never be on the same wavelength. That's not saying I understood why, just that I quit trying to riddle it out.

Eventually I got tired of hurting my own feelings. It just became a fact I'd come to grips with over the last few years.

Unlike me and my family, the bikers didn't appear to have any issues connecting to one another. A pang of jealousy blew through me as I watched them. They were completely at ease with one another. No tension, no awkwardness. They just... fit.

"You ride?"

His eyes—large, brown, and staring into me as if he knew my every secret—snared me the instant I spun around, and an awkward thrill ran through me. The gold flecks floating in pools of warm chocolate stole my thoughts, leaving me silent and fascinated by the twinkle of humor glittering in those eyes.

I wondered for a moment what it was he found so funny, and then I realized it was probably the chick staring at him with her mouth gaping and tongue practically flopped onto the ground between them.

"Ah-I..." I responded, brilliantly.

Suddenly very aware of my thin, awkward arms, I found I had no idea what to do with them. I shuffled my feet and switched between clasping my hands behind my back and laying them down at my sides. Finally, I settled on crossing them in front of me.

He chuckled, shoving his hands into his pockets, and looked out to the group of bikers in the distance. "It's a thrill. Nothing beats it. No job, no responsibilities, nothing to tie us down," he said before giving me a sideways grin. "Not even great sex compares to the freedom of the road. Once you get that engine humming between your legs, I guarantee nothing'll ever measure up."

I could feel heat spreading over my cheeks, my hormones igniting to life. Jesus Christ. It was crass, presumptive, and incredibly inappropriate considering I didn't know this guy from Adam. Yet rather than feel grossed out or offended at his forwardness, I felt strangely... flattered? Intrigued?

I wiped my hand across my cheek, as if that would help clear the blush from my skin and tried for cool and casual.

"I've never ridden," I confessed as he looked away from me, finally freeing me from the intense eye contact.

I was only a few months shy of eighteen, and he didn't look to be more than a year or two older than me; a hell of a lot younger than the rest of those guys across the lot. If one of them had been talking to me like this, I'd have probably called out for my dad.

His hair was cut very short, especially on the sides. A little dip in the center of his chin peeked through the start of a goatee while untamed stubble spread across his jawline and halfway down his neck. Somehow, he made it look insanely hot, rather than just plain dirty.

His eyes found me again, and I swallowed down the hard lump forming in my throat. I quickly looked at the ground, embarrassed to have been caught staring.

"That's a shame. I bet you look hot on the back of a bike."

Me? Sitting behind him? My thighs wrapped around his hips as the bike vibrated under us? The imagery sent my tummy into somersaults.

"Want to try it out?"

Yes, I shouted in my head. *God, yes!* A genuine smile stretched across my face, and tension eased in my shoulders. His hand stretched out for mine, waiting patiently for my answer. I opened my mouth to accept, excitement filling me and violently shoving all rational thought aside.

"Harley!"

We both turned toward the admission gate where my mom, dad, and sister were waiting on me. I hadn't even realized I'd fallen that far behind.

To be completely honest, it looked like they hadn't noticed until that moment either.

"Come on, sweetie," my mother called through the moving crowd. "We got your ticket."

She slid an arm around Lori's shoulders, and they turned to walk into the fair without waiting for me. I glanced back to the guy standing next to me, my smile long gone.

"Maybe another time," he said quietly, though that knowing smile never faltered.

I watched him walk away, moving through the parked cars toward the bikes, and couldn't decide if I wanted to scream or cry. I settled on wallowing in self-pity as I grudgingly caught up with my family.

Locals couldn't resist the pull of the Simmons County Fair. Fairway food, the thrum of electricity juicing the rides, and live music easing through every nook and cranny of the fairgrounds advertised fun, excitement, and some good ol' family togetherness.

Just think 'final number of Grease' minus the *wop-baba-lumop* and *a-wap-bam-boom*.

For me, it was just a lot of noise and bodies. The fair always kicked off homecoming week for Simmons High, the school my sister and I went to, as some attempt to rouse school spirit. I wasn't exactly the spirited type.

I followed my family with my hands shoved into my jean jacket in traditional teenage-angsty fashion, kicking anything my high tops came across. Lori had Mom and Dad engaged in some enthusiastic conversation ahead of me while I just tried my best to keep up with them—at a respectable distance, of course.

We'd been in the games area for about three minutes when I heard the unmistakable squeal of my sister and found them standing in front of the ring toss booth. Lori bounced excitedly as she showed Dad an overstuffed Siberian Husky hanging from the awning. I couldn't help but roll my eyes at the sheer childishness of it. She was eighteen, for Christ's sake, and acted like an overstimulated two-year-old.

By that point, I knew we'd be stopping there to appease the golden child of the Rayne household. Lorelei wants, Lorelei gets. Simple. At least the rigged fairway games offered a small chance of her leaving empty-handed.

It would do her some good to be disappointed for a change.

The simple hope of seeing Lori denied something she wanted kept me close enough to watch the show. I stayed to the side of the booth and waited to see if the fates had any sympathy for me at all.

Okay, so I could be childish, too. Bite me.

Dad and Lori began an uncoordinated assault on the ring toss, and mom cheered them on like a lunatic. They were the perfect picture of a happy family. Just fold me out of the photo and you have a bond that could rival the Cleavers.

"You know these games are rigged, right?" a familiar voice said beside me.

I turned around to find those rich brown eyes and that dimpled chin. The air left my lungs in a violent rush. Nameless Cutie from the parking lot was standing next to me, smiling at me.

"Yeah." I laughed, the sound a little too high as it choked out of me. Trying to pretend it hadn't come from me, I cleared my throat and tried to take back some control of my voice.

"It's stupid. My sister just *has* to have that dumb toy."

He glanced at my family, who were still trying to catch a plastic ring around the neck of one of the beer bottles.

"I see. I bet it'd piss her off if you got it, instead," he whispered, the corner of his mouth lifting a touch higher.

"Yeah, probably. But I suck at this kind of stuff," I said. I appreciated the sentiment though.

He let that hint of a smile spread into a full-blown grin, and it somehow managed to loosen some of the tension in my shoulders. I smiled back, amazed that he could pull it from me so easily.

He didn't say anything else; just pulled a five out of his pocket and slapped it on the counter in exchange for five plastic rings. It was effortless. His hand moved, he flicked his wrist, and each ring flew around a bottle. When all five rings settled around the bottleneck I just stared. It was like he didn't even have to try.

"Winner here," the guy manning the booth shouted. Another plucked one of the Huskies from the hooks, handing it over.

He grabbed the stuffed monstrosity and tucked it under his arm, turning back to me. I chewed my lip, shifting my weight from side to side, and tried to think of something to say.

I felt so squirmy whenever he stared at me. I suddenly became one of those girls I often mocked, full of weak-kneed, heart-pounding feelings.

Gross.

"I'm Frank," he said finally, breaking the tension. "Frank Essex."

He held his hand out and waited for me to accept it. I smiled again and took his hand, giving it a firm shake. A warm jolt of electricity whispered over my hand as he gripped it, his heat creeping over me and chasing away the chill of the night breeze. I had never felt something so intense in my life.

His grin widened, and I couldn't tell if it was because he'd felt it too, or because I was now fidgeting nervously in his grip, stammering like an absolute tool.

"Nice to meet you. I'm—"

"Harley. I remember," he said with a crooked grin. "Not the sort of name a guy like me can forget."

A blush warmed my cheeks again. I was acting like some lovesick puppy. Like all those girls I made fun of in school because their life's ambition was getting noticed by some boy.

"Also, I just learned it like thirty minutes ago, so... that doesn't hurt," he teased, earning an honest-to-God giggle from me. "So, you out on a fun-filled, family adventure?" he asked, and I could hear the mockery laced in his words.

I eyed my family. Dad was the only one playing the game now.

"Something like that," I said under my breath as I rolled my eyes at them.

Frank followed my gaze and just stared for a moment. Finally, he turned that grin back to me and leaned down, lowering his mouth to meet my ear.

"Your sister looks pissed," he whispered with a chuckle, and I glanced at her.

Lori looked like an errant child ready to erupt into a tantrum. Apparently, Dad had not managed to win her the Husky. His arm was wrapped around her shoulders in a comforting half-hug as he tried to smooth things over.

"Good," I said, barely managing to suppress my gleam of satisfaction.

"Well, now. That's not very sisterly of you," Frank teased.

"I couldn't give a shit less about her pissy little attitude. Besides, it's just a—" I turned my head to look at him only to have my train of thought completely derail.

My face was suddenly *very* close to his.

This close, in the glow of the carnival lights, the flecks of gold and honey in his eyes sparkled. They bore into me like they were trying to dig deep down beneath the surface, searching for something.

His face was serious, intense, and barely hung on to that boyish charm he'd been carrying with him so far. I couldn't describe what I saw as he looked at me, but I fell into those deep brown pools gladly, and everything around us seemed to vanish for one second.

All sounds silenced, save for the thick beating of my heart. The carnival around us disappeared in a smoky haze, and all that was left was me, Frank, and the pulse drumming away in my ears.

"Harley," a voice called in the distance, but I was captured by Frank's smile.

"Harley!" This time the voice was crisper, and everything flooded back in a crash of senses. It nearly knocked me on my ass.

I turned my head and blinked confused eyes over at the disembodied voice, until my father came into focus. He was standing closer to us now, his dark eyes narrowed at Frank. I hadn't even seen him walk up to us.

"Huh?" I said as my brain fought its way out of the fog Frank had put me in.

Dad merely stared at the boy next to me while mom and Lori stood just behind him, whispering to one another. Something about my dad's face unnerved me. I looked over at Frank. With his lips pressed into a hard line, the muscles in the jaw flexing, and his eyes hard and unflinching, he matched my dad's stare.

"Come on, Harley." My mom spoke this time. "Time to go."

"But we just got here," I said. I didn't want to leave, not when I just met Frank. "Can't we just—"

"*Now*, Harley." The booming insistence in my father's voice startled me. My dad never raised his voice at us.

My spine stiffened. Why was he being like this? Usually, I was the one wanting to go home while they dragged me around the fair for hours. We'd only just gotten here, and they were ready to leave?

And to top it off, he was acting weird. Almost mean.

I sighed and started away from Frank, trying not to cry. Freaking typical. Whenever Lori begged to do something, to stay longer, to get something, they were only too happy to ply her with everything she wanted. The one time I asked for something, they wouldn't even listen.

"Hey," Frank whispered behind me.

I turned around and stared at him, choking back the anger and jealousy that threatened to spill out of my eyes. He held the stuffed Husky out to me, bumping its big snout into my arm, and smiled.

"She won't always get everything." This time he wasn't as quiet.

I glanced at Lori. Her jaw was clenched, and her nose flared as she stared at him. She looked like she was ready to tear him to pieces. Mom's arm wrapped around her shoulder and pulled her closer. Maybe it was the sight of mom comforting Lori while I was being treated so unfairly that made me reach out and grab the Husky.

I didn't think. I can honestly say that there was no planning or thinking when it came to what happened next. I simply reacted. While one hand grabbed the Husky from Frank, the other reached for his arm and pulled him down a little so I could reach his cheek. I kissed it, the scraggle of day-old-beard scratching my lips; I liked it.

I was suddenly jerked away, and I looked up to see Dad towering over me, gripping my arm firmly. It didn't hurt, but it was just this side of painful.

"Go to your mother. Now." His voice wasn't loud anymore.

In fact, it had returned to its usual softness but there was a finality to the words. I went. What else was I going to do?

My mother's hand found my shoulder and pulled me between her and Lori, using her body to keep me from moving back in front of them.

If there was another word spoken between the four of them, I didn't hear it. Mom was ushering me away, and Lori was pretending to not look at the stuffed Husky in my arm.

My lips were on fire. I knew it was from his stubble scratching them when I kissed him, but it felt like so much more. I brought my fingers to my lips, touching that residual heat and glanced back over my shoulder. Before my dad joined us and blocked him from view, I watched as Frank touched a hand to his cheek.

Chapter 2

July 10th 2008, 10:12 p.m.

"CAN WE JUST RUN away?" I asked, nuzzling my head into the crook of his shoulder.

The stars stretched above us, shining down like a weighty promise that there was so much more to this world than high school politics and a home where I barely felt wanted. Every time I looked up at the night sky, I was filled with the urge to run, to take off and leave everything behind. I craved adventure and freedom, and I wasn't going to find it sitting in my room listening to music.

Frank chuckled, and I watched his chest rise and fall with it.

"I've told you before, Harls. Say the word and we're gone. No questions asked."

It was the same promise he'd made me over and over again. Three months of begging him to take me away from here, and three months of me making excuses why I couldn't go through with it. It felt silly, but as much as my family pissed me off, and they did it often, something wouldn't let me leave. I would be happier if I left, I told myself. So, what was holding me back?

"I know," was all I could offer him.

He'd heard this time and again. At first, he seemed excited at the idea of running off together. The more we discussed it, though, the less likely he seemed to think it was going to happen. It had finally reached the point where he stopped believing me.

I turned my head and pressed my lips to his tan chest, kissing it lightly. He sighed and sat up quickly. I spilled to the ground, still warm where he'd been lying, and looked up at him.

"What?" I asked as he snatched his shirt and pulled it over his head. His movements were rigid and quick.

He mumbled something that sounded like 'Don't worry about it'. I pushed myself up so I could lean on my arm and reached out to touch his back. He twisted away from me.

"Frank, what is it?" I asked again, sitting up a little straighter.

He twisted his upper body to look back at me, his eyes harder than normal. "Are you ever going to make up your mind?"

I hadn't expected that.

"About what?" I asked, though I was pretty sure I knew.

"Don't. Don't play that game with me, Harley. You tell me, over and over, how much you want to be gone from here. I've told you more than once, in more than one way, how we can make that happen. And you pull away. Every time." He loosed a laugh that sounded bitter and jagged. "I mean, I don't think you really want to go. I don't think you want to be with me at all."

"That's not fair. I wouldn't be here if I didn't want to be with you. I love you—"

"I'm leaving, Harley."

His words were so sudden that I choked on my own. "Leaving?"

"Yeah. I'll be gone by morning."

We sat there, on the blanket he kept on the back of his bike, and let the silence weigh down on us. He was leaving? Just like that? A dull ache started in my heart just thinking about being left there without him. He was the only one I could talk to, the only one who understood me.

"Why?" I choked out. Dammit, I wasn't going to cry. Not for some guy who just told me he was going to leave me.

"Jesus." He ran his hand over his hair and shook his head. "Look, I ain't ever stuck around somewhere longer than a month or two, babe. I'm just not built to make roots. I stayed here for you." His eyes softened a touch as he looked at me. "Come with me. For real."

I shook my head and sighed. "I can't. I want to, I do, but I can't just take off like that. My parents would freak out."

"Would they?" he asked sharply. "'Cause here I thought they didn't give a damn one way or the other. That's what you keep bitching about, ain't it? How you're an after-thought to them? How Lori is everything and you're just taking up space?"

I winced as he slung my own words at me. They hurt. Even though I had said them first, hearing someone else say it out loud was like a knife in the heart. A cutting reminder of just how little I meant to Mom and Dad.

That was when the tears betrayed me.

He touched my cheek, smearing the salty traitors into my skin and lifting my chin up so he could look me in the eye. His words hurt, but his eyes were a soothing balm to take the sting out.

"Please come with me, Harley. They might not want you, but I *need* you."

My heart pounded. He needed me. Someone on this earth needed me, and he was right here holding me. He wanted me to run away with him. What could be so horrible about that? What was I leaving behind that could possibly measure up to what he offered me at that moment?

"Take me home," I said, finally. His muscles tensed. He started to move his hand from my cheek, ready to give up, but I grabbed it and held it close. "And come pick me up in an hour. I need to pack a few things."

July 11th 2008 9:57 a.m.

I'd never ridden so long on the back of a bike before. Hell, before Frank, I'd never ridden on a bike, period. The last few months he'd pick me up, we'd ride around town, head out to the lake and back, but that was about it. There were no long road trips, no rides that lasted more than half an hour. It was definitely a much different experience being on the open road. Better in a lot of ways; freeing, exhilarating... but it came with its own drawbacks.

My ass hurt.

That was my first thought when I climbed off the back of his bike. The backs of my thighs were numb, and my spine screamed at me for the torture of sitting so rigid for so long. Frank had assured me it would pass, that with time my body would grow accustomed to the posture. God, I hoped so or it would put a serious damper on the whole *Easy Rider*-outlaw-biker vibe.

I looked up at the sign above the building. A simple white sign with "Curly's" written in red and black. It was worn, the wood peeling on the edges. This place had been here for a while.

Frank's hand found the small of my back, and I glanced at him. I looked back at myself from his mirrored sunglasses, and I looked scared, ready to jump ship. My gray-blue eyes were wide and looking for comfort.

"Don't worry," he said, pressing his lips to my forehead. "Just keep quiet until I can smooth things over."

I blinked up at him. Smooth things over? I didn't get a chance to ask him what exactly he'd need to smooth over before he led me into the bar. It was so much darker than it was outside, and my eyes took their sweet time adjusting to the new lighting.

He led me to a stool at the corner of the bar. I slid onto it and realized the bar was fairly empty. As big as it was, there were only about ten people inside, including the woman behind the bar. I also noticed they were all decked out in leathers and worn denim, chains, bandanas, vests, and buckles.

He'd taken me to a biker bar. Why was I surprised?

"Park here. I'll be right back," he said, and walked away.

He moved toward the other end of the bar, and I just sat and watched him. There was nothing uncertain about him. He was all confidence. I envied it.

"Drink?" a woman asked.

I turned and saw the bartender staring at me from across the bar. Her face was unreadable and dismissive. And here I'd stupidly thought bartenders were friendly. Oops.

"No. I'm fine," I said.

"Suit yourself."

"Who are they?" I asked, jerking my chin to the group of men Frank had joined.

One clapped him on the shoulder as he stepped up to them, another stood behind a man seated on another stool. The man on the stool was much older, and thicker than Frank around the middle, but the way the other men flanked him gave him an undeniable air of importance.

"I wouldn't get yourself too acquainted with anyone here, girl. You'll probably be going back to Mommy and Daddy in a few minutes."

I turned and blinked at her.

"I'm with Frank. Means I'm not going anywhere 'til I'm damn good and ready."

The words spilled out of me before I could stop myself. This chick was almost a foot taller than me and looked like she'd give me a thorough ass-kicking.

Sure enough, she was giving me a stare that looked like she was considering what would be best used to break my head. That was until a smile broke the empty nature of her face. She laughed her face to life. The smile managed to wipe years off her, and I breathed a little easier when I was sure the threat to face was gone.

"Right," she said and turned her back to me, grabbing a short rocks glass from the shelves. "The guy closest to Frank is Paulie. Then there's D'Angelo standing behind the older guy, who would be Chuck. He's the road captain of our little Club here; the Hellhounds," she finished as she sat a drink of some kind in front of me and leaned against the bar.

"Is this a "one for the road" type of thing?" I asked, grabbing the dark drink and sniffing it.

She shrugged, "Or a 'Welcome to Hell' type thing. I guess we'll see."

Her eyes slid back to the men, and I wrinkled my nose at the drink, setting it down. It was strong, whatever it was. I glanced at the guys, straining to catch their conversation. Suddenly, the older guy didn't look very happy.

"Take the bitch home. You're bringing trouble into our family. The fuck is wrong with you?"

"I'm not taking her back, Chuck. Sorry," Frank said, sliding his sunglasses from his face and folding them.

"Are you really being this stupid? I mean.... even for you, Frank." This from Paulie.

"It's not a request or a suggestion, Frankie."

"No," Frank said, and his voice was a touch harder.

I felt small. This Chuck guy had a real problem with me being there. I didn't even know the guy and he was trying to get me the hell away from them. The room grew hotter as the men argued, like someone had kicked the heat on full blast. It was almost suffocating.

"Don't be an idiot. When have you ever got strung up by some bitch? Now this skinny little skank gets your panties all knotted up and you forget your place?" Chuck all but screamed the last, and I couldn't help but wince.

That was a bit harsh. The asshole didn't even know me.

I watched Frank. I was curious how he'd react to that. It was obvious he looked up to this guy. He'd told me about him, back before I had a face to match the name. If all the people he talked about were this charming, I was in for a peachy friggin' time.

Frank's back stiffened under his leather vest. I couldn't see his face, but I could see how rigid the rest of him became. His shoulders squared back, and he seemed to grow an inch or two taller.

"Chuck, we been through hell together. I've had your back in some hard situations," he said, his hands flexing at his sides before balling into tight fists. "But if you call her out of her name one more time, I'll feed you the floor."

The bartender whispered something under her breath and I made the mistake of looking at her. By the time I snapped my attention back to the men, Frank was nowhere to be seen.

Chuck was on his feet now, and I could see that he was a great deal shorter than Frank. He barely gained inches standing up from his stool. Paulie had his arms raised, his hands laced over the top of his head and his eyes closed tight, but D'Angelo was actually... smiling.

When I caught sight of Frank, he was propping himself up on one elbow on the floor, his hand rubbing his jaw.

"She's your problem, Frankie. Her blood comes hunting for her then you're on your own with it," Chuck said as he reached a hand down to Frank. It took a minute, but he finally accepted the help and let Chuck pull him to his feet. Not that he needed the help.

"Yeah, I got it," Frank said.

Before he could step away, Chuck jerked his hand closer to him and grasped his other elbow in some strange half-hug. "You're a beast. A damn good man to have at my back and I'll walk through fire for you," Chuck's voice dropped down a touch, "but if you ever buck up in front of our brothers again... I'll take your fucking throttle hand. Got me?"

He brought his hand away from Frank's elbow and gave a light tap to the side of his face before walking past him. He added, "Hope the tail is worth it," before heading out of the bar, D'Angelo following close behind him.

Frank didn't walk over to me and apologize or make excuses for what Chuck had said. He didn't try to explain what exactly had just happened. Paulie loosed a chuckle that lightened his face a bit and they walked towards a table in the corner, their voices becoming too soft to hear.

"Well," the woman across from me said. She grabbed her glass and moved it over to mine, tapping the rim of mine lightly, "that went well."

As she gulped down her drink I grabbed for mine and brought it to my lips, no longer caring how the smell made my stomach turn.

"Welcome to Hell it is," I whispered into my glass.

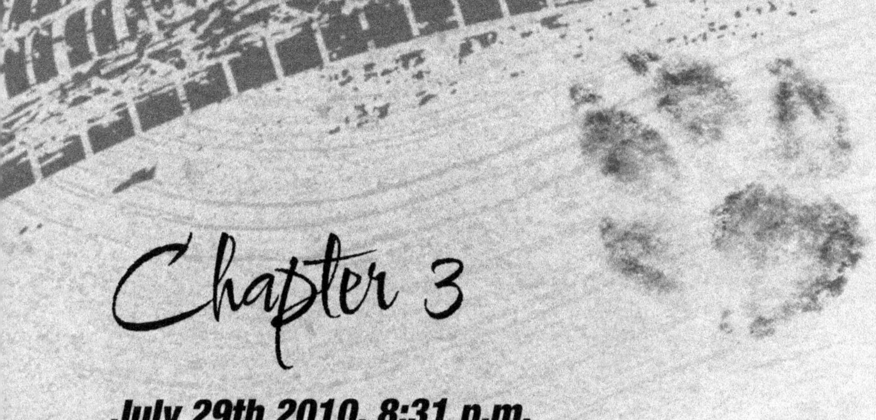

Chapter 3

July 29th 2010, 8:31 p.m.

"I just don't understand why. I mean, you told me you looked up to him. That he was like a father to you or something."

I'd been trying to wrap my head around what Frank had said for some time. Two years in, and I was still scrambling to make heads or tails of this life. Now, he wanted to change things. A 'purging', he had called it.

"I ain't ever called him my dad, Harls," Frank growled from the shower.

We were sitting in a motel bathroom about the size of a closet. We'd stopped on our way to Texarkana to get a couple days of rest, and for Chuck and the guys to handle some kind of business. When I asked Frank what business, he'd told me it was the kind I'm not a part of. It felt like a slap in the face.

I wasn't sure when he'd started keeping things from me, but eventually I just let it go. I knew the crew didn't exactly follow the straight and narrow, so I figured I prob-ably didn't want to know anyway.

"Whatever. The point is he's someone you looked up to, right? Now you're planning some kind of... coup against him?" I pushed off the little sink and turned around, wiping the steam from the mirror. "I just want to understand why, is all. He doesn't seem that bad a guy to me."

"You wouldn't understand. I've tried explaining it to you, and you just don't get it. I know you think he's this great guy. That's my fault, I guess. I talked him up to you. But really, Harley, you don't know him.

"These people need to follow someone who's gonna be a real leader. Who can make the hard decisions needed and not just look for the easiest way out of shit. He can't talk about becoming this powerhouse like he is and then sit on his ass and let shit slide by that make us look weak. It leaves us vulnerable."

He was right; I didn't get it. Make us look weak? Pow-erhouse? Frank had been talking about the Hellhounds like it was an army for some time now.

The water squeaked off, and the room was sudden-ly quiet. I thought about what to ask him as he dried off—something that might get a direct answer from him for a change.

"What is it you plan to do, exactly, Frank?"

The glass door slid open, and Frank stepped out from a billow of thick steam. If he was trying to distract me, it worked. Water clung to his freshly scrubbed skin, drawing attention to every crease and swell of his upper body. Frank was fit. Not in a scary steroid-pumping way. His was much more subtle. A nice surprise hidden under his clothes.

The towel he'd dried off with was slung low around his hips, held up only by the grace of God, himself. I never thought I'd be one of those girls that let a hard body and a charming smile make my brain go soft, but here I was: Jell-O for brains.

Frank awakened things in me I never knew existed. Some days I loved that he was able to do that. Other days, it made me wonder if I would ever be recognizable from the girl I was two years ago.

"Why do you care?" he asked as he stood across the bathroom from me.

"I... I don't know," I finally admitted. "I don't know why it's bugging me so much, but it doesn't change the fact that I want to know. I'm part of this family now. I think I deserve to know why the man we've been following around Texas is suddenly not fit to lead us."

"Oh, babe," Frank said with a laugh. It was the laugh that said I was being silly. Amusing. He'd been making me feel that way a lot lately, and I was growing less and less fond of it. "It's cute. Really. It's sweet that you consider yourself a part of our... family... after two whole years of riding with us."

I managed to ignore the way his bicep flexed as he ran his hand over the back of his head. Mostly. Even the power of his absolutely hypnotic body couldn't withstand the surge of resentment beginning to swell inside me.

Thank you, anger.

"Don't talk down to me like I'm some stupid kid."

"But you are, Harley. You are just a stupid kid, and it's funny that you think you have any understanding of us. Riding bitch on the back of my bike doesn't mean you know a fucking thing. You don't." He stepped closer to me, and I felt my face growing hot with a building anger.

"Fuck you, Frank," I said as I held a hand up to stop him from coming any closer. "I care about you. And about the rest of these guys. Two years, two months, or two days; who gives a shit? So, yeah. If I'm going to go along with tearing down someone I've been following for the last couple years, then I think I deserve to know why and what's going to fucking happen. Give me at least that much or I'll just find my own way."

He stared down at me, his ribs just a hair's breadth from the flat of my palm and said nothing. I don't know if it was because I'd gone off on him or because I'd threatened to leave, but he looked down at me and let the silence fill the space between us. Finally, a little quirk of a grin tugged at his mouth.

"You're sexy when you're mad. You know that?" he said, and moved to wrap his arms around me.

I pressed my hand against his ribs and tried to keep him from coming any closer. "Seriously? I'm trying to have a serious fucking talk and you're going to pull that tired ass shit on me?"

"Aww, what? You don't like it?" he said and managed to lace his hands at the small of my back.

I craned my neck to look into his eyes. My face was as serious and unmoved as I could manage, though his still-wet skin was making the front of my clothes damp. It was seriously distracting.

"What are you gonna do, Frank?" I asked and tried to ignore the press of his hips into mine and the thought of how there was no way that towel would stay on if he kept this up.

He bowed his head and pressed his lips just under my earlobe on the curve of my jaw. My eyes closed at the feel of his breath, warm and tickling, on my skin.

"Nothing, Harley," he whispered. He lowered his lips again and laid another soft kiss along my jaw.

"Paulie and me are just gonna talk to him. That's all." Another kiss landed at my chin and I sucked my lower lip between my teeth. "We're just gonna have a little heart-to-heart. If I was gonna do anything more, I'd have already done it."

"That's it?" I managed through a growing tightness in my throat.

I felt his pulse beating hard and fast against my palm and he wiggled himself between my knees so that we were pressed tight against each other. His heat spread over me, wrapped around me like it had arms and set out to touch every part of me.

"Yes," he whispered again, "but there's something else I gotta do first." His lips closed over my throat and he edged teeth over it.

"Yeah? What's that?"

He chuckled against my throat, his laugh vibrating over my skin and making me tingle in places far, far below my neck. His hands slid over my backside and cupped it firmly, pulling me up to sit completely on the sink in front of him.

Any arguing, any interrogating I may have been getting ready to do, disappeared under his mouth. He always had this insane power over me, over my body. If I'd had any friends back home, they might have told me it was purely physical, this attraction I had for him.

It wasn't true. There was so much more to it. Unfortunately, with my legs wrapped around his waist and his hands sliding up into my hair, I couldn't think of anything else.

I felt a sharp tug at the base of my skull, and it opened my mouth with a sharp gasp. It wasn't pain that made me react like that. No. Far from it.

His mouth sealed over the front of my throat, his hand controlling my head so that he could bend it whichever way he wanted. He was almost animal in this part of our lives and it excited every part of me. All that dangerous bad boy thrill us silly girls just seemed to always be drawn to.

His lips blazed a hot, wet trail down the front of my throat, making a detour to nibble along my collarbone, and then finally nestling into the valley of my breasts. I leaned back, resting my head against the mirror over the sink, and pushed my upper body towards him, giving him as much of me as I could. More. That was all I could think of. I wanted more. More of his lips, more of his heat, more of him. It was an addiction, and one I was nowhere near willing to let go of.

While he nibbled at my breasts, my hand searched down his body. Fingertips played over the still-wet contours of his chest and torso as they traveled down, sliding between our pressed bodies and edging over the wet terrycloth that kept the rest of him from me. Between the movements of my hand and my lower body I managed to loosen the towel enough for it to slip away from him and leave him nude and perfect in front of me. My hand reached further down, and I felt him shudder against it, his lips finally breaking from my body to sigh against my neck, seconds before a sharp knocking came from the bathroom door.

"Yo, Frank! You ready yet?" a male's voice shouted through the door.

"Fucking hell, Paulie," I groaned breathlessly, unable to keep my voice quiet through the pounding of my heart.

Frank stood upright, which sadly pulled his body away from me and left me melted against the mirror and sink. He snatched his towel from the floor and didn't so much wrap it back around him as just hold it in front of the important bits.

He reached for the door and whipped it open. Watching the muscles in his back tense and flex as he moved didn't help me gather myself any faster, but seeing Paulie's eyes stretch wide, his face fall when he came eye to eye with Frank... that did help a little. He looked scared. I would've been, too, if I had just cock-blocked Frank.

Paulie was older, near his 50s if not already ankle-deep into them, and a bit softer around the middle, but he could run with men half his age and not even break a sweat. His reddish-brown beard covered most of his face and pulled down into a thick braid that hung just past his neck. Though he was about my height, he carried himself much taller. He was the type that could broadcast 'I will fuck you up' just by standing nearby. He didn't even have to open his mouth for people to think twice about coming at him, but to the right people he was just kind and good-natured. I, luckily, was one of those right people.

"What?" Just one flat word, but Frank made it sound more like a threat than a question.

"Shit. Sorry, brother. You know I'm the last guy that would pull you away from your old lady's attention, but it's time to go. Chuck should be getting there soon." Paulie glanced over Frank's shoulder to me. "Sorry, sugar. Gotta steal your sex toy away."

I just rolled my eyes at him and hopped off the sink. The damp shirt felt awkward sticking to me now, without Frank's heat pressing against it. I plucked at it mindlessly until the men decided to unblock the door.

"Fine. I'll be out in five," Frank said and pushed his way past the other guy, not even bothering to hide his still very naked ass.

Frank was strange like that. In fact, most of them seemed to not really care about each other's nudity. Sometimes we parked and made camp where there are no showers. The guys had no issues jumping into the water to freshen up. If murky lake water can be considered fresh, that is.

When he left the bathroom, that left enough room for me to squeeze past Paulie and I took quick advantage of it. Paulie stepped back to give me plenty of room. Most of the other guys would have stepped closer or made lewd comments about my wet shirt. Paulie was good people. I felt like I could trust him not to be a total pig around me.

I crawled onto the bed and pulled a pillow against my stomach, watching Frank get dressed and finding myself very disappointed about it. What the hell was so important that Frank had to drop everything—meaning me, primed and ready—and go? All the questions I had been wondering about before Frank distracted me with promises of sex came flooding back, but I was too wound up to ask now. Forget it. Let the boys be boys.

Paulie left the room and Frank sat on the edge of the bed, pulling on his boots.

"When are you gonna be back?" I asked.

"Tonight. Probably late," he said.

He twisted around and pressed his lips to my forehead before hopping up again. He was moving in quick, jerking movements. Something was eating at him, but I knew he wouldn't tell me.

"So, don't wait up then?" I asked, sounding churlish even to me.

"Wait, don't wait... I don't really care how you waste your night," he said. I decided, at that moment, to just drop it. I grabbed the clicker from the bed and turned on the television. He walked out of the room without even saying goodbye. Or I love you.

I hadn't even gotten through one episode of Law and Order before my mind started to wander. I felt out of place without Frank there. Restless. He was right about one thing; I didn't need to sit around and waste my night waiting up for him.

I forced myself out of bed and pulled my hair into a long dark braid that hung to my lower back. Frank loved it long, so I'd made a point to keep it that way, but it drove me crazy getting in the way these days.

Our crew occupied ten other rooms at the motel. I was pretty sure I could find something to keep my mind off the clock and all the things I imagined Frank doing behind my back. I headed out of our room and walked to the fourth door down, knocking on it loudly.

"Suze?" I called out.

I wasn't worried about doing to her what Paulie had done to me and Frank. She was single. Not because she wasn't attractive, or a hoot to be around, but because she wanted Paulie, and it seemed like she was willing to wait 'til the end of days for him to come around.

I knocked again and tried the handle. The door opened, and I stepped inside and found Suzanne blow drying her hair in the bathroom. The room mirrored mine, so I knew that her bathroom wasn't nearly big enough to maneuver around in. I imagined it was harder for the much taller woman to be in there any length of time.

"Hey Suze!" I shouted, catching her attention over the loud hum of the dryer.

She clicked it off and smiled over to me, tousling those wild curls of hers with her fingers.

"What's up?"

"You going out?" I asked her, sitting on the corner of her bed.

"Nah. Some of the girls is just hanging out. Wanna come?" She turned back to the mirror and fixed her hair the way she wanted, grabbing a can of Aqua Net and giving her hair a good coat.

"If you don't mind a tag along."

"Girl, when've I ever considered you a tag along?"

"How about when you, Paulie, and I went to the bar last week?" I asked, smiling because I already knew what was coming.

"Now, that's different. I've been trying to get that man to myself for months," she smiled at me. "How's a girl supposed to get a man to notice her with you standing next to her, batting those pretty blue eyes?"

"Oh Jesus, Suze," I laughed, "you're freaking hot, and you know it. No competition. He wasn't ignoring you because I was there. He ignored you because he's fucking stupid and can't see a good thing when it's right in front of him."

She gave me a look that said she didn't believe a word, but appreciated that I'd said it. I guess men could even make knockouts like Suzanne second guess themselves.

She walked up to me and grabbed my braid, playing with it for a minute before dropping it and jerking her head towards the door.

"Come on. We're meeting in Joy Anne's room," she said with a chuckle.

My head dropped, and I let out a long, low groan. I stood up and sighed, following Suzanne out of her room.

"Fuck. Joy Anne? Oh, this night's just getting better and better."

"What's the matter? Don't like the H.B.I.C.-wannab e?"

"You know exactly how I feel about her," I groused.

"Just remember," she said as she slung an arm around my shoulders, "Frank wanted you. Not her."

Joy Anne was one of those women that grated on your nerves for a number of reasons. For me, the biggest was that she wanted to get her hooks into Frank. Since I came into the picture, she'd apparently gotten even more aggressive with it. For everyone else, well, take your pick. Her abrasive laugh, her need to be in everyone's business handing out toxic advice... and speaking of toxic, the cheap perfume she insisted on bathing in could repel all manner of wildlife. She was just a bag full of charm.

The door swung open, and we were greeted by the eloquent Joy Anne sporting a big grin and dazed eyes. Her dark hair was pulled into a messy ponytail, her makeup done up for vamp on the prowl rather than just a few girls having drinks in a craptastic motel room.

"Suzie-Q! Ya came!" she squealed. I happened to know Suze hated the nickname.

"Hey girl," Suzanne said, stepping past her.

When Joy Anne's eyes found me tagging along behind her, her smile went out like a blown bulb. Oh, yes... this was going to be a great night. Full of fun and laughter... possibly an assault charge. Speaking of which, I couldn't help but notice a deep bruising just under her left eye. Shit. Someone hit her good.

"Hey, Joy Anne. I hope you don't mind. Suze invited me," I kept it as pleasant as I could manage. Go me.

"Whatever," she said finally. "We're just havin' a few drinks. Come on in."

We were only forty-five minutes into the first round of Jager Bombs and Whiskey Sours when Joy Anne had me cornered. There wasn't much room for me to avoid her in this shithole of a room, but I had made a valiant effort.

"So, how's you an' Frankie doin'?" Her whiskey-breath hit me with full force, which was impressive since I'd already had a few, myself.

"We're good," I answered simply, hoping to leave it at that.

"Good. Ya know, I was always worried he'd never find himself a good girl. Not that I didn't offer," she said, giggling. It was that high-pitched kind that made my molars hurt, "but I think we both knew we had nothin' in common, really. Just great sex."

My neck tensed. I knew what she was doing. She'd done it before. Frank insisted they'd never gotten that far with each other, and I trusted him. Mostly.

"Well, lucky for him, mind-blowing sex isn't the only thing we have together," I slung back at her, taking a drink. As I'd hoped, it knocked her big-toothed grin down a notch.

Suze and another girl were playing quarters across the room, and I tried to invest my attention on the game, but

Joy Anne only seemed to have eyes for me. I tried my best to ignore her, which only seemed to push her.

Joy Anne leaned closer to me and whispered, "Ya ever notice how hard he gets when ya suck on his earlobe? It's like concrete."

My smile faded. I wouldn't have put it as crudely as Joy Anne had, but it was accurate. The fact that she knew about it was what hit me hardest. Frank had professed, over and over again, that they'd never been that close. A shared kiss while dancing one night and that was it.

I don't know if it was just being fed up with her shit, the three Whiskey Sours, or what, but it slipped out before I could think about what I was about to do.

"Yeah, I do. You know, he also said he couldn't imagine sleeping with you would be any fun. Said 'what's the point of fucking something that's been so used and stretched out? He needs a woman with some grip.'"

"Ya fuckin' whore! What did you just say to me?" her voice exploded over the din, spreading a sudden silence through the room.

"I said Frank doesn't want anything to do with you or your sloppy ass, so you can quit pretending you two have been together just to try to piss me off." I felt strangely calm as I said it. I smiled at her and held her gaze. "Frank is in my bed. Not yours. That ain't gonna change. So go find some other guy to spread your legs for. Frank isn't interested or available."

There was movement in the room, but I had locked eyes with Joy Anne and wasn't going to be the first to look away. I had challenged her and taking my attention away from her was probably the worst thing I could do.

"Guys, really? Come on, let the shit drop and let's have some fun," Suze said, trying to diffuse the situation.

Joy Anne did something I wasn't expecting. Not in the least. She smiled. It was thin and empty, but it was a smile nonetheless.

"Little girl, ya got no idea what Frank wants. Let alone what a man like him needs. You'll learn that soon enough." She looked away. In a way, it was a small victory. Very small, as her words repeated in my brain.

She relaxed back against the wall and held her cup out to one of the other girls.

"Fill me up. I ain't gonna let this get in the way of my good time," she said, and the tension broke just a little more.

Things slowly returned to a relaxed state, and Suze pulled me aside. We sat in our little corner, playing a half-hearted game of quarters as I let my adrenaline fizzle out.

"Harley, you need to be more careful. Joy Anne might be a dumb bitch, but she's a dumb, *vindictive* bitch," she warned me.

"I'm not gonna just let her walk all over me. Sorry, I don't care who she is. I'm tired of her trying to come between me and Frank."

"I get that. I do. I'd probably feel the same if she was prowling after my Paulie. But, baby girl, you don't know what she is capable of. Just... be careful. Please?" Something about her 'please' made me look at her. There was genuine worry in her green eyes.

"Okay. I won't go looking for trouble with her but," I bounced my quarter and watched it fly off the table, "I don't think Frank is being honest with me about the two of them. I think there's more to it than he told me."

I looked at Suzanne, and she wouldn't meet my eyes. Did she have her doubts, too? Hell, for that matter, did she know something I didn't? I wanted to ask, but she grabbed a bottle from beside her foot and poured more Jack into my glass. By now, it had become mostly Whiskey and very little Sour.

"Let's just try to have some fun, yeah? The boys are off being boys. Let's just kick back."

I sighed and leaned back in my chair. "Yeah, fine," I said.

I was defeated, at least for the time being. What was I going to do? Call Frank while he was out with Chuck and them and tear him a new asshole? Accuse him of lying to me like some insecure little twit? The idea of just getting up and knocking the smug grin off Joy Anne's face sounded like a great way to entertain myself, but Suze was right. Why not just relax and have a good time?

Chapter 4

FRANK'S PHONE BUZZED AGAINST his hip as he stretched out across the rusty old truck bed. He was content to ignore it at first; most likely just Harley bugging him about when he was going to be back, something he didn't feel like dealing with tonight. He needed to distance himself from her a little.

What had started out as a game for him had grown into something far beyond what he'd wanted. She was supposed to be a job. A simple procurement. And he figured, what the hell? If he had to drag her around, why not have a little fun?

She was never supposed to get under his skin the way she had. He hated it, hated the way he craved the salty smoothness of her skin, craved her scent.

And yet, even when he fought to get a little peace and quiet away from her incessant nagging, his body—and something deeper inside—itched and squirmed with her absence. The animal inside him had hungered for her from the moment he'd been turned. It was like a switch had flipped. Once the wolf was alive within him, it had scented her and wanted her. Frank had never questioned his wolf. He'd submitted himself to it in all things, including her.

But that didn't mean he had to like the fact that he was drawn to a woman that drove him crazy in every way he could think of—good and bad.

Nursing the bottle in his hand, he tried to put her out of his mind. He needed a clear head tonight. Distractions could be fatal. As much as he'd like to pretend tonight was an escape with his boys, the truth of the matter was it was so much more than that. Tonight was going to change everything.

The phone nagged at him again, vibrating over and over until he slipped it out of his pocket and flipped it open. The screen nearly blinded him as it lit up, flashing the name "Joy Anne" across it.

Frank sat up, knocking John-Boy from his unstable perch on the Chevy's frame. His brothers laughed as the prospect fell face-first in the dirt, but Frank's attention rested solely on the messages Joy Anne had sent him.

> *he knows*

> *hes hedin straight to u*

> *watch ur ass*

Fantastic, he thought. His grin widened as he snapped the phone shut and shoved it back into his pocket, not even bothering to send a message back. Thank God that bitch could come through when it counted. Not that she'd had any clue she'd been nothing more than some moveable piece in his little game. Things were falling into place.

If Frank were a better man, he might have felt like a shit for tugging her along the way he did. But he wasn't. And he didn't. He needed her to set things in motion and nothing more.

There had been no doubt in his mind she and Chuck would get into it and she would open her mouth. In fact, he was counting on it. He needed her to wind Chuck up, get him so pissed off that he'd fuck up. He'd be looking for blood. As long as he could keep Harley from finding out what he'd had to do, he'd be golden.

He briefly entertained the idea of Harley and Joy Anne being let off their leashes at one another. It was no secret how much Harley despised the woman; something that couldn't be helped when the dumb bitch kept throwing herself at him right in front of her. But then again, she loved to stir shit up. It was as though she was trying to get a chance at Harley. Like she was just waiting for an excuse to sink claws into her. The idea of them fighting it out had started out amusing, but just thinking of Joy Anne hurting his girl made his skin burn hot.

Fucking women. They would be the death of him.

He tossed his empty bottle into the blazing fire, the sound of shattering glass almost musical to his ears. Things could go either way by the time the night was over. Might as well have one last drink with his boys, just in case. A low, almost-menacing chuckle escaped him as he snatched an unopened bottle from Paulie as he passed by.

"Asshole," he said, with a good-humored smile. "What are you laughin' at?"

"Good times. Good company," Frank replied.

Paulie grabbed himself another beer from the cooler and leaned against the truck, tapping the neck of the bottle against the one Frank had stolen. "Good life."

As Frank brought the beer to his lips, he heard a hog approaching beyond the trees. His skin sung with anticipation. *Soon.*

He nodded softly. "It will be," he whispered against the glass before taking a deep, greedy drink.

With the sudden quieting of the engine, Frank laid back again, his worn boot kicked out in front of him while he leaned on one elbow and nursed his Budweiser. Even the danger breaking past the tree line and approaching hard and fast couldn't wipe the smirk off his face. He held it firm as he watched the ball of fury coming his way. He raised his bottle in a silent cheer as his leader stormed towards him, then eyed him over the bottle as he took one last drink.

Frank knew what was coming. The rest of the guys had no clue, but Frank did. He'd made sure to be ready when Chuck reached him. His body tensed, muscles tightening in his arms and chest as Chuck closed those last few steps. He couldn't help himself. He winked before he lowered the bottle away from his face. Oh, he was asking for what was coming, but strangely, didn't seem to give a shit.

"Hey Chuck, there you are. Take a load off," Paulie said, bending down to grab him a bottle.

Chuck's fist crushed through Frank's jaw.

Frank's head snapped with the force of the blow, blood spraying out in dark droplets across the truck bed. Voices raised and glass shattered as bottles slid from the hands holding them. Chuck grabbed Frank by his collar. Thick, meaty hands wrapped in his shirt and used it to pull him off the truck and onto his feet. He laid another blow into his gut, but there was less force to it thanks to Paulie and a couple of other men pulling the two apart.

"What the fuck, Chuck!?" Paulie cried out, stepping back towards Frank.

Frank staggered back a little, catching his balance, while rubbing his jaw. He laughed; a soft roll of chuckles that built into a very male, very deranged, laugh.

"You laughin', boy?" Chuck screamed over the group of men between him and his intended target.

"Fuck, yeah, I am," Frank said, standing more upright.

His jaw ached as he ran his tongue over his teeth then leaned to the side to spit out a little more blood. "You hit hard for an old dog. But this time, I ain't going down."

Chuck lunged again, but his bulk was held in check by the other men. Each of them looked between the pair, con-fused. Out of their depths. Only Paulie slid a knowing look to Frank. Frank glanced back up at him, that ever-present grin still stretched over his lips, teeth tinged with blood that oozed from the cut on the inside of his cheek.

"Shit," Paulie whispered, barely louder than a breath. He leaned closer to Frank trying to keep his voice low, "You really fucking did it?"

"Oh, yeah," Frank said, eyes trained on the threat just behind his friend.

"Whatcha whisperin' for? You afraid the men you call brothers will think less of ya if they know? That they might not trust you to have their backs if they knew you were low enough to go and fuck my old lady?" Chuck's voice was rough and held a slight tremor as he screamed those words.

The men erupted in a symphony of reactions. A couple of them gave Frank impressed glances, one gave a low whistle, while others looked at one another as if wondering whether they should watch their own women.

Theo and Butch, two old dogs that had been with Chuck from the beginning, let their disgust towards this kind of betrayal show plainly in the curl of their lips.

"The question you should ask," Frank said more firmly, "is why would they follow a man who can't control his own bitch?"

Chuck loosed a guttural scream, lunging towards Frank again. The men that were holding him back lost their grip and had to jump on him to tackle him to his knees. They all knew if Chuck got to Frank at that moment, that he would kill him.

Frank might have been an ass, but he knew most of the men they rode were loyal to him. Most didn't think a used-up bitch like Joy Anne was worth such a sacrifice. More importantly, they all knew Frank was right.

Chuck grunted with the force of all those bodies holding him back. "And who do you think they should follow?" he growled. "*You*?!" He screamed the last word as if it was vile.

"Yes," Frank said softly, his voice going empty and cold as his grin finally vanished.

Chuck stilled instantly. His eyes were wide, lips parted. The men holding him turned their attention to Frank now, letting Chuck push himself to his feet.

"You challenging me, Frankie?" he asked, that edge of growl still thick in his voice.

Frank laughed again, his hands flexing idly at his sides. "Yes, Chuck. I am fucking challenging you. I call you out as being nothing more than a squeamish, indecisive, weak-ass, pussy of an alpha."

"You ain't wolf enough to take them from me," Chuck said, a sudden roll of heat coming from him.

"I might not be able to shift like you can, but that don't change shit. I am still calling you out," Frank's grin returned, but it was more like a bearing of teeth than a smile. He moved towards Chuck, closing the distance between them until they were eye to eye. "And I was wolf enough for your girl. I took *her* every way she'd let me."

Chuck surged forward. With no one stepping in now, he hit Frank in a violent crash of bodies. He'd been pushed past his limit. Beyond the betrayal, beyond any hurt, Frank knew the motivating force behind Chuck's attack all too well. Chuck was driven by things that were less human ego and pride and more animal instinct. Kill or be killed. The threat was in front of him, and he would take it down and tear out its pulse so it would never rise up to him again.

Only, this time, Frank was ready for it. He tensed, bouncing slightly on the balls of his feet, waiting for Chuck to make his move. When his body crashed into him with all the power of an oncoming train, Frank took the hit, absorbing the force and using his own momentum to turn them around before hitting the ground.

He landed on top of Chuck, arms locked into one another, trying to control his hands. It wasn't easy. Chuck's animal ferocity was almost impossible for Frank to hold at bay. It was all he could do to keep those anvil fists from slamming into him.

Chuck was a big man. Older, possibly past his prime, but he was a seasoned fighter. This is what he'd done many times before to get to this level among the rest of the men. That, and the sheer fury that raged through him, would make him dangerous.

The world flipped over, and Frank was suddenly underneath Chuck, his bulk crushing him into the dirt. A hand slipped out of Frank's grip, and he threw his forearm up, managing to block the heavy blow. With his head protected, and his other hand still gripping Chuck's dominant hand, his trunk was open to the next hit. Frank's stomach went up into his throat. It hurt. God, it fucking hurt. He coughed, feeling as if he might eject the entire contents of his stomach right there, but he choked it down. He couldn't afford to lose time getting sick. He'd be dead.

Most men might have doubled over, folded in half like a woman, clutching their gut. But not Frank. He had to stay alert, couldn't close his eyes, couldn't give into the pain. He may have been smaller than Chuck, but what he lacked in size he made up for in balls and brutality.

A rough, calloused hand found Frank's throat, squeezing tight. Frank gasped, his throat choking around his breath, as Chuck pushed down on him, not just squeezing but trying to crush his windpipe. Frank's fist beat into the other man's ribs, one desperate blow after another, but he was losing strength. The world was going fuzzy around the edges.

Chuck's grip tightened as the hits stopped. He was going to rip his throat out. He was going to put him down like a rabid dog that bit the hand that fed him.

"You lost, boy," Chuck whispered as he leaned into Frank's ear. "Don't worry... we'll take care of your little bitch when you're gone. I'll give everyone a turn with her before we take her to him."

A deep, rasping laugh squeezed through Frank's throat. There was something almost manic in the sound.

"You... ain't... won...yet," he hissed against the side of Chuck's face.

Chuck turned his head, still hovering against Frank's cheek, and opened his mouth but Frank was too close. Chuck had made a deadly mistake.

As Chuck brought the front of his face closer to Frank's, the younger man wrapped his hands around the back of Chuck's head, holding it in against his face, and opened his maw like a snake ready to strike. He bore down over Chuck's eye, sinking teeth into his temple and hooking his bottom teeth against the soft inner corner of his eyeball, and he bit into him. His teeth scraped along the curve of his eye, pushing deep into the socket, and sank into the soft, meaty flesh of his eyeball before it burst into his mouth like a big, fat grape. It exploded over Frank's tongue and oozed from the corners of his lips.

A scream that should not have come from a man of his age, and size, exploded into the night, echoing among the trees that surrounded them all. Chuck shot off Frank, his hands clasping over his eye. He stumbled back, and a trail of gore oozed down his cheek as he screamed.

Frank drew in a sharp breath that burned his lungs, tightened his throat, and pulled in the thick, gooey liquid that had burst into his mouth. He didn't wait to be able to breathe again to get to his feet. He rolled to them, his eyes shining fiery amber in the light of the fire. Broad shoulders rose and fell as he caught breath, but he never looked away from Chuck. Many might make the mistake of rushing towards the injured man in an attempt to get the upper hand on him, but Frank knew better. You don't corner a wounded animal. That was when they lashed out and tore your face off.

"I'll fucking kill you!" Chuck screamed, moving his hand away from his face to reveal the mangled mess of his injured eye, streaming with blood and thicker things.

Frank held his hand to his stomach, coughing. Fighting past the nausea from the taste of it. Blood burst from his mouth, spraying out to fall to the ground, dribbling down his chin.

"You'll try," Frank spat back at him, still regaining his breath.

A low growl rolled from Chuck's throat. It was a sound that did not belong to a human body. It was the growl that caught Frank's attention and put him back on highest alert. If Chuck shifted, it was all over. He had to keep that from happening if he had any chance of getting out of this alive.

Once claws and teeth came out, he was dead. Those razor-sharp claws would tear through his body like wet tissue paper. He needed to make Chuck want to kill him so badly he couldn't think past it, couldn't focus and bring those claws to bear.

He straightened his back and cleared the dirt from his sleeves and shoulders. To everyone watching, it seemed like he wasn't paying any mind to the man in front of him, might look like he didn't see Chuck as any kind of threat.

Nothing could be further from the truth. Frank honed every sense he had on that raging bulk of a man, and he was thinking of his next move.

"Well, fuck me," Frank said, laughing just the right way to stoke the embers of Chuck's rage.

He looked at Chuck again, hands drawn out, palms up, to either side of him. "Oh, in case you were wonderin', that's how it all started. She came to me and begged. 'Fuck me, Frank... Please'. Hard to deny that girl of yours when she was comin' at me like a bitch in heat."

The men grew eerily silent, struck dumb by what Frank was saying. It brought a mirthful grin to his lips, teeth still edged in red. They set the stage for this, allowing Chuck to see their realization that he was not the strength and power they thought he was. He was going to milk it for all it was worth.

"'Cause she did. You know... beg for it," he said low. "She begged for a real man to fuck her good and hard," he repeated as he reached down and cupped his crotch.

Words are for an educated and civil mind. A way to communicate the complex thoughts and ideas of man. Animals were not so complex. Fear, food, fighting, and fucking. Four simple instincts that drove them. If you weren't afraid of it, didn't want to eat it, and didn't want to fuck it, then you fought it. You destroyed it any way you could before it destroyed you. That was what Chuck's animal scream expressed as he threw himself at Frank.

Frank was ready. He anticipated the attack, waited for the right moment when Chuck was too far gone to change tactics and not quite past the point of 'too late'. Sweat beaded at his brow and neck, drying blood flaked on his chin, and he waited.

He waited, even as his mind urged him to move. To attack or to run. His body knew the plan, listened, told his mind to shut the fuck up. When Chuck seemed like he might weigh-lay into him, Frank stepped back, turning his body just enough so that Chuck hit the fender of the truck head on with a deafening clank.

He was stunned for just a moment, but that was all the time Frank needed to finish this once and for all. He grabbed Chuck by the back of his hair and beat his face into the already dented fender. He loosed a primal and bone-chilling scream as he married the man's face into the truck over and over again, painting it red with fresh blood. Each blow flattened Chuck's face, crushing cartilage and bone alike.

He jerked him away from the truck and tossed him closer to the fire to groan and sputter as he tried to breathe through the ruin of his face. A half-empty beer bottle caught Frank's eye, and he bent at the waist to snatch it up. As he stood upright, he brought the bottle back to crack it sharply against the truck bed. It shattered, leaving a jagged bottle in Frank's blood-splattered hand.

There was movement in the gathering of men. Frank's eyes slid past all of them as he slowly stalked toward the fallen alpha. Faces of horror, of disbelief, of awe, and even disdain met his gaze.

He took note of those that sneered at him, who looked ready to fight for their fallen brother. They would see, soon, just what kind of man Frank was. They thought he was ruthless? They hadn't seen nothin' yet.

Frank stepped one boot over the man on the ground, standing over him like the grim reaper waiting for his final breath. He was a ruin of a man, somehow less than half the size he had started, but he could heal. Frank knew that, if given the time, Chuck could be almost back to full health.

He might not ever save his eye, but he wouldn't need it to tear Frank's throat out. He crouched over the big man, nearly sitting on his round stomach.

"They're mine, Chuck. All of them. Your bitch was just the first. They'll all follow behind me, because they crave a real leader. Thanks for keeping the seat warm for me." He glanced at the line of men that seemed to be pushing closer, watching him.

The sharp edge of the glass bottle bit into Chuck's flesh, just under the sternum. In movies, they always aim just over the heart, but they forget about the ribs encasing that precious organ. He put pressure on it and twisted, cutting and digging into the skin with wet, meaty sounds that were quickly drowned out by ragged screams. Chuck's flesh peeled away like over-ripened fruit, the glass disappearing further and further into him.

As the screams died down to a wet gurgling, Frank could hear a soft, retching behind him. One of the men couldn't hold it in. Too much beer, falling adrenaline, and the sickly-sweet smell of blood and meat made his stomach clench and spill out onto the ground behind him. The rest of the men watched Frank cut their fallen brother away.

The bottle emerged with a thicker, darker coating and Frank tossed it over his shoulder, a glob of viscera landing on the shoulder of his jacket. He glanced at the men, his men, and locked eyes with one still looking at him with a defiant gleam.

Without taking his eyes off him, Frank plunged his bare hand into the tunnel he'd carved under Chuck's ribcage, his fingers digging the rest of the way through.

Muscle and tissue gave way as his hand searched, moved, twisted, and finally he pulled it back out with a thick, meaty heart in his grasp.

He stood, blood slicked up to his elbow, and held the heart out to the side of his body. He stared at the men still gathered, letting them see the life source of their former boss before letting it fall to the ground. All eyes were fixated on this man before them.

"Now," Frank said, his voice gravelly, "shit's gonna change. I know you all loved Chuck. Hell, I loved him too."

A snort of bitter laughter rung out from within the men.

"You got a funny fuckin' way of showin' it," said a slender man with graying hair. His skin was dark in the way only a lifetime of being in the sun could manage.

"This ain't preschool, Theo. You want group hugs and story time get on your hog and blow the fuck on outta here. This is the nature of the beast, gentlemen. If you lead, you fight. If you lose... you die. Chuck knew how it is. He was a helluva guy, but we need more than just a helluva guy to take charge and do what's gotta be done to get the respect we deserve.

"Now, if y'all wanna sit here and bitch and whine about how shit's done, then be my guest. The rest of us are gonna move on to bigger and better things. The rest of us are gonna live life the way it's meant to be lived. Wild and free and answering to no one."

Frank looked from Theo to the rest of the men gathered around the truck. Many nodded at what he had to say and looked ready to fall in line. Some still looked as though they might turn on him. That was fine. Frank had no love lost for the old dogs Chuck had brought with him. None of them were real threats. Weakness like that could be left in the wind as far as Frank was concerned.

He shook his hands at his sides, the last remnants of Chuck's life dripping from his fingertips and started walking towards the trees and the line of bikes parked just beyond them. Those that would follow him would do so. Let the dead weight stay with the dead. As he thought about that, an idea came to mind. He glanced back to the fire and the crowd of men moving towards him.

"Go back and get him," Frank said to two of the men closest to him.

They looked at him with identical expressions of confusion.

"Chuck. Get his body, prop him in Theo's sidecar," he said without elaborating any further.

As Frank went to his bike, the men glanced at each other then back to where they'd left Chuck lying on the ground. They weren't sure what Frank's intentions were, but looking at Chuck's heart lying cold and motionless on the ground, they sure the fuck weren't going to ask him.

Chapter 5

Suze and I pretty much kept to ourselves for the next two hours. She commandeered a couple bottles of Jack and a two-liter of cola, and we stayed in our cozy little corner. It wasn't an ideal way to spend an evening, but it beat waiting alone for Frank.

Her quarter flipped into my cup while the one I threw missed the table entirely and ricocheted off the wall behind her. I was way too drunk for this game.

"Drink up, baby girl. You'll have an iron constitution by the time I'm through with ya," she said, with a giggle.

"I've mentioned how gross whiskey smells, right?" I asked as I pinched my nose and threw back the double shot of Jack. I wasn't a big drinker, in all honesty, but it seemed like Suze was working on changing that.

A sudden crash across the room sent the entirety of the room into panicked shrieks. Most of us launched ourselves out of our chairs, knocking over glasses, bottles, and in some cases, each other. Only Suze seemed to not be scared shitless.

She shot to her feet, all laughter drained from her face, and cut through the rest of the girls. I managed to catch a glance of bandanas and leather spilling into the small, packed room.

"Get the fuck out the way!" Paulie's voice roared through the rise of female voices.

The small crowd parted, and I blinked fuzzy eyes at the men as they scrambled inside. Paulie and Niko, another man that rode with us, were both staggering in, spatters of red all over them. They were carrying something between them, and it took a considerable amount of concentration on my part to realize it was a body.

"Shut the door," Frank's voice called out.

Suzanne hurried to the door and shut it, locking the dead bolt with a sharp click. The boys, who were carrying the body by the feet and shoulders, moved towards me and the bed. Paulie crawled up backwards on the mattress, hoisting the bigger man onto it placing him into full and perfect view. It was Chuck.

Or what used to be Chuck. His face was so swollen and busted up I could only recognize the black Durangos on his feet.

"Oh my God," I said, feeling my stomach start to churn.

"What happened?" Suzanne asked, her eyes wide.

Joy Anne was close behind, her makeup already started running down her cheeks. "Oh my God. Oh my God, Chuck. Please don't be dead! Don't die, baby!" Her voice grew shriller and more painful to hear with each syllable

Chuck's shirt was shredded. There was so much blood I couldn't help but stare at it in numb fascination. The more I stared, the more I started to make sense out of what I was looking at. There was a gaping hole in his chest, the edges of his flesh shredded around it, blood drying darkly inside it. It looked like the exit wound of a close-range shotgun blast.

"What... happened to him?" My voice was barely audible over Joy Anne's sobs.

Frank looked at me, then, and I tore my eyes from the corpse to meet his. His face was hard, unreadable. If there was any grief there, I couldn't see it. Drops of red spotted his chin and drew my eyes further down. He was covered in blood. His arms were coated in it, stomach painted in it. We locked eyes for a minute, and only Joy Anne's shrieking made him look away from me.

"He's gone, Joy Anne." His voice was eerily calm.

I forced myself to move towards Frank. I couldn't tell if the blood on him was his own or Chuck's. I needed to see if he was okay. It was too much blood. Far too much.

"Are you hurt?" I asked. He didn't even look at me. He just stared down at Chuck's lifeless body as it lay on the bed.

"Frank," I tried again but Suzanne cut me off.

"What the hell happened out there? Who did this?"

I tried to touch Frank's shoulder, but he gave a sharp jerk away from my hand. That was when I noticed how hard and fast he was breathing. He had looked so calm, so collected, until I noticed that. Now he seemed wild like he might snap at any moment. What the fuck had happened? He looked to me, then to two of the other girls that were with us. He whispered something I couldn't hear to Suze and she just stared at him, unmoving.

"Get them out of here. Now!" He barked at her.

She stepped back, her eyes going wide, but nodded. She grabbed my still-hovering hand and turned me to the door.

"Come on," she whispered to me, and then raised her voice. "Shelby, Roxy. You, too. Out."

I stared over my shoulder at Frank as Suze all but pushed me out of the room.

"Suze, what the Hell? Talk to me!" I shouted, finding my voice.

She turned me around and grabbed my face in her hands, forcing me to look at her. Her eyes were large, fierce, and alive with an emerald fire I couldn't explain.

"Go to your room. Pack your shit," she said in a hushed whisper. "Take a cloth and wipe down everything. Anything you or Frank might have touched. Do it fast."

"What? What are you talking about?"

"Just go. We're leaving. Don't talk to anyone. Just go. Do what I said and wait for Frank. It'll be okay, alright? It'll be fine."

Things were moving so fast, and I couldn't keep up. Suzanne was already walking the other two girls to their rooms, disappearing around the corner. I wanted to go back, to barge into Joy Anne's room and demand answers, but panic turned me the other way and sent me to do exactly as I was told.

It was the first time I'd been grateful for having so little to my name. My clothes and makeup fit into my backpack, even without taking the time to fold them neatly. Frank's bedroll was already on his bike and everything else of importance was locked in the saddlebags. After five minutes of packing—which was more like me running around in a blind frenzy—I moved onto cleaning up our fingerprints.

I should've taken a moment to stop and ask myself why I needed to do this. Why did our fingerprints matter? I should have, but the truth was I was scared out of my skull. Suzanne was good people, and if she said we needed to do this then who was I to argue with her?

After grabbing a washrag from the bathroom sink, I darted around wiping down everything in sight—the doorknobs, the dresser drawers, the telephone. I ran the cloth over everything Frank and I may have touched, unsure why I was doing it or how it was going to help with the whole "Chuck's dead" situation.

I was scrubbing the remote when the door opened. I dropped the rag, my heart roaring in my chest as Frank stepped inside.

"Oh God," I breathed, throwing myself at him.

His hands went up and he stepped back; a clear message for me to not touch him. He'd cleaned some of the blood off of him, but his palms were still tinted red. Seeing the stains on his palms helped convince me to keep my distance.

"Are you hurt?" I asked, trying to control my voice.

"No," was all he offered before shoving past me.

"Well... what happened? How did he..."

"Drop it, Harley." He grabbed a pack of cigarettes from the side table and slammed them into the heel of his palm.

I stared at him as he took one out then slipped the smokes into his jacket pocket. I barely recognized this man anymore. He never used to be this closed off and hostile toward me. He was hiding something. Something big. I'd seen my first dead body tonight, and everyone's first reaction was to pack up and run. That wasn't right. In fact, it was very, very wrong.

"Drop it? Exactly what the fuck am I supposed to drop, Frank?" The shock was giving way to desperation. "Chuck is dead! What happened to him? Why are we not calling the cops? I don't understand how you can be so calm about all this."

Frank didn't say a word. He straightened his jacket and grabbed my backpack from the bed. It clicked. In that moment, watching him not even give a damn that his friend was dead, I knew exactly how he was keeping so calm.

"Oh my God. You did it, didn't you?"

He looked at me then. It was brief; a mere flash of narrowed eyes, but it was enough. I started towards him, not sure what I was going to do when I reached him.

"You told me nothing was going to happen. That you guys were just going to talk to him." My throat was tight. He continued to ignore me.

I wanted to grab him and force him to look at me. If I stood my ground for a change, then maybe I could finally get some answers from him. I reached out for him again as I snapped, "Frank!"

He grabbed me. Hard. Fast. His fingers gripped painfully into the meat of my arms, and he spun me around so that my back crashed against the door. It knocked the wind out of me, stunned me. Ow.

"Shut up!" he shouted less than an inch from my face. "Just... Shut. Up."

I don't know if it was shock from hitting the wall, or that Frank had been the one to do it, but I shut up. My lips pressed hard together, and I just stared at him. I stared at the face of the man I was beginning to wonder if I really knew at all.

"Chuck's dead. I don't want to talk about it now. I... can't talk about it right now." His grip and his face softened and the roiling violence inside him seemed to be ebbing away. He swallowed hard. "We don't have time. We have to get out of here. I need to get you away from here, now,

Harley. Let me get us safe, get us somewhere where I can think again, and I'll explain."

He let go of one arm and I flinched as he pressed his hand to my cheek and his forehead to mine. His breath came out in a dry sob that turned into a bitter laugh. I didn't see anything funny about this. I had so many questions, and he just gave me so many non-answers.

What I did know was something not good was happening. Whether it was happening to Frank or happening *because* of him was something I'd have to find out in time. But for now, at this moment, he looked desperate, afraid, and in shock. Whatever was coming after us he wanted me away from it.

"Please."

That one word spoke volumes to me. He didn't use it often. Sometimes it seemed like it was a special little word he used only for me, and even that was rare. To stand here pleading to me to go with him—it was the most vulnerable he'd allowed himself to be to me for a while. A long while.

"Okay," I said, finally. "But once we get wherever we're going you talk to me. I need to know what I'm doing in all this."

That was brutal honesty. I needed to know why I should stay with them. Why I should throw my life away to run with Frank and everyone else knowing that they could just leave someone like Chuck dead in a run-down motel?

I went with them for answers and because Frank needed me. For whatever reason, he needed me. The question was, why?

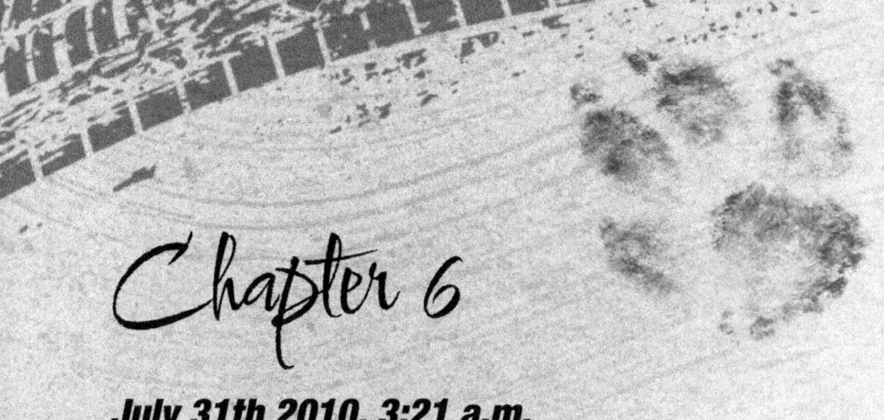

Chapter 6

July 31th 2010, 3:21 a.m.

FRANK

A SHARP KNOCKING BROKE the silence of the motel courtyard. It was late, well past the hour when normal people went to bed and even the crazies called it a night. For Frank, the night was still young and rife with possibility. He'd left Harley in their room to sit and stew in her attitude so he could tend to a little more business before dawn.

Frank leaned against the door frame and rubbed the back of his head as Paulie continued his relentless knocking.

"John Boy, get your ass out here," Paulie growled before looking at him. "Asshole's probably asleep."

"Nah," Frank said with a chuckle, "he's probably in there yankin' his dick."

He balled up his fist and slammed it against the door. The knocks echoed around them, bringing eyes to a few of the surrounding windows. Frank scanned all those windows and all of the eyes staring at the two of them. He was used to it. Hotels were full of people sticking their noses where they didn't belong, and his group was never one to be quiet and inconspicuous.

As he went to sweep his eyes over a break in the building, where the parking lot let out onto the road and the woods beyond that, he caught a sudden flash in the deep shadows. They could have been headlights in the far distance, except they were too close together and way too small. Not to mention they came from inside the bushes just across the road. A quick flash of silvery-blue and they were gone before Frank could really get a bead on them. He stared at the spot they'd been seconds before until another assault on John Boy's door turned him back around.

"Open up, Jackass!" he bellowed before the door whipped open.

A sliver of white skin and red fleece peeked from the cracked door, topped with dark eyes and yellow curls. It was one of the girls from Joy Anne's room. She was new, newer even than Harley. Paulie straightened himself up, backing up a step, but Frank just sighed.

"Tell John Boy to get his ass out here already."

"He's asleep," the girl said.

"And? Get him up," Frank countered, the patience leaving his voice.

A hushed voice came from inside.

"He's not feeling well," the girl said, her voice shaking slightly. "Took some sleep meds. Can't wake him up."

Paulie rolled his eyes and opened his mouth, but Frank was done playing around. He slammed his hand hard enough against the door that it popped open and bounced against the wall inside. The girl balked and nearly lost the grip on the small blanket she was holding around herself, but she quickly stepped out of the way in time to let Frank pass.

After a bit of a struggle, Frank emerged from the room dragging a pale, stark-naked, man by the foot. John Boy clawed at the sidewalk and patch of grass Frank dragged him over. The gravel bit into the exposed flesh as he slid over it, leaving shallow cuts like tiny lipstick kisses all over his skin. His protesting fell on deaf ears.

"Fucking Christ, Frank," John Boy shouted as he lay prone on the ground.

Frank walked over to his bike and unlocked one of the saddlebags.

"Maybe next time you'll be man enough to answer the door yourself. Instead of sending your girl like a little bitch." He grabbed a white cotton t-shirt and pair of jeans from the compartment and threw them on top of John Boy.

"Now put that baby dick of yours away. We gotta talk."

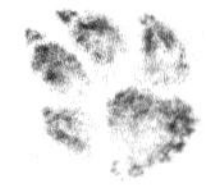

HARLOW

The wolf watched from the trees as the two men dragged the boy from his hotel room and dumped his naked ass onto the gravel lot. Essex certainly wasn't trying to keep a low profile. How many people were sitting in their rooms, watching the display from their windows? It was sloppy. Stupid.

It was everything Frank Essex was.

Mutt.

The animal didn't so much as move until the men rode away on their barbaric machines and disappeared from sight. He could have procured the girl right then. It would have been effortless. Essex had left her alone with a bunch of females and betas, none of which were any threat to him. Hell, he could have run down there, tore his pack of outlaws apart, and been halfway home with the package in tow before the bastard even came back.

Yet he didn't. He knew if he disobeyed his orders, he would be made an example of and some other wolf would be given his role in what was to come. He couldn't have that. He'd earned his place with blood and loyalty. Why throw it all away now to get to Essex?

Even if the thought of him finding his pitiful pack completely ravaged made Harlow's cock rock hard.

Instead of giving in to the urges, he turned back towards the woods. Not now. But soon.

As the tawny wolf padded back to the small clearing and the awaiting BMW, he heard Rizzaro's voice cut through the nocturnal music of the woods. He slowed, lingering just inside the shadows of the trees to listen.

"Yeah, we got in about an hour ago," Rizzaro spoke into the phone with a raspy voice.

The voice on the other end, however, had nothing raspy about it. Harlow could hear the clear and articulate confidence easily from where he waited.

"Excellent. Did you have much trouble finding them?" the voice asked.

"No, sir. They don't really seem to be putting much thought into it. We just followed the stink of exhaust and beer," Rizzaro said with a chuckle.

Green eyes, the color of fresh cut grass, stared out of the window of the Beemer, waiting. Just on the other side of these woods was, yet another, run down motel they'd followed the bikers to. They'd driven past it and saw the bikes grouped out front that suggested this could be the right place. The collective smell of pack strengthened their suspicions.

"He's one stupid fuck if he thought we couldn't track them here," Rizzaro added.

"Or he just does not care. Never underestimate a man like Mr. Essex, Rizzaro," the voice over the phone suggested. "There is a reason I chose him."

The wolf's lips curled at that, baring its sharp teeth.

The line went dead and Rizzaro slid the phone back in his pocket. People like him did not warrant the pleasantries of polite farewells. He was hired muscle. Nothing more. So, he would sit there on that quiet little road and wait for Harlow to come back with confirmation that Frank and his baggage were, indeed, in that motel.

Frank had been sent to get the girl. Now Harlow was being sent to watch the both of them. It was an insult that didn't sit well with him. He was built for better things than babysitting duty.

If Vale had wanted him to come out here after them he should have sent him for her in the first place.

The man pulled out a pack of Newports and slid one between his lips, gearing up to smoke, before stepping out of the car and slamming the door behind him. The wolf raised its snout to the air, scented the filmy smoke snaking its way from Rizzaro, and gave a wild sneeze.

"Good news?" Rizzaro said to the animal before coolly sliding his cigarette back into his mouth.

Silvery-blue wolf eyes locked onto Rizzaro as it reached its fourth step, large paws melting away into pink flesh. Fingers dug into the thick soil, more suited for clawed appendages, and lifted away as the animal's body morphed into something more of the two-legged variety.

The wolf had been replaced with 6'2" of solid muscle and tan skin. A lot of skin. He stood stark naked against the darkness of the trees and didn't even seem to care. Deep chestnut hair danced over his collarbone, long and unbound and studded with little bits of twigs and dead leaves. His cupid-bow lips curled into a self-satisfied grin.

"Very," he said low, his hand stretching out in a silent request for Rizzaro's phone.

Rizzaro shrugged his shoulders and procured the cell from his pocket, tossing it to Harlow. It didn't take long for someone to pick up on the other end.

"Yes?" a single, expectant, word.

"They're here. Saw Essex myself, and he's got a pretty little brunette with him," he said, still grinning at Rizzaro over the top of the car.

"That is very good news. Very good."

"Should we procure them for you?"

"No, not yet. I am curious to see Mr. Essex's next move."

"I don't think the little beast is going to come quietly. Are you certain you made the right choice? Essex seems to be getting far too involved—" Harlow was cut off by a sharp 'tsk'-ing sound.

"They will come in the end. Like dogs to their master, they all come. It just takes a little.... housebreaking." He chuckled. "Do not make any moves on them yet. It is preferable for the wolf to submit willingly."

"And if they don't?" Harlow asked.

"There are ways to make someone see reason." The phone went dead.

Harlow tossed the phone back to Rizzaro and moved to the BMW's back passenger side door, swinging it open and reaching inside. He emerged again with a pair of fresh-ly-pressed charcoal slacks, slipping them on over his mus-cled legs.

"So are we stuck here?" Rizzaro asked him as Harlow flung a crisp black dress shirt over his shoulders, slipping his arms into each sleeve.

He flipped his long hair out from the collar like he'd done a thousand times. He took care with each delicate-ly-sewn button and then tucked his shirt tail in with equal scrutiny. After he was mostly dressed, he reached into the front passenger seat and opened the glove box, pulling out two little foil wrapped packs of wet wipes. He tore into them, cleaning the dirt form his fingers and nails.

Rizzaro shook his head and flicked his half-burned cigarette into the darkness. He dug keys out of his black slacks and opened the door, a crooked grin breaking over his lips as he glanced at the taller man cleaning himself.

"What's the matter, Harlow? Daddy didn't give sweet'ums his way?" he said with a laugh in his voice.

Harlow fixed him with a hard look. It made Rizzaro's smile fade around the edges, and he started to duck into the driver's seat without another word. Harlow's hand slapped the roof of the car, stopping him.

"Talk to me like that again, and I'll cut your balls off and fuck the hole while it's still fresh and bloody," Harlow whispered with an edge of growl to his voice, a smile spreading over his lips.

The smile was one that walked the line between threat and eager anticipation. Rizzaro shut up, as was the intended effect, and got into the car, turning it on. Harlow slid in, slammed his own door far harder than was necessary, and they drove off in search of a place to post up for the night.

FRANK

The bar next to the Fairview Motel was small, even for a hole-in-the-wall dive bar. The bar on the far wall sat two stools, and aside from a few tall tables, it was pretty much standing room only. Most of its space was lent out to the single billiards table just in front of the door. It would have been too small to hold the entire crew, but tonight it was just Frank, Paulie, and John Boy.

John Boy racked up while Frank and Paulie got themselves a couple beers. The place was empty enough; just a bartender, a waitress, and one guy who'd made his way into the bathroom as the trio entered. Small as this place was, the need for more than just a bartender on duty seemed a bit excessive but she wasn't hard on the eyes.

She gave Frank the full effect of her smile, though there wasn't anything remarkable about it. She was short, her dark hair cut into shaggy layers with streaks of purple peeking out, and a little thicker around the middle than the social standard thought as hot, but her curves made up for it. If you're not gonna be stick-thin, then flaunt the assets a plusher body gave you.

Frank gave her a wink before heading back to the pool table with Paulie, sipping on the cold bottle of Budweiser. John Boy had already taken his turn, the rainbow of billiard balls scattered all over the green felt.

"Still open," the kid said as he looked for an ashtray on a nearby table.

Paulie took the stick from the wall and stalked about the table, looking for a shot. Finding the one ball in a near-perfect set up with the corner pocket, he lined up his shot, and took it. He sunk it in effortlessly, the cue ball rolling back to rest almost exactly where it had started.

"Alright, Frank. I don't think you pulled us in here for some nine ball," Paulie said as he sized up another shot.

He hit it, sinking his intended ball into the side pocket, and subsequently lining up a third perfect shot. John Boy sighed, shaking his head. "What's goin' on in that hard head of yours?"

"You know exactly what we need to talk about," Frank said as he glanced at the bartender behind the bar.

He moved towards the jukebox on the opposite wall, clicking a few buttons. The clicking of billiards was the only sound in the place. No way could they talk freely like this. He tossed in a few quarters, hit a random sequence of buttons, and made his way back towards Paulie. Frampton started playing, giving them just enough white noise to talk about things without being overheard.

"He has to be dealt with," Frank said behind the mouth of his bottle.

"Who? D'Angelo?" Paulie said, missing his next shot by a glance.

John Boy made a sound of excitement, drawing the eyes of both men to him. He squirmed a little under their collective stare before moving to take his shot. Frank shook his head and looked back to Paulie giving him a quick nod.

"C'mon, Frank. I mean... Chuck's blood is still warm," Paulie's voice quieted even more with that. "You really think we outta go picking a fight with D?"

John Boy missed his shot, cussed softly, and stood back against the wall again. It almost seemed like he was oblivious to the conversation. That, or he was smart.

"He's a wildcard, Paulie," Frank answered.

"And you aren't?"

"What the fuck do you think he's gonna do, man? Come back to the motel, find Chuck dead, and just go 'oh... well... shit. Guess I better go find a real job'?" Frank shook his head. "Fuck no. He's comin' for me. The minute he figures out what the fuck went down, he's comin' at me tooth and claw. Chuck was too stupid to see past his bruised ego to do what he had to do to beat me. We all know what would've happened if he'd gone all wolf. It'd be me laying on that crusted-up bed. D ain't that stupid."

"But he can't shift either, Frank. It's even ground," Paulie said.

"Exactly. I got the drop on Chuck 'cause he let his bitch get into his head. D'Angelo won't. He thinks, once Chuck's gone, the pack is his. That he's the stronger wolf. Only difference is he ain't distracted by the bullshit. He can just as easily kill me as I can him."

"So what do we do, then? Keep running with our tails tucked?" Paulie asked.

Frank's jaw muscles clenched as he stared down Paulie over the pool table. Paulie looked up from his line-up, stared at Frank for a few silent heartbeats, and then shook his head, cursing softly under his breath. He stood up, not even bothering with the shot now. He leaned on the pool cue, giving Frank the full weight of his eyes.

"He's gonna find us sooner or later. He ain't gonna give up what he thinks is his," Paulie said.

Frank just took another sip of his beer. John Boy stared at him openly. He was young, inexperienced. A mere prospect for the M.C. Chuck hadn't thought was ready to get so deeply involved in things yet.

"Frank, look... I know. You're a beast. Hard, driven, a hell of a fuckin' leader. But this just ain't how it's done," Paulie's eyes had gone from suspicious to worried.

"How it's done," Frank whispered with a bitter laugh. "There are no set rules for this, Paulie. Pretty to think so, but this life ain't built on rules. It's born of chaos. The thrill of the chase and the power to take what you want with force and blood. Chuck had his damn rules and his own limits he placed on himself when he tried to lead us. Look where it got him."

"What if D'Angelo finds us?" John Boy asked. The other two men looked at him in unison and he swallowed hard.

Paulie slid eyes to Frank, shrugging a shoulder as if he were wondering the same.

"Kid's got a point. Now, I love ya Frank, but we can only run away so long. He's gonna come back and find the body. Gonna figure out we took off. Fuck, I still don't get why you wanted to bring the body back. We should have left him in the field and been done with it."

Frank stared between the two of them for a moment as if he were letting it all sink in. They still doubted him. Doubted he had the strength and ruthlessness needed to lead these people. Yeah, they were right about D'Angelo. He would be out for fucking blood. Did that make Frank want to take him out any less? Hell, no. If anything, Frank felt like it might help him prove himself to the rest of them.

"You wanted D'Angelo to find Chuck, didn't you? You're not runnin' away from the fight. You're just buying time," John Boy looked at Frank completely bewildered.

He hadn't expected the kid to figure it out before Paulie did. A smile found its way onto Frank's lips and he clapped a hand against John Boy's back. It was a friendly gesture, though John Boy seemed to lurch forward with the force of Frank's hand.

"How long you been with us now, John Boy?" Frank asked suddenly.

The kid blinked large brown eyes at him, thrown off by the sudden left turn the conversation had taken.

"Like... a year. Maybe eighteen months," he answered.

"Paulie. I think it's time to take the training wheels off, don't you?" Frank said, giving Paulie that practiced grin of his.

Paulie looked at him with suspicion dancing in his eyes, but also didn't push the subject any further. The man had proven himself a damn good friend and loyal pack-mate. Frank knew he would follow him into the flames of Hell itself, and if all went well that would be exactly where they were heading.

Chapter 7

August 19th 2010 9:15 p.m.

THE WEEKS FOLLOWING CHUCK'S death had been a hell of a roller coaster ride. We blew through Texarkana, made our way West on Interstate-30 until we hit Dallas. We spent the night there while the men planned our new route and the rest of us tried to get a grip on ourselves. It was easier for some than others. While I managed to put my head into a nice, blank state and Suze continued to be the rock she was, some of the other girls were still scared and confused.

Out of all of them, I thought Joy Anne would have been the least to give a shit about what was going on, but surprisingly, she was taking the loss of Chuck pretty hard. The tears had stopped by the time we reached the next motel, but no one was home upstairs. She just stared ahead with a lifeless gaze and let Suzanne lead her around. Maybe she really had cared for Chuck. That made it difficult to not feel sorry for her.

Me, pity Joy Anne? I sure hadn't seen that coming.

Sleep eluded me. All I saw when I closed my eyes were shreds of flesh dripping with thick red blood, bed spreads soaked in it, and Chuck's cold dead eyes staring through me as he lay there. Sleep was not an option.

Each day was like that. Ride, park, plan, maybe choke down some food, get a few hours of sleep if my brain allowed, get on the bike, and do it all over again. We must have ridden through two dozen cities in less than three weeks and none of it changed.

And Frank still hadn't given me any answers.

I was lying on the bed in the newest dank hotel room when Frank came in. I didn't look up from the TV. Hell, I didn't have to know it was him. He had this air about him when he walked in the room that let me know he was there. I couldn't puzzle out what had changed in him, but he was different.

He'd always been a force of nature, but now he felt more dangerous; as though he were a tsunami pushing forward to wipe away everything that crossed him. It made it hard to be around him, which only sent me into a deeper spiral. I no longer knew if I wanted to be there with him.

Something I was so certain about had become the most uncertain decision ever, but I felt stuck. What else was I supposed to do? Crawl back home to Mom and Dad? Give Lori even more reasons to feel superior?

Fuck that.

For now, I just made a point to distance myself from the storm as much as possible.

I raised my hand in a half-hearted wave only to feel something soft and cool fall onto it. I lifted my head and looked at what had landed on me.

"What's this?" I asked, pushing myself up and looking at the red fabric.

"Get cleaned up, get dressed, do whatever you gotta do to look hot. We're goin' out."

I looked up at him then. Going out? All we'd done for the last three weeks was ride and sleep, put as much road between us and Chuck's corpse as possible, and now he wanted to go have a good time? Sometimes I wondered if Frank needed medication.

"I take it I don't have a say in it?"

"Not tonight you don't," he said as he snatched the remote from me and hopped onto the bed. "Get to it. I'm sick of the funeral procession."

I rolled my eyes at him and slid off the bed, heading to the bathroom. I had no energy to fight right now. Besides,

I could do with a night away from musty hotels and stale reruns.

The shower was to be expected. Lukewarm, generic-smelling soap and shampoo, over-washed towels. I was clean, though, so little else mattered. Just as His Highness commanded. I dried off and slipped on my black thong and bra that I'd washed in the sink the night before and hung to dry on the towel rack, then grabbed my hair dryer and brush.

The warm air soothed a bit of my irritation. Each sweep of the hair dryer across my scalp melted away whatever tension I was holding onto. I didn't know why I was acting this way. Why was I taking Chuck's death so hard? Like Frank had told me, I didn't know the guy. Not really.

With each careful sweep of my hair, each twirl of my brush under the rushing hot air, I came to terms with the fact that I was mourning an idea, not a person. The father I did have kept me at arm's length while showering my sister with more love and attention than I could ever hope for. Now, I am not saying Chuck welcomed me with open arms, or treated me like the daughter he never had, but he filled a role in my little world. Now he was gone.

The fact that my boyfriend had been involved in his death only made it harder to swallow, even without knowing the details.

I grabbed the clothes Frank had bought me from the top of the hamper and held it out. It was a dress. At least, it may have started its life as a dress before a battle with hardcore drugs, anorexia, and self-mutilation. There was barely anything left of the fabric I was holding in my hands.

"What the hell, Frank?" I murmured.

Untangling the dress was like getting the knot out of a string of Christmas lights. My first try, I think I put my foot through an arm hole, but who could really tell? It slid over me like a second skin that I had long outgrown. The fabric itself was nice, almost silky but not quite silk. It took some twisting and pulling and some rather awkward poses to figure out how it was supposed to sit on my body, and when I had finally figured it out, all I could do was stare at myself in the mirror.

I looked like a Pretty Woman reject.

I mean, it was cute in a way, but it looked like lingerie rather than something to wear out in public. It might have been right up Joy Anne's alley, but for me... I felt like a hooker-in-training.

The red cloth hugged every curve I had, even gave me the illusion of more curve than my thin frame had to offer. It was cut out on each side to show off my skin and the fabric crossed in the back where another larger cut-out was centered over my lower back. An inch lower and I'd be showing the world my thong.

"You seriously want me to wear this?" I shouted through the door to Frank.

"I bought it for ya, didn't I? Lemme see it," he said.

I took a deep breath and found that was a mistake. It was so tight that I could almost hear the seams screaming with tension, threatening to break open. The bustier of the dress squeezed my chest tight as I filled my lungs, pushing my flesh up to almost spill over. Dear God, I wouldn't be able to do anything in this thing without falling out in one way or another.

It took everything I had to force myself out of that bathroom. I opened the door with my eyes clenched tight, arms crossed over the front of me as if they could hide my shame. Perhaps shame was too strong a word, but I certainly wasn't flouncing around the room like a giddy little girl in a new party dress.

"Damn," a whisper more than a word.

I opened my eyes and saw Frank half-crouched on the bed, his mouth hanging open and eyes all for me. I swear I could feel his gaze like fingers raking over me, and it made my stomach tight. I'd seen him lost in passion, but it was never like this. A possessive and almost predatory air filled the room. It was all coming straight from him.

"C'mere," he said finally. "Do a little turn for me."

His gaping maw quirked into a lustful grin, and he crooked his finger at me. What else could I do? I went to him.

My neck was on fire. Embarrassment strangled me as I closed those short few steps to him. I couldn't understand why I felt so awkward. He'd seen me naked before, yet the idea of him seeing me in this little floozy-parade special seemed so much more perverse.

I slowly began to turn, letting him see the full effect of the dress. When I faced Frank again, I risked a glance up at him and realized what was really bothering me about it. It wasn't the dress at all. It was the raw lust in his eyes as he looked at me. That base instinct where male saw female and decided, no matter what, that he would mount her and make her his. It shone openly in those chocolate-colored eyes. It made my throat tight, my neck tense, and pressed a heavy weight in that lower place in my body.

Hands grasped me on either side, rough and warm with fingers digging. I looked down and found that eager face staring up at me.

"What's the matter?" he asked, the words coming out nearly strangled.

"Your face," I whispered.

"What about it?"

"You look like you're ready to eat me alive."

His lips curled even more. His fingers kneaded my sides, thumbs running over that delicate edge of fabric and searching for warm, alive skin. I stared down into that grinning face until he lowered it and pressed his nose firmly against my abdomen. He nuzzled my stomach, rubbing his nose, his forehead, his cheeks against it, those wiry little hairs on his chin catching the thin, fragile cloth.

"You are so unbelievably sexy, Harley. Everything about you. Your skin, your scent, the way you carry yourself. If I could devour you, I would."

His words were muffled into my stomach, breath tickling me effortlessly through the dress, but I heard—and felt—all of them.

"Someday, you might even see it yourself."

I stood frozen as he rubbed his face against me. My stomach hurt. It was so tight and unrelenting that each breath was a struggle. For months his attitude towards me had grown cold and indifferent. Even when we made love it was more for the sake of release than any pressing desire or need for one another. That he was clutching me, expressing his attraction and desire for me, now, had me stunned.

Finally, my hands moved. They rose to cup either side of his face and found his cheeks almost blistering hot. Frank always ran hotter than most people I knew, but this would have edged on feverish compared to his norm. I leaned down, which effectively pulled my stomach away from his face, and pressed lips to his forehead, drinking down that heat.

"Are you sick?" I asked against the taught skin of his forehead.

He chuckled and raised his chin so he could catch my lips with his. He sucked his heat from my bottom lip before pulling away and standing up abruptly.

"Nah, I'm good," he said, regaining his more normal tone, "but if we don't get outta here that dress ain't gonna last too long."

"Where are we going?" I asked as I grabbed my stuff.

"Just this little shit-hole dance club on the edge of town."

"If it's a shit-hole then why did it matter what I wore?"

He looked at me, straightening the collar of his jacket, "Because I want to show these backwoods hicks what a real woman looks like."

"And rub it in their faces?" I asked, actually finding myself smiling.

His grin told me all the answer I needed to know. Frank was a man's man. That meant the other men expected him to have a sexy woman hanging off him. I didn't exactly believe I fit the criteria, but it was flattering. Really.

I followed him out of the room automatically. It wasn't until we reached the Softail that I realized I was going to have a serious problem. I stopped and stared at the bike as Frank moved to get onto it. When he was settled onto it he finally looked over to notice I hadn't moved.

"What's wrong?" he asked.

How the hell was I going to ride in this thing? I was freaking out about sitting down in a normal chair too fast and flashing my ass, there was no avoiding it on the back of a motorcycle! His eyebrows knit closer together as I stood there awkwardly, not answering him.

"One moment," I said finally before turning around and rushing back into the room.

About five minutes later, I came back out. I was still wearing the dress, but black jeans peeked out from under the scandalously short skirt. Frank gave me a disapproving look as I finally made my way to mount the bike.

"Seriously, Harley. You looked good," he said with a shake of his head. "Don't be embarrassed about showing off your body. I'm not."

I hoisted myself up behind him and found that the skirt, indeed, rolled up over my ass. For once, I was right about something. My arms slid around him and I rested my chin on his shoulder, mouth just behind his ear.

"While I appreciate you not having a problem showing off my body, I'm not embarrassed," I whispered. "It's just for the ride."

His body moved against my chest, as he laughed. He probably thought I was being a silly girl, but that was okay. I was Frank's silly girl. He wanted me in spite of my neurotic little episodes, which was more than I could say for some.

I felt stupid for being ready to throw all that away these last few weeks, over something I was sure would make sense when he was ready to talk about it.

I knew I wasn't the sort of girl that guys like Frank sought after, but tonight he was proud I was his. He wanted to flaunt me around, make other men jealous of what he had. In a way, that made all the crap lately seem worth it. It made me feel like leaving my family and that dead-end town wasn't such a dumb move.

The jeans came off almost the second we parked the bike. Frank had given me a look that said it was time to be the dutiful girlfriend and help him make the envy of the bar. That was fine with me. It was a balmy night and with the added heat of the bike's engine, my legs were sweating. I slid them off and stuffed them into the saddlebag.

When I turned around I nearly ran into Frank's chest. He was suddenly just there, staring at me with a strange hunger in his eyes. His hand snaked around my waist and pulled me tighter into him. In the heels, I didn't have to get on tiptoe to kiss him, or have him crane his neck down to meet me. It was a nice change. It let me focus more on the feel of his lips on mine instead of the inevitable ache in my feet.

When he pulled his face away from mine, he sucked in his bottom lip and didn't open his eyes. It looked like he was savoring the taste of my mouth. When he finally released that oh-so-kissable lip, I saw a light stain of red on it. My lipstick had rubbed off on him. I moved to wipe it away from him with my thumb, but he caught my wrist, gently, in his hand and smiled at me past it.

"Leave it," he said with a smile, before bringing my palm to his mouth and kissing it. "I like when I can still taste you."

I didn't say anything. I couldn't. A sudden heat blossomed, not just in my cheeks but in my body. It was just a smear of lipstick, but Frank made it seem so much naughtier. I tried to gather myself again, pulling my hand away from his and smiled at him to let him know he'd won this little battle. How could I argue with that? Why would I try?

The "shit-hole dance club" was about twice the size of my high school gymnasium. There were three bars, each with its own drink theme like Jack Daniels rodeo and Corona luau, an elevated dance floor the size of a large rectangular pool, and an army of pool tables lining the back wall, two deep.

Country music swelled and hit every square inch of the space coming from a DJ booth that had taken me about fifteen minutes to realize was on top of the floating island bar in front of the billiards area. All that was missing was the damned mechanical bull.

"Wow," I breathed, looking all over as I stood under Frank's arm.

He led me to a corner full of tables. Our people stood, sat, and even draped themselves all over the chairs and stools, and I couldn't help but smile. Frank was right, yet again it seemed. Seeing the crew alive with energy, smiling and laughing, I knew that we had all needed this to get out of the grieving mindset. It was best for all of us.

They welcomed us with a round of cold beer and a few wolf-whistles and cat calls, which made me tug down at the skirt every so often. Just like that, we let go of some of that dark cloud that had been leeching off us for days. Frank broke off to talk to some of the guys and I, instinctively, made my way towards Suze.

"Damn, baby girl," she said as she slid out of my hug. "Look at you. You almost look grown up."

I gave her a look and she chuckled, leaning back in her chair.

"Thank you," I said finally, taking the compliment.

"Where'd ya get the dress?" Roxy asked from across the table.

Like me, Roxy was fairly new to the group. One of the other guys had picked her up at a bar a few weeks after I turned up with Frank, and he tried to leave her behind, but she sort of just kept leaving with us. She wasn't pressing him for a diamond ring and wedding bells, but she made it clear she wouldn't just be tossed and forgotten like some piece of trash.

Her hair was cut short, barely hanging past her ears. The cut was cute on her bone structure and hid how dull the brown was. If it had been any longer I'd have called her mousy. Short as it was, it actually complemented her high cheekbones and drew attention to her cornflower blue eyes.

"Frank bought it for me, I guess," I admitted.

"Damn. The man has taste," she said with a smile.

"Yeah, Frankie," one of the men shouted behind me, "who knew you had such fabulous fashion sense."

Frank grappled him around the neck and dragged him towards the pool tables.

About two hours later, I was sitting back watching the couples out on the dance floor. Suze had gotten about four glasses of beer and a shot of tequila in me before Paulie grabbed her up and whisked her away to dance. The look on her face every time they two-stepped past our tables brought a smile to my face.

My life was far from happily ever after, but maybe it was close enough. For Suze, it looked like it was as close as it could get short of Paulie asking her for more than a dance.

While they made their turn around the floor, I watched everyone else. Men swept their girls around, some spun in intricate moves like they've been doing it for years, others stumbled and laughed as they were being taught for the first time, the real veterans spun their way through piles of sawdust in the corners. I'd never two-stepped before but it seemed fun. I wondered briefly if Frank knew how, but was drawn out of my quiet wondering by a loud cheering.

I glanced over to the pool tables where the men, Frank included, were in an uproar over a finished game. Frank and Niko rubbed their win into the others' faces. The other two men paid for the next game and a pitcher of cold beer. I'd be getting no dance from Frank but seeing him relaxed and slipping into the man I'd fallen in love with brought a smile to my face that no half-learned two-step could.

A dark head of hair passed through the men by the pool tables, cutting past them as if she were on a mission. I watched Joy Anne emerge from the crowd and make a bee-line for Frank. Part of me was ready to jump out of my chair and cut her off—a strangely possessive impulse considering I had never really been like that towards any guy in my life. Not that I dated a whole hell of a lot, but with Frank I found myself getting jealous easily.

The other part of me was curious, though. I wanted to see how he acted towards her. There was a lot of talk where Joy Anne was concerned. Now, I might get a little peek into how it really was. I told myself that if there was even the slightest attraction between them, I'd see it when they thought I wasn't watching.

FRANK

Already about two-hundred bucks up, Frank leaned over the table to line up his break. This was a game he enjoyed playing, something he'd always had a knack for. As a kid, he practically lived in the pool hall around the corner from his house. It was where he'd learned to hustle, where he had his first beer, and where he'd first made out with a girl right under her brother's nose. Sometimes, when he played, he could find himself back in that smoky old hall long before the monsters wreaked havoc on his life.

He was just about ready to shoot when a pair of hands snaked their way around either side of him, scarlet red nails shining under the hanging light.

"Hey baby. Wanna duck out of here for a minute?"

Frank turned his neck to glance behind him. Heavily lined eyes stared up at him, peeking just over the top of his shoulder. He could feel her breath through his shirt. He slid a hand over the top of hers as they linked around his stomach.

"No. You go ahead, though," he said, prying Joy Anne's hands apart and throwing them off him.

She stepped back, her arms held up, and stared at him with open disbelief. Frank just shook his head and leaned over the table, lining up the break, and tried to ignore her as she gaped at him. Joy Anne, though, was never a girl easily ignored.

"What's the matter? Worried your girl's gonna find out?" she asked. She was trying for cool amusement, but he could practically feel her temper rising behind him.

"No," he said before taking his shot. "I ain't worried. 'Cause I ain't going with you, Joy Anne. Go scratch your itch with someone else."

"Didn't ya have fun with me, Frankie? I know she can't handle ya. Not enough for you to have any real fun." Her hand reached out under his chin and trailed a slow, tickling nail over his throat as he tried to line up his next shot.

"You need a real woman that can handle all ya got. That can take all of you. Let's just slip on outta here. We can be back b'fore she even realizes you're gone."

Frank dropped his head and breathed out slowly. Joy Anne was a relentless woman when she wanted something, and it was obvious she wasn't about to give up anytime soon. It was one of her more irritating qualities.

With a pointed look to the guys hanging around the table, Frank stood up and placed his cue over the felt. He turned on the spot, resting back against the pool table and facing Joy Anne fully as he gripped the edge on either side of himself. As expected, Joy Anne saw this as a permissive move and stepped closer, pressing her legs against his inner thighs. He didn't move her away.

The guys busied themselves with shots of tequila.

"You're right," he said smoothly. "I need a strong, sexy, badass woman in my life. On my bike. In my bed."

Joy Anne's face lit up, her thin-lipped smile widening. She took the chance at pressing her pelvis against his, her hands pressing against his chest and playing with his shirt. He rewarded this by grabbing her on either hip, his thumbs rubbing small circles, and drew his face closer to hers as if trying to tempt her to kiss him.

"That's why I chose Harley," he whispered.

The light in her face vanished like a blown light bulb. She stared up at him, a wrinkle forming between her eyebrows. With no effort on his part, Frank gripped her hips tight and shoved her skinny ass away from him before grabbing his pool cue again.

"You were just a means to an end, Joy Anne. Fun, but temporary," he said. "Harley's much, much more than that. Best get used to her, doll."

He didn't give her a chance to argue with him. He turned around, lined up his next shot, and sunk three balls in. That was all he had to say on the matter. He'd hoped it was clear in his posture, the banter starting up between him and the other guys, and his lack of attention towards her.

Joy Anne may be persistent, but she knew how it was. He was her new alpha, and he'd dismissed her.

Still, a woman scorned was a hell of a thing. She huffed behind him and he glanced over his shoulder to watch her storm off, rejoining their friends, before catching Harley's intense stare. She was smiling at him, no doubt having seen him refuse Joy Anne's advances, and he returned the smile.

Chapter 8

Frank gave me that sweet, lopsided grin that I'd fallen for time and time again and all the hurt and frustration melted away from me, if only for a few moments. It left me feeling warm, and safe, and loved, and oh-so-right.

I hadn't missed the whole scene at the pool table. Their conversation may have been lost to the noise of the bar, but Joy Anne's body language broadcast her intentions in high definition. She'd tried to sink her skankified teeth into him, and he'd resisted, even pushed her away. That girl could talk all the shit she wanted, but Frank's actions spoke volumes and he was practically screaming 'not interested.'

I watched as she stormed back towards her friends at the bar a few feet away from my table, looking as dejected as I was smug. Yeah. Eat that, bitch.

"Jesus, that looked painful," I heard the girl sitting on the stool to her left say. Oh yes, it really did.

"Shut the fuck up, heifer," Joy Anne snapped. I chuckled.

I was trying not to look in their direction, trying not to let her see that I was watching. Her friend huddled in on herself a little, sipping her fruity little cocktail through a thin straw. If you were friends with Joy Anne, you kept your mouth shut. Never pointed out her shortcomings or failures. It was the first lesson of Sycophant 101.

"Fuck him," her other friend chimed in.

"That was the idea," she growled, turning in her stool to slam back a shot.

I felt the jealousy twist my gut again, but this time it was coupled with a possessive anger. She peered over her shoulder to watch Frank and I glanced over to him, too.

He bent over the table, grinning that crooked grin at me and pressing his fingertips to his lips before he took his shot. When Frank was relaxed he took on a shine of the boy I'd fallen for. I knew he was still there, buried under all the machismo, and when I got quick peeks of him like I did just then, it made my heart flutter.

We could be okay.

Joy Anne plopped in the empty chair in front of me, blocking my view of Frank. I smiled at her, not because I really liked the woman, but because I was a smug little bitch in my own right. Sue me. After that display with Frank, I couldn't help but gloat about what I had just seen. Just a teensy little gloat.

"Hey, Joy Anne," I said with a voice more sugary than a southern grandma's sweet tea.

She didn't say anything at first. Just sat there, chewing her gum and smiling at me for a few moments before she finally let loose a heavy sigh.

"Feels good, dunnit?" she said, stretching backward against the top of her chair.

"What? Being out?" I asked.

She nodded her answer, and I nodded, too.

"Yeah, I guess it does. We've been holed up for a while since," I paused, realizing what I had almost said. I looked to her apologetically. "It's nice to get out and relax for a change," I finished weakly.

She stared at me again, going quiet. I guess she'd caught what I meant. Too soon? Probably. I was never good with the whole condolences thing, and often put my foot in my mouth before I realized it. Miss Sensitive, I am not.

"Frankie buy that dress?" she asked suddenly.

I looked down at myself, smoothed my hands over my thighs, which the dress did very little to cover.

"Yeah," I answered.

"He did good. It's a damn hot dress, I'll tell ya that. Chuck used to shop real good for me when he was tryin' to make up for something he done wrong."

Normally, I'd wonder if she was trying to bait me. Looking at her face as she said Chuck's name, I couldn't tell if she was just reflecting on her lost man or if it had been a purposeful choice of words. I didn't rise to it, but instead kept my tone relaxed as I asked her what was itching in my brain.

"You trying to tell me something?" I asked, simply.

"What'chu mean?"

"I mean, are you trying to say that he's trying to do the same thing? Make up for something by buying me this dress?" Honestly, if he was trying to butter me up this dress wouldn't have been at the top of my guilt-shopping list.

She stared at me, her jaw working in slow motions as she chewed her gum. Finally, she shrugged a single shoulder and leaned back into her chair, staring at me defiantly. God, why did this woman try to make me hate her so much?

"Look, Joy Anne, I am trying very hard to be nice to you. I get you lost something special to you and I am trying to afford you some sympathy, but you aren't making it very fucking easy. Let's be honest with one another for a change. For the sake of trying something new. What aren't you saying?"

Her mouth, which had begun to look much like a cow's chewing hay, quirked into a self-satisfied grin. I felt my shoulders tense at that smile. Nothing good ever followed a smile like that.

"What I lost," she said with a bitter laugh. "God, you think ya know everything. That you just walk your pretty little self into this family, and ya suddenly understand all of us."

"Then fucking enlighten me, Joy Anne. If you have something to say, say it," I said with a desperation and tiredness that had grown so heavy from dealing with this girl.

We stared at each other for a few minutes, me waiting for her to say whatever and her weighing her options, I guess. I was tired of her little games. Either she had something to say or she didn't. As the minutes passed, I was beginning to guess she was just talking out of her ass again.

"Ya know, it's funny," she blurted out suddenly as I started to get out of my chair, "Chuck's always been pretty easy goin'. Hell, he was a fuckin' doormat. Too soft for his own good. Never thought he'd get so pissed off he'd go after Frank like that."

I settled back onto the chair, though I didn't relax.

"Go after Frank?" I repeated.

"Oh yeah. Apparently, he was out for blood," she said, that smile coming back. She'd caught my interest now and knew it. "Rode out to where the guys was at and went straight for him. Woulda killed him too, if he wasn't such a damn fool."

"Why'd he go after Frank?"

"Well," she said as her smile curled even more, "he helped me give Chuck a little payback."

I didn't ask her what she meant. She was milking it. Giving me just enough to make me ask her to go on and on, and I was getting tired of the theatrics. I just stared at her, waiting for her to either spill or shut up. Finally, she got the point.

"Chuck don't take criticism well. We got in a fight, I said a few things to get his goat, and I guess I went too far cause he hit me." Her smile seemed to go a little fuzzy around the edges at this but didn't disappear completely.

"The black eye?" I asked.

"Yeah. Knocked me solid, though I guess he didn't hit me as hard as he coulda. I'd prolly be dead if he had."

"Alright. So where does Frank come in?"

"Well, like I said, he helped me get a little revenge on Chuck. I wanted him to hurt. So, if he thought what I'd said before was a blow to his precious ego, then I took it up a notch. I called good ol' Frankie and told him what Chuck did. Told him I was done with him and wanted to see him knocked off his fuckin' high horse."

Something about that made the little hairs on my arm stand on end. Fear and anticipation flooded into me as I waited. Did I really want to know? I mean, really. It wasn't good. I already knew that. Chuck was dead. That was the bottom line. I knew Joy Anne enough to know she was waiting to drop the bomb on my head.

"So, what did he do?" I asked through the tightness in my throat.

"He fucked me bow-legged," she said, dragging each word out as long as she could to really make me hear it. "He came straight to me and fucked me in the bar bathroom 'til we both was nothin' more than a sweaty, weak-kneed mess, and then I made a little phone call to Chuck."

I felt sick. There was no way. He wouldn't do something as disgusting as that. Not for her. Not to a man he'd followed for years. The tears came, hot and stinging, but I held them back. I would not cry. Not in front of her.

"You're lying," I whispered through my teeth.

I didn't trust myself not to cry if I dared speak up. I could feel the sobs waiting like a dull ache in my chest.

"I told ya, bitch. You can't even begin to give him what he needs. You ain't got it. But he knows where to come for it. He don't have to hold back with me. Don't have to worry about breaking me like he does you," she laughed, and it was thick with triumph. "I almost feel sorry for ya. You don't have no clue what you're missin'."

She was thumbing her phone as she said it. I thought about punching her in the face. Give her a fresh shiner to replace the one that Chuck had given her. My palms hurt, and when I glanced down at them to keep myself from doing just that, I saw little red half-moons in my skin. I'd bit my nails so hard into my palms that I'd broken skin.

I stood, still half not-believing it and half wanting to hear it from Frank's own mouth. I didn't know where my feet were trying to take me, but before I could move past Joy Anne's chair, she shoved her phone under my face.

I stared down at the illuminated screen in horror and disbelief, and yet how could I not believe it? It was staring right at me. He was staring right at me. He was poised behind Joy Anne, staring over her shoulder with his hands gripping, white-knuckled, into her hips. His bare chest was flushed and shining with sweat, his eyes heavy-lidded in a look I knew far too well. Joy Anne's crooked lips grinned at the phone in the most vulgar selfie I had ever seen.

"There's all the proof ya need," her voice swam through the imagery in my head. "I forgot how good he was in bed. I'll have to remember to have a go with him more often. God knows he enjoyed himself. Maybe, if you ask him real pretty-like, he'll let ya watch next time."

I can't explain what I was thinking, because I don't remember thinking anything. One minute I was staring at her smiling face, glowing with sex and heat, and the next I was wrapping my hand in her hair and pulling her head back.

She was still in her chair when I drove my fist into her mouth. Pain exploded in my hand, white and sharp, but I pushed it away. I couldn't think about the pain and hurt her at the same time. The first punch, and the pull of her hair in my other hand, tipped her chair out from under her. She should have toppled with it, but amazingly, she had her feet steady under her.

By the time I moved to throw the next punch, her hands had raised to deflect it. I missed her face but did connect with the side of her neck. She cried out and grabbed me, her grip strong and painful on the tendons in my wrists. She was so much stronger than I'd have ever thought. Sure, she was tough, she had to be to run with these guys for so long, but there is a difference between toughness and strength. She had both in spades.

It came to a point where I either had to let go of her hair or let her break my wrist. I let go, but I knew she'd be coming at me. She still had one wrist in her grip, gearing up to hit me no doubt, but I used the other one to hit her just under her ribs. It was my off hand, so there wasn't much to it, but it was enough to make her let go of me.

She stumbled back a little, arms cradling her ribs, hair hanging over her face. I felt myself jerked back but I wasn't about to look behind me. Not with Joy Anne still standing.

Hands tugged at my skirt, pulling it back down in place. I hadn't even thought about it riding up. The embarrassment helped to pull me up out of the haze of adrenaline just a little. Suze's voice whispered something to me, but I didn't understand it. It took too much energy to concentrate on her and I needed my focus elsewhere.

I felt her pull at my arms, an attempt to guide me away, and I started to walk backwards with her. I almost turned around---convinced it was finished---but Joy Anne started laughing. Not her usual shrill laugh. It was thicker, raspier and reverberated down my spine like a chilling frost. I stopped, heard Suze curse under her breath, and watched as she lifted her face again.

"Oh, I'm gonna enjoy this," she growled.

Her eyes were wide, wild, and glowing an eerie yellow-green in the dim lighting. I was stuck. I couldn't look away. Was I hallucinating? Beer mixed with adrenaline, that had to be it. She stepped toward me, holding a hand out to her side. For a minute, I thought she was balling up her fist to swing at me, but she kept her fingers flexed out. Something was wrong with them, too. They were unnaturally long, the nails sticking out from the tips nearly two inches and sharpened into stake-like points.

I couldn't move, couldn't react. All I could do was stare at this woman as she began to shift and change into something out of this world. This wasn't from beer gone bad. I'd have welcomed that explanation with open arms, but my gut knew better. I felt Suze move next to me, her arm sliding across the front of me like she was getting ready to step between me and this crazed woman—thing—coming at me. I opened my mouth to argue but a blur moved in front of us.

There was a sharp crack over the almost-deafening music. I blinked, my eyes trying to make sense of what was happening and found myself staring at the embroidered Hellhound on the back of Frank's club jacket. Suze's hands tightened on my arms, and I peered past him, trying to figure out what had just happened.

Joy Anne sagged against another girl, unmoving. Blood poured down her mouth and chin, her nose was swollen and bruised. I couldn't tell if she was conscious, but it didn't look like it. Her eyes were closed, her body limp, feet useless. He'd knocked her plain out.

"Holy shit, Frank," Suze said beside me.

She finally let go of me and laced her fingers on top of her head, staring at the unconscious Joy Anne in front of us. Frank growled loudly and shouted to one of the men that were scooping up Joy Anne's dead weight.

"Get her out of here. Pack her shit and drop her at the nearest bus stop. If she comes after Harley again, she'll wish I'd put her down tonight," he warned. "You can tell her that when she wakes up."

They carried her away, parting the crowd of onlookers as they moved past. That was when I noticed the crowd. A cat fight was sure enough to draw attention but Frank's interjection into the fight had stunned everyone silent. Movement across the bar made me look away from the sea of faces around us, and I watched as a small group of black shirts made their way towards us. Shit.

A hand touched my shoulder, and I looked behind me to find Frank. I didn't think. I just jerked my shoulder out of his hand, turned around to face him again. His eyebrows lifted in surprise.

"C'mon. Let's get out before they call the cops," he said.

I didn't say anything to him. I just turned, grabbed my stuff, and stormed towards the door. I tried to put as much space between me and what had just happened as quickly as possible. The more I walked, the more I was able to think about what had led to the fight; able to think of the driving force behind my hitting Joy Anne. By the time I made the door, I was filled with a fresh fury.

I walked right past Frank's bike, not even bothering to stop for my jeans, and made my way towards the road. I had no idea how to get back to the motel, but I was thinking about other things. Things that made my hands shake at my sides.

Frank shouted behind me, but I didn't even slow down. Fuck him. Fuck his lying, cheating, no-good...

"Where are you going?" He was suddenly so close behind me that I nearly tripped on my own feet.

I whirled around, not quite stopping but slowing my pace so that I could look at him.

"You can go to hell. I'm leaving before you drag me there with you," I said, my voice shaking.

"Harls, just... stop. Hey," he stuttered as I turned around again. "Just.... fucking talk to me!"

I stopped then, sharp and sudden, and spun around.

"What the fuck was that?!"

"What?" he asked, stopping short of crashing into me.

"You hit her!"

"Well... yeah! She was trying to hurt you, Harley. What did you want me to do, just wait for her to put you in the fucking hospital?"

"I was handling myself just fine."

A wordless, caveman-like scream erupted from Frank, his hands dragging roughly down the sides of his face. I took a step back and stared at him like the crazy jackass he was.

His body jolted towards me, his hands raised, fingers curled in as if he were fighting off the urge to strangle me on the spot. Seeing the look on his face, maybe he was.

"You don't know shit! Fuck's sake, Harley, how many times have I said it?!" He jerked his hands away from me, away from temptation. "'Stay away from Joy Anne'! Why the hell can't you just do as you're told for on—"

"Yeah, I'm sure you wanted me to stay away from her, didn't you?" I screamed. "You didn't want me to find out. Well, guess what, baby. She told me everything!"

He froze, his face going slack.

"That's right, Frank. Secret's out. I just hope she was worth it," I said, tears burning the back of my throat.

"I don't know what—"

"Oh Jesus. Give it up, already. She showed me the pictures of you two together," I snorted. "Don't tell me you had no idea she took pictures?"

He just stared at me, his face tightening again, jaw clenching. He wasn't denying it. I laughed, I couldn't help it. It sounded wrong in my throat.

"Oh... Oh that's great. How's it feel, huh? To be betrayed like that? Yeah. Looks like Joy Anne's legs aren't the only thing she can't keep shut," I swallowed hard.

We stared at each other in the darkness. He didn't move, didn't make excuses. He just stared at me, silent. I wanted to hear him tell me she was lying, to explain some bullshit circumstance that proved it wasn't him in that awful picture with her, but he didn't.

Her didn't even try to offer some half-assed lie. He just stood there, and I just stared at him until red taillights flared to life behind him.

I turned around, with a shake of my head, and made to walk away from him when he grabbed me by the arm. He made soft, whispered pleas to stop, to let him take me back to the hotel, but I pulled against his grip, the tears falling freely. I shook my head, trying to shake the tears from my eyes, and jerked, slapped, tugged, and shouted at him to let me go.

"No, Harley," he said firmly.

His grip was tightening on me, crushing my arm, keeping me from walking away. I struggled against it.

"Let me go, you worthless piece of shit!"

The back of his hand met my cheek in a burst of white-hot pain. It sung across my skin and he let go of me so suddenly that I fell to the ground. I broke my fall with the palms of my hands, but even the gravel biting into them didn't take away from the stun of his hit.

He hit me. He actually hit me.

I went into a strange sort of hyper-focus as I sat in the middle of the road. All modesty was forgotten. I didn't notice the dress riding up, the cars queuing up on the road next to us, or the bleeding scrapes on my palms. All I could see was Frank. All I could hear was my own breath and the pulse beating in my ears.

He crouched in front of me, his hand coming towards my face. I flinched, ready to fight off another hit, but all he did was sweep my hair from my eyes and sigh. I couldn't read the look in his eyes. Hell, I didn't trust myself to read it right then.

"Go home, if that's what you want. Run back to Mommy and Daddy. Do whatever you think you gotta do, because I'm tired of it. But you ain't walking in the middle of the night in that fucking dress and painting a target on that sweet little ass of yours," he whispered.

When he lifted me up, I didn't fight him. I just went with him. I let him carry me to his bike while I wondered how fast my daddy could drive out here and get me.

I stared at the room's telephone for about an hour. Why was it so hard to just pick it up and dial the number? An action so simple, and yet my body battled with my mind. I wanted to hear my mother's voice. It was a desire I hadn't felt in so long.

Everything was wrong. I was supposed to be happy, now. I belonged somewhere. I was loved. I was equal. At least, that was what I had believed until that night.

How could everything I believed to be true twist and contort into something so unreal, so warped? Funny how one little slap could make me second guess the last two years.

Okay, so it wasn't a little slap. It hurt. It ached even as I sat there staring at the phone. I brought my hand to my cheek and rubbed it gingerly, briefly wondering if any of this was even real. When he'd hit me, there was a sudden burst of hot, stinging pain, but then it just stopped. Maybe it was the shock that he had raised a hand to me, that kept me from feeling it.

Even his repetitive apologies didn't move me.

But now it hurt. Shock was gone, adrenaline subsided, and I was left with the dull ache in my cheek and the shame that I'd let it get to that point. It was very, very real.

Even if my parents treated Lori like the golden child, they'd never not loved me. They never hurt me. At least, not physically. Maybe I really hadn't chosen the lesser of two evils. If I went home now, would things change? Would it be too much to hope that they missed me?

I let out a slow, centering breath. It was just a phone call. I could do it. They hadn't talked to me in two years. Surely they'd be more than happy for me to come home, right? I dialed the number that had been ingrained in my memory, my fingers moving automatically.

"Hello?" a woman's voice answered.

The voice that picked up wasn't the one that I had expected. It caught me off guard and I forgot, for a minute, that I was expected to respond.

"Hello?" she said again, more urgently.

"Lori?" I squeaked out.

Silence stretched on the other end. I could hear her breathing softly, so I knew she hadn't hung up on me. Good sign.

"Harley, is that you?" my sister asked finally.

"Yeah. Yeah, it's me."

"Wow. You're the last person I'd expected to call." Her voice was unmoved. Her words so matter-of-fact that she could have been placing a to-go order rather than talking to her estranged sister.

"I know," I said, resting my head back against the wall. "I didn't expect to be calling either. I was hoping to talk to Mom."

"She isn't here."

"Oh. Alright. Dad gone, too?" I glanced at the clock. Two a.m. and they weren't home? Unlikely.

"Yup." Such a tiny word, yet it stabbed right through my heart.

"Okay. Well... how are you?" I tried to not sound as awkward as I felt.

"Harley, what do you want?" she asked, finally. "Mom and Dad are not home. Are you looking for money?"

She had no emotion to her voice other than disgust. Like I was some mooching pest looking for her next hand out rather than family. I blinked at the receiver before bringing it back to my ear.

"No. In the last two years have I ever called to beg for money?" I asked, sounding as indignantly as I felt.

"In the last two years you haven't called at all," she spat back. The cool demeanor gave way to a hissing anger.

The silence returned, but something told me she hadn't hung up. I waited for her to talk and wondered if she'd be the first to break. After a few seconds, I realized she wouldn't. Did she even care? Was she happy that I hadn't been around? I didn't think that, even Lori, could be so self-absorbed that she'd rather her sister go missing without a trace than share Mom and Dad's affections.

"I need help," I admitted, finally.

"So you do need money."

"No, Lorelei. Not money," I said, feeling the hot sting of tears again. I haven't cried so much in my life, and there I was going for the gold in one night.

"Then what, Harley? You disappear for years. Take off with that piece of shit, Fred, and don't even bother to call and let Mom and Dad know you aren't dead somewhere. No, poor pouty Harley doesn't think about anyone other than herself," Lori unleashed on me, each word dripping with contempt.

"Frank," I said through gritted teeth, fighting both anger and the tears threatening to break through. "His name is Frank," I said seconds before a sob clawed its way from my throat.

"Oh, Jesus," she said flatly. "Who cares?"

"He hit me, Lori."

Silence.

"I want to come home."

"Why?" she asked. It was so not what I had expected.

"Why?" I repeated.

"Yeah. Why do you want to come home? You're a big girl, now, aren't you? I tried to get you to stay. I told you it would break their hearts, but you didn't give a shit about them. All you cared about was that sorry sack of shit. Well, now you see what he is."

She sounded like she was on the verge of laughing, like she was almost happy she could pull the whole 'I told you so' argument on me.

"You wanted to go play house with a criminal. Well, pull up your big-girl panties, if you can spare a few minutes off your back, and deal with it. You made your bed, you can sleep in it. Mom and Dad don't want to clean up your mess."

I opened my mouth, astonished at what was pouring out of hers, but the phone went dead before I could even think of what to say. My cheeks were wet, tears stinging the still-tender skin where his hand had hit, and I couldn't breathe. A weight pressed on my chest, crushing my heart and my lungs. My world was closing in on me.

I was alone. I didn't want to stay here anymore, but I couldn't go home. That part of my life was over.

Chapter 9

I'D FINALLY MANAGED TO stop crying a whole twenty minutes when the door opened. The familiar heavy thunk of hard-soled boots approached the bed behind me, and I squeezed my pillow tighter in my arms. I didn't want to look at him right now. Not when the wounds from my sister's rejection were still fresh and burning.

I had no one. Nothing. And it was my fault. All of it.

When I didn't turn and look at him, Frank came around the foot of the bed. I buried my face into the pillow. The closer he got, the more I hid.

Finally, he whispered, "Harley?"

"What?" I said into the pillow.

The bed sagged by my knees and I could feel his warmth drawing closer to me, but he didn't touch me. He kept at least that much distance between us, and I couldn't be more grateful for it.

"Harley, come out of there," he said, his voice still soft.

I shook my head, which only buried my face deeper into the pillow. If I didn't stop this, I'd suffocate from my own stubbornness.

"C'mon, babe. Let's talk."

"What for?" I asked, finally pulling my face up and looking him in the eye. "You're done, remember? I think we both are."

"You gonna go home, then?" he asked and the emptiness in his voice made my stomach clench tight.

Did it really mean so little to him? Did I mean so little to him?

The truth was, I knew I couldn't go back home. Lori had made that abundantly clear. I couldn't go back, but I didn't want him to know that. I wouldn't give him the satisfaction of knowing I had no one else but him.

"I'll figure it out," I said simply, resting my head back down. "Don't worry about me. I told you I can find my own way."

The minutes ticked on agonizingly slow as we both sat in total silence. I'll admit a small part of me was hoping that he would drop to his knees and beg me to stay.

No, please, don't go. I'll do anything. Blah, blah, blah.

But that was a child's wish. Lori had destroyed that part of my heart that was still back home with Mom and

Dad and left only that which Frank had stolen away so long ago. It was that sad remnant that screamed for him to do or say something, anything, that showed me he still cared. That he still wanted me.

"I don't know how to handle this," he said finally. "Any of it. Joy Anne, as much shit as that bitch talks, she's right about some things. You don't know anything. Not a thing about us. You can't be with us and not really be a part of us. You should go."

The flutter of hope that began once he broke the silence, died away with each word. So that was it. He really was done with me. And agreeing with that horrible piece of trailer-trash... I just couldn't handle that. Not after what I'd seen.

I threw the pillow to the floor and swung my legs off the bed before I could talk myself out of it. Jumping to my feet, I was resolute in leaving.

"Fine. I'm gone."

His hand caught the crook of my arm. It was gentle, but firm enough to keep me from taking another step. Even though he had a captive audience, I wasn't about to look at him. I couldn't let him see how hurt I was.

"You should go," he repeated, "but I don't want you to. At least, not before I let you see what I've been keeping from you."

"I think I saw enough of you and the slut, thanks," I choked out.

"Not her." The finality in his voice did make me look over at him. "This is a lot more than just me cheating, Harley. That shit doesn't mean a damn thing in the scope of it. There are things going on that you can't even begin to comprehend."

"It's pretty easy to say it doesn't matter when you were the one that cheated, Frank." The words came out in a near-hiss.

"Just..." He released my arm, raised his hand as if he were grasping the air beside his head, then breathed out slow and lowered it into his lap, "Hear me out. I'm telling you that I do not want you to go. I want you to see every-thing for what it is. Come with us to the woods tonight."

"The woods?" I asked, impatiently. "What the hell do you have to show me out there? Why not just get it out here and now and be done with it? I'm tired of the mind games, Frank."

My anger and hurt retreated a little, leaving a heavy wariness. That wasn't what I wanted. I wanted to hold onto the anger, not surrender it to the mental exhaustion that often followed Frank's bipolar attitude.

The anger would let me walk out of that room. It would give me the validation of leaving behind the one and only family that I had ever felt I belonged to. Without it, the nag of desperation clung heavily to me and rooted me to the spot; it forced me to listen to him and his request.

He rubbed the bridge of his nose for a moment then, with a sigh, said, "Because I can't just tell you. I gotta show you. It's the only way you'll understand what we've been tryin' to drive into your head from day one. Just... come see for yourself before you take off. Then you can call your parents or whatever."

I glanced over at the phone a little too quickly. I wanted to know what the hell he'd been holding back; the thing that I demanded he tell me that he always managed to sidestep.

I also didn't want to tell him about Lori. What if I didn't like what he had to show me? So far, as far as he was concerned, I was a phone call away from going back home. Telling him I wasn't wanted back home would make it that much harder to break away from him. Until I knew what he had up his sleeve, I would keep my call with Lori close to my chest.

"Fine," I said. "I'll go with you tonight. But, Frank, if I don't like what you have to show me, I'm gone."

"I ain't gonna lie, Harls. You probably won't like it. At first."

I frowned at him, opened my mouth to ask what he thought I wouldn't like, but he cut me off.

"Just... You'll see. You're the one always tellin' me you can handle things. I'm giving you a chance to prove it."

Well, what could I do? He was right. I did always go on about how I could handle myself. If I backed out now then he'd make me a liar, and that didn't sit well with me. If I didn't like what he showed me, I was free to leave. If he finally laid everything straight for me maybe, just maybe, the strain that had taken up residence on our relationship would ease up. Maybe we could work out, after all. I did love him, but was love enough? I figured, by the end of the night, I'd finally know for sure.

August 20th 2010 7:49 p.m.

"You gotta be fucking kidding me. This is a joke, right?" I said as I stared at the man behind the counter.

He didn't so much as look up from his tabloid. His face remained unmoved at my outburst; that bored indifference that said he'd heard this all before and often. Ten dollars for two packs of Pall Mall Red 100s. It was highway robbery.

I grudgingly shoved my hand into my hip pocket. With the price of ciggs getting steadily higher, I was almost ready to quit. Just not yet. I drank, but it wasn't an everyday thing. I've never done drugs. Hell, I didn't even gamble. My vice was tobacco. Someday I'd quit, but not today. Today, I'd shell out more of my hard-won money for something that would eventually kill me.

My fingers pinched the bill and started to pull the money out when the sudden growl of an engine erupted outside. I jumped, spilling change all over the floor. Damn him. As if I wasn't nervous enough about tonight, and what he was going to show me, he had to go and be a dick.

I glanced over to the large wall of windows and watched as Frank threw his arms out in a gesture of his impatience. I replied with a gesture of my own before slamming the twenty on the counter. Okay, it wasn't the most mature response. So sue me. My tolerance for him and his bullshit attitude was wearing thin. Normally, riding was something to lift my spirits and put me at ease, but tonight I couldn't lose myself in the ride. There was just too much to escape from.

I turned to look at the clerk, leaving Frank to stew in his irritation, and drummed my nails across the counter. He was, of course, taking his sweet time counting from the cash drawer. A slew of insults built up inside of me, bubbling and boiling, ready to erupt out of my mouth like a volcano, but I bit my tongue. My bad day was not his problem.

"Yo, Habib!" A male voice called from behind me. "You know how to count American money, or what? Hurry the fuck up already you fucking sand rat. We got places to be."

I felt my anger flush into my cheeks hearing one of our guys talk to the man in such an awful way. I stared at him coldly as he continued to show his ass, speaking gibberish and laughing until the clerk's coworker called him over to his register. At least he wouldn't have to help him. It was a small grace.

"Ignore him. His mom spent too much time looking for a new dad and not enough time teaching him manners," I said, giving the clerk a small smile.

He didn't seem to care what I had to say, and I honestly didn't blame him. Why should he? As far as he was concerned I was just another ignorant fool, tagging along with racist hicks, not doing anything to put them in their place. Silent compliance. And the worst part was he would be mostly right. Why didn't I speak up? Because we rode together? Because he was one of Frank's guys? How much longer would it be before I started to act just like them?

The guilt hit worse when I thought about my own family. While I was pretty white-passing on the outside, the blood that ran in my veins was Shoshone, or at least partly. My heritage peeked out in ghostly traces on my features, hidden behind more prominent white traits. Prominent cheekbones padded by full cheeks, hooded eyes overshadowed by the gunmetal blue irises. Even my nose didn't match my mother and sister's aquiline noses

Unlike my sister, Lorelei, who was graced with the statuesque beauty of our Shoshone blood, I looked like just another white girl. A privilege I could have used in situations like this, but instead I chose silence and excuses just to avoid the confrontation.

It was cowardly, but all I kept thinking about was the inevitable shitshow that would happen once it got back to Frank. That fact alone was enough to buy my silence; and my integrity.

The clerk handed me back my change, and the look in his eyes showed me every bit of contempt he was feeling towards the guy—and towards me by my sheer proximity to him.

All I could offer him was a pathetic, "Sorry."

I snatched the cigarettes and bolted towards the door, beckoned by another roar of the Softail outside. The night greeted me with an assault of stale, hot Texas air. Even the nights made me want to grab a cold glass of lemonade or a chilled beer in a nice frosty mug. I liked the heat and all—it was better than snow and ice—but there was a point where there really was too much of a good thing. Add in Frank's heater-like body temperature pressing against my skin when we touched, and the Texas summer heat could kiss my ass.

"What the hell took so long?" Frank asked as I tossed him one of the little red boxes.

He caught the pack in the middle of his chest without looking. I tucked mine down my shirt and threw a leg over the bike to hoist myself behind Frank.

"Don't start," I begged.

It was physically exhausting fighting with him anymore.

Once I was settled, the bike roared to life and we sped off. I didn't know where we were going, and to be honest, I didn't care. The where wasn't as important as the why.

As we rode along the empty road, my imagination ran rampant. So many scenarios played out in my mind, from a wife and kids he'd abandoned to a hidden plot of land with dozens of shallow graves where he hid dead bodies. Aside from those two possibilities, I couldn't think of anything that would warrant him being so damn secretive.

Before long, I had to stop guessing. I'd find out soon enough. Then I could decide my next move. Instead, I focused on the soothing thrum of the bike underneath us and let it drive out everything else.

His beloved 'Beast'—talk about lame, male machismo—was a 2001 Harley Davidson Springer Softail. A beautiful custom job with flame engraved, 10-inch chrome ape hangers, a custom bench seat with hand-tooled trim, matching solo bag with key lock, and 2-in-1 chrome exhaust. He'd had it custom painted in sweeping shades of navy blues and blacks like the night sky dotted with stars.

On the back fender was a breathtaking graphic of a Native American woman lounging with a wolf.

Lounging was almost too mild a word. She melted her scantily-clad body against the animal's neck, embracing it, her arm thrown over her head to reach back and pet along the wolf's fur. Her face was turned into its neck and it stared outward. Its amber eyes stared into my soul until the recessed tail lights flared to life and would turn the amber eyes of the wolf into bright red glowing things.

The only thing that unnerved me about the paint job was the woman. Frank had it done during the early stages of our relationship, and I wasn't sure if I was seeing things or not, but the woman looked very much like a sketched-out version of me with the Shoshone cranked up.

Still, it was a beautiful paint job and somehow managed to fit Frank perfectly. It was his most valued possession. I really couldn't blame him for his obsession with it; the bike was pretty much my favorite thing in the world, too.

Something about riding cleared my mind and eased my soul. I didn't have to think about where we were going to sleep, the cops catching up to us, or even the less-than-charming way Frank had been treating me lately. The past few months had been pretty bad, but at that moment all I cared about was the feel of the machine vibrating under me, Frank squeezed between my legs, and the wind whipping my dark hair behind me.

The hum of the engine lulled me into a state of complete meditation, and before I knew it, we were there—wherever 'there' was. Frank cut the engine and stood first, years of riding making it one fluidly practiced movement. I began my own less graceful dismount to find him standing against me and keeping me from taking even a single step from the bike.

"Ready?" he asked, the muscles in his jaw working furiously.

I couldn't trust my own voice. No, I wasn't ready, but that didn't matter. Now or never, as they say. I gave him a soft nod before he finally moved away and led me towards the woods.

I needed a drink. That was the first thought that came to me as I stumbled through the trees. I say stumbled because, unlike Frank and just about everyone else we ran with, I had little in the way of grace and balance. It amazed me how easily Frank could move through the overgrown brush. He moved with purpose, cutting through the trees and bushes like they weren't there; like they were alive and parted just for him.

Me? I skinned my knee a little ways back when I tripped over a tree root.

I heard a laugh ahead of me and looked up to see Frank leaning against the trunk of a huge cypress tree.

"C'mon, we're almost there."

"I'm moving as fast as I can," I said breathlessly. "You know, you can always stop running ahead of me. How the fuck do you move like that?"

"I like the woods. It's second-nature to me," he said with a shrug.

"Good for you. My second, and first, nature prefers pavement," I said as I rubbed the rough scrape.

My knee stung angrily, and I had a sudden wonder about how such inconsequential injuries, like scraped knees and paper cuts, hurt like hell. It was a comical distraction while Frank continued to lead me to wherever we were going. Something to keep me from caving into my anxiety. It had been nearly an hour since we'd left the bike, and each step was one step closer to truth. Truth I had been begging to hear for months now.

Finally, the distant sound of voices caught my attention. We'd finally made it. There were so many voices. They were talking, laughing, crying out very male boasts. I couldn't see anyone, yet, but there was a flickering orange glow breaking through the trees.

So, we had stumbled through the woods, in the dark, for almost an hour... for a bonfire?

Frank's body eclipsed the glow as he moved in front of me, his hands sliding onto my shoulders. He stared down at me, and all evidence of laughter that clung to his face moments ago had been replaced by an anxious anticipation. And something strangely close to fear.

Foreboding, maybe?

The sudden change in his demeanor was dizzying. One moment he was the cocky, playful boy I fell for ages ago, and the next he was guarded. Careful. Stony.

"Right. Remember to keep your cool. You asked for this. Just keep that in mind if things get a little... hairy." A ghost of a smile teased his lips, and he brushed a hair from my face.

"Might help if you told me what to expect," I said.

"Well... tonight's kinda big. You know them two guys we picked up in Dallas?" he asked, dropping his hands and shoving them into his pockets. He waited for my nod before continuing. "Tonight, we're gonna make 'em Hellhounds. Officially."

"And you gotta do that in the middle of the forest?" I didn't try to hide the skepticism in my voice.

He ran a hand over his chin, rubbing the coarse hair that covered it. I could tell he was debating how much to tell me. How much I needed to know compared to what I needed to see for myself. Finally, he reached his hand out and draped it over my shoulders, forcing me to walk forward with him.

"Let's just say we got a very particular way of doin' things."

With that, we walked towards the break in the trees where a large fire blazed. Just about everyone from the crew was there, including Suze. Her eyes widened when she looked at me, not with the usual warm welcoming, but with a look of near-alarm.

As Frank ushered me closer, I realized that she wasn't the only one that looked less than thrilled at my intrusion.

More than not, I met unhappy eyes and looks of bemused scrutiny. Some looked absolutely frightened at my being there. These were the people I called friends. I'd ridden with them, drank with them, joked with them... why did I suddenly feel unwanted?

"Frank," Paulie's familiar baritone came more as a warning than a greeting.

Frank's arm slid off me, leaving me standing awkwardly as he drew up to his closest friend. Paulie's eyes were all for me, and though he was one of the friendliest of the men, he looked at me like an intruder.

"Is there a problem?" Frank asked distractedly.

"You sure about this?" his friend asked, still looking at me.

"No. But it's happening. Remember what I said," Frank's voice dropped a bit lower. "If anyone touches her I'll rip them apart myself."

Paulie looked at him. "You're riskin' a lot, Frank. You know how it gets. I like the girl just fine, but even I can't promise—" He was cut off before he could finish.

Frank patted his shoulder. "I ain't askin' for your promises. I'm demanding obedience."

His words floored me. He and Paulie were close. Almost like true brothers. What right did he have to demand so much from his friend? He talked to him like nothing more than a dog at his heels, and what was even more unsettling was that Paulie seemed to be okay with it. At least on some level.

Paulie stared level with Frank for a few minutes. The looks in their eyes seemed to convey words from a language I hadn't learned yet. Finally, Paulie nodded once and broke eye contact.

"Alright. Whatever you say, boss."

"See, that's the spirit," Frank called to Paulie's retreating back before turning back to me.

"I'm not sure about this," I confessed.

The words poured out of me of their own volition, and I instantly regretted saying it out loud.

"Too late for second guesses, babe. You came this far. Don't let that skinned knee of yours go in vain."

His arm slid over my shoulders in that typical possessive way, but this time, I didn't mind it. I couldn't shake the feeling coming over me or the discomfort of all those eyes on me. I hadn't felt this in-the-way since I was with Mom, Dad, and Lori. Maybe I really had been stupid.

Maybe, I didn't belong anywhere. Nowhere at all.

I let Frank lead me to a stack of big, flat stones that couldn't have possibly been positioned that way by nature. It was just a little higher than my waist, flanked by other, shorter stacks of rock, and almost fought with the bonfire to be the focal point of this little clearing. It was just a pile of rocks, but even I found my eyes drawn to them.

Frank led me to one of the shorter stacks and patted the flat surface. I took the cue easily, like there was much to riddle out, and once I sat on the rock he slid himself up onto the taller stack, looking out towards everyone.

The whole arrangement reminded me of a throne with the king sitting higher and more regally than the queen whose perch was less ornate. Less important. I didn't like how that made me feel.

"If you listen to me just one time in your life, listen now," Frank's voice cut down towards me, bringing my eyes up. "Things are gonna get weird. Dangerous. I'm gonna protect you, but you gotta do exactly what I tell you. You have to trust me or you're as good as dead. Do you understand?"

His eyes were bright and shining with something I couldn't comprehend. Protect me? Dead? What the hell was going to happen that I would be at risk of death? I filed that away under 'stuff he could have told me before we got here'.

"Wait, what? Maybe this wasn't..." I started to stand, but he grabbed my shoulder, stopping me.

"No. I already told you it's too late. You wanted answers. You wanted in. This is it."

His voice wasn't angry or even impatient. He didn't say it like some threat. In fact, his words were void of any real emotion. Just stating truth, plain and simple. Okay, maybe not so simple.

I did the only thing I could do at that point. I sat back down.

Even though the warning bells were going off in my head, I didn't run. He was right. How long had I told him I wanted full disclosure, that I was sick of being tip-toed around and left without knowing what the hell was hap-pening around me?

Once Frank and I were as settled as we were going to get, the chatter around us died out. Eyes turned not just on me but to Frank. It was sort of eerie how quickly the silence fell, leaving nothing but the crackling of the burning wood and the night songs of the creatures lurking in those deep dark woods around us. They looked to us, to him, with restrained anticipation.

"Tonight," Frank's voice cut through the quiet so that even I snapped to attention, "is a special night for us. Each month, under the moon's full power, we gather as one family, one pack, and we run. We revel. We hunt. Tonight, even though the moon shift is not upon us, we have cause to celebrate. We have new blood wishing to join our ranks."

I stared at him in a strange mix of awe and bewilder-ment. On the one hand, his voice was so commanding, carrying on the wind with a crystal clarity and authority that not only earned my complete attention but demand-ed obedience from everyone around us.

On the other, the forefront of my mind caught words like 'pack', 'run', and 'hunt'.

Frank had always had a strange way of explaining things that made everything sound more animal than human. I always just considered it an idiosyncrasy of his, but as I looked out at the reverence shining on the faces of those gathered, I realized that he might not be the only one.

As I looked over everyone, I noticed the two new faces Frank had mentioned. They were standing side-by-side near the fire. The man on the left was gorgeous. He looked to be about six-foot-tall with sun-bronzed skin peeking out from a form-fitting ribbed tank. His hair was blond and hung around his ears and fringed his forehead in a too-hot-to-care mess. I couldn't really see his eyes well, but I could see that they were dark and dangerous.

The man beside him seemed similar but different. He matched his companion inch for inch in height, breadth, and muscle tone but the coloring was strikingly opposite. Though his skin was just as tan, his well-toned arms were decorated in thick, black designs. I hesitate to call them tribal, at least in the 'frat boy on spring break' fashion, but there was something very old and primitive about the hard lines and circular markings.

Mayan, maybe?

His hair cascaded down his neck and shoulders in dark, thick waves and his eyes were a striking pale hue that captivated me even from so far away.

Their facial structure, like their stature, were very similar and I wondered if hottie number two's chin was also dimpled under that dark scruff of hair. Brothers? Twins, maybe? They had to be. There was no way they could look so alike without sharing, at least a little, blood.

"Jordan. Levi. You will lead our hunt tonight. Prove that you are worth your mettle by leading your new brothers and sisters to a kill. By sharing the blood of the weak, you will become part of the strong. Now, let's get down to it," Frank's words were emphasized by the raise of voices, each one cheering and praising him.

All except for mine.

Chapter 10

Lead them to a kill?

My pulse sped up, and I looked from all our eager friends to Frank. Did he mean a literal kill? Like going out and shooting someone? There was no way. No, it had to be a metaphor for something. I didn't have a clue what but that had to be it. I just could not wrap my head around Frank openly announcing his plan to kill someone.

As I mulled this impossibility, I realized I was not the only person looking less-than-excited about Frank's little speech. Near the back of the crowd, Theo stood drinking from a can of P.B.R. Unlike the smiles and clapping hands around him, he stood tense and unmoved. His eyes were hidden behind his big, wrap-around sunglasses, but I could see his hand flex at his side, the can denting under his grip.

A hand touched my back, and I jumped, twisting in my seat to find Frank leaning down towards me. His grin was still wide and full of excitement.

"Okay, remember what I said," he whispered. "It's gonna get crazy, more than you could ever imagine. Just be smart, and don't do anything that will get you killed. Don't provoke them."

"Provoke them?" I asked, beginning to think more and more with each passing minute that this was a very, very bad idea. "What'll provoke—"

That was the first time I felt it. That electrical charge in the air, searching for something to grasp onto. It was like the air itself was alive and sentient. It crackled with that warm charge, spreading out towards me and licking over my skin, crawling up my arms, my neck. I fought past the suffocating energy that fought to push past my lips and pour down my throat.

A sharp, melodic howling drowned out my words as well as any ability to think. It was so loud, so close, just like in those terrible horror movies when the audience shouts for the dumb blond to not look. I slowly turned back to face our friends.

Two large wolves stood in the crowd now. And by large, I mean bigger than I'd ever seen or thought possible.

Both were pitch black with almost luminescent yellow eyes and roughly the size of a Great Dane. Maybe even bigger.

I couldn't even process what they were doing there before their strange presence was overshadowed by one of the men standing next to them dropping to his knees as his body thrashed in violent spasms. His light skin darkened into a tawny brown and with a strangled groan, his head jerked back. His clothes split from his body in thick ripping sounds and gave way to fur that spilled over him. If I hadn't watched it, I'd have said what happened was impossible. Okay, I still say it was impossible. The man had turned into a great, huge wolf.

I jumped to my feet so fast that Frank barely managed to grip his fingers into my shoulder.

"They won't hurt you. I've ordered them not to touch you," he said.

He was making disapproving sounds behind me, but I didn't pay him any attention. My attention was all for the people in front of us. If I could call them people anymore. One by one, friend after friend turned into impossibly large wolves until the last of them, Theo, shifted into a particularly menacing white and gray wolf.

The two black wolves shot off into the woods, followed by one, then two, then the rest of the beasts that had changed. Even a few people, who were still people, ran with them as if they bore two extra legs. Just as quickly as the wolves had appeared, they were gone.

My chest hurt. My brain shut down. I was too afraid to even scream. This was impossible. Impossible! Every fiber of my being, that wasn't trying to convince my brain that it had just been tricked, was shouting at me to run, to get the fuck away from this. Fast.

"Harley," Frank said. "Harley! Look at me."

I did.

"They're... it can't..." I couldn't even form a simple sentence.

"I told you," Frank said, bringing his hands up to cup my face. "You had no idea. Now you do. Harls, you were never supposed to find out about this. You weren't supposed to last that long. You have gone against everything I consider normal in my life."

Did he just say his life was normal?!

"I need you. I've needed you the moment I found you, and I still need you now. I know this shit is beyond belief, and I don't expect you to be okay with it right away, but you are a part of my life that I cannot let slip through my fingers. I won't."

I just stared up at him. His voice had gone dark and edged with a deadly growl. Or, maybe, those impossible wolves were still playing with my head.

He hadn't gone all fury and four-legged. He was still human. And still, there was more danger in those brown eyes than the entire pack of wolves that had just run off. It was frightening seeing that much raw emotion in them. It went beyond happiness, sadness, or even insanity. It was aggressive, possessive, and deadly. In that moment, I wanted to get away from Frank.

Not the wolves, not Joy Anne's bullshit, but him.

"You're mine," he said, pulling me closer so that he could breathe the words against my forehead. "And you aren't goin' anywhere. Are you?"

The heat of his touch fought against the cold chill his words brought me. It wasn't a question or a request. As far as he was concerned, I was here to stay.

I had mere seconds to weigh my options. What would he do if I called him a freak, a lying bastard, and told him to go to hell? Would he sick his wolves on me or would he kill me himself? Would I be able to pull out of his arms and make a run for it? Probably not. If I tried, with his hands cupping my face like this, he could probably snap my neck. I didn't know what he would do if I told him what he didn't want to hear. That was the scariest thought of all.

If I had any chance at getting away from him without him hurting me, I had to put space between us. He pulled back enough to look down at me, his eyes imploring. I knew what he wanted to hear.

Even though my heart threatened to come out of my throat I forced myself to smile up at him. To hide the new-found aversion I felt for him. I smiled and shook my head slowly, not trusting my own voice.

That seemed to satisfy him. He smiled at me and pulled me into a slow, deep kiss. Once upon a time, that kiss could make me want to give him anything he wanted. Now, all I wanted to do was pull away from him and scrub my lips.

When he finally released me, he brushed his fingers across the side of my neck, pulling my hair away from it with his other hand.

"Good," he said softly. "Good. Then we can finally move past this. We can move on to better things. Pretty soon you'll be one of—"

"Frankie!" A deep voice cut through the trees followed by one of the guys that had run after the animals. "Need you, Boss. One of the pups is losing his shit."

"God dammit, I knew that mother fucker was too green for this," Frank said, letting go of me. "Harley, stay here. Don't leave the fire and you'll be safe."

He snapped the order at me and took off running before giving me a second look. I listened to the sounds of crunching leaves and shaking bushes until they were too far away to hear. It was my shot. Either I ran now, or he'd come back and make me go back with him.

I allowed myself the brief hope that one of the wolves would turn on him, take care of my problems for me, but I couldn't rely on that. The wolves heeded him for some reason. Unlike them, he was a man, but they followed him like dogs to their master.

I spared a quick glance back to where he and his friend had disappeared and quickly decided that running was my only choice. I had no idea where I was going or even where I was. Frank's little jaunt into the woods had me turned around until I couldn't tell what was forward and what was back, but it didn't matter. As long as I was going the opposite direction he'd gone, I was good. Eventually, I would find the other side of these trees. I would find a road or a house, and with that, help.

I pushed my way through the trees and bushes. They were just as unforgiving now as they had been earlier. The sharp tips of branches cut across my arms and legs, but I couldn't stop until I was somewhere safe. Somewhere I could sit and figure out what to do next.

How could this—any of this—be real? I was the girl-friend of some monster wrangler. Werewolves. Oh, Jesus, I was losing my mind. Werewolves! I was actually considering the existence of fucking werewolves!

But I had no other word for them. I had watched people I thought I knew, friends and companions, change from human to furry uber-dogs. No, I had to be high. Or drunk. Or I was cracking up.

Yeah, that had to be it. All this shit that's happened in the last 24 hours was getting to me. Joy Anne, Frank hitting me, all the booze from the club, the call with my sister... I had finally had enough, and the only way for my brain to cope with all of this crazy stress was to snap. I was officially a nut-case.

I just needed to lie down and wait for the men in white coats to come pick me up in the wacky-wagon and cart me off to a padded room.

A vicious snarl echoed through the air, bringing me to a stumbling stop. The trees and bushes surrounding me were still and silent. Only the hazy lullaby of insects and the wind sweeping over the treetops made a sound. The silence seemed harmless enough, but the hairs on my arms stood on end. I looked around me, half expecting a wild animal to jump out at me and tear me to bits, but there was nothing.

See, I told myself. I'm hearing and seeing things. I hoped that when I woke up tomorrow, all of this would have been a bad nightmare and Frank would be his usual self. A major asshole with a God complex, but normal.

As I was battling with my sense of logic and reasoning, I turned at a large oak and found myself face-to-face with a giant, snarling, white and gray wolf. His ears laid back and his fur rose around his neck and shoulders. Ivory teeth shone out from a snarling snout, dripping with thick drool. He was staring straight at me. I went rigid.

I knew better. That's all I could say for what I did next. I knew better. The one thing stated over and over again about wild animals is to not run. If you run, they chase you. They are faster, they have teeth and claws, and they are driven by instinct to chase down their prey. Running will only encourage a predatory animal to chase you. It will catch you, and it will hurt you, maybe even kill you. I knew this, but when that wolf lunged and snapped its teeth at me I took off. I ran, and it ran after me.

I didn't get far before it appeared in front of me, blocking my path. I'd turn around and run the other way, and it was there with gnashing teeth ready to sink into me. No matter where I turned, it was ready to drive me back the other way until, finally, I broke past it.

I ran harder and faster than I ever had in my life. If the woods fought against me, I didn't notice. All I could focus on was getting away from the monster behind me. Even though my body wanted nothing more than to give out, to fall and heave up everything in my stomach, all I could do was run. I could do all of that later but not if I was torn to pieces in the middle of nowhere.

The trees began to grow thinner as I moved until I finally broke through them and saw a building ahead in the darkness. Just as I reached it, a distant howl erupted behind me. Not wanting to wait for the wolf to catch up, I rounded the front of the shack and pulled at the door until it jerked free, allowing me to slip inside.

The place looked like something out of a Saw movie. There was very little light, and the little that was there was flickering ominously. The wood looked to be splintered and weak; a good sneeze could knock this place down. Any minute now, I expected Mike Myers to jump out and stab me to death.

Sidestepping away from the door, I moved deeper into the room. As I thought, there was nothing but a single hanging light, flickering on and off, clinging to that little bit of juice that kept it burning. There was a spattering of benches cluttered with various things ranging from paper to chunks of gnarled metal and rusted power tools. A rusty hook hung down the center of the room, swinging from a thick chain that came from the center beam and snaked through and under the piles of junk on the benches. It might have been used to pull engines out of cars; a sort of makeshift mechanic shop.

If this had been a business, then maybe there was a phone. There was electricity, obviously, so it stood to reason a phone wasn't too impossible. I had no idea who I would call once I found one, but right now it was the best hope I had. Even if I'd sound like a lunatic.

Hello, 911. I'm sitting in one of Freddy's nightmare rapehouses hiding from the Big Bad Wolf, who was once a man, and I'm pretty sure he's about to huff and puff and eat me and my chinny-chin-chin.

Most likely they would send some men from the local asylum, but hey, whatever works. Either way I would be the hell out of here.

No luck on the benches. All that seemed to be under the chaotic piles of dusty papers was more dust and more junk. If I could just find a cord, then maybe it would lead me to the receiver. I moved to the wall and searched for a phone jack, an outlet, anything that indicated this place had a phone somewhere.

My foot tangled in something on the floor and I bent down to find the jack. Better yet, a cord was still sticking out of it. With a breath of relief, I crawled across the floor, using the thin wire to guide me, until I came to the other end, which was frayed and lacking a vital part of the phone. Like, the phone itself. I cursed, pushed myself to my feet, and backed into something very tall and very solid.

I couldn't help it. I screamed, loud and ragged. It echoed in the room which creaked as if the sound alone would bring it down around my ears. Spinning around, I flung my fists out to strike but they were stopped by large, strong hands.

"Whoa, whoa, whoa! Harley!" his voice rang out, quieting my wordless protests.

I stopped fighting and looked up at the familiar face that I hadn't seen since the night Chuck died.

"D'Angelo?" I asked, squinting to try and make his face out in the shadows.

"Yeah, girl. It's me. Damn, what's got you all spooked?"

I swallowed hard, my throat dry and stinging from the screaming. He let go of my hands, and I stepped back, glancing back over my shoulder towards the door I'd come through.

"There's... a wolf. It chased me in here," I said.

"A wolf? Girl, are you on drugs? What are you even doin' out here in the middle of fuckin' nowhere? Where's Frank?"

"He's," I sighed, unsure what to say. I mean, D'Angelo had been part of our crew. What if he dragged me back to him? Then again, he hadn't been around for weeks. "D'Angelo, where have you been?"

"Me?" he said, his lips curling into a smile. "Oh, I've been trying to catch up to you assholes. Y'all rode out before me and the others made it back to the motel. You know, the one you left Chuck to rot in."

"Chuck?"

"Yeah. Been looking for Frank for weeks now. Got unfinished business to handle with him." His eyes bore into me, and I took a step back. "You wouldn't know where I could find him, would you?"

He matched me, step for step, walking me backwards towards the middle of the room. There was fierceness in his eyes that made me uneasy.

"Why would I know where he's at?" I asked, lamely.

"Because he doesn't leave you alone. Not for very long, anyway," he grinned down at me again. "Which is exactly why Theo chased you out here in the first place, sweet thing. If we got you, he'll be sniffing you out in no time."

A low, dangerous growl rumbled behind me. I spun around to find the pale-colored wolf staring at me, effectively blocking my exit. His tongue flicked over his nose, eyes trained on me, following every minute movement. I was staring down the wolf that had jumped right from the pages of a Brothers Grimm story when something solid cracked hard and fast against the back of my skull.

A crash jolted me awake. For minutes, though it seemed longer, everything sounded distant. Dull. The first thing that felt real was the cold, dirty floor under my cheek. The coolness against my face felt great in the muggy air of the woods. If I could just stay here and keep my eyes closed, then nothing could hurt me anymore. It was a foolish hope. A hope that was destroyed as the rest of my senses returned to me.

Another crash, the grunt of male voices struggling, and the underlying smell of something sickly sweet forced me from my self-made escape and thrust me back into reality. I opened my eyes and saw a puddle in front of me. It was dark and wide and seemed to be spreading as I watched it. It spread itself wider and wider until it reached my outstretched hand and pooled around my fingertips. It was hot and thick; much thicker than water. I lifted my hand and watched it drip back to the floor.

Blood. It was blood. It wasn't mine. I finally found the strength to lift my head, my vision blurring in and out of focus. My eyes followed the trail of blood to the man only a couple of feet away. An older man with gray hair and deeply tanned, almost leathery, skin lay sprawled on the floor. A familiar man. A naked man.

"Theo?" I whispered.

His eyes were open, staring straight at me, looking at me as if he had been looking to me to save him in his final moments. I had seen many things in those eyes. Laughter. Anger. Disgust. Now they were empty.

Before I could stop myself, I let my eyes wander down his naked upper body to the source of the bleeding. His insides had become his outsides. Thick, meaty ropes dangled out of ragged flesh. He had been completely disemboweled.

Somehow managing to not shriek in horror, I threw myself back from the still-advancing blood. My brain pounded from the onslaught of questions. At first, I thought that D'Angelo had killed him, but then I remembered they'd been working together. He'd said that Theo had been the one to chase me into a trap for... Frank.

I shot to my feet. More crashing and shouting came from deeper in the room, and I made my way towards it using the wall behind me as a guide. As I rounded the line of benches that blocked my view, I saw Niko and Paulie near the back wall laying into another man.

Niko was decades younger than Paulie and almost a foot taller. He stood at a staggering six foot five, the tallest man I had ever known, and slender. Most people I've met above the six-foot mark were either built like brick shithouses or were lanky and awkward, especially if they were young. Niko was just barely twenty-one and there was nothing awkward about him. I could see every muscle in his arms, chest, and abdomen flex and ripple as he fought. He was like a statue of a gladiator, each contour of muscle carved deeply into toffee-colored marble.

He was also deceptively dangerous. Where Paulie just let his danger roll off him like a heavy cologne, Niko made people think he was a boy scout before shoving a knife into their back. At first glance, he came off as a great big flirt, a womanizer above all else. But there was something dark hiding behind those light brown eyes of his. Something evil.

Niko had something long and thin gripped in his hand. As he raised it over his head, ready to strike, the light caught the metal just enough so I could make it out. It was a tire iron, and by the looks of it, it had already made a messy introduction into someone. I winced, pulling into myself, as he brought the piece of metal down on the face of his opponent.

I caught a flash of something in the corner of my eye. It pulled my attention back to the middle of the room. I saw Frank being tackled to the ground. Panic flooded through me, but even the impact of a man twice his size landing on top of him didn't stop Frank from fighting back.

For a moment they were locked against each other, so close neither one of them could get a good punch in. If Frank lost the upper-hand, even a little, the guy could crush him. Frank could boast all he wanted, but the man had a good hundred pounds on him, easy. Perhaps my prayers had been answered, after all.

I don't normally wish harm on other people, but Frank wasn't a person to me. Not anymore. Even without the fur and claws, he had been more frightening than any of those monsters I used to call friends. I shuffled towards the door, trying to slip out without his notice.

As I reached the door, I glanced behind me. Frank had turned the tables on the other guy. He rolled the two of them over until he was sitting on top of him. The light spilled over the other guy's face.

D'Angelo.

Frank started plowing one unforgiving blow after another to his face. My insides tightened painfully. Each meaty sound of Frank's fists slamming into D'Angelo's nose was accentuated by the sound of bones and cartilage snapping. I watched as a spray of crimson splattered across both him and Frank, who continued to beat into the bloody pulp of flesh blow after blow, hit after hit, without so much as a pause for air.

D'Angelo's face glistened where the blood poured out. Frank was a mess of red, splattered in small droplets all over his face and arms. I watched his face as he continued to throw his weight into each punch, even as D'Angelo went limp beneath him.

His eyes were wild. Their natural cocoa brown seemed to be alive with an amber fire that was all violence and madness. I knew Frank was a violent man, but I never thought he would fall this far down the rabbit hole.

With one last powerful blow, Frank fell across his old friend's unmoving body and caught his breath. I couldn't believe what I had just seen, even as I stared down at the aftermath. My breath caught in my chest and I tried to hold back the intense urge to scream or vomit or both. I tried to make out any sign of life. His chest never rose, never fell; his body never moved.

I was no doctor, but from all I could tell, he was dead. Frank had beaten him until he was little more than a lump of bleeding flesh. We'd ridden beside this man for the last two years of my life. We drank with him, had eaten with him, and followed him over the open road. I'd bought him drinks on his birthday and watched girls I was friends with get close to him.

And now he didn't exist. Frank had killed him; beaten him unrecognizable. If I hadn't watched it happen, I'd have never known that was someone I knew lying in that growing puddle of blood.

Boots scraped across the dirt floor and tore my eyes from the corpse to the man now getting to his feet. He brought his arm across his face to wipe the blood away, but he only managed to smear more across his brow.

The air wouldn't leave my chest. It was snared in a net of fear and nausea and built into a scream that nearly ejected itself from my body. Somehow, I managed to keep it down. Survival first, throwing up later.

I took the chance to try and run out before he saw me, taking my eyes off of him for only a moment to try and navigate over the hanging door but I never made it. I felt the tight grip of Frank's hand on the crook of my elbow. He spun me around, fast and relentless, and I had to grab him to keep from stumbling, barely missing the blood that coated his forearm like a wet glove.

His face was a bloody mask of feral rage that scared me down to the marrow. He looked wild, crazed. It reminded me of the animal documentaries and the predators that would chew on their meals after a long chase, basking in their triumph. It made my throat tight, making it nearly impossible to swallow down my fear.

"I told you not to run." His voice was deeper than normal, like he was trying to choke down some of that primal anger he'd unleashed on his old friend.

"I... there was..."

"You never listen to me. Come on, let's get out of here," he commanded with a tightening of his iron-like grip for good measure.

I loosed a whimper of pain as he led me out of the building and back to the bikes. He shouted something to Niko and Paulie, but I was too busy trying to wrap my mind around everything to even hear what he said.

With a rough shove towards his bike, he released my arm, making me stumble until I could reach out and steady myself using the seat of the Softail.

"You killed him, Frank!" The words spilled out of me while he circled around to the other side.

Frank rolled his shoulders back, his eyes staying on the bike and his hands, anything he could do to not look at me. How could he care so little about this? This wasn't just some bar room brawl. This was murder. Cold, violent murder. This wasn't just real time in prison; it was also living with taking the life from another human being. No one should be able to shoulder that burden and not care.

"Get on the bike, Harley," was all he said as the Beast roared to life.

How could Frank expect me to go with him after that? Did he expect me to just get on the bike and pretend it never happened? Pretend I hadn't just seen the inside of a D'Angelo's skull?

The other men ran past me and jumped onto their own bikes, speeding off without another word. I wondered, briefly, if the man they had been fighting was still alive. Did they show mercy, or did they crush his skull, too? As I watched Niko speed off down the highway, I knew the answer. Paulie might have left him crippled but Niko... Niko would have made him suffer before ending his life.

I'll be the first to admit I've done some fucked up things in my life, but cold-blooded murder was not something I could just forget and move on from.

I could feel his cold stare trained on me while I sorted out my own conscience. His patience was wearing thin, as it often did these days. When I finally looked him in the eye, I quickly wished I hadn't. His skin went tight, and his lips curled back as we stared at one another.

A low, barely-audible growl rumbled in his throat and he jerked a thumb back behind him before snapping a forceful, "Get on!"

I didn't really have a choice. It was either go with him or stay here with a corpse and no clue how to get home. With much reluctance, I hopped onto the bike and settled in behind him. It would be an uncomfortable ride if

I didn't just let my body relax into him, but I couldn't do it. I didn't know if I could bring myself to cuddle in against murderer. I awkwardly pressed myself against his back, snaking my arms around him to hold on more for safety than for affection, and tried to ignore the tacky feel of D'Angelo's blood sticking my arms to his shirt.

Chapter 11

MY BONES ACHED BY the time we reached the Perry Lake Motel. If I had been able to just sink into Frank, then maybe I could have saved my back a world of hurt, but snuggling up to Charles Manson was not exactly easy. It was all I could do not to run away screaming once my feet touched the ground.

I needed answers and this time he wasn't getting out of it.

Frank climbed off the bike and ran a hand through his hair, talking with a few of the guys. I loved to run my hands through his thick brown curls. He'd even started growing it out for me when I'd told him how much I loved it—just a small victory he'd allowed me.

I mourned him in that moment. Mourned the loss of what used to be and what could have been if he hadn't turned out to be a raging psycho.

I stopped staring at his hair and took in the bigger picture in front of me. The three of them were just standing there, acting so normal. Just chit-chatting like he wasn't covered in another man's blood. Like they were just discussing the weather.

Move along. Nothing to see here, folks. Nothing's out of the ordinary. Nothing at all.

He finally moved from the men and made his way over. Frank was all confidence and swagger, from his short beard right down to his worn leather boots. In the past, that alone could make me swoon like some idiot, but tonight was different. Tonight, my hands trembled with fear as he walked up to me, grabbing a clean corner of his shirt and pulling it up to wipe the red from his face and lips.

"We need to talk," I managed to chirp past the lump in my throat. He just gave me a sideways grin as he pushed past me.

"No, we don't," he said.

"Frank, you... You killed him," I said. I glanced around and dropped my voice to a low whisper. "You didn't just beat the shit out of some guy at a bar. You crushed his skull in. He's dead."

The grin disappeared. He sucked in his bottom lip as he looked around and shoved the key into the lock, pushing the door open. I barely had time to brace myself before he grabbed my shoulders and shoved me into the room, slamming the door behind him.

"You just don't get it," he said, his words slow and careful. "Yeah. I fuckin' killed that son of a bitch. So what? No one's gonna miss a piece of shit like him, Harls."

I steadied on my feet and turned around to face him. The whole throwing me around like a ragdoll thing was getting fucking old and fast.

I forced my breathing to settle, to calm myself back down as I watched him toss his blood-stained jacket across the bed. The sight of all that blood smeared on the bed I'd been sleeping in made my stomach clench.

"Who the fuck are you that you get to make that decision?" I snapped. I was done. Completely and utterly finished with this shit. "I'm leaving. I am not gonna be a part of this. I won't be dragged into whatever hell your life is."

He blinked slowly at me, disbelief painting his features. Moments ticked by and we both just stood there staring at each other in silence. He actually looked surprised that I might leave him. That I couldn't—and wouldn't— just put all of this past me and forget about it.

Frank finally walked into the bathroom, and I allowed myself the brief, and possibly foolish, hope that he was thinking things over. Maybe he would even do the right thing and call the cops. Yeah, even I knew that was pretty damn naive.

"You know, Harls," he said from the bathroom, "you never understood me. We've been together two years now and you... You just don't get it. You don't get what I do for us. For the pack."

When he walked out of the bathroom he swung his arms upward, grasping the top of the door frame. It drew my eyes and showed off the muscles straining and tensing below his skin. On the surface, it was a very natural and automatic pose, but Frank never did anything without purpose. He knew exactly what he was doing.

There was no denying he had an appeal that was all raw masculinity and seductive danger. My eyes couldn't keep from following the line of his body, from the small glimpse of his rock-hard stomach peeking out from his lifted shirt, up to the bulging muscles of his arms as they stretched overhead.

The sight distracted me until he opened his mouth again and added, "I'm not a bad guy, babe."

That made me squirm in my skin. Sure, he wasn't a bad guy. The men we called friends, some of the toughest sons of bitches I knew, were terrified of pissing him off and he had just beaten a man to death with his bare hands. Oh, and he seemed to be leaving a string of corpses behind him these days. He was just a misunderstood guy; a real boy scout.

He pushed his body through the door and let go of the frame, letting his arms slap lazily against his sides. A smug grin tugged at the corners of his mouth again as he prowled towards me, and I began to feel less awed by his dangerous masculinity and more fearful of it.

"Doesn't matter what I think, but what you should do is go to the cops. If you're really not a bad guy, then do the right thing. It was self-defense. If we tell the cops that they ambushed us, then maybe they won't charge you with anything."

"You really think they're going to believe we weren't there doing something illegal? We just happened to be in a shit-hole outside town and these guys jumped us for no good reason?" he asked.

"Well... maybe," I offered, unable to even convince myself.

He laughed at that, one of those rich, throaty laughs that came from being truly amused. Apparently, I was a real knee-slapper tonight.

"God, you're so naive sometimes. It's cute. No. No one is going to the police, Harley. I did what I had to do. We'll put it behind us, and we'll move on like we always do. No need to dwell on it."

"We can't just sit on this," I said. I was tired of being cute and amusing. I wanted to be heard. I wanted him to hear me. "Maybe if we—"

Before I could finish the thought, Frank lunged at me, forcing me back against the door. He had me cornered like a spider and I was a juicy fly stuck in his web. I had nowhere to go except to press back against the door as hard as I could. Wood splintered beside my head as he punched a fist through the door, locking both arms on either side of me so I couldn't move. I couldn't run away, even if my feet and brain weren't both frozen in terror.

His face, still marred with droplets of dried blood, was so close that we were touching noses, his brown eyes locking onto my blue ones. There were no more playful grins or flippant remarks. It was all raw, explosive rage and a tiny thread of control holding all that anger off of me.

"This is the last time anything is said on the matter. No one is going to the cops. I did the world a favor. I did you a favor by scraping that piece of shit off this earth. You should be kissing my boots with gratitude for that." His face softened ever so slightly after he said that, but the dangerous gleam remained in his eyes, a wicked grin returning to his face.

"In fact," he whispered. He took a couple of steps back. "Why don't you go ahead and do just that?"

"What?" The word came out as nothing more than a tremble.

"Kiss... my God. Damn. Boots. Show me that you still love me. That you appreciate what I did for everyone by getting rid of that son of a bitch."

There were no words. Nothing would leave my throat. It all lodged under the huge lump that was steadily growing there. I almost asked if he was serious, but found it pointless. Of course he was serious. He was always serious.

I could feel the sting of tears burning the backs of my eyes. I watched him waiting—ever so patiently and expectantly—for me to obey him. To demean myself to him. Had I ever truly meant anything to him? If I had, how could he make me do this? How could he want me to do something so disgusting?

I'll admit there had been times I had to make a choice: poke and prod and question him to the point where he might come unglued on me, or keep the peace and walk away unharmed. I wasn't proud that I allowed fear to win over reason at times. In hindsight, I was even more ashamed that I hadn't sat back and wondered why I was with a man that made me make such a choice. A man that made me worry, at any point, that he'd somehow hurt me.

At that moment, I realized it had been a long time since love held together our broken relationship. Frank was the first man I ever loved, and I had been his for the last two years. I was just a girl when I first laid eyes on him. He was all I knew. While that might never change, there was also one bigger truth to come to terms with. With the love fading away, the only reasons I had been staying by his side and putting up with his shit was because I was afraid of being alone.

I wanted to belong. I wanted to be loved. I wanted to matter. I needed to be needed by someone. Frank didn't need me. He wanted to use me, to possess and control me, but he didn't need me. Not in the way I had needed him. With this epiphany stoking my confidence, I squared my shoulders, stood tall and unmoved, and said something to him I had never before dared to say.

"No," I said, stunned by how little emotion was in the word.

"Excuse me?" he asked.

He took another step towards me, backing me back against the door again. Only, this time, my hand reached for the doorknob. His eyes darkened, anger beating off him in hot waves.

"No. I'm not going to be your bitch anymore. I'm done."

His hand shot out at me and made me flinch so hard that I missed the knob completely. I'd expected his fist to crush into my face, but instead his fingers dug into the back of my skull, wrapping in my hair.

As if I were nothing, he shoved me towards the middle of the room. I managed to not fall flat on my face, but a sharp pain was shooting up my forearms from catching myself. I started to get to my feet and was met with another shove.

"Don't you fuckin' move," he bellowed as he rounded on me, taking my hair again and making me look at him. "You ungrateful bitch. I kept you safe. I took you away from your meaningless existence and brought you in at the expense of my own blood. I let you in and let you see the parts of us we've killed better men over.

"Do you really think after all the time and effort I put into you, after the blood spilt for you, that you'd just be able to get up and walk away from me? I told you before, Harls, there's no turning back now. You belong to me. Everything you are... is mine."

His face contorted into something monstrous, something edging on insanity. Even with the multitude of horrors I'd witnessed in just a few hours, this was the most frightening. A man I once loved, that I let close to me, was a dangerous stranger. His smile made my stomach tight. There was too much satisfaction in it for what was happening.

"Now," he said softer, taking my silence as acceptance, "do as I say."

He shoved my head down until it hovered just over the top of his boot. The smell of worn, dirty leather turned my stomach. I was not going to do this. Let him beat me to death like D'Angelo. I didn't have much going for me in my life, but I was going to hold on to my dignity as long as I could. I dug my nails into the tightly looped carpet fibers, fighting against this disgusting display of abasement.

I could feel his eyes bear down on me like a bitter cold wind. My face remained down, facing the floor in probably the only smart thing I had done all night. It kept Frank from seeing the disgust I felt towards him. His impatience weighed down on me, but I held strong. I would not do this. I would not debase myself.

I did, however, allow my stupidity to take charge, and I spit on the toe of his boot.

A sudden flash of hot, white light burst behind my eyelids. An explosion of pain erupted in my cheek. I flew to the side, landing across the floor in a heap, my hands flying to my face as I slid across the carpet. When I dared to open my eyes again, everything was an unfocused blur of color.

"Hard headed to the core. Go get cleaned up. When you're ready to play nice, come to bed," he said in a hollow tone, all signs of mirth and sick amusement gone from his voice.

I managed to find my way to the bathroom by the time my vision started to return. My face was screaming in pain, and it felt like all the meat in my cheek would just burst through the tender skin at any moment. I locked the door behind me and gripped the edge of the sink to force myself to stay upright. It wouldn't do any good to faint now. I would get little sympathy.

I was stupid to not have seen that coming. I had to have been lying to myself to believe it would have ended any other way. Sometimes, I was my own worst enemy.

Get cleaned up, he had said. As if soap and water would wash away all the pain and abuse. I leaned over and ran a hot bath, ready to melt into the steaming water and hide from the ruin I'd made of my life for about twenty minutes.

As the tub filled, I glanced at the cracked mirror hanging over the sink. My cheek had already swelled twice its normal size. By tomorrow it would be worse. I couldn't take refuge in the hope that our friends would see it and help me. I'd seen it way too much with the other women to believe that they would cross Frank.

Most of the girls would feel sorry for me, but no one would speak a word about it. It would be a week or two of staying in while everyone else went out and had a few beers or got some food. Just long enough so that Frank's trophy girlfriend could heal and look presentable to flaunt around again.

Frank might have been a jealous and possessive son of a bitch, but he was also proud. His pride usually took precedence over all else. If he could show something off, he did. I was no different. I was just a coveted toy to show off to the other kids.

I pressed my tongue gingerly over the inside of my cheek and winced at the sharp sting. The meat on the inside was split almost wide enough for me to stick the tip of my tongue into it. My tongue moved away with a metallic taste. I leaned over and spit into the basin of the sink and watched the white porcelain ruin with bright red droplets. What started as a slight tinge of blood now filled my mouth, like I had been sucking on a mouthful of pennies.

With one last good spit, I looked back up into the mirror. I had one of those moments where the face looking back doesn't make sense anymore. My eyes stared back at me, lifeless. There used to be light in those eyes. I'd found my fire after I took up with Frank.

The cynical and pissy girl my family's treatment had turned me into had finally melted away with my newfound freedom. I'd learned to enjoy life, to live it up with friends. Two years later, and Frank had managed to snuff the fire right out of me and leave me hollow.

Dull, gunmetal blue stared back at me with a defeat-ed, nearly deadened, sadness. They'd never been much to write home about but with the right makeup the color would pop and let more of the blue shine through. Lately, even the most expert make up couldn't hide the exhaustion around my eyes. Or maybe it was all in my head.

I felt so tired and run down that I thought I was beginning to show on the outside just how exhausted this life was making me. The youthful innocence had slowly drained into something older and harder and I had a sudden clarity on why women in this kind of life looked so much older and worn than they were.

I knew Frank would be more than happy to drag my name through the mud with his if I really pushed him, so I didn't push. I didn't want to go out that way. The more I thought about it, turning him into the police would only bring me down with him. He'd do or say whatever he could to make sure I suffered just as much as he did.

And the wolves. I couldn't even begin to understand what had happened earlier. I mean, we've all seen the movies. Heard the stories. But never would I have believed they were fucking real. I mean, two years is a long time to not notice something as weird as my friends going all furry once a month.

The more I thought about it, the more it sounded like a bad acid trip than anything that could be remotely possible. Maybe he had dosed me somehow. I knew the kind of shit Frank had his hands in, so the idea of him slipping me something wasn't too far fetched. And I had woken up in the shack.

Maybe everything that happened up to the point where I regained consciousness was some bad dream.

The water was nearly to the edges of the tub before I remembered it was running. I moved to turn the water off but stopped when my fingers brushed against something cold and metal. Glancing down at the sink, I saw the keys to Frank's bike resting under my hand. I stared at them for a moment, the beginnings of an idea forming in my head. Truth was there was only one way out of this situation without being swallowed up in it myself.

I looked around the small bathroom, first at the door between me and Frank, then to the tub, and finally a small window above it. My heart was racing as I mapped it all out in my head. I would have to leave the water running or he would probably hear me open the window. As it was already threatening to spill over the sides, I didn't have much time before it would flood over. The last thing I wanted was for him to check on me and find me hanging halfway through the window making a grand escape.

My heart raced in my chest, my heartbeat echoing thickly in my ears. I propped a foot on the slick porcelain, using the wall and sink to steady me. After wobbling a bit, I steadied and swung my other foot across the water to the edge of the tub against the wall.

The keys jangled in my hand as I moved, and I sucked a breath in through my teeth. If Frank saw me now, it would be all over. I wasn't sure I would survive the beating he would give me if he thought I was running off to turn him in. Betrayal was not easily forgiven by Mr. Essex.

I waited a breath or two, listening for any sign of movement in the other room. When I heard nothing, I tucked the keys into my pocket and worked on opening the window. I jostled it until it was finally freed from the years of built up rust.

It wasn't easy, but I managed to push up and squeeze through the narrow opening and shimmy down to the dumpster outside and waited to see if any of his friends were walking around outside the rooms. Finding myself alone, I hopped off the dumpster and made a break for Frank's bike, jumping onto the seat and sliding the key into the ignition.

I said a small, silent prayer to coax myself into finishing what I was starting. If I stayed, eventually I would be dead. I knew this. If I went to the police, I would go to jail. Or Frank would find me and kill me. Again, dead.

This was it. Either get out now or prepare my own funeral. With a last glance over my shoulders, I let out a soft sigh.

"Thanks for the ride, baby," I whispered.

I started the engine. I had a split second before he would come running outside and find me. There was no way I was giving him the chance. With as much gas as I could give the bike, I peeled out of the parking lot and shot gravel in every direction, speeding off into the night and towards the freedom ahead.

Chapter 12

July 2nd 2011 2:36 p.m.

"Do you ever miss sex?"

Liz's question came so unexpectedly I had to clamp a hand over my mouth to keep my soda from spraying all over the steering wheel. It burned my nostrils, all those tiny fizzy bubbles threatening to shoot upward and outward.

I blindly set my cup in the cup holder and took the rough paper napkin Liz offered me, dabbing at my nose.

"Miss sex?" I asked, though I'd heard her loud and clear.

"Yeah. I know you're kinda in a dry spell. I'm just curious if you miss it or if you even think about it."

"Do you miss it?" I threw back at her, knowing she wasn't getting her cookies either. It had the desired effect. A glance to the side found her tugging at a blond curl, her lip captured in her teeth.

"Yes. I mean I guess I do," she answered shyly. "I've never been the sex-starved type, but I don't know how much longer I can go before I explode."

Oh. Okay.

So, we're actually going to have this conversation.

Her openness surprised me. She was my best friend, and these were the things best friends were supposed to talk about, but the fact that she was being so open about her sex life was something I could not empathize with.

Unlike her, I couldn't chit chat about my sexcapades. It was just something I preferred to keep private.

Honestly, I hadn't even thought of Liz as a sexual creature until recently. She was too small, too introverted, too... Liz. It seemed wrong to think of her getting all hot and sweaty with someone.

Not because that someone would have been female—I honestly couldn't give less of a shit about that—but because she'd become like a kid sister to me.

So, when she'd asked me if the club I danced at was looking for dancers, I'd been completely thrown. It so didn't fall in line with how I saw her. But since she asked, and I didn't want to see her starve, I pulled a few strings and got her an audition. To my complete surprise, she not only went through with it, but she'd nailed it. Andre was so happy he'd been gushing about her debut for the last few days.

Liz's sudden silence was unsettling. She looked embarrassed at having said what she'd said. She was tensed up, her knees jerking and fidgeting in the small leg space on the passenger side.

"Sometimes," I offered her, "but it's never been something that I needed."

That was a lie.

With Frank I always seemed to need his touch, his kiss, his warmth. I craved him in a way that edged on desperation. It scared the shit out of me.

"I mean... I know what it's like to need a specific person, but when I don't have a guy to paw it just doesn't seem to bug me."

"How can you dance the way you do every night and not feel all revved up? It doesn't turn you on to know you're the object of desire for those men in the club?" The question was innocent enough, but it brought a slight burn to my cheeks hearing it like that.

"It's an illusion, Liz. Dancing doesn't turn me on. It's just something fun to do. Afterwards, I don't need a cold shower for anything more than cleaning the sweat and smoke off my skin," I shrugged as the car started forward again. "Why do you ask?"

She went quiet beside me. I counted about three city blocks before she drew breath to answer.

"I don't know. Just... wondering," she said, but she sounded utterly defeated about something.

"Do you ruminate about my sex life often?" I flashed her a toothy grin for the use of my newest four-dollar word.

"I just mean," she started again after rolling her eyes at me. "We've been friends for a while, and I don't think I've ever seen you with anyone. A date, a fling, nothing. That's a long time to hold it all in without even a little..."

I was suddenly very interested in my steering wheel.

Was she getting at what I think she was getting at? Liz had never come onto me before, but she was beating around the bush about something. Too nervous to get the words out.

"I... Liz, I..." I couldn't get my mouth to cooperate with my head. "You know I love you. I just... I'm not... into women. Nothing against it, but it's not my thing and you're like a... a sister to me, you know?"

It got dead silent on the other side of the car. I couldn't help but feel guilty for having rejected my friend, but it was better than leading her on. I'd never expected her to have those sorts of feelings towards me. Then again, maybe she was just trying to be a friend in offering to ease some of my tension. It was a sweet gesture, even if it made me feel a bit awkward.

I risked a sideways glance and found her staring at me with those large blue eyes. Her face was tense, eyes wide. When I pulled into the parking lot, I saw her turn forward, resting her face down into her hands, her shoulders beginning to shake. It was slow at first, but soon her shoulders bobbed up and down at an increasing pace.

"Shit," I whispered before pulling into the nearest empty spot, cutting off a black Lexus that was getting ready to pull into it. I ignored the honking and colorful insults outside my window and turned as much as my seat belt would allow.

"Liz. Liz, I'm sorry. Please don't cry. I just," but the sound that suddenly came out from those hands sounded nothing like tears.

A high cackling erupted from her, and her hands dropped away. Liz wasn't crying. She was laughing with a face-splitting smile.

"Oh my God... you wish," she said finally, her baby blues shining with tears of laughter.

I stared at her completely dumbfounded.

"Ohhh... Please don't cry. I'm just not that way. I like sausage, not tacos." Her voice was high and teasing, and honestly didn't sound like me at all, thank you very much. I narrowed my eyes at her as she laughed at my expense. "Jeez, ego much?"

"Not fucking funny, Liz," I said, shortly.

"Bullshit. It's hilarious. Your face."

"Ha, fucking, ha. Way to make me feel like a jerk," I said, snatching the keys from the ignition.

Liz opened up her door and I followed, looking at her over the top of my Toyota.

"I wasn't trying to at first, but you started getting all weird. I couldn't help myself. Don't be a bitch about it. It was funny. Albeit maybe a touch homophobic," she giggled, meeting me behind the car.

"Homophobic?? How would I possibly—"

"What, just because I'm gay I gotta be ready to pounce on all girls I see?" She waved her hand at me. "Please, I'm a lesbian, not a man."

I glared at her, shook my head, and pretended to be mad. In all honesty, I wanted to laugh, because she wasn't wrong. Not at all. I just wouldn't give her the satisfaction.

"Tell me why we're here again," I said, attempting to divert the subject to something less embarrassing.

I wasn't complaining, exactly. The air-conditioned shop felt amazing after the twenty-minute ride in my junky old car. Typically, the lack of cold air didn't bother me. Freon was a luxury my limited budget couldn't afford. However, today was a scorching 97 degrees, and even I felt the sweltering misery after five minutes in the tiny car.

"I told you, I need some clothes. Can't a girl spoil herself?" Liz smiled at me over the circular rack of bedazzled ribbed tanks.

"When you got the money to splurge, why not?" I said as I idly began thumbing through the clothes.

The shop was one we frequented often. Full of low cost, secondhand clothes that weren't in season anymore. There were even some vintage dresses and accessories behind the counter. I loved to find a good buy and modernize it, mix and match things to make cute outfits. I liked to be creative in my fashion choices as long as we weren't counting my studded bustier and leather chaps I wore at work.

"Oh, damn. Check this out," Liz exclaimed as she pulled a hanger from the rack.

I walked around until she came into view, clutching a deep red dress in her hands. Despite her momentary excitement, her face had a look of disappointment on it as she stared down at the dress.

"Damn, they don't got it in my size," she looked up at me, sized me up, then smiled. "You should try it on!"

"I'm good," I said.

"Harley," my name came out in a whine, "you'll look hot, I promise. Just try it on. Humor me."

She was being unusually pushy.

With a roll of my eyes, I snatched the hanger from her and headed towards the fitting room. I could hear her bobbing along behind me excitedly, and even imagined she was clapping her hands together gleefully at my surrender.

It was hard to fight her. Lizbeth was really, truly, one of the sweetest girls I'd ever met. Most of the time I wanted nothing more than to see her happy. But then there were times like this where her happiness would come at my expense.

I ducked into the fitting room and locked the door. As I undressed, I looked at the red thing hanging against the wall beside me. My stomach tightened as the slip of a dress stared back at me, tauntingly.

I didn't like it. In fact, I made a big point to avoid wearing anything red ever again.

"So," Liz called out from the other side of the door, "you're going to think this is funny."

I quirked my eyebrows at that before pulling the dress off the hanger, "Why do I have the feeling that is so not what I am going to think?"

She completely ignored me.

"You remember that guy I was telling you about last week? Braedon?"

"Sure."

"Well, turns out his ex that dumped him is already engaged to another guy," she said.

"Damn. Didn't take long, did it?" I said, not really thinking anything of it. I was too busy slipping on the little red dress and trying to zip it up.

"Yeah, that's what I said. Anyway," her voice became uncertain, "I thought, maybe, it was time for him to move on. Find a good girl to take his mind off the heifer. I figured... maybe you two could..."

"Not interested, Liz."

"I know you aren't really into the dating scene, but he's really sweet and charming and really, really good-looking. I mean, if you're into men and all."

"Liz," I said, searching for any excuse that would get her to drop this insanity without hurting her feelings, "I don't have time to date. Dinners and movies and dancing aren't really something I can do with my schedule. You know that. I work all night."

"I know," she said confidently before her voice wavered again. "That's why I told him you'd meet him for an early supper tonight."

It took a full thirty seconds for her words to register. I stopped craning my arm back to try and catch the zipper pull and just stared, open-mouthed, at the door between us.

Is she out of her mind?! Why would she set me up on a blind date without even asking me first?

"Liz!" I finally shrieked, unlocking the door and swinging it open, "you didn't!"

Liz stumbled as the door she'd been leaning against was no longer there to support her weight. Her hands caught on either side of the door and she looked up at me with a timid smile. That smile faded as she saw the dress on me.

"Holy shit, Harley. You're fucking smokin'," she breathed.

Unfortunately for her, I didn't care. One, I hated the dress. It brought back memories of Frank. Two, I was more worried about the fact that Liz had set me up on a blind date. And as a rebound chick, no less!

"Liz, I can't go on a date with this guy," I said, swallowing my irritation.

"Why not? He really is a good guy, Harley," she said.

"And that's good for him, but I am not in any state to be in a relationship with anyone. I don't need or want it."

"Oh, Jesus, Harley! What is so bad about meeting a cute guy? No one is making you marry him. Hell, you don't even got to sleep with him!"

"How generous of you," I said dryly.

"Seriously. You never have fun. You work, you study, and you stay home, alone, all day. When was the last time you just did something out of your routine? That you let your hair down and enjoyed the freedom of being an unattached grownup?"

The truth was I'd had enough 'fun' for a lifetime. Reliable routine was a blessed thing; not having to answer to or rely on anyone else was a godsend. Sure, it could get lonely. I was still alive. I had needs. I just refused to pay the price that comes with it. I opened my mouth to tell her that, but Liz's pleading blue eyes stopped me.

"I thought you wanted me to see you dance tonight," I said, trying another tactic.

"You can come to the club after," she answered way too quickly.

"It's your first night—"

"And you'll be there to support me like a good best friend. After your date."

"Liz..."

"One date. He's a really good guy and he needs a night of fun as much as you do. Just... have dinner with him. If you don't like him after tonight, you never need to talk to him again, I promise." Her eyes fell to the dress again, and she smiled. "Hey, you can even wear that. He'd be putty in your hands."

I turned around and looked at my reflection. The dress wasn't nearly as hookerish as the one Frank had given me, but it was the exact same shade of red. My new honey-blond hair and the deep red color of the dress made my skin look tanner than usual, and she was right, it looked amazing on me, but I just could not shake the memories. I couldn't function while wearing the thing.

"Fine. I'll go. But I am not wearing this. I'll wear something out of my closet, and he'll either like it or..." I stopped, shrugged. "Honestly I don't care."

Liz erupted behind me, throwing her arms over my shoulders and hugging my neck. Her giggles were musical and the warmth in her voice as I conceded made me smile. I liked her to be happy, even when it was at my own expense.

A few hours later, I pulled up to The Java Jive. When I first moved into town, I'd gotten a job there as an early morning barista. It was the worst week of my life.

I wasn't exactly a morning person to begin with, but add in dozens of high maintenance, snooty, rude ass customers and that was a recipe for disaster. Thankfully, I'd found the club before I went postal and was able to find a taste for coffee again.

Why am I doing this? I asked myself. I could have just stood the guy up.

No, I chided myself.

It wasn't his fault I was a mess. I could imagine, after the ordeal his ex had apparently put him through, how he would feel sitting there waiting for me. The idea of crushing someone's self-esteem didn't sit well with me. I'd had my fill of feeling unwanted and cast aside, of being unimportant as a person. I couldn't do that to another human being. Against my better judgment, I parked the car and headed inside.

According to Liz, I was looking for a clean twenty-five-year-old man with dark brown hair and dimples that tugged at my heart strings.

The fact that she listed 'clean' as one of his strong suits made me wonder what sort of men the girl thought I was drawn to. Just because I was an exotic dancer—Okay, a stripper—that didn't mean I was drawn to the oily, sleazy, scumbag types.

So, Frank wasn't exactly wholesome and clean cut, but I had never divulged that part of my life with my friend, so she could hardly hold that against me.

A hand waved at me from the corner of the coffee shop. There, sitting in a window-side booth, was Braedon. His hair was shining and well-styled. Emerald eyes sparkled with delight as he flagged me over. All right. Clean was definitely a good word for him. He practically sparkled with good grooming.

As I drew closer to the booth, he stood. No kidding. The man actually stood like an honest-to-God gentleman and waited for me to sit down.

"Wow," he said. His face and tensed shoulders gave me the impression it had slipped out before he could stop himself. "Sorry, Hi. I'm Braedon."

"Harley," I said, forcing a smile.

"Well, it's nice to finally meet you. Liz told me a lot about you."

"Did she, now?" I asked, quirking my brow.

That was interesting, considering she hadn't even told me about this date until today. He looked at me, fidgeted a bit, and finally laughed. It was soft, and with it, he released a breath he'd been holding.

"No, actually," he admitted. "She just told me your name, that you were single, and that you were gorgeous. She obviously downplayed that last bit."

Now, I'd had some horrendously cheesy pickup lines thrown my way before. So much so that there was barely a line a guy could say that would give him any credit. However, the smooth way the compliment flowed from his lips, which were a very kissable pout by the way, reached that jaded part of me and thawed it.

I smiled at him. Not the tight lipped, I'm-only-doing-this-to-be-nice smile that came from doing a friend a favor, but a genuine smile that I felt in my cheeks.

So maybe Liz hadn't done such a horrible thing in setting this up. He was handsome enough and seemed sweet. If anything, I could enjoy myself for one night and maybe make a new friend. No harm in that.

"Alright, can I make a tiny confession?" I asked him, easing back into my seat.

"Oh, already? I thought confessions and soul bearing would come after a few cocktails but," he breathed bracingly before flashing me a perfect smile, "Shoot."

I laughed.

"I didn't want to meet you," I blurted out.

"Ouch," he said with a grin.

I laughed again. It felt good.

"But... I am going to do something completely out of character for myself. I'm going to ignore all my instincts and all the negativity I like to hold onto, and I am going to allow myself to have fun." That earned another smile from him. "But if Liz asks, I was completely moody and sarcastic the entire night. Just really miserable to be around.

"In fact, I cursed her name more than once and nearly drove you to tears with my snarky attitude. Whether or not you actually ended up crying from heartbreak," I wagged my hand back and forth. "Eh, I'll leave that up to you."

"Well," he laughed, his eyes twinkling, "I think that is doable. But, if you don't mind, I didn't cry until I made it home. Crying in public really isn't a good look."

He had an ease about him that I really found refreshing. He didn't bristle at the implications against his manliness or take offense to what I'd said. He simply let it roll off his shoulders and took it in stride. He was so comfortable with himself that he didn't feel threatened by it. Didn't appear to need to defend his virility.

Maybe there was hope for the opposite sex, yet.

"Now that we've gotten that out of the way," he said, "let's get that coffee."

"You know what," I said with a glance to the little menu under my hand. "I really don't like coffee that much anymore. I'd rather have a cocktail. You wanna go grab some real dinner?"

He flashed that perfect smile again, and while he considered my offer, I considered him.

Now that I wasn't fighting against myself, I was able to really appreciate the man in front of me. He really was handsome. Not in the rugged sense, nothing like Frank, but in a softer way. Soft in the way that he'd had an easy, cushy life where nothing more than a broken heart wounded him. His eyes glittered with his smile and made me almost wish I could let him pull me into that serene happiness.

"Yeah," he said. "I think I'd like that. After you."

He stood and waited for me to move away from the booth before he followed. Never able to truly let go of my paranoia, I glanced over my shoulder to look at the man behind me. He was laying a folded five-dollar bill on the table and tucking his wallet back into his pocket.

"What are you doing?" I asked.

"Tip."

"But we didn't order anything."

"No. But we held their table up when they could have been making money," he said before catching up to me.

I was completely thrown by the gesture. Good looking, funny, and generous? Oh, Liz... and it's not even my birthday.

It almost seemed like this guy was too good to be true. That thought took the wind out of my sails a little, but I tried not to look too much into it. For once, I wanted to relax and have a good time. That fact, alone, surprised me.

Chapter 13

FRANK

TRAFFIC ALONG SOUTH QUENTIN Avenue began to slow as the night dragged on, allowing him an almost-unobstructed view inside the restaurant across the road. Only the occasional car driving past broke the scene before him, robbing him of a few seconds of her flirtatious smile.

He'd been standing there for nearly two hours, and it looked like they weren't going to be leaving any time soon.

God, she was beautiful. More than she'd ever been, if it was possible. Her face was alive and vibrant as she spoke, her hands animated with whatever story she was sharing with the man at her table. For once, it looked as if she had thrown all of her worries aside and allowed herself to live in the moment, to enjoy life and all it had to offer her, and he hated her for it.

He hated the way this man could bring that coy smile to her lips, the way she fluttered those eyelashes at him, and lightly touched his arm as they talked.

He'd been looking for her for several months. Every city they passed through, he couldn't help but wonder if she was nearby, if she was right under his nose. Like most things Harley did to him, her running off had made him crazy. He didn't know what she'd done with his bike, if she'd gotten herself hurt, or worse, if she'd moved on. Watching her with this guy, it appeared as though she had done just that.

A waiter set a plate between them. The man grabbed his fork and dug it into the fat slice of chocolate cake then offered it to Harley. Rage roiled within him as she leaned over the table and let the guy feed her.

Oh, but that bitch was gonna pay. She would pay for what she put him through, how she made him feel, but first, he was going to tear that jackass limb from limb.

Frank's cell rang in his jacket pocket, and tamping down his anger, he answered it on the third ring.

"Yeah," he growled.

"Where are you?" The voice was impatient.

"Who are you, my mama?"

Harlow growled over the line. "Don't start with me, Essex. You're on thin ice as it is, you know. Now, if it were up to me I'd have skinned you alive the night you let the girl ride away on your little toy. You had one job to do, and you fucked it off. However, my father thinks you'll be worthwhile, yet."

"Is that so?" Frank laughed derisively. "Man, it must really twist your nuts knowing daddy likes me better."

"Don't get too cocky, jackass. You're about one wrong move from being on his shit list. Please," he said the word with longing. "Please, give him a reason to send me after you."

"Sorry, dickweed. You're not my type," Frank breathed as his eyes moved back to Harley.

She was reaching over and wiping something off the guy's lower lip. Frank's grip tightened on his phone so hard that it began to creak in protest.

"What the fuck do you want, Harlow? I'm a little busy right now so if you just called to bust my balls—"

"Have you found her yet?"

Frank stared at the woman in the restaurant. Her hair was different. Blond and shorter than before, but there was no doubt that it was her. It was tragic, really. So many memories of that long, thick, dark hair as it tickled down his body—sliding silkily over his skin as she teased him. So many memories of her and the things she could do. His dick hardened at the mere thought of it.

"No," he growled as he watched them together. "Still no sign of the bitch."

There was a disgusted snarl on the other end of the phone.

"I knew you were useless. How hard can it be to find one little girl?"

"Pretty fuckin' hard when she don't want to be found. I don't see you or Vale pluckin' her off the street."

"Funny, I don't see you doing much of anything. Are you even trying to locate her?" Harlow asked.

"She's got my bike, dick. I want to find her just as much as you."

"No, see... that's where you're wrong. I don't give a shit about her," Harlow hissed. "But my father wants her. He wants you to find her and deliver her like you should have done ages ago. You were supposed to bring her to us, not play house with her and make her your little biker bitch."

"Play house," Frank snorted. "Trust me. She's more of a headache than you know. I was tryin' to make her more pliable. You think she would've just dropped everything and let me drop her off on the doorstep of some guy she never met? You gotta tame 'em, first. Then they'll do what-ever you ask 'em."

"Sounds to me like she was the one doing the taming, Frankie-boy," Harlow laughed smugly. "Tell me, did she at least give you your balls in a jar when she neutered you?"

"Fuck you," Frank growled.

He hung up on the sound of deep, self-satisfied laugh-ter.

When he let his attention return to the window across the street, he saw an empty table. Damn it. Daddy's boy had gotten him so distracted he didn't realize they were leaving. Hoping they hadn't left the restaurant, Frank pushed off the lamp post and hurried across the street. A car honked as it nearly clipped his leg, and he cursed. The last thing he wanted was to draw attention to himself.

When he was tucked safely in the shadows again, he rolled his shoulders and waited, watching the entrance. Harley's laugh erupted from around the corner, and they stepped out onto the sidewalk, heading the other direc-tion. They were walking towards that beat-up car he'd seen her driving around town.

He found it amusing that she drove here separately. Apparently, she hadn't trusted this jerk as much as she'd like to think.

Feeling a deep satisfaction at that thought, Frank carefully trailed the pair. He didn't have to follow too close to hear them. Or smell them. The night was breezy and warm and carried scents to him easily. The scent of Harley's perfume, and beneath that, her salty-sweet skin made his stomach tight, his mouth dry as he remembered the taste of her under his tongue. So many months and the thought of her stretched naked under him could still overwhelm his senses.

He loved it and hated it all at once. Loved that the memories were recalled so thoroughly that it was like she was right there with him. Hated that she could distract him so easily. So fully.

It was the second scent, though, that turned him from lusting flesh to lusting for blood. It was an earthy musk. Damp and strong like forest dirt after a heavy rain. It was the smell of kin.

The smell of wolf.

It blew past Frank's human logic and poked at the part of him that wanted blood. He would rend the wolf's flesh from his bone for daring to go near his territory.

He wouldn't move, yet, though. Not until they'd parted ways. It was the only way he could swoop in without bringing down the entirety of hell around his head. Patience and timing.

They hovered next to her Toyota for a good ten minutes, just laughing and talking. The subtle nuances of her body language were flirtatious and inviting, but there was still a tension in her shoulders and neck he could see in spite of the distance between them. She wanted to pretend things were normal and easy, but she knew better. She could never trust easily again, and Frank was satisfied in his hand in that. Finally, the man leaned forward and kissed her.

A low, feral growl trickled from Frank's throat as he watched this dog violate her mouth. This would not be tolerated. He would pay, dearly, for touching her.

They finally separated, and Harley moved to get into her car. Frank waited eagerly for her to pull onto the street and drive down the road. If only she knew how close he'd been.

Keys jangled beside him, drawing his gaze back to the man who had been pawing her. He flicked his cigarette to the road and pushed away from the wall, moving with swift determination towards the wolf. He was just sliding his key into his car door when Frank reached him and grabbed the back of his hair, throwing his face forward into the top of his car.

Braedon 's nose cracked with the force of the blow, spilling thick, hot blood down his face and throat. He started to grab at his face as he spun around, only to barely duck his head to the side before Frank's fist smashed through the car window, raining pieces of broken glass down on him.

He fell to his side, catching the ground under his hands, and quickly crawled away from Frank trying to get back on his feet. He staggered back, still stunned from the blow to his face.

"Who the fuck are you?" he shouted, blood spraying from his mouth.

He was answered by another strike to his cheek, which rocked him to the side but didn't knock him down. He blocked two more hits before thrusting his own fist up into a powerful uppercut that connected with Frank's jaw.

Frank fell back against the car, his knuckles sliced to bloody ribbons from the broken glass and peeling away with the force of each blow he laid into Braedon. So, the dog did know how to throw a punch. This would be much more satisfying than he'd originally thought.

He didn't move as the guy stepped into him to throw another blow to his face. Not until he was close enough for Frank to jerk his knee up and crack him in his groin. A howl of pain screeched from the guy and Frank laughed, standing up easily.

"Oof. Now that... that's gotta hurt," he taunted as he walked towards him. "But not as much as it will when I'm done with ya."

He grabbed Braedon by the hair again and dragged him into the darkened alley before grasping his pants and lifting him from the ground. With a grunt of effort, he tossed the man headfirst into the brick wall, watching as he crumpled into the pile of trash bags below.

"See, now that's a start," Frank said with a clap of his hands as he approached him. "Now that I've got your attention, I've got a little story to tell you. You see, there's this woman. This hardheaded, pain in the ass, want-to-choke-the-life-out-of-her woman. She's hot. I mean, smokin' hot. Guess the gods felt that this was the only way to make up for the incessant, belligerent nagging she dealt out like her life depended on it."

Braedon crawled out from the trash and was trying to get to his feet again, a dark trickle of blood seeping down his forehead. He'd barely managed to reach out and brace himself on the wall when Frank's boot cracked against his ribs. He sprawled out on his back on the ground, coughing wetly.

"Jesus, and she is a wildcat in the sack, I mean," Frank touched his pointer finger and thumb together, extending the other three fingers as he gave a low, appreciative whistle, "mind-blowing, gold star fucking pussy. And this woman, well, she sort of made some bad decisions. The biggest mistake of all was that she left a man that would, quite literally, kill for her. Someone who can protect her from things she doesn't even understand. Someone who really, really hates when other men, and most especially other wolves, sniff around his belongings."

"I didn't touch her," he mumbled, clutching his ribs.

Frank lifted his foot and lowered his knee down into the man's chest, putting weight into it. He was rewarded with a grunt of pain.

"How long, wolf?" Frank asked.

"W-what?"

"When were you bitten?" he asked again, his tone almost bored.

"Two m-months," Braedon wheezed through the pressure on his lungs.

Frank's mouth twitched, "You're just a pup, ain't ya? No wonder you don't know how to fight. You've barely had time to learn what to do with all the strength you've been given."

Braedon didn't say anything. He simply stared at Frank with a look of self-righteousness that sickened him. Oh, fantastic. Another wolf that would rather play human. The idea of trying to pretend to be normal was laughable at best. But mostly, it was just pathetic.

Frank leaned forward, bracing a hand on the ground next to Braedon's head until he was hovering just over him. He pressed his knee harder into Braedon's chest, grinning as he watched the terror shine in the boy's eyes.

"Let me teach you a little somethin', then. Most alphas can smell dishonesty on you. It's not easy to pull the wool over our eyes." Frank's voice dropped low and quiet. "The fact that I saw you two doesn't help. I saw you kiss her. Saw you put your filthy, fucking lips on hers." Frank actually moved his hand to Braedon's face and rubbed his thumb across the underside of his lower lip.

Frank heard the guy's pulse speed up as he stared at the red smear of lipstick that rubbed off on his thumb, sniffed it, and then growled low in his throat.

"I'll end it. I swear." Braedon swallowed hard. "I won't go near her again. Man, I wouldn't have kissed her if I knew she was yours. Please."

Frank grabbed Braedon's bottom lip between his fingers and ripped the soft flesh clean from his face. Blood sprayed the front of him, and the man's chilling scream echoed in the alley. He flung the strip of severed flesh to the ground and reached forward, hooking his fingers into Braedon's blood-drenched mouth, gripping his fingertips into the back of his lower gums. Braedon cried out, tears pouring from his eyes to mingle with the flow of blood as it pooled around his head.

"Oh, I know you won't. No one touches my girl," Frank growled in his face before he pulled his head up from the ground by the jaw and slammed it into the asphalt.

His skull shattered, the asphalt breaking beneath his head. Frank released his mouth and wiped the blood on his shirt as he caught his breath, swallowing down the rage and need for blood.

It was getting easier now. Long ago, the idea of killing another human being would give Frank pause. Then it would haunt him. As time went on and the realities of his life came to surface, it was almost nothing to him to snuff out the weak. Just the nature of the beast.

Frank started to move off him but stopped when he heard a light, melodic ring. He looked down at Braedon's lifeless body, searching for the source of the sound until he found a small flip-phone tucked into the inside pocket of his jacket. He flipped it open and saw a text alert from a woman named Lizbeth.

So? How'd it go?

Did Harley show up tonight or will I have to knock some sense into her?

A wicked grin spread along his face as he replied.

It was killer

He stared at the screen for a few seconds, thumbing through the various apps and settings until he found the address book. There, tucked in the H's, was Harley's number. Another grin stretched slowly over his lips.

Well, well. Wasn't that handy?

Clicking the phone shut, he shoved it into his pocket and pushed himself to his feet. He heard voices drawing closer and knew that the guy's scream had been heard. It was time to get out of there. Fast.

With a new spring in his step, Frank made his way back to the motel room he'd bought for the month. He delighted in anticipation of Harley's face when she realized he'd found her. How she'd react to knowing she'd never escape him, and that this whole new life of hers was nothing more than a distraction that let Frank plan his next move. Soon, he'd have her, and everything she was, at his whim.

Chapter 14

I PULLED MY CAR into the parking lot of The Velvet Rope nightclub and did a few laps in search of a decent spot. Tonight was a busy night, it seemed. They'd been advertising the debut of their "Nightingale". That was the hook they were trying out for Liz. She had won the admiration of my boss with an enticing fan dance and Andre, creative genius he isn't, thought the large feather fans made her look like some exotic bird.

Personally, I don't know how a bird can be considered sexy, but either way, I was proud of her.

Liz had almost no confidence when I first met her. She was quiet, rarely made eye contact with anyone, and always second-guessed herself in everything she did. It pained me to see such a beautiful girl try to take up so little space in the world. Especially when I could just tell she was hiding a really large, and amazing, personality behind her sheepishness.

I don't know what made her behave that way, and to be honest I haven't asked her. It was probably a childhood thing, and I was in no position to analyze her. All I could do was try my best to boost her self-esteem and coax out the woman I knew was hiding inside.

I'd helped her practice for her audition—such a pretty word for our line of work—and was surprised by how well she moved. She was a natural. Once she had the confidence she needed, she would be spectacular.

The air conditioning hit me at full blast the moment I stepped inside. It sent a shiver over my skin as the cold air hit the small beads of sweat that had formed on my neck and back.

"You're just in time, sugar. Liz just stepped onto the stage." A deep baritone voice greeted me when I stepped out of the entryway and into the main room.

Jackson was six-foot three, and about as wide as two of me standing shoulder to shoulder. He was bald, but it was hard to tell if it was the kind of bald that came from genetics or if it was just his preferred style. He didn't look old enough for his hair to be falling out, so I assumed it was just a force of habit from his time in the military.

He had two heavy-looking hoops dangling from his earlobes and some smaller ones which ran all the way up the curve of his ear. If there was ever an incentive for the patrons to be on their best behavior, it was an intimidating, pierced-up, ex-marine watching everybody's every move.

I smiled at him as he stepped down from his stool by the door. While most people would shrink within themselves at his looming size, I knew that behind the grind-your-bones-to-make-my-bread appearance he was just as sweet and cuddly as a carnival teddy bear. All the girls adored him. He was a complete gentleman, thanks largely in part to his southern upbringing.

I wrapped my arms around his midsection, but my hands barely met behind his back. He was all hard muscle behind his thinly-stretched Velvet Rope Security t-shirt. Burying the side of my face against his chest, I let him hug me back, though he held a certain air of caution when hugging us girls.

Maybe he thought we would shatter in his arms.

Pulling away from the hug, I stared up at him and smiled. "Thanks Jackson. Come have a shot with me on your next break, okay?"

He smiled and nodded before taking his post back at the door and jutting a hand in front of an entering male.

I left him to check ID's and found a small table near the edge of the stage. The music was sensual and slow and took me to a place of exotic flowers and waterfalls. Carefully sliding into the small chair, I turned my attention to the performance.

Liz was dancing with two oversized feather fans in a deep blue color. The middle of the fans, where she held them, were sparkling with rhinestones that glinted and played in the lighting above her, almost as if they were alive and a part of the show as well. She held one fan in front of her and the other behind, encasing her nimble body in the soft plumes of the feathers.

Every few seconds, she would lift the fan in front of her, allowing her captive audience to peek at her scantily-clad body. She was all jewels and feathers wrapped in navy blue silk. Her stomach was adorned down the center with more rhinestones, giving the impression that she, herself, was a fan like the ones she held in her hand.

Darker blue feathers lined the top of her bustier, only giving the audience a tantalizing peek at her cleavage. Her skirt was done in the same fashion, but had more feathers than silk. Her legs, all lean muscle and fair skin, were wrapped in blue fishnet stockings held up by a rhinestone garter. Her heels were strewn across the stage already kicked off.

One of the cocktail waitresses brought me my usual Amaretto Sour, but I paid no notice to it. I was too busy watching my friend work her magic on stage. I wished I could have taped it to play back for Liz, because I knew wouldn't she believe how incredible her performance was. Everything we had practiced together, Liz did with flawless perfection. Every tease and every expression was pure art.

She danced her way towards an ornate chair that sat in the middle of the stage, her hips sashaying hypnotically, and swung one leg over it, spreading her thighs wide so she could sit backwards in the chair. She trapped her fans together between the front of her body and the chair, giving the crowd the full pleasure of her long, flawless back.

Her arms rose slowly over her head and she tugged her elbow-length gloves off in time with the music. Once her arms were bared, she wrenched her right arm behind her, reaching up her back towards the clasp of her top. With a deft snap of her fingers, the clasp popped open, and without missing a beat she twisted her upper body, so she could look at the crowd over her shoulder.

The look on her face made me laugh. It was a very comical, and yet still sexy, look of feigned surprise. As if she had no idea how her top had just undone itself. She slowly smiled, gave an exaggerated wink, and turned to face the back of the stage again.

Her arms disappeared in front of her, almost crossing over her chest, and I knew that she was about to give a swift tug to one strap. To those seated directly behind her, it would look as if the strap pulled down her arm by an unseen hand. It was all part of the teasing and entertaining. Another look of false surprise, this time over her other shoulder, and the second strap did the same as the first.

With her back completely bared for the horny masses to feast upon, Liz began to move her upper body in slow, rhythmic circles. Again, her hands shot up in the air, but this time she fell backward off the chair. Her back arched deep, and she let her body go limp so that she could hang backward off the seat.

With such a sudden motion, the audience thought they were about to be rewarded with a complete baring of her breasts, but her large feather fan fell back with her, keeping her chest covered and drawing sounds of disappointment and appreciation from the men.

Her next move had impressed me when we were practicing. It was a testament to the true core strength of the human body. Something I would never be able to do, my-self.

Fully extending her legs on either side, Liz spread-eagle before using her abdominal muscles to lift her lower body, very slowly, off the chair while her head and hands braced her on the floor. She remained in a half-split half-hand-stand for a few seconds before pulling her legs and pelvis forward, rotating her hips until she could lower her pelvis down to the floor.

Anyone else would've done the last part quickly. Liz, though, had the most amazing control I had ever wit-nessed. She continued to move at a slow, steady, impressive speed until her ass touched the ground, and she pulled her upper body up once again.

She stunned the entire room into silence for a few heartbeats. What she had done was amazing, beautiful, and the imaginations of the men around me thrust into overdrive as they bore witness to her body control. To put it simply, she'd become the sexual fantasy of every man sitting in there. Such an irony considering Liz preferred women—though, I guess to be fair, that was a fantasy unto itself.

When Liz finished by falling sensually across the chair, one fan spread over the front of her hiding her near-nudity,

I felt an overwhelming sense of pride. I clapped, and the rest of the room joined me in a thunderous roar.

Finally taking a drink of my Amaretto Sour, I leaned back in my chair and let the taste settle on my tongue. I felt like a proud mama watching my best friend nail that dance so perfectly. Liz would be making a name for herself here; that much was certain.

It wasn't a terrible place to work either, as far as gentlemen's clubs go. It was the most prominent strip club in Houston. Sure, they had their typical strippers and topless dancers, but they also had the Burlesque girls like me and Liz. We were what set The Velvet Rope apart from your garden-variety titty bar. It brought in deeper-pocketed clientele and kept the business a "respectable" one.

As respectable as half-naked women could be, anyway.

Aside from the club's reputation, actually working in the place was pretty good, too. Our boss, Andre, was a pretty easy-going guy. He wasn't a dog like some club owners who thought they were pimps and their employees were hookers they could sell to the highest bidder. He actually cared about the girls' safety and well-being almost as much as he cared about the reputation of his business.

I'd wandered so deeply into my own thoughts that when an excited, "Harley!" erupted from behind me, I nearly jumped out of my chair.

Lizbeth was a lot shorter than me, standing at a petite 5'2", but was well put together for her size. She had every proportion just right. Her perfectly-blond curls cascaded down to her waist like a small cloak of silken softness. They were the type of curls someone could get tangled in and be completely at peace with their predicament. Even I found it hard to resist running my fingers through them.

Her cheeks were well defined, unlike mine which were round and full, and her face seemed like it had been created by a master sculptor. Her bright blue eyes were large and shining and kind.

One of the reasons I had been instantly drawn into our friendship was because of how sweet and kind Liz was. She could almost appear naive at times, but I often wondered if that was just for show. There was something hidden deep inside of those eyes and I'd always wanted to pick at it and find out what it was.

Liz threw her arms around me and squeezed my neck to near asphyxiation, still fighting off the excitement from her performance. Once she was able to compose herself, she released her grip and sat in the empty chair next to mine.

"Did I do good up there?" The confidence from her time onstage was beginning to disappear. "I think I got all the steps down. It felt like it."

"You did great, Liz. It was beautiful!"

"I thought I was gonna fall on my ass, but... thank you so much, Harley. I wouldn't have had the guts to do that if you hadn't pushed me."

A smile tugged at my lips, and I grabbed the top of her hand, "I like to think of it as persistent persuasion. Besides, all I did was crack your shell. It was all you, Liz."

We giggled and smiled at each other, drinking in the excitement of the moment.

"So, how'd it go with Braedon?" Liz asked with a knowing smile.

Yeah, I actually flushed a bit as I thought about the date. I didn't want to admit to her that she had won this particular argument, but I couldn't stop the smile crawling on my face. Rather than admit defeat, I turned in my chair and gestured to one of the waitresses.

"Can I get two shots of Jack, please, Amy?" I turned back over to Liz, who had finally managed to calm her breathing down. "You're going to have a shot with me before you go back to work."

"I'd love to have a shot with you lovely ladies," a voice chimed in from behind us.

A skinny, disheveled man stood behind us, beer in hand, grinning down at the two of us. He wasn't a regular, that I could tell, but it wasn't uncommon for people on vacation to come by and see the show before going back home. Normally, it was men on business trips separated from their wives by thousands of miles, but no one could mistake this guy for someone that even owned a suit.

Most of his face was covered by an unruly mess of hair; not like he had been growing out a beard, but more like he had forgotten to shave for the last week. Just under the beard, on the side of his neck, three long scars disappeared into the twisted collar of his denim jacket. My skin went cold as I stared at the scars, unsure why they were making me feel uneasy.

I tried to put on my best polite smile as I said, "Sorry, but this is sort of a private celebration."

"Harley," Liz whispered over the din of the crowd, "maybe it's best if I just go back to work and take that shot later."

"Harley?" the man repeated loudly, before giving me his full attention.

He looked me over a moment, and I could almost feel his eyes raking over every inch of me. After a few moments of silent contemplation, he stepped up to me and placed his hand at the back of my neck, making the hair on my arms stand on end.

"Hey, come outside with me real quick. I have something you need to see."

I smacked his hand off of me, scooting my chair away from him a bit. While I'd gotten better at controlling my temper, I did not appreciate being touched by some handsy drunk. The only thing that had kept me from full-out punching this guy was the fact I was where I earned my check and I really couldn't afford to not work.

"I think I'd rather not, if it's all the same," I said, trying my best to hold a pleasant expression.

I turned around to speak to Liz, hinting to the man in a not-so-subtle way to leave, but he didn't take the hint. I felt hands grasp high up on both of my arms, yanking me out of my chair and knocking it to the floor with a loud clanking sound.

"No, girly. You're coming with me," the man growled in my face as he pulled me to him.

He no longer had a drunk, flirtatious look on his face but one of determination and near frenzy. Whatever it was he wanted, he had decided he wouldn't—or couldn't—leave without me in tow.

Personally, I didn't give a damn. I raised my hand up and raked my fingers across his face, the only thing I could reach in the grip he had me in. As I pulled my nails across his skin I shouted as loud as I could, hoping to draw security's attention, "Get your hands off me!"

He cried out from the strike, thin red lines showing up across his face, filling with blood. He shoved me from him so hard I flew into the table, knocking Liz off her chair in the process. I was certain he was going to go after me again, but as he moved to throw his fist he was pulled back by some unseen force. Large, thick arms wrapped around the skinnier man's body, encasing him in pure muscle.

His feet lifted off the ground, and I helped Liz up, putting myself between her and my attacker. Once I was on my feet, I saw that Jackson had restrained him and was trying to drag him outside.

"Now, now," I heard Jackson's voice cut through the excitement of the crowd. "That's not the way you treat a lady. I think you need some air."

And then they were gone.

The people inside the club were abuzz, and the staff worked double-time at calming the crowd back down. Andre gave complimentary drinks to smooth things over with his customers, and most of them went on about their business. The DJ cued the dancer to resume her set on stage, and after about five minutes everything was as it had been, though the topic of conversation was universal throughout the room.

"Jesus, Harley," Liz said breathlessly. "That happen here a lot?"

"No. Don't worry, it doesn't," I assured her as I squeezed an arm around her shoulders.

The two of us helped one of the bouncers pick up the table and things that had spilled on the floor. Surprisingly there was no real damage, if I didn't count the bruises I could feel just under my skin. He had an incredibly strong grip for someone who looked like they could be knocked over by a gust of wind.

I handed a broken glass to one of the waitresses and glanced over at Liz. "Shit, Liz. Your top is ripped."

Liz looked down at herself and cursed. I grabbed her hand. "Come on, let's get you changed. You can borrow one of mine in my locker." We started towards the dressing area when a shot rang from outside.

A symphony of screams erupted from the front of the club. I ran toward the door and pushed through the mass of bodies collecting near the entrance, leaving Liz behind inside the club.

"Out of the way!" I shouted as I forced myself between two onlookers.

Somehow I knew, deep down, what I would find before I even reached him. It was one of those gut moments where I knew that everything had just gone to hell, and there was no way to stop it. A scent in the air, so to speak. As I made my way past the last wall of bodies, I looked down at the pavement in front of me and choked back a scream.

I fell to my knees, grabbing Jackson's large, meaty paw in my hands. Someone was at his head, apparently telling me to back off, but I didn't really hear anything he said. I just stared down at my co-worker, and friend, as the tears started to seep into my eyes.

"Jackson. Jesus, Jackson I'm sorry. I'm so sorry."

He blinked up at me and gave me a weak smile, his normally powerful southern drawl strained. "Well, heaven must be close by. I have an angel crying for me."

His breath hitched, his eyes began to close, and before I could ask him what happened, he went completely limp.

Chapter 15

July 3rd 2011 1:23 p.m.

THREE HOURS. THAT'S HOW much sleep I managed to get. After Jackson was taken away by the paramedics, I'd stayed behind to answer a few questions and help out the staff any way I could. A lot of the customers had skipped out on their bills, and the chaos had left a bigger mess than usual.

The police were still taking statements when Liz asked me for a ride home. She'd been shaken up a bit, but physically she was okay and cleared to go. I drove her home and stayed for a few hours while she calmed back down.

In all honesty, she probably could have driven herself, but I think we were both looking for comfort after what happened. I know I was.

I was still trying to forget the sight of Jackson's blood staining the sidewalk.

We talked a bit about her future at The Velvet Rope, but I couldn't help but wonder if she was having second thoughts about working there. After everything, I was pretty sure Liz was scared off for good, but it was just one of those things I would have to wait and see.

By the time I had gotten home, it was three in the morning and it took another couple of hours to fall asleep. When my eyes opened at 8:15, all I wanted to do was yank the covers over my head and shut out the world, but my body wouldn't let me sleep any longer.

I drove up to the small yellow house and parked on the opposite side of the street. After taking a moment to pull my face together, I got out of the car and walked up the stone steps to the front door, clutching a small arrangement of yellow carnations to my chest. My finger hesitated over the doorbell for a moment, but I forced myself to push the small button, hearing the sharp buzz inside.

A tall woman, somewhere in her mid to late-twenties, opened the door and stared out at me. Her hair was brown, straight, and gathered in a messy loop at the back of her neck. Her face, though pretty, was void of any makeup which made her eyes seem small and worn compared to the rest of her features.

When I didn't greet her, the woman's brow knitted together, and she cleared her throat.

"Yes?" she said. "Can I help you?"

"Sorry. I'm Harley. I just wanted to, uh... stop by and," I moved the flowers in my arms as I spoke, hoping to show her what I couldn't seem to verbalize.

The woman gave me a soft but tired smile and pushed the door open wider.

"Of course. Won't you, please, come in?" She held her arm out offering to let me inside.

I gave her a tight smile and stepped in, looking around the living room as the door shut behind me. The house was warm and inviting, but the ghosts of harder times hung in the air. The woman stepped out from behind me and reached for the flowers, politeness and kindness still in her voice.

"Let me put these in some water, I'll be right back."

"Alright," I said, relieved to get another moment to compose myself.

When the woman disappeared into a side room, I let myself take in the full view of the living room. I stepped over to the empty fireplace and glanced over the array of pictures arranged on the mantle. In a few different frames there were pictures of nameless people. Some were celebrating, others more demure. There were three photos of the woman who had let me in, but her face was brighter. Happier. One picture, in particular, made me smile.

The woman and Jackson were laughing hard; a candid shot. Both of their faces had a green and white mess smeared across them and their hands held plates and small pieces of cake. Jackson's scary, towering form was a lot gentler and his bald head was adorned with a green party hat.

I'd never seen Jackson look so playful. He was a sweetie, and a joker, but this was downright endearing.

"Is that my angel?" a voice called from the next room.

I turned and walked towards the open French doors, leaning on them with a delicate cross of my arms. I smiled at the large bear propped up in the window seat and shook my head.

"Never pictured you the type to sleep with teddies, Jackson."

I looked over at the small couch resting against the wall. I hadn't been able to see Jackson until I stepped all the way into the room, but when I finally saw him my smile widened a bit. He looked pretty good. Surprisingly good for having been shot. The fact that he was already home and not hooked up in a hospital was miraculous. Jackson pushed his feet from the couch and sat up, still looking impossibly large on the small loveseat.

"I prefer a pretty lady, but sometimes you take a good cuddle however you can get it."

He was teasing me now; another sign that he was in as good of spirits as he was physically. The image of the giant snuggling an oversized bear as he slept was too much for me to even try to process. Biting back the urge to giggle, I strode over to the couch and sat on the other end.

"You look good," I observed as I sunk back into the soft cushions. "Not that I'm complaining, but how did you get released from the hospital so quickly?"

"Ah. Well that is the funny part. It was pretty superficial. Just a grazer."

"But all that blood... by the time I had gotten to you there was already a puddle spreading around you," It hurt deep in my chest just to recall the sight of him lying there.

I was curious now. Even the paramedics seemed concerned at the amount of blood he had lost. The average man has about 10 pints of blood in his body. Jackson looked to have lost about 15 pints in a matter of minutes. Of course, he was the size of three men so maybe he just had more to spare.

His lips curled in a mischievous smirk, "Hemophiliac. Paper cuts are hell."

He let the smirk shift into a full-blown grin, and it was incredibly infectious. I laughed a bit, even though I knew he was full of it, and patted his knee. Patting the back of my hand in return, Jackson let out a soft sigh.

"So, Harley, what do I owe this pleasure? I don't think I've ever seen you outside work. You look... different."

I could tell by his tone that it was meant as a compliment. I did dress a bit differently when I worked, a lot more sequins and thongs. I looked down at myself and slid a hand over the pink button-up blouse, smoothing out wrinkles that didn't exist. My jeans were a deep shade of navy blue and hung loose around my calves. I looked relatively normal.

"Well, I think I clean up nice, don't you?" It was my turn to tease him a bit.

"Oh, definitely. I like the costumes and all, I'd have to be dead not to, but you look really good."

"Thank you," I said with a gentle nudge of my elbow.

My gaze moved to the doorway, and I listened to the movements in the other room. Looking back to Jackson, I smiled and added, "Your wife is really pretty, Jackson. Why didn't you tell me you were married?"

Jackson let out a thunderous laugh, covering his face with his hand. That kind of exertion should've hurt someone who'd just been shot in the stomach, but then again, he had said it was just a graze. I felt my brow quirk at him.

Finally getting under control, he shook his head, laughter still glittering in his eyes. "No darlin'. A thousand times no. That's my sister, Gina."

My eyes went wide with embarrassment, "Oh, shit. Sorry Jackson she just... I just assumed that you both lived here." I leaned over, buried my face in my hands, and groaned. Sitting back up, I sighed heavily, giving in to the embarrassment I had caused myself. "Sorry."

"It's ok. You didn't know," he laughed and patted my knee the same way I had done to him a moment before.

The doorbell buzzed again, making the both of us turn towards the wall at our backs like we could see right through the drywall. I turned to Jackson, whose face had gone from light and warm and full of laughter to alert, serious, and cautious. He was usually so calm and collected. I realized, for the first time, that he may have been more affected by the attack than he was letting on.

We listened to his sister walk back to the door and open it. Her voice, as well as that of the new visitor, remained low and indiscernible, but Jackson seemed to relax a little beside me. I watched the muscles in his neck and shoulders soften, and he sat back against the arm of the loveseat, his eyes moving from the wall to the door behind my back.

Gina walked into the office, the shadow of another person looming behind her, and smiled at her brother. "Jackson, there's a detective here to talk to you."

She gave him a look that almost seemed like a warning to play nice.

A man walked out from behind Gina's slender frame, thanking her, and turned toward us on the couch. His casual demeanor stuttered a bit when he noticed me sitting next to Jackson. Maybe he hadn't thought anyone else would be in the room. Trust me, I wasn't too keen on being there at that moment either.

"Sorry to barge in like this, but I had a few more questions for you, Mr. Tate."

A curtain was drawn over the cop's face, shifting it from blind-sided back to a pleasant professional smile. Pleasant, but practiced.

"It's alright. Though, I have to admit, I'm a bit surprised to see you so soon. Did you guys catch the asshole that shot me?"

"No, not yet. Actually, there are a few more questions we need to get out of the way. Some loose ends to tie up."

He didn't even look the least bit worried that the guy was still on the loose.

Why don't you focus on the loose end running around shooting people, I thought.

If I didn't leave, my mouth was going to get me in trouble.

It was beginning to feel a little crowded in that room anyway, with me, Jackson, the detective, and his badge, gun, and handcuffs. It was time for me to get out of there. I glanced over to Jackson and gave him a half-hearted smile.

"I guess I should go. I'm running late for the gym anyway. I'll see you at work though. Take care, Jackson." I leaned over and gave him a small hug before standing.

"Later, Harley," he said as he let me slide from his arms.

I moved to step around the detective, let the men talk, but he held his hand out in front of me so abruptly that I nearly ran into it. I took a quick step back, my skin tightening with a flush of cold.

"Excuse me. Sorry." He looked a little embarrassed at his sudden block and let his hand fall to his side. "Your name is Harley? You worked at the club last night during the altercation?"

I shook my head a little. "No, I wasn't working. I was just another customer last night."

"Okay. Do you have any extra information that might be helpful?"

"I gave my statement last night. He hit on me and my friend and got a little handsy which was why Jackson escorted him out. I didn't see what happened outside. I was still in the club." The knot in my gut loosened a little as I repeated the statement I gave the cops last night.

He made a face that looked tiresome. Not necessarily that he didn't believe me, but more like he was hoping to hear more than what he already read from all the statements taken. Reaching into the inside of his jacket, he pulled out a small business card. It had his name, Det. Riley Sheppard, and a couple of numbers where he could be reached.

"Alright. If you think of anything else, get in touch with me. The fact that this creep was tossed out because of you means you need to be careful. If you hear or see anything, anything at all, call that number." He pointed at the top number directly under his name.

I wasn't too thrilled at the fact that he was indirectly blaming me for what happened, but I nodded and tucked the card into my pocket. Besides, like it or not, if I hadn't gotten into it with the guy then Jackson wouldn't have had any reason to take him out. Not that refusing to wander off with some stranger was irrational, but it did mean I had set off a chain of events that ended with Jackson almost getting killed.

I glanced over to Jackson, who was giving me a sympathetic look, and gave a wave of fingers before showing myself out of the house.

I walked out to my car a little shaken, a little irritated, but no worse for the wear. I stared at the unmarked police car with its not-so-hidden lights in the back window and crossed the street to my Toyota. Even after all this time, the authorities made me squirmy.

Last night was easier to handle because I was wrapped up in Jackson's condition and the chaos around the bar. It hadn't even occurred to me that I could be recognized for my less-than-exemplary past. Now that I knew Jackson was safe, I moved my concern to my own skin.

I'd kept my nose clean since I left Frank—not so much as a traffic ticket—but that didn't mean shit. Not really. I was still a marked woman in my mind. I could stop the rap sheet from getting any thicker, but it didn't erase what was already tucked away inside.

I opened the driver's side door and slid in, ready to put as much distance between me and the badge as I could. What I had told Jackson was true. I was going to head to the gym, but I was grateful for the opportunity to leave the detective behind me. Letting out a long, slow breath, I pulled out onto the road and drove towards McKinley's.

McKinley's Gym sat in the heart of downtown Houston. Andre insisted, upon my hiring, that I join up with a local gym to keep in shape. Now, it wasn't as sexist as it sounded. Truthfully, it was a requirement of all his employees.

Most of the women from the club went to the YMCA across the street and did the whole cardio/yoga/Pilates thing. It was great for working off calories and keeping lean muscle. However, after three days of the whole girly thing, I had been making my way to my car and noticed McKinley's. Jackson and some of the other guys had mentioned it in passing, and I knew the male half of the club preferred it to the Y. I could hardly blame them.

After watching the inside of the gym from the safety of the sidewalk, I caught sight of something really interesting. Two men were sparring on the large ring in the middle of the floor. Their movements were hypnotic. Watching them, I knew what it was I needed, and it wasn't sitting on a yoga mat or finding my Chi.

I'd been a regular at McKinley's for about eight months and so far, only one other female has ever joined.

She didn't come in often, but I heard the men talking about her. It was pretty typical talk coming from a bunch of sweaty, muscled, no-necks, and I managed to block out the sexist banter for the most part.

What I couldn't block out I simply ignored.

What else was I going to do? Get up in their faces about it? I didn't know her; she didn't know me. I could only assume they talked the same about me when I was out of the room. I just preferred ignorant bliss at this point. The only one that had managed to not get the 'let's try and guess the chick's cup size' memo was Marcellus, my trainer.

I hit the mat with brutal force, bouncing off of it once before landing fully. It knocked the air out of my lungs and sent a sharp shooting pain up my spine. Fuck, Marcellus was fast. Of course, I hadn't expected him to be anything other than perfect.

This month, we were touching base with some Jiu-Jitsu throws. I'd made some progress, but Marcellus' experience still intimidated me to the point of hesitation. Hesitation is not an ally in self-defense.

I laid sprawled on the red mat, my knees bent and my eyes staring up into the hanging light above us, trying to catch my breath before it ran away from me in the form of rapid, shallow panting. The mat felt so cool against my back. I seriously considered just staying there for the rest of my life, but the bright yellow light above was eclipsed by a round silhouette. Marcellus stared down at me, beads of sweat dotting his forehead, mouth stretched in a satisfied grin.

"You're getting better, but you leave too many openings."

"That's what she said?"

A soft chuckle followed a shake of his head. "Out of the gutter and onto your feet. You're getting close, but you won't get it done lying on the ground in defeat."

"I like it down here. It's cooler. Less... flippy."

"You can get up yourself, or I can make you get up. Your choice."

I closed my eyes, an exhausted smile pulling at my lips, and made no attempt to move from my newfound safe haven.

"Alright," he said. I thought, maybe, he accepted that I was just done.

Good. Mr. Bossypants can take a hint. I'd get up eventually, but it would be on my own time, dammit. The blinding light returned forcing my eyes to clench tighter, and I knew he had moved away.

After a few moments, I opened one eye, risking a glance to see where he had gone. I shouldn't have done that. The moment my eye found him, I was doused by a bottle of cold water. I jumped to my feet, coughing and sputtering, my sinuses burning from the water rushing up my nose.

I swiped the water from my face, shaking my hands and spreading droplets all over the mat.

"What the fuck, Marcellus!" I screamed, stopping the gathering of bodybuilders in the room mid-rep.

"You wanted to cool off, right? Thought I would help you out a bit. Now let's go."

His tone changed from playful to commanding, but not in a threatening way. It was more of a teacher and student type of thing. Still, now I was agitated. I stared up at him through my eyelashes, my brow creased in the middle, water dripping from my chin and hair.

"Yeah. Let's go."

Chapter 16

July 3rd 2011 5:17 p.m.

It had been a pretty good day, all things considered. Marcellus said I was coming along nicely. A "real improvement" since he started teaching me six months ago. I never really pictured myself as the type of girl to take self-defense training, but with the shit that tended to get thrown my way, it really couldn't hurt.

I already knew how to fight, but it was just the dirty bar-fight type stuff. Nothing with any sort of discipline or forethought; something Marcellus called out early on.

My speed and endurance had surprised him when we started training, but he'd made it clear that I didn't know what to do with any of it. Go figure. I could blame all of it on the same source.

Running with Frank meant I needed to know how to handle myself. It was just part of the lifestyle. I didn't go out looking for fights, but if I wanted to go out with the guys without running into the cops, then I had to know how to fight my way out of a shit-storm.

Or at least how to run like hell to keep from ending up in a pair of ugly steel bracelets.

With the time and distance I'd put between us, I also came to many hard truths about how he manipulated me. He often encouraged my anger, antagonizing me or making bad situations worse until I let it take control of the wheel. You couldn't have both rage and control. It just didn't work.

McKinley's technically didn't offer self-defense classes. Marcellus was just a regular weight-jockey that liked to spar other guys on the mats. It was just a happy circumstance I came in the same day he was sparring with someone. I guess my interest was what eventually led him to offer to teach me various techniques.

In truth, he wasn't just good at basic fighting and jiu-jitsu. Trained in aikido, judo, Muay Thai, and of course, karate, Marcellus was one scary mother fucker. I would never want to be on his bad side. And yet, there I was sparring him twice a week and letting him knock me around like a rag doll.

After drying off from a much-needed shower and slipping into my pajama pants, I decided it was time to bite the bullet and get cracking on my homework. My arms and legs were sore, as they always were after the gym, but sore muscles would not be accepted as an excuse by my English-Lit professor.

I had already put off the assigned reading for two days. Any longer and I was pushing it. It was due in three days, and I still hadn't started reading it, let alone write a critique on it.

Hours ticked on as I hit the books, pouring over the copy of Pride and Prejudice I checked out from the public library. By nine o'clock, my head was pounding. There were so many obsolete words and nuances to the long-forgotten linguistic style.

And the day-to-day lives of women back in those times were horrible. Marriage was the most important thing for a girl to look forward to in her life. Watch her sisters get married off, marry a man—typically twice her age—and then marry off her own daughters.

Wash, rinse, repeat.

While I had to admit Elizabeth Bennett was a woman ahead of her time, from what I'd been able to follow, even she was of the mind that a marriage was the main event. The only thing that set her apart was her bold tongue and desires to marry someone of her own preference. I couldn't imagine thinking of nothing else in the prime of my life than which man I would serve until death.

I slammed the novel shut, letting my frustrations out on the well-worn cover, and raised my arms above my head in a delicious stretch. I had sat down for far too long. My back was stiff and achy from the mixture of the afternoon training and not moving for the last couple of hours.

As I bent backwards, appreciating a good stretch to my tensed up back muscles, I caught a glimpse of my calendar out of the corner of my eye. Two very large brown eyes were staring back at me with a depressingly pathetic plea to be adopted. Liz was convinced I needed a pet or something to keep me company. Apparently, this Humane Society Puppy Calendar she bought me was supposed to convince me to save one of the animals in the local shelter.

"Shit," I cursed as today's date caught my eye.

Trash night. I had forgotten all about it last week. Honestly, I always forgot about it.

The truck was an invisible entity, a real ghost story because it came very early in the morning and I had never actually seen the thing. Lecturing myself to be a damn adult and get it done while I was thinking about it, I moved about my apartment and collected the trash in every room and moved to the door.

The musical chime of my phone erupted in the kitchen, stopping me for a moment but the weight of the bags urged me forward. Let it go to voicemail. My hands were full.

My apartment was actually one-fourth of a quadruplex sitting on the edge of the city. I'd lived in the upper right apartment since moving to Houston. The area was quiet, a little more secluded than the hustle and bustle of the city proper, and rent was cheap. Perfect for a single gal trying to keep a low profile.

The other upper level apartment was vacant, and had been for a few months, and the bottom two were rented by a couple of cousins or something. Actually, I wasn't sure how they're related to one another, but I'd seen the massive get-togethers where people spill out from both apartments and into the courtyard between them.

The only thing I hated about my apartment, other than the time-bomb water-heater, was the stairs. Narrow staircases outside my front door lead to each of the top-level units. Hauling anything up or down the steps, especially in some of the shoes I own, is a near-death experience. Dragging down more than one 13-gallon trash bag was not my idea of a good time, either.

With one slung awkwardly over my left shoulder and the other dragging heavily across each step, I only just managed to not kill myself or tear the bottom of the bag open to rain trash down on my neighbor's porch.

It took a few tries, but I was finally able to toss both bags into the dumpster around the corner from my side of the building. Thank God the trucks were coming the next day since it seemed that they were fuller than normal. Last thing we needed was a bunch of wild animals scavenging from our trash.

I turned to make my way back upstairs but stopped as a glance upward brought the night sky to my attention. It was clear and beautiful.

This was another reason I preferred living on the edges of the city. While the stars weren't quite as brilliant as I had seen in smaller towns, this was as clear as I could see them out here. The trees were plentiful in this area, but they were far enough from my building that it put me right in the middle of a broad clearing, leaving the sky to full exposure.

The night sky always seemed to have a calming, some-times clarifying effect on me. It soothed my mood and allowed me to shrink away from all those outside forces of trouble. Made me feel like there was no way trouble could find tiny insignificant me under something as large as the heavens.

A gentle rustling interrupted my moment of meditation. I glanced over my shoulder, looking out towards the trash cans with a deep sigh. I knew it. Probably a raccoon or stray cat looking for a quick meal. I made my way back to the dumpster and made a sharp hissing sound through my teeth in hopes of scaring the animal away.

"Pssst. Go on... no dinner here."

Another thunk against the side of the bin urged me closer, my eyes searching the darkness for the animal. As I neared the edge of the trash, I gave one last attempt to scare it off, clapping my hands hoping to spook it away. Instead, I was met with two eerily glowing yellow eyes.

I stopped and stared at them. They were much higher off the ground than a raccoon or opossum would be, and their menacing glow raised the hair on my arms. I'd never seen a dog's eyes reflect so brightly in the dark. I hadn't seen any animal's eyes do that. The thought barely passed through my brain when it hit me.

That wasn't exactly true.

I thought about running upstairs. For the moment, the thing seemed to be okay with just watching me. No sudden movements, I repeated to myself. Don't give it any reason to get worked up. If I just stayed very still it might realize I wasn't a threat and move on.

The eyes shifted, and I hoped it was turning to scamper the other way. Instead, a large furry paw stepped out of the shadows and into the barely luminous glow of the neighbor's porch light. My skin tightened around me, a cool flush creeping down my skin as adrenaline mixed with dread.

No, it was bigger than a dog. So much bigger. A low growl rolled from the animal's throat as it eased its face into the light.

Its advancing forced me back a step before I could stop myself, and I cursed under my breath. The animal stared at me, neither one of us making another move. Now that its front half was bathed in the soft light, I could tell that this was absolutely not a dog but a wolf. Fear gripped me as I stared at it.

Ever since the night I left Frank, I'd been trying to convince myself I hadn't seen what I thought I'd seen. It couldn't have been real, and every time I thought about it I felt more and more crazy.

It was a stress-induced hallucination, a terrible mix of too much drinking, too much fighting, and too much craziness in my life. Everything had finally caught up to me and created this wild and unfathomable delusion that my mind used to finally push me to do what I should have done long before. It gave me an inarguable reason to leave Frank.

Given everything I'd seen, real or otherwise, my anxiety skyrocketed any time I saw a wolf. This one in front of me was real, it was huge, and it was slowly coming toward me.

If I ran, it would most likely chase me down. However, the longer I stood there the louder and more menacing its growling became. It was going to attack me no matter what. I could feel it in my bones. That impending dread pulsed against my brain like a buzzer telling me I hit the nail on the head.

I scanned around me and the wolf in search of a weapon, shielding, something. I whimpered as the animal drew closer. He was about to pounce. My skin was cold, my brow damp, and my heart raced impossibly fast.

Beneath the stairs leading up to my apartment, I noticed a piece of wood, about 3 feet in length and the only thing within reach that might persuade this wolf to leave me alone. I knew it would be on top of me the instant I moved for the board. I had to be quick.

With one last glance at the wolf, I shifted my weight to my left foot, twisting my body so I could jump to the board. A ferocious snarl erupted behind me. My arm stretched out for the wood, but I judged it short. My fingertips brushed the edge of the plank seconds before I felt a powerful jerk at my pant leg, dragging me backward.

I watched my weapon retreat from reach and flipped over on my back, staring down the line of my body at the wolf as he dragged me across the ground. My throat burned, but I didn't remember screaming. My eyes darted to the driveway, hope filling my chest. I thought maybe my neighbor would have heard and come running to my aid.

He wasn't home. I was all alone. My ankle suddenly dropped to the ground, and I snapped my attention back to the rabid animal. The wolf leapt, all strong muscle moving under that coarse fur, and lunged toward me. My foot connected hard against its ribcage, sending it flying in the other direction.

I didn't waste a precious second to see where it landed. I scrambled to my stomach and crawled as fast as my hands and knees would let me until I snatched up the board. I flipped back onto my back, grabbed it near each end and held it across my chest. Once more the wolf leapt toward me. I held the board at arm's length, hoping to block its snarling, drooling snout.

The board nearly connected with it, but another growling bark erupted at my side, and a light-colored blur crashed against the side of the wolf, knocking it to its side on the ground and skidding the pair of them across the pavement.

I stayed on the ground, paralyzed by fear, confusion, and adrenaline and strained to see what was happening in the shadows of the driveway. Another wolf had intervened. The snarling, the snapping, the sound of teeth and claw and solid muscle hitting the ground echoed as the two animals fought. The lighter-colored wolf kept the darker one at bay, pouncing on it and clenching teeth around its neck.

Slowly, my senses came back to me, and I remembered the stairs. The second wolf had given me an opening to get away, and I was gonna take it before both animals turned on me.

Scrambling to my feet, board in hand, I clamored to my stairs and climbed as quickly as my feet could carry me. My turned to jelly as I reached the top, barely holding me upright. My door was within reach; only a couple more steps to safety.

A sharp, sudden, whine sounded from the driveway below, forcing me to turn around. The darker wolf was running away from the apartments towards the line of trees across the road, the other...

I stared down past the railing and watched the second animal limp around the driveway. She was hurt. Hurt from protecting me. I stared down at her, unsure of what to do. It was just another wild animal, right? Just like the first one that had tried to rip my throat out.

Large blue eyes turned up and stared at me, imploring. Pleading.

My hand gripped the rail as I tried to convince myself that it would know what to do for itself. It's lasted this long on its own. Obviously, it wouldn't have survived if it didn't know how to take care of itself. No sooner than I moved toward my door, the wolf fell to its side.

There was no more thinking, no more debating. I gripped the board in my hand and fumbled down the stairs, alert for signs of movement. If that other wolf came back, I wanted to be ready this time.

I rushed over to the wounded animal, slowing just out of reach of it. It looked so helpless lying on the ground, its side rising and falling in long breaths. Slowly in, quickly out. It was struggling to breathe. She was much smaller than the other one, almost the size of a normal wolf. Not small, exactly, but not the same as the massive monsters that had been haunting my dreams for months now. Not as big as the one she had saved me from.

Her eyes stared at the darkness ahead, wide but unfocused. Her cream-colored fur looked so soft until it reached her front paw and the side of her neck where light fur became matted in dark crimson tangles.

My heart hurt for the animal. All of this pain, all this damage, was because she tried to save me.

I needed to see if I could help her. I thought about throwing her into my car and driving to the animal shelter off the highway, but Liz popped into my mind. She was completely anti-shelter. The more I thought about it, I knew they would put this wolf down. I couldn't deliver her into the hands of death now.

I glanced upstairs and sighed. Maybe the damage wasn't as bad as it looked. If I cleaned her up, wrapped a bandage around her leg, maybe she could heal on her own in the woods. If anything, she seemed exhausted from the fight, and I could at least keep her safe until she was ready to fight off whatever came after her. Sleeping out there, wounded and fatigued, the other wolf might come back and finish the job.

I was upstairs only five minutes before I came back down with a belt and an old sheet. I laid the sheet out behind her back and walked back around to her head, kneeling slowly with the belt in hand. If I was going to do this I wasn't going to take any chances. I needed all of my fingers after all.

I laced the tip of the belt through the silver buckle. The wolf's eyes moved to me, watching me as I inched the loop towards her muzzle. She locked eyes with me and we stared at each other for what seemed like eternity before she moved her eyes away from mine. It seemed like she was giving me permission. God, I hoped so.

I moved the belt and wrapped it around her snout, pulling the loop tight until it was snug to her muzzle, and clasped it shut. Her eyelids closed, and I let out a shaky breath.

"I'm so sorry, but I'm going to have to roll you over onto the sheet." I said.

I didn't want to touch the injured leg, and I wasn't sure grabbing a wild, already skittish, animal by the hind legs was a smart move. Hell, moving a wild animal was already stupid, but here I was.

Me and smart choices just don't seem to add up.

I decided to use her midsection to roll her over onto the sheet. I wasn't strong enough to lift the animal in my arms and carry her upstairs, but the sheet would allow me to drag her a little easier. I would have to take extra care on the steps. Images of the poor thing rolling down the stairs played through my head, made me hesitate, but what else could I do?

Crouching down between her front and back legs, I placed my hands onto her belly, her fur surprisingly soft under my hands. With a small prayer, I shoved her, rolling her over with little protesting on her part.

I held the corners of the sheet in both hands as I stared up the narrow and tall flight of stairs. What the hell was I doing? I could barely take two trash bags down these stairs. Now I was trying to drag a good 70 pounds up them. I closed my eyes and took a deep breath.

"Alley-oop," I whispered before taking the first step and tugging on the sheet.

She was so heavy, and I thought, for a moment, I wouldn't be able to get her to the top. My shoulders screamed at me. I released my breath and relaxed my grip on the sheet. I hadn't even gotten her off the ground. I stood two steps above her and shook my head. It wasn't going to be easy, but I was going to do it, dammit.

About thirty-five minutes later, I managed to climb up the 20ish steps with the wolf in tow and dragged her through the threshold of my apartment. I slammed the door behind us and rested against it, sliding down to the ground. My lungs ached, and my breathing came out in harried pants; my skin was coated in sweat.

Remembering the reason for the whole test of strength, I jumped to my feet and went to the bathroom to find anything that could help me with her. A few minutes later, I emerged with a bowl of warm water, a small stack of wash cloths, and an old clean t-shirt. I set the bowl of water down on the floor and knelt next to it, dipping a washcloth into the water and ringing it out.

I'd never done wound care on an animal before, unless we're talking animals of the human variety. There were countless times I'd patched up Frank after one incident or another. Still, I doubted triple antibiotics and Band Aids were going to be of much help.

Wash it up, wrap it, and let the wolf tear the rags away at her leisure. That seemed to be the best I could offer. So, I spent the next hour trying to clean the blood away from the wound and return her fur back to the beautiful cream color it had been. When I looked closer at her leg, I found a set of small punctures in a row. The other wolf hadn't appeared to rip any of the skin, thankfully. It should heal easily.

I grabbed my shirt, ripped a three-inch-wide strip from it, and wrapped it around the wolf's front leg. Happy with my work, I tended the other wound. I could clean it, but I wouldn't be able to bandage around her neck. Just cleaning it out would have to work. Her fur still had an orange tint around the neck and leg, but I'd done my best.

"There you go, girl," I whispered, sliding my fingers through her fur.

I had always imagined wolves having coarse, brittle fur. Hers was surprisingly soft. She stared up at me as I pet her, and I smiled down at her, amazed that she was allowing it.

I stood and stretched my back. It was almost midnight, and I needed some sleep. The wolf lifted her head, watching me sidelong while I locked my door and picked up the soiled cloths and the bowl.

"You can sleep in my house tonight so that big bad wolf doesn't get ya." Again, I was talking to a freaking animal. "Just... Don't eat me. Please."

I put the washcloths in my hamper and dumped the red water in the bathroom sink before heading to bed. I froze as I passed the television on my dresser.

The volume was set low enough so it didn't distract me from studying, but loud enough to give me that comforting white noise in the background. What I saw staring back at me, though, was as far from comforting as one could get.

Braedon's handsome face was on the screen. Seeing his picture on TV was enough to distract me, but the headline accompanying it made my heart stop.

"Area Man Found Dead in Alley Behind Castro's Bistro."

"Holy... Shit," I whispered.

While they interviewed the police on the scene, I ran into the other room and snatched my phone, dialing Liz while I returned to the television. The news had already moved on to the next story, but Liz had to have seen it. He was her friend. Surely, she'd know what had happened.

She didn't pick up. I cursed and plugged my phone into the charger as questions whirled around in my mind. What had happened to him? Was he mugged? And right after he saw me off? The thought made me sick to my stomach with all the 'what-ifs' that revelation created.

I crawled into bed and pulled the comforter up, and dropped onto my pillow. What should have been a sweet, blissful sleep turned into tossing and turning. I reached an arm over to my nightstand through the darkness and started to nestle back into my bed, but the sound of my door creaking shot me up again.

"Hello?" I called out into the empty darkness.

My heart began to race again. A thousand possibilities rolled around my imagination. I lived alone so there was no reason for my door to be moving. All of my windows were shut, my door locked, and I hadn't heard anyone trying to get in. My blood went cold as I thought of other possibilities, and Frank suddenly popped in at the top of the list.

Oh God, had he found out where I was? I didn't want to think of what he would do if he ever did.

I slowly reached my arm back, squeezing my hand between the headboard and the wall. My fingers brushed the holster, and I was a hair's breadth from pulling my gun, when a soft whine squealed from the side of my bed.

I looked down to find the wolf staring at me, her eyes flicking to my awkwardly angled arm. My relief blew out of me at the end of a deep sigh, and I pulled my arm back in front of me to reach down and pet the wolf.

"Okay. But on the floor," I conceded to that imploring stare.

As if understanding me, she padded in a circle, limping slightly, and lowered herself gracefully to the ground. I laid back on the bed and pulled the covers up to my chin, ready to welcome the greedy clutches of unconsciousness.

I hadn't thought of Frank in a while. I mean really thought of him, as opposed to a fleeting memory here and there. He was always in the back of my mind. If I let my guard down too much, I was just asking for trouble, but the longer I'd gone without him the easier it was getting to move on with my life. It had also gotten easier to forget just how much he scared me until moments like this.

With that all too familiar paranoia clutching at my chest, I drifted into a restless sleep.

Chapter 17

The rush. The exhilaration of running, of my hands and feet digging into the damp soil of the forest floor, of my heart racing impossibly fast with each powerful stride. I was searching. Looking for something that I could taste just on the tip of my tongue. Something delectable. Som ething... satisfying.

It was close. I could smell the sickly-sweet aroma in the air mixed with the scent of freshly disturbed earth and wet leaves. An almost metallic taste on my tongue. Almost there. My stomach clenched with ravenous hunger. It was so dark and yet I could make out every tree and bush, every single leaf in my path. I could see it all.

The huddle of brown and taupe and black fur stopped suddenly as I eased away from the bushes. Their heads lifted and stared in my direction, masks of red across their eyes and snouts, mouths dripping with something thick and crimson.

They waited as I made my way closer to the group, that wondrous aroma getting thicker in my nostrils. Each step found the dirt wetter and wetter, until the earth was saturated in something much warmer than rain. It coated my palms and soles in the reddest red, and dirt clung to my skin possessively.

The wolves in front of me parted, and in the middle of the gathering, on the blood-soaked floor, was... me. At least something deep inside me told me that I was staring at myself, because what lay on the ground was unrecognizable. Honey blond hair was matted with chunks of flesh and tacky blood. Her stomach—my stomach—was torn open. Sinew and entrails ripped apart and strewn along the ground around my body, dark blood glistening in the moonlight as it poured effortlessly from the wound. An arm stretched out across the forest floor limp and appeared lifeless at first, but as I stepped closer it reached up to me, pleading to me.

There was the distinct scent of fear—of blood, too, but mostly fear. The aroma of my terror, of my blood and meat, was intoxicating. It reached every crevice of my being, and I was drunk with the need to feed.

I stared down at the body I had known for so many years and felt... nothing. No sympathy. No regret. No affection. No loss. Just hunger. I looked into the eyes of my former self, wide and smeared with my own blood, and without mercy I lunged and sunk my teeth into my throat. Blood poured like wine into my mouth. Meat melted between my teeth and I ate. I feasted to my heart's content with the wolves around me.

Chapter 18

July 4th 2011 8:26 a.m.

MY EYES FLEW OPEN and I sat straight up in my bed. I'd woken myself with my own screams. My stomach was heavy, the room was spinning, and before I could even manage one linear thought, I was out of bed and running to the bathroom.

The entire contents of my stomach emptied right then and there. I hovered over the toilet bowl, my arms draped over the top, and I swear I could taste blood and raw meat in my mouth. It was thick, and rancid, and the mere thought of it made my stomach tighten and forced me into another heaving fit.

When I was certain the vomiting was over, I splashed my face with some water and brushed my teeth with extreme scrutiny. Even when the taste of vomit was gone, I continued brushing until the taste of blood was a hazy memory. It was the most intense dream I'd ever had. So real, so vivid. I could still feel the dirt between my fingers and toes. Could still feel the exhilaration of the run, of the hunt. The kill.

Thoughts of the wolves in my dream turned to the animal sleeping beside my bed. God, did I even want to look at that thing after the dream I had? I needed to. I know I did, if for nothing else, then to let it out of the apartment.

I peered around my bathroom door and listened for movement. Silence. She was probably still sleeping.

"Wolf?" I called out softly, making my voice as soothing as possible.

My toes flexed over the carpet anxiously, but I found reassurance in the absence of blood-soaked dirt.

The last thing I wanted to do was startle it. What if it was more hurt than I thought? The idea of some poor animal silently dying on my apartment floor, especially one that had gotten hurt helping me, all but broke my heart and gave me the extra push I needed to round the bed, the nightmare long forgotten.

"Wake up, girl," I coaxed as the spot I'd last seen her came into view.

What I saw knocked the wind right out of me.

Naked! There was a naked woman on my floor! How did a naked woman get in my apartment?! Why was there a naked woman in my apartment?! I stared down at the curled-up legs, the blond curls running down her back and around her shoulders, thankfully covering the more private bits from view. A white rag was wrapped around her forearm, smeared with dark red smudges.

Oh... fuck.

Not again. My mind railed at the sight of the woman lying where I had left a wolf. God, I had spent so many months trying to convince myself that I was crazy, that this shit couldn't be possible, and then this falls into my lap.

I raised my arms and laced my fingers behind my head while my mind went berserk. Who was she? Why was she here? Well, she was here because I brought her up here, but why had she come? Why protect me? I didn't recognize her as anyone running with Frank's pack, but if she didn't belong to him then where did she come from?

My foot moved of its own volition and gave a gentle shove to the bottom of her bare foot.

"Hey..."

I tensed, but she didn't move. This time I shoved a bit harder, my panic and confusion fueling the anger slowly building inside of me. I hated being clueless. With another rough kick, I repeated, "Hey! What the hell are you doing in my apartment?!"

The woman flailed, her curls hanging over her face and body as she swiveled around and got to her feet in a strangely graceful movement. She flung herself back against the bedside table, knocking my lamp over and busting the bulb. Fantastic. She just cost me six bucks, gave me a strong compulsion to shampoo my carpet and... Wait, is she growling at me?

I snatched the duvet from my bed and tossed it violently at her very exposed body.

"I don't know why you're in my house, or who sent you here, but get the fuck out before I shoot you in your bare ass!"

"Harley..." A soft, scared voice squawked out from behind the blanket.

My head pounded, my stomach was still tight from the very generous vomiting moments before, and I had just found a naked chick in my room. My eyes locked on the blond hair peeking out from the top of the blanket as she clutched it not only to her body but to her face as well.

I waited for her to say something else, but she stayed silent.

"Who the h—" But my interrogation turned into stunned silence as two very large, very blue, eyes appeared from behind the blanket through the mess of blond curls.

"Liz?" I could barely squeeze the name out of my throat.

"I'm sorry Harley." Her voice was strained, holding back the emotions that kept trying to force its way out with each syllable. "I didn't want you to see me like this. I had hoped—"

I held a hand up at her, silencing her. I couldn't speak.

"Harley," Liz whispered. I answered her with a step backwards.

"Harley," she repeated a little louder.

"No. No, not you. Not you, Liz," A sense of utter betrayal hit me like a punch in the gut. I kept moving away from her, and she stepped toward me. "Don't," I snapped, my throat tight. "Don't come near me."

"Harley! Please, stop and listen to me!"

I stopped at the front of the small hallway and stared at Liz standing in my bedroom door with her arms crossed tightly across her chest. Her cheeks were wet with tears as she stared back at me, a complete mess from head to toe. We stood motionless in a long stretch of heavy silence.

My eyes dropped to her forearm, wrapped in the bloody bandage I'd put on the wolf last night. Her eyes followed suit before she moved her arm slowly behind her back, her eyes locked on her feet, and that was when I noticed the red smeared at the side of her neck too. It wasn't as dark as the blood on the rag, but lighter like it had stained her skin. Skin that was completely unbroken.

"I didn't mean for you to find out like this," she hesitated.

"Find out what? That you've been lying to me this whole time? That you've been spying on me? What, Liz? What didn't you want me to find out?" My voice grew louder with each word, the emotional floodgate inside me starting to crack and crumble away.

A soft sob broke from her throat, and she covered her face with her hands. This was hard for her, that much I could see, but I didn't feel anything but rage. I couldn't.

She lifted her face from her hands, the tip of her tongue darting nervously over her upper lip. She couldn't look at me. That was fine with me. Quite honestly, I didn't want to look at her either.

"What the fuck are you, Liz?" I demanded.

She winced like I'd hit her. I could see the struggle within herself as my words seared her. A small part of me hurt for bringing such a stricken look to her eyes, but I was pissed and hurt, too. I didn't know what was real and what was a lie anymore.

"The term," she whispered, so softly that I actually had to move closer to really hear her, "is werewolf."

It started off slow, quiet. A whispery titter of sound bubbled in my throat and rose into a full-on assault before I could choke it down. I laughed good and hard, the tension breaking from my chest, the corners of my eyes getting wet.

I don't know why I laughed. Maybe it was the only way my brain could cope. Maybe all the stress and restless nights I'd endured since Frank revealed what he really was finally caught up with me. Whatever the reason, I completely lost it; laughing myself to tears until my brain shut that shit off so abruptly the sudden return of oxygen made me swoon and catch myself on the doorframe.

I forced out a deep, calming breath and moved across the room to sit on my bed. I sat on the edge and folded myself in half placing my head between my knees. I was disoriented, so blown away by Liz's confession that I couldn't even stand upright.

Even though the words came from someone I trusted completely, my brain was in full mutiny mode. It downright refused it.

This dear girl, who had never given me any reason to distrust her before, was telling me that she was the animal

I had bandaged and cared for last night. She was one of the monsters that had haunted me for nearly a year. Even with everything we had been through together, my brain was calling her a liar and a fraud and every insulting name in the book.

"You're screwing with me. Right?" I finally managed, though my voice was slightly muffled. "Please tell me you broke into my apartment this morning, took the wolf out of here, and set this up to fuck with me. Tell me this is a cruel, sadistic joke."

My pleas were met with tense silence. I lifted my head from my knees and stared across the room at Liz, who was now wearing a t-shirt and pair of shorts from my dresser. I hadn't even heard her move.

"Lizbeth," I stated more sternly, using her given name for probably only the third time since knowing her. "Tell me that I'm crazy. Please."

"You're not crazy," she said.

She curled up on the window seat in my bedroom and drew her knees to her chest. Her thin arm wrapped tightly around them holding on as if it was the only thing keeping her from running away in shame.

"How?! You tell me how it is even remotely possible that you... that you're a..." I couldn't say it.

It stuck to the roof of my mouth like a fat glob of peanut butter. No matter how much I tried to force it I only spread it around making it more difficult to get it out.

She rested her forehead on the tops of her knees, her shoulders shuddering ever so slightly. Was she crying? I don't think I had ever seen Liz actually cry before, and it disarmed me almost immediately. I got to my feet on pure instinct and made my way over to her, sitting next to her on the bench and wrapping a comforting arm around her shoulders.

"Hey... I'm sorry," I said and instantly couldn't believe I was the one apologizing.

She mumbled something I couldn't hear, and I swallowed down that small lump of anger that wanted me to snap at her to speak up. Instead I just waited. I forced myself to practice patience with her because, even if I was angry and confused, Liz appeared to be having a serious struggle within herself. I could practically smell the pain and shame oozing from her every pore.

After a few brief moments of contemplative silence, she lifted her forehead from her knees and rested her chin in its place. A soft breath blew from the small 'o' her lips had formed and she swallowed hard.

"I am an honest-to-God, howling, furry, dangerous, two-natured creature of the night. A monster."

I stared at her for a good long moment, waiting to see if she was going to continue and hoping my brain was going to catch up sometime soon. My first instinct was to laugh, but I didn't want to laugh in her face again. Not when she had such a pained look in her eyes. Instead, I decided to ignore the anger, for the time being, and forced myself to be the calm and collected one.

Fuck, when did that happen?

"You're not," I said, barely convincing myself. "I don't know what you are, but I could never call you a monster. You're just... Liz." Maybe if I said it out loud I would start to believe it myself.

Now it was Liz that was laughing, but something dark coiled around the sound. Something bitter, cold, and defeated. It felt like tiny blades cutting at my heart. I never wanted to hear anything like that coming from my dearest friend.

"You really don't know anything about me, Harley."

"Okay, fine. You're right. We've only been friends for... what... almost a year? Obviously, I don't know a damn thing about you. So, tell me. How long have you been a werewolf?"

Liz blinked at me, her jaw slack. I guess she wasn't sure where I was headed with that, or if I was biding my time until I could hurt her, but eventually she shifted in her seat and glanced down at her toes.

"My whole life. I was born like this."

"I thought werewolves became werewolves from bites or something," I recited my oh-so impressive understanding of storybook werewolves.

"Well, they can," she hesitated, wringing her fingers, "but I was born a wolf."

"Alright." I nodded and stood up, crossing my arms and turning to look down at her. "So you've been a werewolf the entire time I've known you. You're pretty damn good at hiding it."

Silence.

"Do you change at the full moon?"

"Yes."

"Well, that will make work difficult for you, won't it? I don't know if many of the men that come in are into bestiality."

She made a face of absolute revulsion. A little piece of me, deep inside, found relief at her reaction. That same part of me was ashamed at being so harsh toward her, but what was I to do? I was trying to cope.

"Last night wasn't a full moon," I said with a flat stare.

"I change on the full moon. I can also change whenever I feel like it. It's just that I don't have a choice when the moon is full. It pulls the wolf out of me, whether I want it to or not. Any other time I can shift at will or," she hesitated, "sometimes I can't help it."

I stared at her as she went on, unsure of what to say to her or if I should even say anything. When I realized she wasn't going to continue I let out a soft sigh.

"Okay, fine. So yesterday you shifted, and this morning you shifted back. On my floor," I remembered the rag around her arm, just like the one I had used on the wolf's injured leg.

"Let me see your arm."

Liz sighed and held it out but hid her face in her shoulder. I tentatively reached for the soiled cloth. The blood was dry, the cloth brittle. My fingers worked the knot clumsily, afraid of what I might uncover. When the ends of the rag were finally freed, I quickly unwrapped her forearm.

I don't know what I expected to see. For a minute, when my guard was lowered, I thought I was going to find the bite marks I had seen last night, but that's not what I saw. The skin was tinged red, and was damp. Indentions from the rag were a purplish color, giving her skin a weird ripple effect, but other than that the skin was unmarred and flawless. It was whole. Not even a scratch.

I released that apprehensive breath that stuck in my chest and dropped her arm suddenly, pushing it away from me.

"I could have told you. I heal when I shift back..."

"Oh, of course," I gave an exasperated laugh. "How convenient."

"Well, if you want to know the truth, it is. It is pretty damn convenient. You know what would be inconvenient? Bleeding to death," she snapped.

My eyes met hers, and it was like two stubborn forces slamming into one another. Part of me wanted to tell her to get out and just leave me alone. I was through with games—had been since Frank—and all this was doing was making me more and more angry with each passing moment. The rest of me wanted to hold her hand and tell her everything was okay. I didn't understand that. I was the wronged party here. So, why did I feel the overwhelming urge to take care of her?

"Are you hungry?" I found myself asking without thinking.

She blinked up at me in complete bewilderment, "What?"

"Food. Werewolves still eat, right?" The word formed a knot in my throat. "I mean I'm not about to find you some roadkill or anything but..." I trailed off, realizing how mean I was being. If I needed further proof of that, looking at her hurt eyes drove the truth home. "I don't know how to react to this right now, Liz. I just don't."

She used her fingers to comb her hair up into a ponytail and grabbed a hair tie off of my dresser, her face tight and eyes distant. The tension in the room was heavy, a pressing weight on my shoulders threatening to crush me if I didn't do or say something, but I couldn't. I didn't want this conversation to continue.

"Okay," she said finally. "Let's just get some food."

I tried to force myself to smile at her but barely managed. With a quick nod, I went and changed into a pair of shorts and a tank top, slipped on my own flip flops, tossed her a spare pair, and grabbed my purse. Maybe after we got some food in our stomachs I would be able to wrap my head around this.

Though, something told me things weren't ever going to be normal again.

Breakfast was awkward. Neither one of us talked about that morning's events, but then again, neither of us said a word to one another aside from asking to pass the Sweet N' Low. So many questions built inside me, but I refused to re-ring that bell. Not yet.

We ate in deafening silence, barely looking at each other, before I took my leave. I had classes all day and I was back on stage later at work. It would all just have to wait. Maybe if I took a little time to myself, I could figure out what to do.

I wanted to go back to thinking I'd been crazy this whole time, and what I had witnessed a year before was a mental breakdown of some sort. I wanted to laugh and smile at my best friend and mean it. Most importantly, I wanted to know why this had caught up to me again. I needed to know if she had sought me out or if it was an unlucky coincidence.

I paid both of our bills while Liz was finishing her food and left. I don't think I had ever left her without saying goodbye, but I couldn't talk to her right now. Maybe, by the time work came around, I'd be ready to delve deeper into this. Could I ever be truly ready?

Chapter 19

July 4th 2011 9:45 p.m.

Fourth of July at a strip club could get interesting. There were lots of patriotic costumes, red, white, and blue sequins, pyrotechnics, and more than a few sparklers. One of our newer, more ambitious dancers had petitioned our boss to do an act that made me cringe in pain just thinking about it.

Not only would shooting off a roman candle be against fire codes, but the way she wanted to hold the giant fire-stick would probably haunt me every Independence Day from now until the day I died. Some things just were not meant to be seen.

Tonight's music selection ranged from "American Woman" to "Cherry Pie" to—gag me—"Firework" from Katy Perry.

Yes, Andre knew how to milk the holidays for all they were worth. To me, it was predictable and cheesy, but I wasn't the one in charge so there was little I could do about it. I simply followed the Independence Day spirit in my own little way.

I rebelled by gothing-out with black latex, spikes, and heavy liner and dancing to "Blood" from In This Moment. Andre had grouched about it, but eventually gave up. He had twenty other girls to be his little dolls. I was a lost cause.

Unlike the playful music the other girls danced to, this was raw and angry. Maria Brink's growling voice unlocked that box I'd carefully tucked my anger into. Everything from the shitty way I'd allowed myself to be treated in the past to the feeling of betrayal from my best friend got shoved in there and locked away until I let myself get lost in the dancing. For a few hours, I let it all spill out through my body in a sweet release of endorphins and sexuality.

Once my set was done, and my tips cleared from the stage, I ducked into the back and changed into my floor outfit. I had a few different ensembles I used when I walked the floor during the other girls' sets. It was pretty common to see a girl in two or three outfits each night. Kept things fresh and fun, I suppose.

I slid into a pair of black pinstripe shorts that fit like a second skin and were scandalously short. Bend over too far in them and a guy could almost see my ovaries. A black lace bra fit snug against my chest, helping to push up that supple bit of cleavage. A matching fedora and suspenders that hugged my curves finished the look, and I was ready to make my way to the main floor.

First a drink at the bar, and then a walk through the club, looking for anyone wanting a dance or even just a little flirty conversation. Tonight was already pretty good as far as tips went. Anything else was just icing.

I slid over to the bar, smiling and flirting my way through the crowd, and hit the bartender up for a shot of whiskey. When I looked ahead of me, I found that Liz was there waiting for me, drink in hand.

"That was a refreshing change," she said as she sipped on whatever fruity cocktail she was trying out tonight. I had to love her for braving the tension between us right now.

"Thanks," I said awkwardly.

I wanted to just forget about everything that happened that morning, wanted things to be like they were before all the crazy. I wanted that easy friendship back. "I thought I'd break the whole 'Born on the Fourth of July' trend."

"Well, it worked," Liz laughed. "That was a pretty... harsh song."

"Not if you really listen to it."

"How so?" she asked. "She's basically asking her guy to be a jerk to her."

"That's not how I hear it. To me, she's saying she hates all the good things he does because it's what makes her love him even when he's really just a bad guy."

"Hmm," Liz said as if she really didn't get it. "So why thank him for the toxic shit, then?"

"Because, that's what finally gives her the courage to break away from him," I said, my smile long gone.

I sat and thought about that for a moment. That song really did strike a chord with me. I hadn't thought about it much before, but it was exactly how I felt about Frank. He'd made me fall in love with him then hurt me. Over and over again. It wasn't until he finally showed me the real monster he was that I was able to leave him. I just couldn't pretend to not notice everything he did after that.

Liz gave a slow, considering nod before sliding an appletini in my direction. It wasn't exactly my favorite drink, but I decided to humor her. Who was I to turn down, what I assumed was, a peace offering?

"So, about this morn—" I started, ready to apologize.

"Harley!" A man's voice cut me off. I turned on the stool and found Andre moving through the crowd towards me, a suspiciously happy smile stretched over his face. "Hey, doll. You have an admirer."

My eyebrow arched, but the open skepticism didn't seem to derail the cheeriness of my boss. He looked like he was picking canary feathers out of his teeth.

"A young gentleman just paid a pretty penny for a private dance. He requested you."

"A private dance? Andre, you know that's not really my—"

"Harley, it's a done deal. He wants you and he paid a vulgar amount of money for a half hour of your attention. I don't ask you to do this often—hell, ever—but business is business. Just be a good girl and give him a dance and a show then collect your tip and get out. Thirty minutes. Hardly seems worth arguing about."

Andre's tone was gentle yet authoritative. There would be no backing out of it. The customer already paid, and I was who he paid for. Andre even held a valid argument. He rarely asked me to do VIP dances. Every other girl here would get six or seven VIP's a week, at least, and most of them were more than happy to reap the benefit of a larger purse.

I stared at him, letting him know from my expression that this was only as a favor to him. Sometimes I just knew I was being stupid and difficult. What did I expect? I wanted easy, fast money, didn't I?

With an apologetic look at Liz, I downed the rest of my appletini and set the glass down on the bar.

"We'll talk later," I told her. The guilt for the way I talked to her was beginning to eat away at me.

"Get that money!" I heard enthusiastically from the bar as I made my way to the room.

I stepped into the VIP room, pulled the door closed behind me, and tugged softly on the string that held the red curtain open, letting it fall over the window. The mystery of what went on behind closed doors was part of the appeal. People paid the big money to explore the darker, more exclusive, side of the club.

The interior of the room upheld that promise. Red backlighting ran the entire space of the room, bouncing onto the crimson walls from a small black rail that ran the length of each wall, breaking only for the space of the door. Though the coloring of each private room was different, each one had an overstuffed loveseat, upholstered in soft velvet, and a small circular stage with a pole in the center. The floor of the stage was also lit with a red light. The only break in the color scheme was the white light that hung over the loveseat, pointing at the stage to give the customer a good view of their dancer.

A pair of legs stuck out from the shadows of the couch, covered in faded denim jeans. I gave the shadows my best flirtatious smile and walked towards a small table in the corner of the room.

"Hey handsome"

I made my voice purr in that throat way that guys—for whatever reason—seemed to expect when things got hot. What girl actually talks like that during sex? And what causes guys to think they do, if not porn?

Talking to the customers wasn't my strong suit. I'd rather just dance and pretend they weren't real people with real thoughts. I grabbed the small, credit card-sized remote to the stereo and pushed the power button.

"Just sit back and relax. I'll take good care of you." Oy, what cheesy bullshit. Men really get off on this stuff?

The stereo played a low, heady beat that was commonplace in strip clubs. It was too cliché for my taste, but then again, the men weren't drawn here for the music. I tossed the remote back onto the table and prowled towards the small stage, putting on a show for my customer.

"So, what do you like?" I asked as I grabbed the pole and pulled myself onto the stage slowly, pressing the front of my body against the cold metal.

"Actually," he said, the timbre of his voice making the hairs on my arms stand on end.

He pulled his feet out of the light and leaned forward, letting the soft white light spill over his face. Ice shot through my veins, my hand tightening around the pole.

"You should know exactly what I like." The grin that spread across his face was cold and dangerous. "Hiya, Harls."

"Frank," I managed to force out on a shaky breath.

I was frozen, staring at him like a deer caught in headlights. Eleven months I'd been free of him, and he still managed to grip me with fear as strongly as the day I left. Just saying his name aloud made my blood turn to shards of ice, cutting me up from the inside.

Frank apparently found triumph in catching me off guard. His lips curled with a self-satisfied grin as he drank in my reaction.

"Blonde, huh?" he said finally as he straightened up in his seat, pulling on the collar of his jacket. "Have to say, the darker hair was better, but I guess I could get used to it."

The idea of him being around long enough to get used to anything made me squirm.

"What the hell do you want, Frank?" I finally managed to say, though my voice seemed less confident than I had tried to make it.

Frank simply continued to smile at me, his ruggedly handsome face full of mirth and something much darker. If I didn't know better, I'd say he was absolutely giddy that we were in the same room again. He rubbed a hand over the back of his head, which was covered by a black bandana.

"What do I want?" he repeated, dropping the hand to hang between his legs. "Well, I want what I paid for. A dance."

Alarm bells rang out in my head. I needed to get out of there. Get as far away from him as I could manage. I wished Jackson had been working so I could run to him and tell him that I was in trouble, but he was still home recovering.

I'd seen this man crush a skull like a pop can. I wasn't sure any of the other bouncers were big enough, or strong enough, to take him down. All I knew was the longer I stayed there the more he was going to get into my head and that never ended well for me.

"Go to hell." I finally managed to peel my white-knuckled grip from the pole and step down off the stage. "Find somebody else to dance for you."

I turned and stepped towards the door, ready to make a run for it. Maybe I could withdraw all my cash and get my things out of my apartment before he caught up with me.

"Well that's fair, I guess," he said the moment I gripped the doorknob. "Wouldn't wanna cause problems. I'll just ask for that pretty little blond you were talking to at the bar."

My spine went stiff, and I stopped, my eyes peering through the cracked door and falling on Liz. She was laughing with the bartender. Carefree and completely unaware of the danger she was in because of me. He knew he had my attention.

"She's cute. Small. Doesn't look like she'd give me too hard a time. Tell me, Harls... She a good friend of yours?"

It sounded so innocent. Just small talk from anyone else, but coming from Frank, I understood the underlying threat that question held. I stared at Liz for a moment, my jaw clenched. Even though I'd been angry with her this morning I couldn't let him hurt her. She hadn't been spying on me for him because he was trying to use her as leverage against me. I closed my eyes as his question loomed in my head. He had watched us, and he was using it to his advantage.

"Fuck!" I growled, pounding the side of my fist into the wall just inside the room. I took a step back and slammed the door behind me, rattling the decor hanging on the wall.

"One fucking dance," I said through clenched teeth. "Then you get the hell out of my life."

I walked back to the stage and Frank's awaiting grin. I'd have loved nothing more than to slap the smugness right off his face, but that would only make things worse. I wanted to get him out of there not give him a reason to continue to fuck with me.

"Of course," he said.

Frank relaxed into the couch as I stepped back on the stage. I hadn't had this much trouble getting my head into dancing since my first night. It was hard to be sexy when I wanted to run away screaming. I tried to keep my breathing even as I wrapped my fingers around the pole and slowly began to walk around it. I closed my eyes and let the sound of the music fill my head, anything to push the thought of the man watching me from my mind, but I still found myself having to force one foot in front of the other.

"No," his voice cut through the music, stopping me before I even got started.

I looked past the pole to him, waiting for him to explain why he stopped me. He shifted in his seat again, leaning forward.

"I don't want a damn robot dancing for me. Dance like you did on stage earlier. Seduce me."

I stared coldly at him, wondering now just how long he had been watching me. An hour? All week? Or had it been longer? Had he let me believe I had actually gotten away from him? I stepped in front of the pole and started to close my eyes again when he made a disapproving sound, stopping me once more.

"Look at me." The teasing was gone and now his voice held a more serious tone.

It was lower, commanding, and held just a hint of that dark desire that was pure carnal instinct. It was the tone he used when he wanted me to do exactly as he instructed. To please him.

I bit back a few words that I wanted to throw at him. Fine. He wanted me to dance for him? I would give him a dance like any other faceless Schmoe and get the fuck up out of there. I pushed against that last shred of iron will I had and forced myself to do what needed to be done.

My hips began to sway slowly, and I locked eyes with him. A deep, penetrating stare in which I pushed every bit of cold, seething loathing I could muster. I wanted him to feel the burning hatred I held for him. My body moved, drinking in the music.

His face looked unmoved.

"You look like you're having trouble getting in the moment," he said. "Need a hand?"

The curl of his lips told me that would be the last thing I wanted. I needed to get a grip on myself if I wanted him out of here faster. I tried to shift my focus on the parts of him that didn't make me want to put an entire country between us, and concentrated on the physical. The more I managed to do that, the easier it got to turn on the sex appeal.

Rough, rugged, and oozing masculinity from every pore, there was a time when that man would drive me absolutely wild. I thought about his broad back and shoulders, the way his body tapered into narrow hips, the rock-hard biceps under smooth tan skin decorated with beautiful ink. I recalled the taste of that skin. The earthy, salty flavor of him when I'd nibble the underside of his jaw. The way his day's growth of beard scratched over my tongue and lips.

A little more inhibition slipped away, and I rolled my body against the steel pole, bringing a knee up, eyes still fixed on him. I twirled once around the pole before stepping down in front of Frank, going to a knee and dropping down into a languorous crawl. That simple movement made him shift in his seat again, and his body made it very clear he was finally enjoying it.

Reaching his feet, I pressed my hands to his shins, sat back on my legs, and slid my hands slowly up to his knees. I grabbed his knees and pushed them apart, so I could slide my body between them. He let out a restrained breath and my hands explored his legs and thighs, working him up like any other man who walked into the club.

I knew he was much more than that. In the years we'd been together, there had been no shortage of heat and passion. We couldn't keep our hands off one another, and I let the memories of those distant days fuel the dance.

He felt just as I'd remembered. Solid. Strong. I let my fingers play over every inch of rock-hard muscle through his jeans and t-shirt, remembering days when even the thinnest cloth was too much barrier between our bodies.

The more I stepped into my memories, the easier it was to be the temptress I was being paid to be. I walked a fine and dangerous line. Where it helped me get in the right frame of mind to get this over with, it also brought me dangerously close to the feelings I had once held for him. Feelings I stuffed into that psychological back pocket to keep from running back to into the bitch seat. I needed to take care not to step over that quickly-thinning line of control.

I pushed myself up to my feet, sliding the front of my body over the front of his. The feel of his body beneath mine made my stomach clench. He felt like home. The one and only place I had ever felt as though I belonged.

The way his neck and shoulders tensed as I slithered over him showed me that I was giving him exactly what he asked for. I was holding up my end of the deal, and in my own little way, exerting my own type of control over him.

I reached eye level with him and pulled my knees up, sliding them on either side of his hips until I was straddling his lap. I rolled my hips, pressing our lower bodies together until I felt the hard length of him rub me through the thin cloth of my shorts. It made my body shudder, and I had to grab his shoulders to keep from falling backwards.

He made soft, eager sounds as I rolled against him to the sultry rhythm of the music. Using him to keep me balanced I bent back, my spine arching deeply, and continued the provocative hip rolls, mimicking sex as closely as I could with my clothes still on.

I felt a hand slide over my belly, barely touching my skin at first, but as it curved around my side it clung more desperately. My skin drank in the rough, calloused hands that rubbed small, greedy circles on my sides, guiding my body into a fluid rhythm. His skin was always so much warmer than my own and the more he touched me, the more I moved, the hotter his touch grew.

I thought I might melt in his hands.

Before I could stop it, my excitement rang out in a throaty groan, and Frank reciprocated with a whispered grunt of his own. He must have taken it as consent because he sat forward, grabbing me at my ribs, and pulled me towards him. His face pressed against the soft mounds of flesh peeking out over my bra and tugged at them with lips and teeth. His hands slid around my back and up my spine, his fingers tangling into my hair.

He growled into my chest with a gentle tug on my hair, "Come home. You belong with me." Though his voice was muffled against my body, the mix of desperation and triumph rang clear in my ears.

Just as I was riding along that dangerous edge, my eyes flew open. My body stilled under his hands as his words replayed over in my head. I stared down at the top of Frank's head, his face still buried in the softness of my breasts, lost in his desires.

Come home? Controlled and pushed around by a ruthless, sadistic criminal? I'd lived that life for so long that it all seemed perfectly normal. Get up in the morning, play a con to get a little bit of gas money, and head out to a new town by dusk. Did I belong with Frank and his pack? The thought of the others, of the wolves, helped to push me back into my head and clear the haze of desire.

Pressing both hands on either side of his shoulders I pushed away from Frank's hungry lips, sliding my feet back down to the floor. With a measurable step backwards, I stared coldly into his unfocused eyes and let all that burning desire frost over once again.

"Belong with you? Don't you mean to you?"

I pulled my bra strap back over my shoulder and took another step away as Frank sat back, running his fingers across his lower lip as though he was trying to wipe the feel of my skin from it. He looked just as lost as I had felt moments ago curled up on his lap. Perhaps it ran both ways. Or maybe Frank was just another horny asshole, and any girl would have made his head spin.

"Get out of my fucking life, Frank. Stay away from me or I'll tell the police everything."

With the threat shaking on my voice, I turned and all but ran to the door. As my fingertips grazed the doorknob, the air around me stirred, and I was suddenly pushed into the door, a solid weight pressing against my back. My cheek crushed against the soft curtain that covered the window and hid what was happening in the small room from the public eye. His arms encircled me, trapping me in that one small space between him and the door.

"You'll tell the police, huh?" Fingertips pressed against the side of my face as he spoke, his voice a low, threatening rumble. "And what exactly will you tell them, Harls? That you watched men turn into wolves? Or that we killed people while you watched and did nothing to stop it?"

"Please," I managed to whisper through the pulse in my throat.

His fingers slid up the side of my face into my hair and pressed my head harder into the door.

"See, I don't think they'd believe you." His breath was hot on my cheek now, his lips so very close. "And if they did... well eleven months is an awfully long time to confess to murder."

"I didn't kill them."

"No, but you were an accessory. You could've went to the cops when you got back to town, but you didn't. You helped us get away with murder."

I forced my eyes open, but I saw nothing but his shadow. If he was trying to intimidate me, he was doing a damn good job of it. Still, I'd seen this show. I swallowed hard, still trying to come out on top of his threats with a little more strength than I had shown him before.

"You can't scare me anymore, Frank." I almost believed it.

A bone-chilling laugh erupted in my ear.

"Is that so?" Frank closed what little distance was left between us and breathed in deeply, his nose buried in my hair. After a few silent moments of him smelling me, he pressed his lips to my ear and whispered, "You sure smell scared. It's intoxicating."

He grabbed me by the shoulders and spun me around to face him making my stomach lurch. Fear held my voice captive as I stared into his eyes. An amber glow flickered behind his irises, like fire behind a stained-glass window.

"Let me tell you how it's gonna go down. You'll go tell the pigs about what happened. I'll get arrested, taken in for questioning, and then they'll ask me who else was involved. You with me so far?" His eyes bore into me, searching for my tell. Something that would let him know he had me where he wanted.

His thumbs rubbed my collarbone as he continued, "See, I've been around the block with cops, babe. They're gonna want names. So, being the helpful guy I am, I'll tell them everything. How you went along with me and my guys to a drug deal, how you didn't even try to stop me and just watched as I killed some poor bastard, and how you helped me cover it up. Then BAM!" He clapped his hands centimeters from my nose, making me jump. "They'll slap a pair of bracelets on you, too, and drag you off to prison just like the rest of us. By the time you get out, you'll be good and ready for some of me."

My eyes met his again; full of the cold hatred I'd built up over the last year. I wasn't surprised he would spin a yarn like that. Embellishment was just another talent in Frank Essex's bag of tricks. Even though I was completely innocent in what happened that night, he'd twist it into some ugly tale of aiding and abetting.

My lips curled back, exposing my teeth. "You are un-believable."

A smile stretched over his face but there was nothing friendly about it. "Thanks. I am pretty badass, aren't I?"

His hands slid over my neck and up my cheeks, brushing a hair from my forehead and holding me so that I had no choice but to stare into his handsome, smug face.

"That's option A. Option B... You forget about this little lie you've made for yourself and come back with me. Where. You. Belong."

Each word he spoke was a breath closer to my lips, raspy with growing desire, and before I could take in a full breath his lips were crushing against mine.

He didn't kiss me so much as feed at my mouth, his tongue sliding between my lips and filling it. I cried out around his tongue, trying to pull away, but his hands gripped the sides of my head, holding me still so he could ravish my mouth fully. Frank's desire poured into me and I found myself caught between wanting to kiss him back and wanting to bite his tongue off.

If one good thing could be said for Frank, it was that he was an amazing kisser. There were times when I felt starved for the taste of his lips. One kiss could make me forget everything I had been worrying about and leave me in a state of bliss for hours. But that was before. All I wanted now was to escape his hungry kiss before I said yes to option B.

It was harder than it should have been. His hands roamed all over me, exploring places that hadn't been touched in a long time. The line of his body pressed against mine and I could feel the length of him grow against my hip, pushing just that much harder at the resistance that was already glass-thin.

My body betrayed my mind, reacting to his touch. It ached for him, having missed his attentions for so long. If I hoped to break free of his influence, I would have to do something quick. Something to snap me out of it before it consumed me.

I pushed against his shoulders, breaking the kiss. His eyes were half-lidded and unfocused, drowning in lust and desire. With every ounce of strength I could gather, I pulled my hand back and slapped him sharply across the cheek.

Stunned, Frank stared down at the floor between us, still pinning me to the wall with an arm on each side. He glanced up at me, the silence stretching on for far too long, and then the corner of his mouth turned up into a wicked grin.

"Oh, baby, you do remember what I like," he taunted as he brought a hand to his cheek and rubbed at the pink welt my palm had left behind.

The cat and mouse game was getting old. Beyond the incessant need to make me as miserable as he could, there had to be something else keeping him there. He had to have known I wouldn't go back to him willingly. So why was he still there toying with me? What did he really want?

Tired of the games, I ignored his comment and asked him exactly what I was thinking, "What do you want from me, Frank? The truth."

The humor receded from his eyes a little, and he looked at me as if I'd surprised him. His hesitation cemented my suspicions. There was something else after all, and I had called him out on it. Just a small wrench thrown into his plans, but like always, he recovered quickly. His hands dropped to his sides, allowing me a little more breathing room, and he shrugged his broad shoulders.

"Fine. Down to business it is." He locked eyes with me, and all the humor and playfulness in them was long gone. "You took something of mine when you left. Something very precious to me. Give it back and I'll let you get on with your glamorous little life here."

"I have no idea what you're talking about."

"Oh," he shook a finger at me, taking a step back with his mouth twisted in an annoyed sneer. "See you really shouldn't lie to me, Harls. You took the Beast, remember?

Hopped right up in my seat and drove like a bat out of hell. Probably thought it was pretty funny too, huh? The guys sure thought it was." He stepped back into me until we were nose to nose, his breathing faster. "But let me tell you something... I didn't!"

He screamed the word in my face, making my pulse trip over itself. I prayed that he had been loud enough to catch the attention of someone outside, but as minutes passed and no one came, I let go of that small glimmer of hope. No one was going to come to my rescue. It was too loud out in the main room to hear any of the screaming back and forth. The curtains were drawn down to cloak us from sight. As far as Andre knew, I was giving him a hell of a party and making him more money. No one would come until one of us left the room or the club emptied; whichever came first.

I let my face go slack, sliding into bored indifference. I was growing tired of the meek, helpless girl I used to be, and the new, more confident woman was ready to get this shit over with.

"Aww, what's the matter, baby?" I spit the words out like bitter venom. "The other kids making fun of you now that your girl decided to get off the bitch seat?"

"Harls, I fuckin' run the pack, remember? The last guy that tried to prove something to me is rotting in the dirt. No one is stupid enough to run their mouth at me. No one but you." He brought his hand up to my face, stroking my cheek slowly. I tried to move out of reach but there really wasn't anywhere to go.

"Just give me the bike. Or I'll send some of the guys to get it."

"I'll tell you what. I'll give you the number of the chop shop I sold that piece of shit to. Maybe you can find all the pieces and Humpty Dumpty that shit back together again."

His nostrils flared at the mention of his bike being in pieces. I could see the force it took to control his urge to lash out at me. Anger shifted into mild amusement and the look made me swallow hard.

"Nice," he said. "I almost bought it. Quit fuckin' with me, baby. Just tell me where it's at."

"I already told you. I sold it."

"To who?"

"Hmm. Don't remember," I said.

My heart was racing. I knew what would happen if Frank found the guy I sold his bike to. It didn't matter that he was innocent. Frank would work him up just for touching his property.

He let out a bemused chuckle. "You stupid, stupid girl. God, you really are a stubborn one. But hey, I like that. I really, really do."

One moment I was standing against the door staring at Frank, and the next he grabbed me by my arms and flinging me across the room to topple onto the couch. It rocked back, and my body slid down the soft velvet until my ass was just barely on the edge of the cushion. I grasped the edge of the cushions tight as he approached unbuckling his belt, my eyes trained on his movements.

He slid the buckle from his belt and maneuvered it in his hands. I strained to see it more clearly, and when I did, my racing heart stopped altogether. The buckle was actually a small, silver dagger that fit in his palm. He wrapped his fingers in the loop, poising the tip on top of his knuckles so he could punch the blade into his target. Which, I was assuming, was me.

"We were good together, Harls. Given just a little more time, we would have been unstoppable. Then you had to go and fuck it all to hell," he said as he leaned into me.

He moved the blade dangerously close to my eye, forcing me to push my head back into the sofa as far as the cushion would allow.

"I didn't fuck anything up. I ran away from a cold, murdering bastard." Probably not the best thing to say with a fucking blade trained on my face.

"You just... you don't get it. Not at all. You didn't even stop to ask why it happened, did you?"

Something glimmered behind his eyes, something softer than I had seen in years. The look he was giving me didn't translate to what was happening right then, and I couldn't read it. As quickly as it had appeared, it was gone.

Whatever I thought I might have seen, Frank realized I'd seen it and the storms returned to his eyes. He lowered the blade in a long, slow line down the center of my chest, the sharp edge tickling over my skin, and stopped just over my sternum.

"Just tell me where my bike is," he repeated.

"I'm not gonna sic you on some innocent guy, Frank. The bike is gone."

"Fine. Just remember, you made me do this," he said as he snatched my left arm and pulled me off the couch, spilling me to the floor in front of him.

All of the fight in me came surging back. The time for talking was over. I kicked and tried to pull free, but Frank seemed unmoved. A flash of white caught my eyes and brought my attention back to the small blade as he pressed it into my forearm. I cried out as he slowly and expertly cut a line across the width of my arm, near the crook of the elbow.

"I don't want to do this, Harley. Just give me the name and this will all be over." He stared down at me, lifting the tip of the blade from my arm.

"No... please!" I cried out as the blood began to well up in the thin cut and spill over my skin in warm streams.

Frank shook his head and pulled my arm to him again, pressing the cold steel back into the skin. No matter how hard I fought against him, he somehow managed to hold my arm perfectly still, absorbing all my wild thrashing with his own body.

He carved two more lines into my flesh until my forearm was adorned with a bloody 'F'. He stared down at his work with a strange mix of emotions on his face, but through the tears that were spilling generously from my eyes, I couldn't make it out. The floor was spattered with droplets of crimson under my arm.

When my throat was too hoarse to scream anymore, I pressed my tear-stained face into Frank's legs, sobbing softly into them. "Costa's... on Phoenix Circle. Please. No more."

Blood streaked down my arm as Frank cradled it to his body. He said nothing. Just an expanse of silence broken only by the sound of my soft, erratic sobbing.

He stared down at the bleeding wound taking in his work. He bent forward and brought his mouth to my arm and licked the blood up in one long, slow motion. It stung and unnerved me for more than one reason. With the taste of my blood rich on his tongue, he dropped my arm and wiped the steel on his jeans until it shined.

"Good girl," he whispered as he put his buckle back into place.

I turned a tear-stained face up to him, my good arm reaching up to clutch the bottom of his shirt.

"Don't hurt him. He didn't know it was stolen. Now will you please... just please leave me alone." I pleaded with him, staring up into his eyes, trying to ignore the look on his face.

He turned and lowered himself down to my level and wiped a stream of tears from my cheek. Grabbing the side of my face he leaned forward and pressed his lips to my forehead.

"Pick yourself up Harley. You're better than this," Frank whispered before rising to his feet.

His face was twisted with a look of sad victory. "I'll be in touch. We have a lot of catching up to do."

His dark promise hung in the air as he walked towards the door. He looked back only once as he stepped over the threshold and out of sight.

A woman's scream rang out from the other side of the door, and soon Liz and one of the other bouncers rushed inside to find me in a heap on the ground, blood smeared all over from my arm. I looked up at Liz with exhausted eyes, red-rimmed and swollen from crying.

"What happened out there?" I managed to ask as the bouncer lifted me to my feet.

Liz ran her teeth over her bottom lip as she saw the crimson 'F' carved into my arm. "Shit. He, uh... He sucker punched Andre. Grabbed a wad of money out of his shirt pocket and took off past security. Jesus, Harley, what did that guy do to you?"

For the first time since this morning I didn't think about how Liz had lied to me or how I accused her of spying on me. At that moment, she was the only safety in my world. I let her arms wrap around me, holding me close as the bouncer raised my arm up to slow the bleeding.

I wanted to tell her that he did what he had always done. That he had broken me. That some guy was going to get hurt because I gave Frank what he wanted. But I didn't. I didn't want to see her pity because I didn't deserve it.

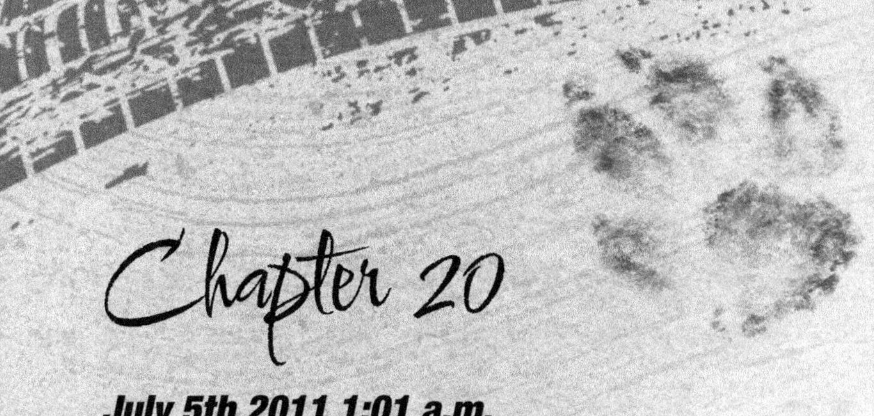

Chapter 20

July 5th 2011 1:01 a.m.

I STARED DOWN AT my dangling feet, zoning out to a place far away from Frank and blood and promised threats. Liz was curled up in the small metal chair beside the gurney, her suede jacket laid over her like a blanket. She'd drifted off long ago. I told her to go home and get some sleep, but God love her, she was too stubborn to leave.

The emergency room was cold, bright, and way too clean to even pretend to be comfortable. I would have been discharged long ago, my wound already cleaned and bandaged, but I had to make a statement to the police, and they were taking their sweet fucking time to get there. The idea of being in a building filled with death and sickness wasn't the only reason I felt uneasy.

I did my best these days to steer clear of law enforcement. While I wasn't exactly a big-name criminal, like Mr. Essex, I had been involved in some things that might lead me back to a very bad place. That paired with the lies Frank had threatened to give the police had my nerves shot.

"Ms. Rayne?" A gentle, strangely familiar, voice inquired before the sound of the door closing brought my eyes up from my feet.

"Yes?"

"Sorry to keep you waiting. I'm here to take your statement about what happened tonight." He was cautious as he spoke to me. Not wanting to spook me, maybe? Too late. I was pretty spooked before he even got here.

"I just want to go home," I said, the exhaustion dragging at my body and echoing in my voice.

"I can understand that. Unfortunately, this is the second time a violent attack like this has occurred at your club in a very short time frame. We're still investigating the assault on Mr. Tate, and anything you might be able to tell us about your own incident might shed some light on our search."

Finally looking at him, I considered him a moment before recognition dawned on me. Shit. It was the detective from Jackson's house. Still investigating the assault, he'd said. I guess that meant they still hadn't found that bastard. I would bet my ass he probably thought Frank was his guy for that one, too.

"Did you know the assailant, Ms. Rayne?" His voice ripped me from my thoughts.

"Huh?" Shit. If I said yes, that might open a door I couldn't close again. "No," I finally answered, perhaps a little too quickly. "I mean I've seen him around before, but I don't, like, know him."

"Has he been to the club before? A customer, maybe?"

"No, I've never seen him in the club until tonight," I answered easily. There. Some truth to camouflage the lie.

"Right. So, he wasn't the same man from before. The one Mr. Tate bounced from the club because of you?"

"Whoa! Hold up. Because of me?"

Like I could have known the guy couldn't take rejection to the point where he'd shoot someone. The victim-blaming completely floored me, yet I should have known better. Whether this guy's misogyny stemmed from my being a woman or my being a stripper, I couldn't say. Truth was, it didn't fucking matter.

"Are you seriously implying because I didn't let some drunken asshole play grab-ass with me that I'm responsible for what he did to Jackson? That it's my fault my friend was shot by some coward who can't handle rejection? I bet I was really just asking for it, right?"

"My apologies, I didn't mean to offend you," he said, though his tone told me professionalism apologizing rather than any form of chivalry. "But isn't playing grab-ass sort of your job out there?"

"Isn't catching criminals sort of your job? Tell me, Detective. Is it good old-fashioned sexism, or do you just have a thing against strippers?"

His eyes darkened, only for a fraction of a second, before he slipped into an unexpected smile. "As I said before, Ms. Rayne, if you answer my questions it might help us catch your friend's attacker. Though, I'm surprised you're more worked up about Mr. Tate's attack than your own."

I opened my mouth, shut it, and took in a deep breath. Counted to ten. Maybe twenty.

"And I'm surprised you're still just a lowly detective with all that charm," I said as sweetly as I could.

I didn't know what I'd done to deserve this attitude. No matter his reasoning, he could go fuck himself.

Liz stirred in the corner, drawing both of our attention. When I looked back over to Det. Sheppard, his face was back to that pleasant and polite blankness. Unreadable cop face. Liz's eyes blinked open and stared curiously at the detective until her neurons snapped back together and brought her back to the here and now.

"So, can you tell me what caused him to attack you? Was he making unwanted advances? Did it happen before or after the dance he paid for?"

I absentmindedly ran the back of my fingers along the white bandage on my arm and replayed the events in my head. I was looking for anything I could tell him without throwing myself into a larger shit-storm. A huge part of me wanted to tell him everything, but Frank had planted enough doubt in my head that I wasn't sure I wouldn't come out of it unscathed.

Hell, if I was smart I would've told him it was the same guy he was looking for with Jackson's case—completely throw him off my scent. Unfortunately, the detective had proven to me seconds before that I couldn't trust him. He would never believe I was innocent in everything. If I couldn't fully believe it, why should he?

"I really don't know. I mean I went in to dance and next thing I know he's all over me, keeping me from leaving the room."

"Did he sexually assault you? Try to get more than what he paid for?"

"No. It wasn't like that." Even as I said it, my lips burned with the memory of his kiss.

"So why did he keep you from leaving? Why not just watch you dance then leave?"

Jeez, he was pushy.

"I wish I knew. Maybe he's just a sick bastard that likes to hurt girls. Maybe he doesn't get enough attention from his wife and is taking it out on disposable women. I can't really say for sure. We really didn't delve into his psyche and analyze memories of his dear old mommy and the screaming lambs."

Again, with that sidelong smile. I wanted to wipe it from his face, but assaulting an officer was probably not the smartest move.

"Harley, he's just trying to find out why this guy attacked you." Liz's sweet, rational voice came from behind me.

I glanced over my shoulder and saw the worry etched across her face. I hadn't told her much of what happened in there, either. The truth was if I wasn't going to share it with Liz, I wasn't going to spill to anyone. Not the full truth anyway. Her soft blue eyes soothed the snark and anger that was trying to climb out of me like a savage beast, and with a sigh, I glanced up to Detective Sheppard once more.

"That's all I really know. This guy seems like a real psycho if you ask me. Serial killer type stuff. I mean who cuts the freaking alphabet into women's bodies? Makes you wonder if there's an A through E out there somewhere." That sounded nice and clueless. God, I wanted to go home.

"Alright. Did he say anything to you that was strange or something that might point us in any direction as to who he is, or maybe his whereabouts?"

"No, he spoke in sonnets and soliloquy as he dug the knife into my arm." Liz touched my shoulder lightly.

Chastising or comforting, I really couldn't tell. Maybe both. Either way, I sighed and dropped my gaze to my hands like a scolded child. "Really, Detective Sheppard, that's all I know. He babbled something, but all I really could concentrate on was how fucking scared I was and how I thought he was going to kill me. So, if you don't mind, I would really like to go home and get some sleep. "

He stared at me a few moments, his face unreadable, but seemed to drop whatever was rolling around in his head. He tucked his pen and small notepad into his inside jacket pocket and nodded.

"Well, I assume you still have my card from before. If there is anything else you would like to share with us, don't hesitate to call. Really, anything you know just might get this scum off the street." He opened the door and stepped halfway out of the room.

Looking back, he glanced at me then looked past me to Liz who was still standing with a hand on my shoulder. "You ladies have a good evening. Be careful out there." And with that, he was gone.

His departure released a breath I hadn't known I was holding the entire time he questioned me. I relaxed more, and I think Liz noticed it, too. With a gentle squeeze on my shoulder, Liz wordlessly walked past me and gathered up our bags and jackets. I stared out of the room, thinking about what the detective had insinuated before.

Was this all my fault? This and Jackson's incident? I hadn't really considered it before. If I hadn't been so abrasive with that guy maybe he would have eventually just left me alone. Then Jackson wouldn't have been stuck outside with an angry, armed drunk.

I just couldn't forget the look of panic in his eyes when he really got a good look at me. His sudden determination for me to leave the club with him, like his entire world depended on me following him wherever it was he wanted me to go.

And then I remembered something. The tiniest detail, but it was there.

The three thin scars, about two inches in length, stacked on the side of his neck. I don't know why it hadn't clicked before. Maybe the heat of the moment had clouded my judgment, or maybe I was getting too relaxed, too comfortable in this new life I made.

I had seen it so many times back when I ran with the Hellhounds. A handful of the men in his pack, Frank included, all had the same brand on their necks. Some sort of club thing, I'd assumed, like wearing colors or patches. A man I had never seen before knew who I was. He was the reason Frank knew where to find me.

The two incidents were connected, and both were my fault. The scuffle in the club, Jackson being shot, Andre's broken nose... It really was all because of me.

Chapter 21

WHILE I DIDN'T QUITE like being forced to take a few personal days before returning to work, I was grateful that Andre hadn't fired me over this mess.

After the cop pointed out that I'd been in the middle of both incidents, I thought my boss might also have this revelation. Though neither of them had the insight I had on just how connected they were, it was a short jump from victim to liability.

I had no idea what to do with myself for three whole days. I didn't really have a lot to clean because, living alone, there just isn't a lot of mess accumulated. At least not for me. I would have classes, but that would be no different from any other day. It was after classes were over that I found myself idle and clueless.

I sat at my computer desk, chin resting on my palm, and perused the internet for a while waiting for inspiration to strike me. All I found were seven friends announcing what they were having for dinner on Facebook and a spam email telling me, in rather large and rude shouty capitals, that I no longer had to suffer from Erectile Dysfunction.

Oh yes, a day well spent.

Switching off the computer, I leaned back in my chair and let loose a long-disgruntled sigh. I was completely and brain-numbingly bored. Some might think, because of my line of work, I had a ton of friends and parties to go to. That I was a creature of the night and there was never a dull moment for me. Well, obviously, they would be wrong. I was not my chosen profession. Stripping, or burlesque dancing, was not a way of life for me like it was for many of the girls I worked with. It was a job to put food in my house and to pay rent. That's all.

I didn't rock and roll all night and sleep all day. I was up at seven in the morning and going to classes at the local college until about four or five in the evening. I took a brief nap or studied until about eight, and then got ready for work so I could be there by ten and normally didn't get home until three in the morning only to start it over again. There was no time for parties or a girl's night out. There was just the unchanging routine of my life. To be honest, it was a godsend after a nomadic life of uncertainty.

Many people have asked me why I chose stripping. Wouldn't it just be easier to get a "legitimate" job at a fast food place or a call center? To them, my life would have been easier and more manageable than hardly sleeping and staying out all hours of the night.

My response to them was usually one of two things: One, there was nothing illegitimate about my line of work. I didn't get paid under the table and I paid my taxes like I was supposed to. I offered a service and received compensation just like any other person.

Two—and this is the big one—I liked dancing. It not only paid my bills faster than any minimum wage or entry level job could offer, but I actually enjoyed it. I refused to apologize for the high I felt when I knew I was playing to the fantasies of others, be they men or women.

When I was on stage, I became a living fantasy and god damn if I didn't love the idea of that. Call me a whore, call me easy, but the people who spewed that kind of venom were only spouting their own insecurities, not mine. To me, stripping was the best thing for me until it wasn't anymore.

However, without a night at work to look forward to, I came to understand that my life was little else than studying and stripping and that was a bit unsettling.

I glanced at the phone sitting on my computer desk and debated on calling Liz. Normally, I wouldn't think twice about calling her to chat it up, but after the other morning, I was still trying to think of what to say to her. How much longer could we go on like nothing happened? Eventually one of us would crack, and we'd have to deal with this. Better to be sooner than later, I guess.

My hand reached over slowly, my fingers touching the hard plastic case then pulling back. I couldn't do it. Not now. Besides, she was more than likely at the club working. I placed my hand back into my lap, but as soon as I did the sharp chirp of my phone erupted, and I lunged toward it.

"Hello?" My God, I felt like a ravenous cat pouncing on a mouse.

"...Harley?"

It was Liz. I recognized her voice instantly but it sounded unsure, careful.

"Hey, Liz. I thought you were working tonight."

"No, I'm off. I asked Andre for it actually. I really feel like we need to talk."

There it was; exactly what I was trying to avoid. I could feel it in her voice. She didn't want to just talk about this week's episode of Vampire Diaries.

"Oh," I said, because I really didn't know what else to say to that. "Okay. We can go to the deli on Forest if you want."

"No, I'd rather... This is something I want to keep private if you get my meaning. Can I come over to your house?"

I really didn't want her to. I wanted to meet in public where she would be less apt to bring up werewolves and all that nonsense again.

"My house is a real mess. We can—"

"Please."

That single word stopped me. There was so much hope, so much desperation, in that one word that I was hopeless to fight against it. "Sure, come on over," I said in defeat.

"See you soon," she said and hung up before I could say good-bye. Well, I had wanted something to do tonight other than sit alone doing nothing. Careful what you wish for, I guess.

We sat at my small kitchen table drinking coffee. The silence was louder than any harsh words could hope to be. I hated feeling this way about Liz. She had always been a good friend to me, was always there to lend an ear or help me with school when I wasn't getting it. She even trusted me enough to come out to me. But obviously it hadn't been the only secret she'd kept.

At first glance it would be hard to tell if we even noticed one another. We simply sat, drinking our coffee, until Liz broke the dam of silence.

"Are we ever going to get this elephant out of the room?"

Her voice pulled me from my in-depth examination of my coffee cup. She wasn't looking at me. "You mean the big, furry elephant that likes to play during the full moon?" It came out much more aggressive than I intended.

Liz flinched as if my words were as sharp and biting as a whip. "Yeah... That one."

Another few moments of dragging silence stretched on.

"Liz," I said finally, because this awkwardness was seriously starting to wear me down. I had no clue what I was going to say, but thankfully I never had to get that far before Liz spoke up.

"Look, Harley, I know how bad it sounds. I know there is no reason on this God-given Earth that you should just believe me. But I wish you would." She looked back down to her coffee and took a slow drink. When she set her cup back on the table, she finally locked her blue eyes on mine, seizing my attention. "Because I am a werewolf. Straight from the story books, but so much more real. No amount of logic will explain it; no amount of disbelieving will make it not true. You should have never found out. I made a mistake by letting it happen, but I'm also still me. I'm still the girl who will set you up on blind dates against your will and who will protect you because you do it for me all the time. I'm still your friend."

I stayed quiet because she was spilling her side of the story, and I really did want to understand her. I wanted to accept her, wanted to pretend she wasn't the same kind of monster as Frank.

As far as Liz knew, it was the fact that werewolves were real, and that my best friend was one, that I was having trouble coping with. I'd never shared with her anything from my past. I'd never told her about Frank and what he showed me. About what he'd done. Jesus, I really was a terrible friend. I still couldn't tell her, so I gave her the chance to let it all out. At least one of us should feel the weight lifted from our shoulders. I could give her that.

"Show me," I said finally.

Her shoulders tensed, the muscles in her jaw clenching tight. "No," she said softly.

"Why not?"

"No, Harley," and this time her voice was more commanding.

I waited a few moments, thumbing over the rim of my coffee cup.

"If you want me to believe you, then you need to get over yourself and fucking show me. I mean, what you're asking me to believe is... it's insane."

She looked away from me then, her eyes dropping down to her hands as they lay on my kitchen table. She seemed to visibly struggle with herself over this.

"Fine," she grumbled under her breath and I felt my own muscles stiffen. She stood to her feet, taking a step away from the table and began unbuttoning her dress.

"Whoa," I said, holding up a hand. "Why are we getting naked now?"

Liz sighed, rolling her eyes at me like I was being a silly child and simply continued to undress.

"I like this dress too much to ruin it. Sorry, you're just going to have to deal with it."

I didn't look at her as she folded the dress and set it on my table. I would've just tried to maintain eye contact, but since she was refusing to look me in the eye that made it difficult.

"Just remember, you're the one who asked for this. Please don't freak out on me."

Truth was I needed to see it. Though I'd had it happen around me I'd never actually watched the whole transformation take place. I needed to see it to understand it. Or at least to try to.

I started to feel something prickling in the air. Something familiar that settled in my stomach like a lead weight. An electrical charge filled the air—the same as the night Frank had revealed the pack to me—and searched the room for something to grasp onto. It was as if the air itself was alive and sentient. I fought past the suffocating energy that fought to push past my lips and pour down my throat, trying to focus on the small blond woman in front of me. Only there was no more woman.

The thin frame of my friend filled out before my eyes, each lean muscle in her arms and legs appeared to grow and thicken. Her legs seemed wrong. They were twisted slightly at the calf in a very inhuman way. Even her back and neck were stretched longer than normal, and her shoulders hunched forward.

Her eyes were still very blue and very human, and they bore into me with an overwhelming sense of despair. She hadn't wanted me to see her like this. She'd said that before, but this wasn't the wolf I had seen before. The muscles around her eyes strained, and I knew she wasn't done.

A shrill howl of pain erupted from her throat, almost a scream, and she thrashed in on herself. Whatever was happening to her, she was fighting it tooth and nail to the very end. I didn't remember this part with Frank's pack.

My skin went cold. That strange energy seemed to suck all the heat out of my body and pull it toward her.

I watched as, before my eyes, Liz shifted from the girl I knew to the wolf that rescued me the other night. The wolf stared up at me, a sad sideways glance of uncertainty, and didn't move. We both just stood still, staring at one another, too afraid to spook the other.

They were real. Werewolves were fucking real. Not an illusion, not a hallucination, not a metal break of any kind. And my best friend was one. Holy shit.

I had no idea what to do. Should I scream? Should I be afraid? Afraid of Liz? Of course, this wasn't Liz in front of me. Or was it?

"Oh my God," I finally whispered, the only sentence my mind could piece together. As soon as I was able to say that, the neurons in my brain began to spark to life again, and I could feel my pulse speed up, my hands shake, my eyes stretch impossibly wide.

"Oh my God!" I shouted this time, taking a step back only to catch my knees on my chair dropping me onto the seat.

I clutched the back of the chair to keep from falling but my eyes never left the wolf in front of me. Her head lowered, and she slowly sunk her large graceful body to the floor, resting her snout between her paws. She stared up at me, and I swear I saw tears in her eyes.

This was beyond reason, beyond my wildest imagination, and yet, here she was. Everything I had seen, everything I had wished to be nothing more than a bad head trip, was real. Everything. Frank, the pack, Liz... they were all fucking werewolves. That, and everything that came with that unshakable understanding, hit me like a savage punch to my stomach.

"All this time..." I managed in a trembling voice, fighting to stay sitting instead of running out of my apartment. "I trusted you. I fucking trusted you and the entire time you were a... a..."

I couldn't bring myself to say it.

A soft whine sung from her nose, and I couldn't tell if that was in agreement or argument.

I shot up to my feet, but amazingly didn't run for the front door. Instead I ran straight to the cupboard above my sink and grabbed a half-full bottle of whiskey. I tried to pour a shot with trembling hands, nearly spilling it all over the counter.

Not wanting to waste the alcohol I so desperately needed, I decided straight from the bottle was best and tipped it back, swallowing a large, burning gulp. When I turned back around, I wiped my mouth with the back of my hand and looked down at my best friend, who was still whining pathetically in my direction.

One more drink.

Hissing through the burning in my mouth, I moved back to the chair and sat down with the bottle clutched in my hand as if it were my last lifeline.

I brought the bottle back to my lips for my third swallow and felt that warm current-like energy push at me again, but I was just too mentally spent to fight it. Let it swallow me whole, who fucking cares? I kept my gaze on the bottle in my hands, chugging down two, three swallows before pulling it from my mouth.

"Harley?"

I licked the sweet yet fiery alcohol off my lips, which only fueled my thirst for the entire contents of the bottle. Liz's voice was barely registering past my sudden need for that drink.

"Harley, talk to me. Please," she tried once more.

What did she expect from me? Everything, right down to the laws of nature, had just been proven, in no uncertain terms, to be a big fat lie. Everything I knew about Liz, everything I knew about reality, was shattered. Did she expect me to open my arms in welcome to this realization? To not mourn over whatever truth I'd known? What did she want from me? Talk to her, she'd said. What the hell did she want me to say? I said the only thing I could right then.

"Get out, Liz."

Chapter 22

July 10th 2011 3:45 a.m.

THE NEXT FEW DAYS were a blur, and I wasn't sure if it was partly due to my newfound appreciation for Jim Beam. I hadn't talked to Liz since kicking her out of my apartment, but my phone had been going off non-stop.

Most of the calls were from her. Calls every couple hours starting the morning after she left, voice-mail alerts, and unread texts filled the void left by her absence. I couldn't answer. I couldn't bring myself to talk to her or listen to the many voicemails she'd left. I didn't want to hear what she had to say. Not yet. I thought I'd been ready to accept it and move on, but as it turned out, I still needed time to process this.

Even Jackson tried to call me, and while I was itching to hear how he was doing, I knew the topic of his call would be Liz. He was the Velvet Rope's unofficial mediator. He wanted to see everyone happy. Unfortunately, I wasn't ready to accept what I'd learned about our friend, and I couldn't just tell Jackson why I was so upset.

I could only imagine the explanation Liz was giving everyone for our little spat.

I went back to work, and she was nowhere to be seen. I was able to glean from the other girls that she had called in for the next few days; family problems or something like that. I knew her family lived out of state, not sure where, but I also knew that they didn't get along. Knowing exactly what that was like, I seriously doubted that was what was going on.

I tried to remember when the last full moon had been. Was that why she called off? Maybe it was that time of month for her, a phrase which took on a whole new meaning now. Or maybe she had called off because of me.

It wasn't until I was cashing out that I was able to remember the moon had been just past its first quarter when she'd saved me from that wolf attack. There would still be another week or so before the full moon, which meant Liz either really did go see her family or she really was avoiding me at all costs.

Why did that thought make the tears flow?

"Harley, is everything okay?"

Jackson appeared behind me. I must have been really out of it to not have heard him. A man that large should be heard coming long before I saw him.

I turned in my stool and wrapped my arms around him, as far as they would go, and pressed my face into his chest squeezing tight. I could feel him tense under me, could feel the stiffness in his muscles before my memory snapped back to me.

"Oh my God, Jackson! I'm sorry you're still hurt!" I released him instantly.

He laughed softly and relaxed with my release, shaking his head and making the large hoop earrings lining his earlobe clang against one another.

"I can take it, angel. You don't pack that much of a punch."

He flashed me a wry grin before it vanished again. His large hand moved to my face and knuckles wiped at the wetness on my cheeks.

"You should call her," he said with that mysterious understanding he always managed to have.

I could argue that it wasn't about Liz, but then what else would it be? It had been a hard stressful week, sure, but not having my best friend around to relax with, to cry with... It was unbearable.

I turned away from him, wiping my tears away as I collected my tips for the night and put them into my wallet. I had been the one avoiding her calls for the last two days. So why was I so upset that she skipped work to avoid me?

"I can't. Not yet."

"Harley—"

"It's complicated, Jackson. I know it's cliché as fuck, but it's true. I can't even begin to explain it to you."

His hand rested between my shoulder blades, making me look back at him. He was smiling down at me. "You would be surprised what I can understand, angel. If you would just trust me."

I stared up at his towering form for a few heartbeats, trying to understand what he meant. His face was impassive. Kind as always, but giving nothing away. His words nagged at me for a while, but he simply squeezed my shoulder and moved past me, disappearing behind the bar.

What about this situation could he possibly understand?

There was nothing else said for the rest of the night. Jackson busied himself with his closing tasks, and I finished cleaning up my locker in the back. I bid the rest of the ladies goodnight, leaving them to their after parties and hookups, and made my way outside. It was straight home and to bed for this little cock tease.

The parking lot was pretty bare by the time I left the club. There were a few of the employees' cars in the back lot with mine, Andre's Navigator included, and even an abandoned car in the front lot, which usually meant either it was broken down or the owners were too drunk to drive themselves home. Most likely, it would be gone by tomorrow.

I unlocked my driver side door and threw my oversized bag into the passenger seat. A series of short honks sounded, and I saw a glimpse of one of the other girls' hands waving at me as she left the lot and pulled onto the street. I waved back and ducked into my car, ready to head for a date with my favorite blanket and some mind-numbing television.

I pulled from the space slowly, but something instantly did not feel right. I lightly pressed the brake and stopped mid-turn. The parking lot was empty, eerily so, without a sign of life in sight and still something was nagging me at the back of my mind.

Deciding I was losing my mind, I shifted the car into drive and made for the road, but as I accelerated more and more I felt the back end of my car begin to wobble from side to side. I hit the brakes again, cursing under my breath as my back end protested against the sudden stop.

A flat tire? I had just gotten all four replaced two months ago.

I got out and walked around to the back of the car. The tire on the driver's side was fine, so I moved across the back to check the other side. The tire wasn't just flat, it was shredded. It looked like someone had gone to town on it with a knife, slashing and ripping it over and over.

"Fuck!" I screamed, feeling my blood begin to boil.

Who the hell would do something like this? Even Frank wasn't the type to just slash someone's tires. He was more creative than that.

My foot connected with the fender, putting a small, foot-sized dent into the side and subsequently snapping the heel clean off my shoe. A strangled scream of pure rage and frustration growled from my throat as I hobbled on my uneven shoes and bent over to grab the heel from the pavement.

As I crouched near the back corner of my car a small dark puddle caught my eye. At first, I thought it was motor oil left behind by another car, but this was even thicker than that. Something inside me told me to touch it, to see what it was. In hindsight, my instincts are real jerks.

My hand moved towards the dark liquid, but before I could swipe my fingertips into it another drop dripped down into it. It was coming from my car.

I followed the source of the dripping, my feet shuffling in my crouched position to move around to the back of the car. The dark substance was sliding down the bumper through the seal of the trunk above.

My heart went to my throat, and I stood up, looking down at the trunk. I tried to swallow but couldn't manage. My mouth was dry, my heart beating in a rapid cadence of fear. I moved, slowly, to grasp the handle, and before I could talk myself out of it, I pulled it open.

I jumped at the sea of red. Not the deep crimson of blood but bright and vibrant cloth. My trunk was filled with the strange fabric and it was covering something. I didn't want to lift the cloth, to peek and find out what Pandora's Box was hiding underneath, but my body was on autopilot.

Oh God, Liz. She hadn't been at work. Oh God, no. Please, no.

"Harley, is everything okay?"

Jackson's voice was distant, foggy even, as I lifted the red fabric. My voice strangled in the back of my throat, and I let the fabric drop back down into the trunk. I had uncovered enough. I swooned backward only to fall against something solid... something warm.

Jackson's hands wrapped around the tops of my arms, holding me steady. His breath hitched slightly as I stared at the poor deer, its throat a glistening shredded mess of sinew and blood. I felt my stomach twist and contort with the urge to vomit. Jackson's grip tightened on me as he stared down over my head at the animal bleeding out in my trunk.

"...the fuck?" he said, moments before I hurled forward and lost the entire contents of my stomach to the asphalt.

I stood off to the side of my car, bent at the waist with hands propped on my knees to keep me from falling face first, and waited out the wave of heaves that followed. My stomach clenched threateningly, in rapid succession, trying to force out food that was no longer there. When I thought I might be safe enough to stand up again, the smell would hitch a ride on the light breeze and start it all over again. It was sickly sweet, and I remembered it was the same as in my dream. The smell of blood and carnage.

"Jesus..." Jackson stared down at the mess in my trunk and grabbed at the red cloth, taking a look further under it.

Good for him. Personally, I didn't care to know how much worse it got.

"And you're sure this wasn't here earlier? You didn't smell anything strange when you were coming to work?"

"I think I would remember the smell of a deer rotting in my trunk, Jackson." Choking back the retching blunted the harsh tone of my voice. "Just get rid of it."

"Who the hell would put a dead deer in your trunk?"

My affirmation that it couldn't have been Frank shattered with Jackson's question. Slashing tires? No. Slashing tires so I discovered the gruesome gift in my trunk? Yes, I would have to say that was very Frank, which meant he, or one of his lackeys, had been here while I was working. They had been that close.

Out loud I said, "I don't know. Someone with a sick and disturbed sense of humor?"

I could feel his stare on my back. He wasn't buying it, but he wasn't pressing me for the answer either. I turned and glanced over my shoulder to find him shaking his head, but he dropped it. I moved to the passenger side and opened the door to dig some mints out of my bag, hoping to mask the residual taste of vomit.

As I dug in the hopelessly large bag, I felt the car lift slightly on its frame and knew Jackson had lifted the animal out of the car. I decided to stay right there, hunkered inside the Toyota, until he managed to drop the deer off in the surrounding wooded area.

I didn't think I could bear seeing the mutilated carcass again. It reminded me too much of the dream I had a while back. Its throat was torn out, its stomach eviscerated, just like mine had been in the nightmare. Maybe I was projecting, but I did not want to look at it again.

After about ten minutes, I heard Jackson's shit-kickers approaching again. I felt bad that the poor thing had to be dumped so uncaringly in the woods, but it was its natural habitat, and I needed it as far away from me as possible.

"Harley, check this out."

I almost told him no. Hell no. I did not want to see any more. Instead I bravely peeked my head out of the open passenger door and looked down the length of the car to find Jackson carrying the red cloth the deer had been wrapped in.

"Oh God, Jackson! Why didn't you just leave it on that thing? It's all covered in blood and gore and... Bambi bits."

"Just look at it, girl. Damn."

I groaned but did as I was told. He held the cloth up at its full length, just at his sternum, and used one hand to lift the top up. What he held was not just some cut of fabric, as

I thought, but a cloak. An honest to God red winter cloak complete with hood. It looked like something Little Red Riding Hood would wear. My throat suddenly went dry.

"Why the fuck would they wrap it in this?" he asked, his steely eyes staring at me and swimming with as much confusion as I felt.

I stared at the cloak as it hung from his hands, my veins icing over from the fear creeping over me. There was something else about it. Something off about the way the fabric looked in the center of the back. I stood up and turned my body towards it, letting the light from the street hit it at another angle.

There was a pattern to it, something that stood out with straighter lines beside the smudges and dampness of the blood. As my eyes followed those unnatural lines of blood I felt my heart nearly stop.

"Get rid of it," I snapped, slamming the passenger side door.

"Well that's a no brainer, but we need to—"

"Get rid of it, Jackson!" I made my way around the front of my car, my keys gripped in my palm, "Throw it in the dumpster, the woods. Burn it. I don't care but get rid of it."

I opened my door and turned on the car. I gave only a glance in my rearview mirror as I tore out of the parking lot. Jackson held the red cloak in his hands, and I drove until I could no longer see the heart drawn on the cloak with the deer's blood. A love note.

Chapter 23

I PULLED UP TO my apartment in record time. I wanted to be as far away from the club, as far away from that cloak and the mauled deer carcass, as quickly as possible. Hell, I barely remember getting on and off the highway.

I grabbed my bags, made my way upstairs, and locked every deadbolt and chain I had as I shut my front door. Though I normally don't open my windows I still went around to each one and checked, making sure it was locked tight and the curtains were drawn. At that moment, I was the poster child of paranoia.

Once everything had been checked, I made a mad dash to my bedroom and sat on the edge of my bed with a forceful bounce. I ransacked the side table drawer until I found my emergency stash of smokes and pulled one free of the cardboard with shaky hands. I had quit a few months ago but couldn't bring myself to throw the leftover pack in the trash. I was praising my foresight as I lit the cigarette.

I let the nicotine calm my nerves, a cough erupting from lungs that were out of practice. The mixture of the coughing and the nicotine hitting at once brought a nice little buzzed sensation to my brain. After a few moments, I was able to quell the coughing and breathe in the smoke easier. Just like riding a bicycle.

Everything came crashing against me at that moment. Liz's earth-shattering confession, our falling out, Frank's reappearance into my life—I couldn't tell which was worse. The image of the deer bleeding out in my car turned my stomach. That was a lie; I knew exactly which was worse.

I still had no idea what Frank wanted from me. If this was just about his bike, then I'd greatly underestimated his need for a round of psychotherapy. "Psycho" being the keyword.

I swiveled on my bed, bringing my legs up to lay straight in front of me and rested my head back against the wall.

And Liz! What did she want from me? Had she really thought I wouldn't freak out about it? I don't know a single person in their right mind that wouldn't have done what I did. This wasn't her ruining my favorite skirt or bringing my car back with a mysterious dent in the fender.

Hell, it didn't even bother me when she told me she was gay, but this was something I couldn't just put in a box and shove away.

I remembered the feeling in my stomach when I saw the blood dripping from the trunk of my car. The despair and fear creeping up my spine as I remembered she hadn't shown up for work. Just the thought of what could have been was enough to make me lose it completely.

I fished my phone from my pocket and pressed my thumb to the little icon with her picture to dial her cell.

A hard sigh pushed through my lips. The phone had rung long enough that I began to doubt she would pick up. Maybe she was still mad at me for how I reacted. She had told me not to freak out and that was exactly what I'd done.

"Hello?" A small, irritated voice picked up the other end, forcing a billow of smoke out of my mouth before I had even had a chance to breathe it in properly.

"Liz? You're okay?"

"What? Yeah, I'm fine. Why wouldn't I be?"

I felt my heart flood with relief. Thank God. It wasn't as bad as I had thought it would be.

"Just... hard night. Look, Liz, I just wanted to apologize." The words were so simple, but the moment I said them aloud I felt a weight lift from my shoulders.

"Don't bother. You can't take it back, and I don't want to hear it."

That was all it took for the moment of relief to shatter.

"Oh, come on. I was a bitch, and I'm sorry. I freaked out. You don't understand why I'm being like this just, please. I have a really good reason for it and I'll explain everything to you."

"Harley, just... don't call me again."

The phone went dead.

I pulled the cell from my ear and stared at it in silence. She hung up on me. Okay, so I was a stupid bitch in how I handled the situation, but really?! Never talk to her again? Now who was being irrational? And, for the record, my reaction was completely rational, thanks.

Oh, what's that? You're a werewolf, Liz? Well, this is a surprise. Still on for coffee?

That would be irrational.

The phone rang as I moved to set it on the bedside table, and my heart jumped into my throat. Maybe she realized she was being a little harsh. Without looking at the screen, I answered it.

"Liz?"

"Hey babe. I was hoping you'd pick up. Voicemails are so impersonal."

I forgot how to breathe.

"You there, Harls?"

"You sick fucking bastard," was all I could say. I had no need to ask who it was.

"Ouch," he breathed. "What'd I do to deserve that one?"

"You know what you fucking did. Quit playing head games with me, Frank. Did you think I wouldn't know it was you? Putting a dead fucking deer in my car? That's beyond sick."

"A what?"

"The gutted deer in the Red Riding Hood cloak, Frank!" I screamed into the phone. "Enough with the innocent act. We both know you're nothing more than a sick, disgusting piece of shit."

Silence answered me as I sat there trying to control my breathing. For a minute I thought he'd hung up on me.

"Harley—"

"How did you get this number?" I managed to squeak out through the tightness in my throat. I was met with derisive laughter.

"The hows and whys are so boring. Especially when there are more important things to discuss. Why don't you just tell me somewhere we can meet up, so we can handle business?"

"We have nothing to talk about. I told you everything I knew about your bike. Now it's your problem." I paused, thinking about the poor son of a bitch I'd put in his crosshairs. "You didn't hurt the guy at the shop, did you?" I held my breath as I waited for his answer.

"Jeez, Harls. You really do think I'm a monster, don't you?" Most people would have sounded offended at the implication. Not Frank. He actually had an amused lilt to his voice. "He'll think twice when he buys his bikes from now on. We'll just leave it at that."

I felt something burning against my fingers, red hot and painful. My cigarette had burned all the way down to the filter, leaving my fingertips burnt and my lap littered with flakes of ash.

I snubbed the smoldering filter into an empty pop can and pushed it into the opening.

"What the hell do you want, Frank? Obviously, you got what you wanted; you got your precious bike back. So why aren't you gone?"

"That hurts, babe. Really. This isn't just about the Beast, Harls. This is about reclaiming my property. All of my property," he said matter-of-factly. The humor was gone from his voice now. No more games. I could only hope.

"I'm not yours anymore, Frank. I never was."

"Oh, but you are so wrong about that. You were mine. You are mine. See, I picked you. Out of all the women in this world, you are the one that I chose to ride behind me. We belong together, Harley. It's destiny. You are meant to rule beside me."

"Rule? You really are out of your fucking mind. You can find a hundred women that would be more than willing to be your old lady. Let one of them rule with you. I'm not a part of it anymore."

"Baby, you have no clue what you're a part of. Not even in your wildest dreams. But you will. Soon enough, you'll see what I'm offering."

"Please, Frank. Just let me live my life in peace. I haven't done a damn thing to you. I haven't told anyone what happened. Please."

"You think I'm afraid of you calling the cops? They're only men, Harls. Call 'em. Let them come after me. That's not what's important. What's important is you coming to your senses. You will, you know. Soon enough you'll be ready to come back to me. All I gotta do is wait. And baby? I got all the time in the world."

He wasn't going to stop until I was back at his side or dead. That seemed to be the only other option he would accept. Well that wasn't going to happen. Not without a fight.

"Then I guess you better get settled in, because you're in for a nice long wait."

I didn't wait for him to react. I hung up and tossed my phone on the bed before twisting around and sliding my hand between the headboard and wall. I fumbled around blindly for a moment before feeling the cold metal and slid it from its holster.

I pulled my 9mm from the back of the headboard and sat back against it, cradling the gun in my hand. When I was with Frank, I had used a gun once or twice. Well, I'd held a gun. I'd only shot once, and it was at a can of beer with Frank's arms around me helping me aim.

A shudder ran over my body from the memory of my back tucked in tight against him, the heat of his arms against mine, and his strong grip around my hands as we held the gun steady.

His memory was everywhere and in everything. I couldn't hide from it. He had completely invaded my existence until I had nothing left that was just mine and mine alone.

No. That wasn't true. For the last year, I'd been working to create a life for myself, and I refused to let him steal any of it from me. Damn his memories. That's all they were.

I'd taken it upon myself to learn how to shoot properly and had gone to the gun club downtown to practice religiously. I didn't want to risk being at his mercy unprotected, and I knew the lessons he'd given me were bullshit. Just a false security he'd created. I realized that the second I'd started shooting at the range.

He'd made me believe he was giving me power when the truth was the power was mine all along. It was something I had to find in myself, not borrow from him.

If only I'd just been smart enough to use it then.

I stroked the side of the chamber tentatively as I forced the memories of him away from me. This gun, and all the training behind it, was all me. I had done it, not Frank. Remembering that helped clear my head enough to breathe again.

I reached into my nightstand and pulled out the small key that went to the trigger lock and unlocked it, tossing it and the key into the drawer. I opened the action and made a visual check of the chamber before reaching into my drawer once more.

I pushed all of the collective crap towards the front of the drawer and shuffled around until I found my magazine and loaded it into the butt of the Beretta with a loud click. The sound of it clicking into place echoed in my empty room and made the hair on my arms stand on end. I pulled the slide back to feed one into the chamber and let out a tentative breath.

Yes, I had been taught better than to keep a loaded gun when I wasn't actively using it. My trainer at the gun club would be lecturing me into oblivion, but I had no idea what Frank had up his sleeve. For all I knew, he could have been watching me at that very moment. I'd rather be ready to point and shoot than get caught fumbling around for my ammo.

Clicking the safety on, I slid the gun back into its holster behind my headboard, leaving the strap undone in case I had to draw it quickly. No second chances.

Chapter 24

July 12th 2011 10:26 a.m.

FRANK'S LITTLE CALL KEPT me on edge to say the least. Every sound made me turn and look behind me. Every head of sandy-brown hair walking in front of me made me reach my hand into my purse. I had gone to classes, work, and even the post office with my 9mm tucked away in my bag, loaded and ready for anything. The sound of a motorcycle passing me on the highway nearly made me swerve off the road as I reached for my purse.

This was no way to live, and I hated Frank even more for stealing away the little bit of fortitude I'd managed to build over the last few months.

If those had been his intentions—and I'd be stupid to think they weren't—then he succeeded. I hated that he had. He robbed me of my sense of self; something that I was only just beginning to discover.

I went to class but couldn't concentrate. I went to work and was only half there. The only time I managed

373

to throw myself completely into something was when I went to train with Marcellus, and even then, Frank was the driving force behind it. I even arranged to meet with him two extra days a week. If I could get away without using the gun I would be a lot happier, and the only way of doing that was getting a handle on the stuff Marcellus had been trying to literally beat into me.

I tied my shoelaces on the bench, my skin coated in sweat. My breathing was heavier than normal, and Marcellus took notice.

"How long you been smoking again?" he asked casually, handing me a cold bottle of water.

He was the reason I quit to begin with. Complete anti-smoking advocate. Plus, he'd refused to train someone that couldn't breathe halfway through the session. On that, I didn't really blame him. It was a complete waste of his time and effort.

"About a week, maybe. Really bad the past couple days," I had no reason to lie to him. Not about something as inconsequential as that.

He nodded and took a drink of his water, pressed his towel to his forehead. He didn't look at me, and I couldn't help but wonder if I was seeing indifference or disappointment. Did I really care at this point? Yeah. Sad to say, but I did.

"Everyone has weak moments. It's picking yourself up that makes you strong."

"Has anyone ever told you you kinda talk like Yoda?" I teased him because his words actually settled me slightly. He wasn't judging me for picking up a bad habit. He just wanted what was best for his student.

His laugh was rich and real, and it made me smile. "Mmmm... two packs a day you smoked and your lungs, blacker than Mickey's asshole they were"

I laughed. That was unexpectedly playful for Mr. Discipline.

"Wow," I said through the laughter. "That was, uh...impressive... and really, really, gross." I giggled and took another sip of my water. "Seriously, though. I know it's not good. I don't plan on picking back up the two a day habit, you know. Just... trust me."

He smiled at me and shrugged, pulling the towel off his shoulder and slinging it to the bench.

"Alright. I'm just saying. This too shall pass. Now finish up this break, and let's hit the mat again. I don't know what's gotten into you, but you're killing it tonight. I want to show you some new moves."

"Alright, I'm coming," I said as I finished my water.

Though I knew my body would be screaming at me for hours, I also knew this was a necessary evil. Knowing how to shoot was nice, but I needed to be ready for anything Frank might pull.

July 12th 2011 8:40 p.m.

Two days had passed since he called. Two full days of anxiety and paranoia. Sometimes I would let myself think it was just a bluff, but then I would look down at my forearm. The scabbed up 'F' set me straight. Frank didn't bluff. He threatened, he warned, but he never bluffed.

Still, it would be like him to make me cower for days, weeks even, before showing himself again. Perhaps the knowledge that I would be jumping at every noise and looking over my shoulder with every step was his way of tormenting me.

Yeah, that would be typical Frank. He found just as much sick enjoyment from inflicting mental anguish as he did physical pain. Maybe even more so.

I threw my purse into the passenger seat and ducked in to set the paper sack of groceries down. I nestled them down onto the floor board to keep it from tipping over, a lesson I had learned after causing one too many fruit avalanches while turning. It's a pain in the ass to brake when there is a baseball-sized orange stuck behind the pedal. It's an even bigger pain in the ass having to pull over on the side of the highway during rush hour to put them all back.

I shut my door and made my way around the front, fishing my car keys out of my skirt pocket. It was that perfect time of day when I could nearly smell the sunset and the wash of violets and pinks splashed over the sky in a perfect painting of dusk.

I squeezed between the side mirror of the van next to me and my own and opened my driver's side door, stopping before sliding in to close my eyes and breathe in that wonderful scent of summer sunset.

It was these moments I missed—small breaks in time where I didn't worry about Frank or his chaos and could just enjoy existing in the world. I hated that he stole that away from me so easily, and just to spite him, I allowed myself to take in that temporary serenity and the scent of summer dusk.

The grind of a sliding van door broke the enchantment of the moment and startled me enough to make me drop my keys.

I leaned forward and squatted down to pick them up, intent on jumping into the Toyota and giving the people in the van some room, but when I stood up again the sudden appearance of a large man pulled a startled shriek from me.

Iron-like hands gripped my shoulders and shoved me into the open van, my knees catching the step and throwing me back onto the floor of the emptied cargo area.

I had no time to think, to plan, or to wrap my head around what was happening or why. My foot jutted out as hard as I could manage. It wasn't the most effective method of self-defense, but Marcellus hadn't exactly showered me with tips about how to fight back an attack while hanging halfway out of a van. I was shooting from the hip.

My foot connected with something solid. With the second kick he caught my ankle in his meaty hand, pulling me across the floor of the van with a sharp tug that threatened to pull my hip right out of its socket. He pulled my legs against either side of his body, taking away the threat of my kicking feet. My skirt bunched around my hips as I slid across the van, leaving me exposed and vulnerable and pulled against him. I lashed out with hands and fists and nails, refusing to let the sick son of a bitch finish what he started.

"Oh, keep wiggling, sweetness. It feels nice," the man said with a salacious grin.

I fought as hard as I could, considering the less than advantageous position I was in. All I could think about was just keeping him from finishing the job, keep him from pushing me all the way inside the van. Someone would come outside, someone would hear me. I screamed as loud as my voice would allow.

Another hand clamped over my mouth and only when the first man pinned both wrists beside my head did I realize the hand over my mouth had come from someone else. My eyes rolled up to find an almost sickly-thin man stretching over from the driver's seat to shut me up. His scarred-up face was half hidden by the shadows of the van but didn't hide his panic.

"Dude, she's gonna bring the cops down on us. You were supposed to pull her in!" he said to the gorilla on top of me.

"Fucking bitch is fighting me!"

"She's 90 lbs. wet. Harness the power of the fat ass and get her in here!"

When I looked back to the one holding me, I could see the damage I'd done to his face. Two scratches on his right cheek, another on his forehead, and one smaller one at the tip of his chin. When he turned his eyes on me they were dark and cold and made no attempt to hide the vengeful thoughts swimming around in the darkness. I couldn't let them get me all the way into the van.

"He wants her there tonight. I sure as fuck ain't coming back without her now move, fat ass!"

"Fuck you! You think it's so easy why don't you come over here an—" but the gorilla's words were cut short as the hand holding my mouth was suddenly ripped away.

"Jonas!" the man crushing me screamed. When I looked back up above my head, he was gone.

Fatty went still above me, his hands pinning my arms, my legs still useless against him. Jonas suddenly reappeared in the driver's seat. His face was slack, eyes wide in terror. Blood dripped easily from his hair onto the van's floor and I knew he was dead.

"What the fuck?!" fatty screamed as he let go of my arms, staggering back at the sight of his buddy.

The sudden space between us was all I needed. I reared my knee up to my chest and shot my foot out with a forceful growl, connecting to his chin with a loud crack.

He fell back against my car, and I scrambled out of the van while he tried to wrap his head around the pain of a possibly broken jaw.

"You fucking bitch!" he screamed and pushed off my car, using it to throw him close enough to me to grab me by the hair and mouth.

I screamed against his sweaty hand, my hands reaching back behind my head searching for his face, his mouth, nose, eyes... I didn't care what I grabbed.

I felt a sudden jerk backwards and thought he was pulling me back to the van, but he screamed behind me, pulling me off my feet as he was crashed into by something else. I fell to the ground and twisted around to see a smaller man on top of the gorilla, sitting on his chest and pounding the back of his head into the cement until he went still as the grave.

The parking lot was a wash of dark liquid underneath them.

Frank stood up, dragging a boot over the man's mountain of a torso and walking towards his head. He reached down and grasped the man under the arms, dragging him effortlessly towards the painted curb behind him. I knew Frank was strong, and that his strength came from something other-worldly, but seeing him move the giant so easily still seemed impossible. When fatty's bald head reached the curb, Frank pushed him to his side propping the side of his head to the curb.

Oh God, no.

Seconds after I realized what Frank was going to do, his foot came crashing down onto the top side of his head, crushing it between his boot and the concrete. I looked away, but not before I saw his head dent in or before I saw the blood and thicker things force its way out of his skull through any opening it could find.

I curled into a ball on the ground, my knees pulled to my chest in an effort to not throw up. A hand gingerly touched my shoulder, and I jumped, my fists flying only to be caught by Frank. We struggled a moment, me sitting on the ground and him on a knee beside me, but he didn't speak or hit back. He let me lash out at him until I couldn't any longer, then he wrapped his arms around me.

I fought against his embrace but either exhaustion or defeat took hold of me, and I melted into him, resting my head against the hollow of his throat. I'd thought the he the men had referred to was Frank, but then there he was saving me from whatever fate they had in store for me.

It was safe to say, if he—whoever he was—had wanted to invite me to tea or a light chat that he wouldn't have sent two thugs in an unmarked white utility van to procure me from the street.

The arm at my back shifted, and I felt Frank's hand slide over my hair. He pressed his lips to my temple with a soft shushing sound. We sat there for only a moment, but the fact that there were two dead bodies nearby meant we couldn't stay here. He shifted and lifted me up to my feet to let me stand on my own.

His hands moved to my hips and smoothed down my skirt. If I wasn't so shaken I might have been embarrassed. My hands moved down to finish fixing my skirt while his moved to fix the twist in my blouse then rested on my shoulders.

"You okay?" he asked, his voice unusually soft and full of concern.

His thumbs kneaded my collarbone as I looked up at him. There was no snark, no contempt. It was the soft expression of the man I had fallen in love with so long ago.

"I... Yeah. Yeah, I'm good."

His eyes darted behind me, and I glanced over my shoulder to find people walking out of the store. They were looking around them, a group of about five shoppers and two employees. They were coming out to see where the screams had come from.

Yeah, that would have been helpful a few minutes ago.

"Shit. Come on," he said, and for the first time in a long time, I listened.

I followed him towards the exit of the parking lot, to where his bike was sitting. It was his Beast. He really had gone back and gotten it. My stomach sank, but I didn't have time to think about that.

The first scream from the crowd erupted, and Frank pulled me onto the bike, not behind him but in front of him. With a kick, he started the engine and we were gone. By the time the sirens could be heard, we were already making our way onto the old highway.

We drove in silence for about a half an hour. The shaking in my hands had finally eased but my heart was still thumping painfully in my chest, and I didn't think it was from the near-kidnapping. His chest was so hot against my back that I started to sweat. The sun was nearly settled into the horizon now, the pinks and purples giving way for heavier shades of violet and navy blue. Under other circumstances this would be my heaven. Or would have been, long ago.

We pulled to the side of the road, and my body tensed. I didn't want to stop. When the bike settled, and Frank cut the engine, he let out a long-exhausted sigh; the first sound

I had heard him make since we left the store. I turned to look at him, and he gave me a thin smile that was little more than skin-deep.

"You thirsty?" he asked.

As I cleared my throat I realized that I was. The screaming had turned my throat into a barren desert.

He slid his hand into his bedroll and pulled out a bottle of water. He unscrewed the cap, took a drink, and handed the bottle to me. My hand slid over his and something inside me stirred. A warning, maybe? Long forgotten feelings? Who knew? All I knew was I was damned thirsty. I just didn't know if it was that kind of thirst.

I brought the water to my lips and took a deep drink, the plastic sucking inward on itself. I gulped it down, the coolness easing my throat, and ran my tongue over my lips to collect the stray drops before brushing over them with the back of my hand. I stared at Frank and he stared back at me with a weightless relief in his eyes.

"Thank you," I started, though I wasn't really sure what else to say to him.

I was struggling with the fact that mere hours ago I was looking over my shoulder, afraid to see his face, and now I was standing alone with him and strangely calm about it. It didn't make sense, but I couldn't lie to myself. If it was between Frank and some random ass fucker trying to kidnap me, I would choose the evil I knew.

"I don't know why you were there. I don't think I want to know how you were in the right place at the right time, but thank you for saving me."

His thin smile spread into a wider, amused grin. He looked down, recapped the bottle, and looked back up at me with a tilt of his head.

"You always did call me on my bullshit," he laughed a bit and combed his fingers through his hair and I realized, for the first time since he'd forced his way back into my life, that he'd grown it out. It was a good four or five inches longer than I had last seen and curled wildly around his ears and neck.

His beard, too, was much longer and fuller than that wispy goatee from when I'd met him. I realized that the youthful, carefree boy I'd fallen in love with what seemed like ages ago, had grown up.

"Yeah, I was watching. Really didn't plan to be the knight in shining armor, I can tell ya that."

I should have been creeped out that the only reason he had been there was because he was basically stalking me around town. Truth was, it did make my skin crawl but could I really be mad that he was there tonight? If he hadn't been there I would probably be dead or worse. Yes, I do believe there are worse things than death.

"So why did you?" I asked finally, exhaustion creeping up on me fast. My adrenaline must have been crashing because it was becoming difficult to move. "Why not just let them take me and get rid of a recurring problem in your life? Who were they, anyway?"

"My guess? They probably work for the same guy who put that deer in your car," he said. I opened my mouth to ask what he meant, that I'd thought he'd done it, but he cut me off, "I honestly don't get it Harley. I don't see why you think I would want you out of my life. I've said it again and again... I want you back with me."

"Why can't you just let me go, Frank? No," I said as he began to open that charming mouth of his. "I know why you say you can't. I want the real reason. It wasn't like our relationship was a love for the ages."

"Didn't you love me, Harley?"

The question was so left-field that I stumbled over my words. "I... That doesn't matter," I protested, trying to stick to my point.

"I think it does, actually. In fact, it's probably the most important question to ask. Did you love me, Harley?" He stared into my eyes, and I couldn't help but squirm under his scrutiny.

"Of course I did. I wouldn't have stayed through all the bullshit you put me through if I didn't. But that's exactly the problem. You put me through so much shit. Every day it was something else. Another fight, more violence, more running. You drove me away from you long before I left." I prayed he would accept this. I didn't want to love him, but I had. Sometimes I thought that masochistic part of me still did.

"I told you, I had my reasons. You only got half the story, Harley. If you loved me once you can love me again. I can tell you this much, I have never stopped loving you, and I have never stopped needing you."

I started to argue, but I couldn't piece together a cohesive thought. I felt like I could just curl up and sleep right there on the side of the road. My hand lifted, and it was weighed down like a ten-ton anvil. Before I could manage to press it to the sudden throb between my eyes, my body went limp and I was suddenly in Frank's arms.

"Easy," he whispered as he guided me to his bike again. "This is a long time comin', Harls."

I blinked up lazily at him and tried to force myself to stay conscious. The motorcycle shifted under me and the engine sounded so very far away. I wanted to fight against the nagging sense of sleep, but it took hold of me and coaxed me into blissful darkness.

Chapter 25

RILEY

"JESUS CHRIST, IT LOOKS like a wild animal tore them apart," the nasally voice of one of the uniforms said loudly over the murmur of the crowd.

Riley shook his head at him. So much for discretion. They had a double-homicide in the middle of a suburban shopping complex. People gathered all around the scene trying to get firsthand news on what had happened and dipshit-in-blue over there was shouting about wild animal attacks.

A glance around the civilians proved that they were already posting and tweeting about it thanks to the carelessness of one man. Some men just shouldn't wear a badge.

"Someone get that jackass off my crime scene," the detective ordered.

While they escorted the uniform to his car, Riley returned to the van. He leaned into the open passenger side door as the techs took pictures of the body slumped behind the wheel. There was a lot of blood on him. Most of it undoubtedly came from the gaping arm socket on his left side—they'd found a detached arm on the lot beside the van—but it looked like he'd had his head slammed a few times, too. Just not to the extent of his friend a few yards away.

Animal attack my ass, he thought.

An animal might tear you apart, but they don't beat a man's skull open. While he couldn't fathom the strength, or sheer determination, it would take for a human to rip a guys' arm from his body, he'd seen drugs make people do unbelievable things. Unless there was some crazed gorilla running around the city, this was all man.

"Recognize him?" another detective asked.

"No," Riley said, shaking his head, "but I'm pretty sure we'll find a hit somewhere. He looks like a career criminal."

"You mean, like, a hit man?" a rookie asked him from the other side of the van.

"Not professional. Just someone who's probably been in and out of the system a few times. I'm sure we got his prints somewhere," Riley explained as he used the tip of his pen to gently nudge the dead man's head aside.

His face had been pretty badly scarred, but the three on his neck stood out from the rest. There was nothing outwardly strange about them other than how perfectly similar they were. He looked at the tech and nodded his head towards the guy's neck. While she snapped pictures, Riley looked at his partner.

"Just the two, then?" he asked.

"Yeah, we didn't see the girl anywhere," his partner answered. "You think she could have been the one to—"

Riley shook his head, "No. I've met her before. No way she has the strength to do this kind of damage. No signs of a weapon. It was done by hand." Even he knew how insane that sounded.

"Jesus," his partner breathed.

"Yeah. Any word on her friends?"

"We got a hold of a Liz Logan from her address book. She's on her way down."

Riley let the man's head drop back into place and turned on his partner. "Down here?" he watched the man nod. "The last thing we need is a panicked woman seeing two dead bodies, Harris. What the fuck were you think-ing?"

"I told her to come to the precinct tonight, but she wouldn't listen. Hung up on me before I could tell her anything else."

Riley cursed. Fantastic. He had two stiffs, a missing woman, some kind of super-strong maniac, and now he was going to have to play babysitter because Harris wouldn't wait until they cleared the scene to call her. As if on cue, a white Dakota pulled into the lot outside of the yellow police tape. A blond woman spilled out of the truck and ran towards them.

"Beautiful," Riley growled under his breath as he made his way towards her.

As he reached the girl, the driver got out and started up behind her. The man actually surprised the detective. He hadn't expected to see him with her.

"Mr. Tate," Riley called out. "Didn't expect you to come with Miss Logan, here."

"Detective Sheppard," Jackson said with an inclination of his head. "We all work together. I was with Liz when Detective Harris called."

"Where is she?" Liz blurted out, skipping pleasantries.

"We don't know. Car appears to be abandoned. Looks like she just got done shopping, but we haven't found her anywhere nearby," he said.

"Was she hurt?"

"Again, we don't know."

"Well what do you know, Detective?" Liz's tone was sharp and dangerous, and it stunned Riley. She'd been so soft and sweet when he'd seen her at the hospital with Harley.

"You really shouldn't have come out here. We could've waited and talked tonight," he said, trying to keep a calm tone with her.

"Like I was going to wait. Every minute you don't find her is another minute he has to hurt her," Liz said before Jackson placed a gentle hand on her shoulder.

"He? Do you know who might have taken her?"

"The guy that hurt her at the club, maybe? Wouldn't he be at the top of the list?"

Riley sighed softly, "Yes, ma'am, he would be. But we need to make sure we don't miss anything by focusing on just one person. Now, is there anyone else you know that might have been threatening her? Might have wanted to hurt her in any way?"

"Detective," a tech shouted from across the lot.

Riley looked behind him and then sighed as he looked back to Liz and Jackson. "Stay here. I'll be right back."

God, he hated dealing with civilians. It was the same old dance every time, no matter the scene around them. Once kin got involved it was all emotional riptides and threats of lawsuits. One father had even cold-clocked him when he refused to answer his questions. Whenever he could manage it, he avoided dealing with the families and friends of the victims. Walking towards the tech, he made a mental note to take a crack at Harris for calling them in.

"Did you find something new?" Sheppard asked, shielding his eyes from the setting sun.

"Wallet. No ID, credit cards... We bagged a phone we pulled from the driver, but there's nothing else here. Gonna take some samples of the blood, see if any of it belongs to our missing person."

"Well, there's plenty of it around here. Thanks." He looked at the sprays of blood dripping down the side of the van and shuddered.

Whoever did that was one brutal son of a bitch.

He made his way back to the girl's friends but hesitated behind the van when he heard them talking. Blondie sounded worked up. No big surprise there, but what she was saying had Riley completely thrown.

"Liz!" Jackson hissed, seemingly trying to keep his voice low. "Girl, are you crazy?"

She didn't answer him. Riley moved to look through one of the darkened van windows, careful not to catch their attention. Liz had moved to the little car and was looking inside. At first he thought she might be trying to steal evidence, but as he watched it looked more like she was pressing her face to the seats.

He listened as she breathed in deep enough for him to hear it, like she was trying to smell something buried deep in the layers of fabric. She might have been cute, but that chick had a screw loose. After a few moments of watching, her blond curls popped up and swirled around her as she turned to face the van.

Sheppard ducked down quickly, sucking in and holding a breath as his pulse raced over his nearly being seen. The van rocked gently as he pressed against it, straining to hear what was being said. There was something off about those two. Something they were hiding.

"It's him," he heard her say.

"Him?"

"The guy that hurt her at the club. I smell him here. I can smell him on the dead guy, even. He did this, and he took her." Panic flooded her voice.

"It's okay, Liz," Jackson said, grabbing her hands, "we'll find her."

Smell him? She really was sniffing Harley's car. So much crazy in such a pretty package. Crazy girls aside, she had said "him". She definitely knew something more than she was letting on. Riley would never understand why people held back information when someone's life was on the line. And they were supposed to be her friends? Tired of being lied to, the detective stood up and walked purposefully around the back of the van, rounding on them.

"Hey!" Riley shouted. "What do you two think you're doing?"

Liz gasped, looking from Jackson to Riley. "I... I know who took Harley."

"Who?"

"It was the man from the club. It was him," she said imploringly.

"What makes you say that?" Riley asked.

She hesitated. He watched the struggle play on her face, openly and loudly. This girl sucked at lying. Her flushed cheeks, the compulsive gnawing at her lower lip as she looked from him to the big guy, and her eyes darting nervously to the dead man was like a song and dance of guilt. She nudged her chin at the corpse in the van.

"The scars on his neck. I've seen them before. They were on the guy that attacked Harley in the club. I was sitting right in front of my boss when he came out and hit him. I had a clear view of it before he took off."

Riley let out a long, tired sigh. "Well... it's a start. Now we just gotta figure out who he is so we can track him down."

"His name is Frank Essex," Jackson said suddenly. Both Riley and Liz looked up at him in surprise before he elaborated further. "Harley used to run with him and his people before she moved up here. Part of some outlaw motorcycle club. He was her boyfriend. I didn't know for sure if it was him who'd come into the club that night, but Liz just confirmed it for me. That's a mark the Hellhounds use. Like a brand."

Liz blinked at Jackson as if she'd never seen him before. The detective didn't miss that, or the fleeting glance Jackson gave her before he looked away. Something was seriously not on the up and up.

Riley shook his head and gave the pair a reproachful look. If the girl had just told him it was her ex-boyfriend, then Riley could have found the bastard before it escalated to this. Why the hell did these kinds of women protect those that hurt them? It made him sick to his stomach and he held very little respect for anyone that would take such abuse to coddle a piece of shit like this guy.

It seemed that woman left a trail of wreckage in her wake because, what? She didn't want to be alone? She loved him? Who would she let get hurt next to protect Essex?

"Anything else you care to share now, so we can track down this bastard?"

"He's a drifter. They went from town to town. Didn't stay too long. Check local motels for a biker in his mid-twenties. May be alone, but could be with an entire crew," Jackson said before adding, "and he's dangerous. Very dangerous."

Riley nodded and released a long, slow breath. "Alright. In the meantime, take this one home. We'll call if we find anything, and you do the same if Ms. Rayne contacts you."

Jackson started to lead Liz back to the truck, but Riley tried to keep a discreet ear on the pair of them as he took a few steps towards the other officers.

"What? No, we need to go! He'll kill them! They're just hu—"

"He's a cop," Jackson said, cutting her off and glancing quickly to the detective. "Frank might be what he is, but he's not invincible. Regardless of what he thinks."

Riley glanced over his shoulder at them, watching Jackson try to calm her down and quiet her.

"How do you know about him?" she asked. "Did Harley tell you?"

Jackson glanced up from Liz and straight at Riley, his mouth pressing in a tight, thin line before he physically turned her away from the crime scene and towards the truck. A man that size could have easily thrown her over his shoulder if he had to, but he gave her the choice. He had to respect the man for that. Riley wasn't sure he'd have had the patience not to give in and caveman her away, given the opportunity. Jackson seemed to have more restraint.

They both lowered their voices enough that he could no longer hear bits and pieces of their argument. Just as well. He doubted he could get anymore from them right now. They could go round later, but right now he had a missing girl to find.

Chapter 26

I opened my eyes and saw nothing but indistinct shapes and lights. I couldn't keep my eyes open. It hurt too much. I tried to press my hand against my throbbing forehead, but I couldn't. I tried again but something was keeping both arms from budging even an inch. This time my eyes flew open, and I fought past the urge to close them again until things came back into focus.

The room was dark, save for the 40-watt hanging over my head. It hung still, no movement or sway whatsoever, telling me whoever had turned it on had done so some time ago.

Rope scratched across my skin each time I tried to move. A rag rubbed painfully against the corners of my mouth. I cried out, but the sound was muffled. It took a minute to realize I'd been gagged.

I twisted my body, testing the mobility of whatever I was tied to. It rocked, the sound of metal scratching across itself broke my skin out into gooseflesh, but it didn't move. Another jerk of my body, this time backwards, and I could feel it shift slightly in the same direction before settling back into place. It was on wheels, but by the looks of it the front wheels were taken off. In fact, the raw edges next to my feet looked like the metal had been cut through. After a little more inspection, I realized I was sitting in a dismantled sidecar.

My heart climbed into my throat.

Everything had happened so fast. Why did I let my guard down? How could I be so stupid? I knew exactly what kind of man Frank was, and yet I stupidly let him make a fool out of me. Again.

My eyes searched the darkness beyond the light bulb's reach, looking for a way out, a sign of rescue... hell, even Frank. I had no clue what he wanted from me, but maybe I would be able to stall him until help came.

But what help would be coming for me?

No one knew where I had been when he'd taken me. Liz still wasn't speaking to me; she wouldn't even know I was missing. How long had I been unconscious? An hour? A day? If I hadn't been gone but a few hours, then no one at work would think anything of it. This is what happens when I make a point to not have a social life of any sort. No one knew I was in trouble.

No one.

I heard a boot scrape across the sawdust-covered floor and the panic rose again. He was coming. Coming to do what, I still didn't know, but I was pretty damn certain it wasn't to kiss and make up. If the fact that he had me immobilized wasn't indicative to something much worse than a friendly chat, then the gag in my mouth was the nail in the coffin.

People don't normally gag their friends. It's bad manners.

A door opened behind me, the hinges sighing with years of neglect. It was probably safe to say, wherever he'd brought me was just as forgotten.

I listened to the heavy footsteps approaching behind me. I knew the swagger, the rhythm of that stride, quite well. One, two, three... He kept coming without even a pause. Eight, nine...

Nine steps and he stopped. His heat beat against my back. How close was he?

"Sorry 'bout the R-2. I just needed to get you somewhere to talk. You haven't exactly been cooperative, you know. Are you comfortable?"

I pulled at my restraints again, my wrists jerking painfully against the scratchy fibers of the rope. R-2, I thought. He fucking roofied me.

A few months before I took off, Frank procured a shipment of Rohypnol for a local frat house. I guess he'd kept some of it for personal use.

Lucky me.

It all clicked into place, then. Why he had looked so relieved when I took the water, the exhaustion. But he had drunk it too. So why wasn't he affected by the drug?

His breath caressed the side of my neck, sending a shiver of warmth along my skin. I turned my head, but he wasn't there. Fingers traced along my other shoulder, and I turned to find him smiling down at me with that ever-cocky grin.

I breathed for a moment. Just concentrated on filling my lungs and letting it out. I wanted to slow my pulse, to keep that satisfaction from him even if he couldn't actually tell the effect he was having on me. Sometimes, I wondered if he could.

"You know, I really didn't want it to come to this. I mean I'm all for tying up a beautiful woman, but I usually like to keep it in the bedroom. You just left me no other options, Harls," His tone was soft, calm, and completely out of place for the situation.

He moved his hand from my shoulder and stroked the back of his fingers along my jawline. "I told you and told you. I just wanna talk. We have a lot to discuss and now, thanks to your stubborn ass attitude, we don't have a lot of time."

Don't have a lot of time? What did he mean? Was he going to kill me? So many questions ran through my mind as I sat there, completely stripped of my ability to voice them.

His fingers found the gag and traced along the edges of it, giving the barest of touches to my lips. I had to close my eyes to keep from seeing his face as he did. There was something wrong with how much he seemed to enjoy what he had done to me.

"I know you're not as stupid as you like to make people believe. I mean, at first I thought you were. Sure," he smiled. "But you are so much more than even you realize."

His hand dropped back down to my shoulder, and I felt his fingertips grip over it. Not painfully. Just firm enough to let me know he was there. I opened my eyes then, feeling it was better for my health to not make him feel like I wasn't listening.

"I've had plans for us for a long time, Harley. I was going to open your eyes to a world you could never imagine. Give you power you never, in your wildest dreams, thought you could have. But I wanted to wait. I wanted to wait until you were ready. Then you stole that opportunity away from m."

His gentle massage of my shoulder grew harder as he let his frustration out on my skin, his fingertips digging in with bruising force now and I whimpered into the rag.

"You surprised me. I haven't been surprised in a long time. I had no idea you had the guts to take off like that. To lie to my face and tell me you weren't going anywhere. But I gotta ask. Did you really think I wouldn't find you?"

I stared up at him. He gave that rich yet raspy chuckle of his.

"Sorry. Forgot," he said, and for a moment I thought he might take off the gag.

No such luck. His hand snaked into my hair, rubbing fingertips almost possessively against my skull before he grasped a handful just in the back. The yank pulled a soft, distressed sound from me, and he maneuvered my head so that I was looking up at him, his face barely an inch from mine.

"You really should learn to close that beautiful mouth of yours more often. Take a minute to listen. Maybe it wouldn't have had to come to this." His breath danced over my lips, and he tapped a finger against them.

I didn't dare break eye contact. A gleam of darkness I'd never seen before, not even at his worst, filled his eyes. Something violent and dangerous was moving just behind the surface of those beautiful brown eyes, waiting to be freed.

"Now be a good girl, and cooperate, and I'll take it off." He let go of my hair and moved to the knot holding the rag in my mouth. "You can try and scream, but it won't do you any good. No one is close enough to hear it. So, do yourself a favor and save that voice of yours."

My head tugged back a bit as he worked the knot, but after a few moments, the gag loosened. I leaned my head forward and let the thing fall away from my mouth as I stretched my lips and moved my jaw around.

I didn't scream for help. Goodie for me. Mostly, it was because I knew he had no reason to lie about us being secluded. He wouldn't waste the energy on lying over trivial things like that. If Frank Essex wanted seclusion, then he found seclusion. Was I scared that his plans were something absolutely horrible? Of course!

But underneath that fear was the desire—no, the need—to understand why he was doing this. I wanted to know what drove him to kidnap me and tie me up, what fueled him to treat me the way he had been these last few years. He'd opened the door, and now I wanted to peek inside.

"So? What are you going to do?" I asked breathlessly. I'd settled for a direct approach. If I gave him direct, maybe he would do the same for me. "I mean you keep telling me about these big plans, but you've yet to act."

Something must have been showing on my face because Frank pressed his fingers softly under my chin and coaxed my face up to meet his again. His silence was deafening. Those large brown eyes bore down into mine, searching for an unspoken answer. Maybe he found one because those lips turned up into a knowing smile.

"You didn't know, did you?"

I wrenched my chin away from him. "Know what?"

"Interesting," he said softly. He stood for a moment and mulled something over. "I'd only met one other like you before. I figured you could feel it or sense it or something, but you really don't know what you are, do you?"

"What I am," the words came out in a desperate raise of my voice, "is sick and tired of your bullshit. In every way,

I am done with you. With all of this. So, if you are going to kill me then fucking kill me. Grow some fucking balls and finish—"

The back of his hand crashed against my mouth, silencing me. I breathed, deeply and evenly, as I reigned in the surge of fury coursing through my veins. Lashing out would, obviously, get me nowhere but hurt. My tongue darted out and I hissed at the stinging pain on my lower lip.

"How long?" I whispered so softly even I barely heard.

"What?" Frank asked.

"How long?" Louder this time, my eyes rolling up to stare at him through my lashes. "How long have you been a werewolf? From the start?"

He stared down at me, rubbing the back of his hand as if trying to rub away the feel of his knuckles crashing against my face.

"No. Not really. When we met I was still human."

So, I had gotten to see Frank, the real Frank, without the monster. Was it time as this animal that had driven him to become the monster he was today? If that were true, Liz couldn't have been the sweet and kind girl she was. She'd been this way since birth, according to her. She was a werewolf longer than Frank and she wasn't a raging bloodthirsty psychopath.

"So, you were turned," I said. It wasn't a question. "Who turned you?"

His eyebrows rose slightly. Maybe it was a personal question, like asking a woman how much she weighed. His brow relaxed again, and he shook his head, a strained smile forcing itself on his lips.

"We're getting sidetracked. We don't have much time, babe. I told you there's a lot I want to tell you. That little nugget will just have to wait for another day."

He moved to me once again, this time lowering down closer to my level. I just stared at the man I thought I knew. Two years. I had been with a werewolf, sleeping next to a dangerous blood-thirsty animal, for two years. Without a word, he lifted the rag up again and wedged it into my mouth before I could argue, sliding his hands along the cloth to tie behind my head again.

When he had me effectively silenced once more, he crouched down—elbows resting on his knees, fingers steepled in front of his mouth—and just stared at me. The rag in my mouth tasted dirty, like engine oil. It was suffocating and infuriating, and I let him know just how pissed I was as I stared into those brown eyes.

"I'm gonna do something for you I don't do for anyone. Take it as proof of what you mean to me. I'm going to tell you exactly what happened that night. You know, the night you ran out on me. This is a once-in-a-lifetime opportunity, so listen up."

Like I had a choice.

"I got a call from some guys down in Atlanta. Been talking to them for months, discussing the pack's future. They were supposed to join up. Fall in line behind me and mine. The brothers you saw lead the hunt, Levi and Jordan. They were part of that pack."

There was something in his eyes then. Someone had made a fool of him. No one gets away with that. They just don't. Hell, I thought I had managed to. Apparently, I was dead fucking wrong.

The silence stretched on for a moment, and I thought maybe he was just going to stop. Leave me with a magnificent lead up and then leave me dangling like a hooked fish. I wanted him to keep going. I was ready to hear, after all this time, what had driven him to murder a friend in cold blood.

"Turns out," he continued, "I wasn't the only one talking. Theo knew we were gonna take them on a hunt and got in touch with D'Angelo. See, D wasn't exactly thrilled about Chuck. In his mind, when Chuck died the wolves should have been loyal to him. So, he used the hunt, and you, to ambush me. He wanted to take the wolves with blood."

He wouldn't meet my eyes. Instead he focused on the scarred and calloused knuckles on his hands, running thumbs over each knot and scar. I remembered how D'Angelo's head looked little more than a gelatinous pile of meat when Frank was finished. There was so much blood it had been hard to tell what was Frank's and what had belonged to the corpse.

"Hijacking packs ain't exactly a new trend. You beat your challenger down until they cow to you, they depart with their tails between their legs, and you just wait for the next challenge. But it was what that mother fucker said..."

He took a deep breath. The air between me and him got hotter.

"He said, 'You're gonna give your wolves over, or I'll take everyone you ever loved and make them one of us. In fact, I'm gonna start with that pretty little piece outside. She'll be my bitch in every way by the time I'm done with her.' He was a dead son of a bitch."

His eyes darted up to meet mine, and the blood drained from my face. Those eyes were aflame with rage, pure unadulterated anger burning like amber fire. I had never seen such a look of murderous intent before. I thought I had, but I was so wrong.

"I wasn't gonna let him take you from me," he growled through gritted teeth. "Not after I had put so much time into you."

I stared at him in disbelief. If I was to believe what he was telling me, then he killed that man to protect me. Trying to take over packs was normal for werewolves. That hadn't been what pissed him off. It was the thought of this guy doing, whatever it was he'd meant to do, that sent Frank over the edge.

But this wasn't some romantic hero saving the damsel in distress. This was something deeper. Something I was not yet ready to understand. Frank had laid claim to me on an animal level. Put time into me, he said. Time for what? What were his plans?

He stood up, breaking my train of thought. Was that it? He had explained himself, explained his actions, and now what? Kill me? Why would he do that when he had gone so far as to kill a man over me?

A pop, a hiss, and a yellow light erupted from the other side of the room. A cloud of smoke swirled up and around his head as he took in a drag of his cigarette. I found myself wanting one. What an odd thing to think while strapped down and gagged.

He took another drag, and his eyes slid back to me before he plucked the cigarette from his lips, sucking air in through his teeth and pushing the white smoke out of the corner of his mouth. God, I wanted to talk, to ask him the millions of questions floating in and out of my head.

"So, I took care of business. As usual," he started again before letting loose a bitter laugh. "I killed that son of a bitch to protect you, and you just took off on me. I'll admit, I was impressed. Pissed... but impressed. I didn't think you had the balls to take off like that. To steal my bike and ride away. You surprised me, Harley. I've said it before. Not many people manage that."

And he'd killed the last guy that did.

While that unspoken truth hung in the air between us, I watched him. He took another drag of his smoke and rolled his shoulders. He was on edge. I recognized the body language. Something was distracting him from his thoughts, a persistent niggle in the back of his mind that he was trying to push aside.

He spun around quickly, his eyes tracking something unseen and unheard by me. He shushed me with pursed lips even though I had said nothing. I couldn't, but he still found it necessary.

Frank walked out of the room, leaving me alone with the hanging light bulb and a tangle of emotions in my head. His movements were so careful as he slipped out of the door that he reminded me of an animal stalking prey. Maybe he had heard something outside? Werewolves had super-hearing or something, right?

I realized I really had no idea what werewolves could do. Other than what little Liz had explained, of course. I wrestled with the probability of getting whoever's attention. I could scream or try and rock the sidecar around until they heard me and came. If our visitor could hear me, then Frank could too, and it would bring him right back here.

That was the last thing I wanted.

The door eased open, and my eyes snapped over to it, expecting Frank to waltz in. Instead, another figure moved silently into the room.

"Shit," he whispered when he saw me.

He kept his body partially crouched and stepped out of the shadowed doorway. It was Detective Sheppard. I growled against the rag in my mouth.

"Shhh," he demanded as he slipped behind me, resting his gun on my shoulder and training it on the door across from us. His free hand worked the knot behind my head. "I got you, Harley. We're getting out of here, I promise."

He was trying to be reassuring. Bless his heart, but I wasn't completely assured. Not with an obsessive, were-wolf ex-boyfriend lurking around. The rag dropped from my mouth and I spit out the grease and grime that plagued my tongue.

"Untie my wrists," I said in a harried whisper. I tried to look at him over my shoulder. "He'll be back any second. You need to get me undone and get out of here—"

A heavy clunk rang out behind me, and I watched the detective drop to the floor like a sack of flour. I twisted around as much as the chair allowed and saw Frank staring at me, eyes wild.

He disappeared for a second before I heard something dragging over the concrete floor. He pulled Sheppard's body around me by his ankle until he lay completely in view. His other hand held an old, metal, dented gas can which he dropped to the ground next to the cop's head.

His eyes bore into me, a wild jealousy burning in that stare. They screamed his outrage at the detective trying to take me away from him. That was not allowed. Me leaving on my own terms was apparently one thing, but having another man steal me away was something completely different. It was a call for violence of the worst kind. He pulled his gaze away from me and looked down to the offender for a few heartbeats, visibly trying to keep his temper in check.

"Pack or prey, Harley," Frank finally said, nostrils flaring with his deep and measured breaths.

I stared at him, completely swallowed by my fear. Afraid to say something. Afraid to stay silent. I was afraid to make the wrong move or give him the wrong answer. Not only was my skin on the line, but now Detective Sheppard's was as well.

"What?" I settled for simple, honest ignorance.

"I said," his voice was edged with impatience, but he paused to swallow it down, "pack... or prey. You have a very simple choice to make. Let me turn you. Let me bring you to the life you were born for. I know I haven't been the easiest guy to be with. I'm not an idiot, Harls. I know what I've done to you. You need to believe me that there was a purpose to it. I needed to be sure. I needed to know you were strong enough to handle this."

I stared at him in stunned silence. He wanted me to turn into a werewolf like him. That's what all of this was about? But why? I guess he took my silence to heart because he continued then.

"Or if you don't want to be pack, then you'll be prey. Whether it's by me or by your... mystery admirer... the result will be the same. Something is coming for you Harley. So, you can either take the strength and backup I'm offering, or you can continue to be the weak little human. Fragile and always afraid."

I watched him carefully. His intentions were laid on the table, and now he was waiting for an answer. Pack or prey. Not much of a choice if you ask me.

Sure, Frank. I think I am going to go with being eaten to death. The problem was I really did not want option A, either. My choices were pretty much to die or to be a monster for the rest of my life. Could I pick door number three?

The detective groaned, and it drew both mine and Frank's attention back down to him. Frank whispered some obscenity under his breath and reached to his hip, drawing out his knife.

Shit. He was going to kill him. Or maybe he was going to toy with him a bit first. Make him suffer. The different scenarios played in my mind as Frank made his way over to the still body and bent at the knees to get closer. He moved the knife towards his face and the glint of light reflecting off the blade made me cry out to him.

"No!" I shouted. "Please Frank, don't kill him!"

He looked at me over his shoulder as he hovered over the detective's unconscious body.

"Why shouldn't I? He's trying to take you from me. Just like D'Angelo. Just like that pretty boy outside that restaurant."

I choked on my pulse, my stomach dropping at the mention of Braedon. It had been Frank. Somehow, I already knew but I hadn't wanted to believe it.

"He found us, didn't he? It's only a matter of time before he connects you to me. Why would you let him live knowing you're probably going to go down for all the shit we've done?" He asked with an air of genuine curiosity. It was like he couldn't understand why I wouldn't let him kill the detective to make sure I didn't end up in handcuffs.

"He's trying to save me." I wasn't exactly sure how to get him to understand.

"And as soon as he's got you safe and sound he's gonna slap cuffs on you and cart you off," he argued as he swiveled a bit on the balls of his feet. He wasn't moving away from him, but he had lowered the knife. One victory at a time.

"You killed a man, Frank. If you would kill a man just for threatening me, then why would you kill a man for trying to keep me safe? Please..."

Something shifted in his eyes. I wasn't arguing or telling him what to do. I was pleading, asking him for a favor. The fact that he had pulled back enough to hear me out was a good sign, but he was still too close. Still had his blade in hand. He was considering it... but I needed more. At that moment I came to an understanding. I understood why he had killed before. I even found myself agreeing with it. If someone intended to hurt someone I cared about then what would stop me from doing everything I could to stop it?

D had invited death by threatening Frank's loved ones, and realization dawned on me that I was the only one who fit the bill. Frank's definition of love may have been warped, twisted even, but in his own way he cared about me. And it was enough to drive him to kill for me.

But Detective Shepard had no intent to harm me. It was nothing more than the fear of being caught that put the knife in Frank's hand now, not the instinct to protect someone he loved. I couldn't watch him kill another innocent man. Wouldn't.

"Pack," I said. My jaw clenched tight, and I tried to breathe past the rising strain in my chest. "I choose pack. Turn me, but only if you let him go."

His eyes stretched wider. He honestly hadn't expected me to cooperate. Whether or not he would have turned me regardless of my consent, I will never know. He probably would have, but now I owed him. Instead of having me hate him for doing something against my will, I would be indebted to him. My life for the cop's. I couldn't put blame on him now that it was my choice. My decision.

My fault.

"Alright," he said, sliding the knife back into its sheath on his belt and standing up once more.

The wide-eyed surprise slid into that all-too-familiar grin. The grin that said he won, once again. He made his way over to me and leaned forward, resting hands on the sidecar behind my elbows in order to hold himself eye level with me.

"I'll let him go. This time."

His breathing was labored, his breath fiery as it beat against my face. The room lit up as the moon slid closer to the height of its ascension, breaking the clouds to filter moonlight down through the holes in the roof. The energy in the room was strangling me. A thick blanket of heat that flowed from the man in front of me and from the moon above had snaked its way down my throat, coating my lungs.

His body jerked violently, almost pulling the sidecar off its wheels. When he opened his eyes again his face was paling, his brow slicked with sweat. While he didn't appear to be doing much of anything on the outside, the exhaustion in his eyes and sweat on his brow told me there was much, much more going on inside of him.

It hadn't been like this with Liz. Her shift had been fluid, easy, natural. Frank looked as if he were boiling on the inside, waiting to explode from within.

And that is almost exactly what happened.

He staggered back away from me, his fingertips digging into the sidecar and my arm as they slid across. He was fighting to let go, not hold on. His arms, all taught skin and flexed muscle, cradled in against himself. The veins in his neck throbbed so large I could see them from my seat.

The first thing to change was his eyes. That burning amber fire spread further, taking over the near entirety of his eye, his pupil shrinking. He turned those monstrous eyes, those wolf eyes, to me, and a fleeting sense of panic and desperation pleaded in them before an inhuman scream threw his head back and broke our gaze.

His jaw pushed out, his teeth elongating to curve over his top lip. The bones and muscles moved beneath his skin with a life of their own, stretching and bulking in all the right places and shrinking in others. He grew six inches between his spine and legs, the calves snapping backward with a sickening pop. The urge to scream was very much present as I watched his body contort and disfigure. A body I knew very well, or used to think so anyway.

His upper lip and nose caught up with his lower jaw, stretching in a rounded snout; protruding much further than a human's should, but not quite as long and narrow as a wolf's. A succession of cracks and crunches beat along his spine, the vertebrae pushing out of his back, revealed as he grew out of his shirt. He had shredded most of his clothes and now stood before me completely nude. As nature intended, if nature had meant to make his bones longer than his body and his form a strange mix of man and beast.

I was thankful, so thankful, that I hadn't eaten today. I was afraid I might lose anything I'd eaten.

When all movement finally stopped, he stood in front of me silent and breathing heavily. He was unlike anything my mind could imagine. Unlike Liz, who had shifted into a slightly larger version of a common wolf, Frank remained on two long legs. His neck was long and thin holding up a head that was man in the skull and wolf in everything else. Sandy fur covered him from his football-sized feet—or were they paws?—to the tips of his erect, pointed ears. Only his torso and... other regions... appeared to be bare flesh.

I wanted to scream, to let loose as it forced its way up my throat and begged to shoot out around me, but my throat tightened around it and wouldn't let it free. All of the wolves I'd seen so far looked like real wolves. He wasn't a man anymore, and he wasn't wolf. He was a monster.

His eyes zoned in on me, and we locked eyes. His shoulders, if werewolves had shoulders, rose and fell deeply with each breath. I could barely breathe.

The detective screamed as he scrambled on the floor. He looked like a small animal scurrying away, trying to run from the big bad meat-eater coming for him. Apparently, I was not the only one that thought it, because Frank shifted his weight and stepped towards him.

"No!" I shouted, turning his attention back to me instead of the midnight snack on the floor. "We had a deal."

This stopped him, though he didn't look at me just yet. He stared down at the detective for a heartbeat, his face turned so that I couldn't see it, but I didn't need to. The sudden paleness in the man's face told me everything.

"Hey. I'm over here," I felt like he wasn't listening to me. Could he control his instinct to hunt while in this body? It made me wonder just how much of the wolf took over when they shifted. "Come on, baby. I'm all yours. Leave him alone."

He turned and looked at me. Relief swelled in my chest as his attention was redirected away from Detective Sheppard. I just tried not to dwell on what it had redirected to.

He took a step towards me, and I could feel my spine recoil. He was so much bigger than I thought and seemed to grow even bigger the closer he got to me. Or maybe I was just feeling very, very small tied down to this seat. Either way.

His nose pushed into my hair and breathed in. It made my skin crawl, but anything was better than him turning on the detective again.

A metal click focused my attention on the man in the corner again. Sheppard held up his gun, training it on the wolf at my side. His grip was shaky, much shakier than it should have been for a trained marksman.

For a moment I felt like maybe this would all go away. If he shot Frank now, then I wouldn't have to do this. I would be free of all the bullshit that came with him. I would be free of everything. And then I remembered Liz and her wounds when she revealed herself to me.

They'd been deep. Killing blows for any normal human, and yet there was nothing to show for it now. Just smooth, unmarred skin where she'd been torn open.

"Don't shoot him! It won't help!"

Sheppard's gaze flicked from the monster to me, and I didn't miss the indecision in his eyes. I couldn't believe I was saying it myself, but I just couldn't live with myself if he shot Frank only to have him react in the bloodiest way possible.

"Please," I said to Sheppard's unspoken question. "You shoot him, he'll kill us both. I'll be fine."

I almost believed it.

Frank had moved behind me while I was dealing with Sheppard and brushed his fingers up my shoulder, tracing up the side of my neck to push my hair aside. The heat of his breath followed in the wake of his sharp nails, his muzzle hovering over my shoulder as the hand continued to move around the back of my neck and curled around the other side.

"Flesh to fur, Harley. The moon will bind us." The words were hot against my neck and were coated in a deeper growl than I'd ever hear in Frank's voice. "As beast is one with man, so you will be one with me."

His teeth sank into my shoulder and tore a scream from my throat. Dozens of razor-sharp blades ravaged skin and muscle. Heat spread through the bite, setting my blood to boiling as it ran out of the wound and over my shoulder. My screaming stopped when my throat grew hoarse and I crumbled into hysterical sobs.

It hurt. It hurt so badly. I had never, in my life, felt anything so horrible, so all-encompassing and complete as this. Pain became the only thought, the only feeling my body could wrap itself around and it didn't stop there. A deep burning sensation spread throughout my muscles and through my veins, reaching every part of my body until I was enveloped in white-hot agony.

I used the detective as my focal point to anchor me and keep me from succumbing to the void that tugged at me. I stared at him while he stared at Frank, or what used to be Frank, and watched as he mirrored what I must have looked like when Liz revealed herself to me. Every muscle in Detective Sheppard's body was tight as steel, frozen in place as the overwhelming shock took control of him.

The last thing I felt, other than the sharp suck of his teeth pulling from my body, was a large, hot, disfigured hand sliding over my hair and then I released my tether from consciousness, giving in to the pain.

A distant voice called my name. Once. Then again. It sounded far away, like someone was standing at one end of a tunnel with me at the other. It took far too long for me to connect Sheppard's voice with his face as it hung over me. He stared down at me and he was saying something, but the sound didn't quite seem to match with his lips.

I'm here, I thought. But my arms couldn't move. My mouth couldn't form words.

I heard him say, "Stay with me," but didn't understand. I was right there. Where did he think I was going?

Chapter 27

FRANK

HE KNEW HE SHOULDN'T stay too much longer. Once the cop snapped out of it, they'd be combing the area for him, but Frank needed to see her first. He needed to know he'd been right to do it.

Blue and red danced across the side of the ramshackle building, illuminating the door. Would they be bringing out Harley, or would they be bringing out a body bag? Impatience gnawed at him as he waited.

Come on, Harley, he thought. I know you're too damn stubborn to die on me now.

But what if he was wrong? He'd made her life hell, but not everything was for his own twisted amusement. Would she see it now that her eyes had been opened? Honestly, it wouldn't surprise Frank if she died from her injuries just to spite him.

Pain-in-the-ass woman.

It took every ounce of will he had left to leave her there, freshly bitten, bleeding, and tip-toeing across death's door. He should have been by her side as the curse spread inside her, been there when she woke up. This wasn't the way this should have gone down, but if he hadn't left he'd have ended up having to kill the cop. If that happened, he'd lose his hold over her. He'd lose her...

A low, disgruntled growl rolled through his elongated teeth. Nah. That bitch thinks she can ditch me? She'll seek me out before her shift. I guaran-fucking-tee it.

Movement just inside the building pushed Frank's thoughts aside for the moment. His claws dug into the tree trunk next to him as he squeezed it, watching anxiously as they wheeled out the stretcher.

When he saw her beautiful, heart-shaped face instead of a zipped-up black sack or white sheet, the iron band squeezing his heart eased up. He kept a bead on them as they rolled her into the back of the waiting ambulance and hooked her up to an I.V. They wouldn't bother if she weren't alive.

For just a moment, Frank let himself feel the relief spilling out of him. She was still alive. He knew she could handle it.

There was always a chance that someone wouldn't survive a bite. The fever that quickly overcame them would sometimes be too much for their bodies to take, or if a wolf wasn't careful when biting, they could do too much damage and cause the person to bleed out. Healing on Frank's level didn't occur until after the first shift.

When the doors to the ambulance closed, Frank sank back further into the brush. The detective was leaning against the building, huddled in on himself as he spoke with other officers. They were too far for even Frank to pick up on their conversation, but he knew the gist of what was to come.

The trees would only hide him for the moment, until the police began to pour into them in search of the monster their detective would no doubt tell them about. Whether or not they believed his wild claims, they were beat cops and he outranked them. So, they would follow orders.

He hoped the cop would remember the warning he gave him after Harley had passed out. Though the animal in him had wanted to rip the man apart as he ran to her and put his grubby mitts all over her to check her vitals, he'd quelled the urge for the moment.

"Remember what she just did for you," he'd warned before slipping out the back door.

It was the only recompense Frank could give Harley. Hopefully, should the detective ever feel the need to come after her, he would remember that he was indebted to her. Who knew when that very fact could come in handy for him, as well?

Chapter 28

THE SCENT OF THE woods after a healthy rainfall has always been a favorite of mine. It's so earthy and rich, making me feel like I could just breathe in the forest itself. Breathe it right into my lungs and become one with it. There were many times, when I was a little girl, where I wandered off into the woods behind my parents' house after a storm passed. It had been an escape years before I found it on the back of Frank' bike.

My feet sank into the mud and grass, as it had so many times, and I smiled as I lost sight of my toes in the dark muck. It felt just like my old patch of woods. Like nothing had changed.

Only my feet were much bigger now, my weight heavier and pushing me deeper down into the earth with each step. I don't know where I was going, but I was heading somewhere. I was searching for something.

The trees thinned out ahead of me, and I already knew a clearing was on the other side of the last of them. My clearing—the one with the creek that filled ankle-deep after the rain, where I would chase after frogs and lizards. Where I would go because my parents were too busy with Lorelei, and I was too restless to sit indoors and wait.

My steps hastened as I neared my clearing, and a smile stretched over my face. It had been so many years since I'd last been here. I had wanted to bring Frank back to it, once upon a time, to show him my little secret place and share it with him. We just never made it to that point, I guess.

I wondered how much it had changed. Had the years changed it into something sad and unrecognizable, or did it really have the magic I always imagined it had as a girl? Would it be the only thing on this earth that was untouched by time? God, I hoped so.

I broke the tree line and delighted in what I found. It was as I remembered. Still that special hideaway I held so tenderly in my memories. Except I didn't remember fireflies ever showing up this deep in the woods.

I stared at the two lights ahead of me and realized they were moving in exactly the same way, never getting any farther apart. I had never seen fireflies move together in such a way before and it drew me closer.

I walked towards the creek, closer to the lights of the fireflies and their odd dance, absolutely enchanted. It was only when my foot snapped a small branch that they stopped.

The lights were coming closer, growing larger inch by inch as they crossed the creek. They were moving right for me. I don't know why but it made me take a step back, the hair on my arms standing on end.

The clouds parted, breaking to allow the moon to shine down on the world and illuminate the small drops of rain that still clung greedily to the woods. A beam of silvery mist shone straight down in front of me, tendrils of it reaching out to the approaching lights. When the moonbeam hit, a silhouette of a wolf came into view. The lights were not fireflies at all but were the wolf's eyes and they were staring right at me.

My first thought was to run. To run away from this animal that could eat me alive. However, my feet would not move. I was glued to the spot, my muscles amazingly relaxed.

The wolf made another step toward me, but this time I didn't feel threatened by it. Its head was lowered as it stared at me, its feet moving lightly along the forest floor. I can't describe what moved me, but I found myself dropping down to a knee as it came closer. I wasn't afraid of it, I wanted it to come.

And it did.

I stayed perfectly still as the animal trotted up to me. It seemed as curious about me as I was about it, and I let us both give in to our curiosity.

Its fur was such a rich, dark color that it almost looked like my hair. My natural hair color, I mean, not the six-dollar boxed-blond I'd made it.

As it moved, I could see slight tints of dark golds and rust, glinting and peeking with each powerful movement of the wolf. Its grey-blue eyes were almost glowing in the moonlight. I wanted to run my hands through the fur, to see how it felt. Would it feel like Liz's had?

She sniffed my hand, alerting me to the fact that I'd actually raised it up without realizing it.

I didn't move yet. I simply let her scent me, become familiar with me. I waited for her to decide I had no ill-will towards her before I made my move. The last thing I wanted to deal with was another wolf attack. Not on such a beautiful, peaceful night as this. When she seemed satisfied at what she smelled, I moved my hand to pet her.

Nothing.

My hand literally moved through her as if she weren't more than air. I jerked my hand back and stared at the wolf wildly. Was I hallucinating? Was I still drugged and in that garage with Frank? The serenity that had been cloaking me disappeared and I was refilled with panic.

Oh, God. The detective! Was he still alive?

I shot to my feet and turned to run, but a long, shrill howl pierced the silence of the woods and when I turned back to look at the wolf she was lunging towards me. I threw my arms up to protect my face, but as my hand had gone through her moments ago, she jumped through me now.

No, not through me. Into me.

Again, came the warm serenity, and I could feel a light filling me up from the inside.

It coated the underside of my skin, stretching throughout every nook of my body until I was wearing the light like a suit. It was blissful, wonderful, and I felt at peace for the first time in my entire life. I hadn't even realized my feet had left the ground until I opened my eyes and saw the warm light pulsating from my fingers and toes and everything in between. Even knowing I was hanging in the air by an unseen force, I was at peace. The light was safety and truth. A riddle for me to puzzle out later and take ease in now.

I closed my eyes and let the energy of the wolf lull me into peaceful sleep.

Chapter 29

July 14th 2011 7:35 a.m.

THE FIRST SOUND THAT found me, after the wolf's howl, was a strange mechanical beep. It was slow and drawn out. A rhythm that promised nothing and kept me waiting even still. Slowly, my body came back to me. Or maybe I came back to my body. I am not quite sure which.

My eyes fluttered open to an attack of bright fluorescent light and slammed shut again. Don't make me look at that bright light again. I want to go back to the woods, to the wolf and the scent of fresh rain. I thought, maybe, if I just could keep my eyes closed then I could find my way back, but a shuffle of feet drew me back to that damnable light.

"She's waking up," a soft voice rasped, and I heard more shuffling on the other side of me.

"Harley?" a deeper voice said, and I could cry at the hopelessness in it.

"Harley, wake up babe. That's right, just wake up. We're here. We're waiting for you," the softer voice said again. A woman. Something about that voice made me want to jump for joy, but I still couldn't control my body.

My eyes fluttered open, fighting against the harsh white light. I moved my head to the side of me from where the woman's voice was coming. She was a blur of yellow and pink. I tried to ask her something, but the words garbled together in my throat and refused to come out.

"Shit, she really is waking up." The deeper voice sounded panicked, and then I heard a louder, "Nurse! Come on, angel. You can do it."

Something shifted at the other side of me and another light shone suddenly into my eyes. No, I want to see Liz! Get that fucking thing away from me!

"Ms. Rayne, are you there? Ms. Rayne, you're at St. Theresa's. You're in the hospital, honey. Can you open your eyes all the way for me?" She sounded different than the first voice. Louder, like she was shouting at me.

"Fff... li..." I tried to will my lips to move. "If.... ligh..." The lights, I screamed in my head. Turn the damn lights off and I will!

"Is she going to be ok?" Liz asked.

"She should be, now. We didn't get the labs back before she was taken into surgery, so we didn't know about the Rohypnol before we put her under. It could have been a very bad complication, but it looks like she is trying to come out of it. This is a good sign. Ms. Rayne can you squeeze my hand?"

What I wanted to do was flip her off, but I couldn't lift my hand. I did, however, try and squeeze her hand when she slipped her fingers into my palm. I didn't do much, but whatever I managed to do brought an outburst of relief from one of the people around me.

I opened my eyes a bit more, trying to make out the yellow and pink blur to my right. The other woman told the man in the room some things I didn't quite hear. I was too busy trying to focus on the woman now holding my hand.

My vision sharpened, and after a few moments I could make out Liz. Oh, she looked like hell, but there she was.

"Liz," I finally managed, and the single word made Liz fall over me. Ouch.

"Harley, oh Jesus! I've been here all night. We weren't sure if you were going to wake up at all the way they made it sound..."

I was slowly coming back to full consciousness and could see the back of a very large, bald man at the foot of my bed speaking with a woman in a white coat. Jackson, too? I watched him over Liz's shoulder as he turned around and moved towards us, his hands not going to me but to Liz. He pulled her off me and chuckled a bit, though it seemed empty. Nervous.

"Girl, are you crazy? She just had surgery and you're going to bust her stitches."

"Oh, shit. Sorry." She looked at me again and her eyes looked even bluer than usual with the red skin rimming them. "Sorry Harley."

Jackson draped an arm over Liz's tiny frame and hugged her into him as he looked down at me. I couldn't tell if it was to comfort her or to protect me from another over-enthusiastic hug.

The doctor left the room with the nurse after a few moments. Apparently, she had been asking me some questions, but I hadn't really been able to focus. It wasn't that I didn't want to answer whatever questions she had for me. I just needed to talk to Liz. I needed to find out what all happened after I passed out.

Liz sat my bed up, and Jackson tried to get me a small glass of water. The dutiful nurse outside stopped him. I wasn't allowed to ingest anything yet. Not until they were sure I wouldn't vomit it back up. I had vomited, or nearly vomited, enough in the past week that I was grateful for the precaution.

"How did I get here?" A natural question to start with. It was Jackson who answered.

"That cop that came by my house after I was shot? When you were visiting? He found you and brought you here. God, I am so sorry, Harley. I knew something was wrong, I just couldn't find you." His thumb ran over my hand.

"It's okay, Jackson. No one could have known what happened. It's not your fault."

I tried to reassure him, but he looked so ashamed of himself. I couldn't understand why he was beating himself up about this. He wasn't responsible for me. He couldn't have stopped it.

"No, I should have known that asshole had something to do with this but," he stopped suddenly and shook his head. It was Liz who offered him a one-armed hug.

"Is the detective okay?" I finally asked.

"A bump to the head and a couple of bruises, but he's good. He was checked out and released yesterday." This from Liz. "He just left about an hour ago."

This bit of information surprised me. "He was here?"

"Yeah, he was hoping you would wake up. Seemed really shaken up about it. He didn't say a word except when he asked the docs about you. I guess he was afraid you wouldn't wake up. We all were."

"And Frank?"

"Gone. Slipped away while Detective Sheppard was trying to keep you from bleeding out is my guess."

My gut twisted painfully. Frank was still on the loose. And why would I have expected anything different? It was just me and the detective there when it all went down. I could only imagine he was still trying to wrap his head around what he'd witnessed while Frank made his grand escape.

"I guess I owe him some explanation."

"You don't owe him anything, Harley." Jackson spoke up, his eyes intent on me. "Nothing more than a thank you. Anything more and he might start to dig into things he doesn't need to know about."

I looked at him for a moment. What an odd thing to say. Jackson didn't know Frank or anything about my past. What did he think the detective would dig up? Liz's hand patted Jackson's shoulder and his face softened a touch. What was going on?

"Harley, I think what Jackson is trying to say is we don't need him trying to figure out anything about our kind. That bite is pretty vicious. The hospital has it on record as an animal attack, but I don't think a man like Detective Sheppard is going to be convinced."

"You know about Frank?" I asked.

"I do. I have since he came into the club. I could smell him from the bar. If I had known this all would have come from that I would've asked for Jackson's help sooner, but—"

"Wait." My hand moved away from Jackson's and I looked to him. "Why would Jackson matter in this? You know about... about what Liz is?"

He didn't say anything. All he gave me was a slow, uncertain nod.

"And... what would you be able to do to help with all this?"

My question hung in the air for a good while as they turned their eyes from me to each other. Neither one of them wanted to answer, which only made the realization I was having that much more concrete. I closed my eyes and let out an exasperated sigh.

"Jackson, are you a werewolf too?"

I opened my eyes and watched as he nodded again, his eyes swimming with apologies.

What could I do? The truth of all of this was too much to fight against anymore. Werewolves were real. My ex-boyfriend was one. My best friend was one. Another close friend…yeah, he was one too. Apparently, werewolves were not only everywhere but a lot of them were a part of my life. I would just have to accept it and move on because I sure as hell couldn't replace Liz and Jackson.

Jackson took Liz home a little bit later. And when I say that, I mean after about six hours and not without generous amounts of protesting and coercion. She didn't want to leave my side, but the doctors and Jackson all thought it best if I had as little excitement as possible.

I was completely on board with that.

I managed to talk a nurse into detaching my I.V. leash long enough for a bathroom trip and was getting back in bed when my room phone rang. After an hour of sterile silence, it nearly startled me out of my hospital gown.

Poor Liz. She felt even more guilty than Jackson. No matter how much I tried to argue, she felt that her giving me the silent treatment was the tipping point in all this mess. I hate to break it to her, but this was a volcano just waiting to erupt and she had very little hand in it. Still, she seemed to be trying to make it up to me by calling me every ten minutes.

Jackson might have been able to usurp her from my room, but I would like to see him try to pry her cell away from her.

"Hey, Liz. I'm still breathing," I teased into the phone, finally settling back into my pillow.

"Good to know," the voice on the other end countered.

It wasn't Liz. In fact, I would have never anticipated this particular caller. Her cool, emotionless voice chilled the playfulness I had been feeling seconds before.

"Lori?" I asked.

"Yes, Harley. It's me."

"What- How did you know I was here?"

"Well, it was really just a matter of time before you wound up in the hospital, really. The kind of life you lead..."

I pulled the receiver away from my ear and blinked down at it. Forgetting the fact that that had been a really bitchy thing to say, Lori had made it clear our family was done with me. How did she hear about me being here? And why did she care enough to call?

"Look, let's not make a thing out of this. This isn't a social call," she said as I put the phone back to my ear again.

I was still wrapping my head around the fact that she called me. "Alright, then why did you call? Were you checking the morgue? Haven't quite made it down there yet. Sorry to break the bad news to you."

Her sigh echoed in my ear. Hey, I hadn't been the one to start with the bitch Olympics, but I could be a contender if she wanted to push it.

She didn't say anything. Neither of us did. I could still hear her breathing on the other end. After about three minutes of nothing, I couldn't take it anymore.

"Alright, well, this has been a lovely chat but—"

"Mom's sick," she blurted out. "Really sick, Harley. You need to come see her. Before..." She trailed off, unable to finish what I honestly didn't want to hear her say anyway. It was a small mercy.

"Mom and Dad made it pretty clear that it didn't matter if I was around. Why would she want me there now?" I asked through the dull aching in my chest.

"Things change. Mom and Dad never wanted to keep you in the dark, but it just wasn't allowed."

I never really understood the whole "gut feeling" thing before. In the past, I would just chalk it up to someone trying to save face by pretending they knew something before it happened. I don't know why. Maybe they got some sort of validation from it. Maybe they just didn't like the idea of being just as clueless as the rest of the world. I could sympathize with that.

For the first time, though, I realized that it was a very real thing. I could feel it deep down in my belly. A twisting anxiety in my gut that was telling me something wasn't right; that I was about to find myself knee-deep in something.

"What wasn't allowed?"

She sighed again. "Mom wants you to come home. She wants to see you become a part of the pack before she dies."

I hung up, but not before getting an address from Lorelei. I had yet to process any of it and was instead moving on autopilot. Lori hadn't gone into any detail after she dropped the bomb on me, but then she never felt she owed anyone—me especially—any explanations. Those would have to wait until I was home.

Home. Was there even such a thing?

All I ever wanted was to belong somewhere. I wanted a home so badly that I spent years looking for it. The house and family I was born into treated me like an afterthought. The man I thought I loved had brought me nothing but pain and death and violence. Even the friends I held dearest to me had been lying to me about what they were. Anytime I thought I'd found a home, I had only found lies.

And monsters.

A stinging pain shot through my shoulder. The bite was covered by a thick white bandage, but I knew it was there. Frank had turned, he had bitten me, and I'd told him to do it. I couldn't pretend everything was normal anymore. There was no such thing as normal.

I'd fought against the reality of my life for a while, but there was no going back. I couldn't ignore the truth anymore. I needed to start believing in the monsters because now I was one of them.

Thank you for reading! If you enjoyed *Pack or Prey*, please take a moment and leave us a review at your favorite retailer.

Please Follow us on:

Tiktok: @MadisonChaseBooks

Facebook: http://facebook.com/MadisonChaseBooks

Instagram/Threads: @madisonchasebooks

Blusky: MadisonChaseBooks.bsky.social

TomeBooks: MadisonChaseBooks

-Or-

Check out our website and get the latest news, updates, and randomness that you can find!

Also Join our mailing list if you are interested, though please be forewarned we are human and may not get to this every time, if you are cool with that expect at least a monthly update from us. ;)

www.madisonchasebooks.com

Explore our other stories set in this universe!

Five years after a vicious attack changed her life, Charlie Brant faces her greatest battle yet: resisting the devilishly charming man who just won't leave her the hell alone, and just happens to be the devil.

Wolfblooded Playlist

- **Twisted**
  MISSO

- **Devil's Backbone**
  The Civil War

- **Had Some Drinks**
  Two Feet

- **Joke's On You**
  Charlotte Lawrence

- I Hate Everything About You
  Three Days Grace

- **RUNRUNRUN**
  Dutch Melrose

- **Red Riding Hood**
  Elysian Fields

- **I'm Trying to Be My Own Friend**
  Laeland

- **Jekyll and Hyde**
  Five Finger Death Punch

- **Sorry**
  MEG MYERS

- I Ran (So Far Away)(Epic)
  Hidden Citizens

- **Lose You To Love Me**
  Selena Gomez

- **Blood**
  In This Moment

- **Becoming The Beast**
  Karliene